Sparrow

Sparrow

MARY CECILIA JACKSON

TOR TEEN

A TOM DOHERTY ASSOCIATES BOOK
NEW YORK

SPARROW

Copyright © 2020 by Mary Cecilia Jackson

A Tor Teen Book
Published by Tom Doherty Associates
120 Broadway
New York, NY 10271

www.tor-forge.com

Tor® is a registered trademark of Macmillan Publishing Group, LLC.

The Library of Congress Cataloging-in-Publication Data
is available upon request.

ISBN 978-0-7653-9885-7 (hardcover)
ISBN 978-0-7653-9884-0 (ebook)

Our books may be purchased in bulk for promotional, educational, or business use. Please contact your local bookseller or the Macmillan Corporate and Premium Sales Department at 1-800-221-7945, extension 5442, or by email at MacmillanSpecialMarkets@macmillan.com.

First Edition: March 2020

Printed in the United States of America

0 9 8 7 6 5 4 3 2 1

For my husband, William,
who always believed
this day would come

Sparrow

Perdition catch my soul, but I do love thee!
And when I love thee not, Chaos is come again.

WILLIAM SHAKESPEARE, *Othello*

The Valley of the Shadow

What's past is prologue.

There are two kinds of people on the planet. Hunters and prey.

I thought I would be safe after my mother died. I thought all my nightmares would be buried with her, coiled like serpents in her bloodless arms. I thought I would be able to breathe, to watch the silver moon rise, to look out my window at the distant blue hills without always listening for her footstep on the stairs, for the sound of her screaming. I thought I could stop searching for new places to hide.

But you can't escape what you are, what you've always been.

My name is Savannah Darcy Rose.

Everyone calls me Sparrow.

And I am still prey.

1

March

Running down the hall, phone pressed to my ear, I raise my eyes to the huge clock above the library doors. It offers no hope.

"Where are you, Birdy?" Lucas says. "Levkova's going to slaughter you! She's already doing that thing where she's standing near the piano with her arms crossed, looking at us like we're a bunch of zoo animals."

I take a corner too fast and my elbow hits the lockers. I run faster.

"Are you seriously talking to me in the studio? Put your phone away, or she'll murder you before she even gets to me!"

"I'm not that stupid. I'm in the hall, but even out here I can see her eyes turning all frosty. You know how they get, like freaky little balls of ice."

"Oh my God, it's almost two forty. I'm going to have to drive like a fiend to get changed in time."

I'm breaking the Eleventh Commandment, incised into our

brains for the last three years: Thou Shalt Not Be Late for Ballet Class.

"Holy crap, Birdy, you're still at school? You'll never make it! You know you won't get in if you're late. She loves locking that door at three o'clock, hearing the cries of the damned on the other side."

"I'm going as fast as I can! Try to stall her."

"Oh, right. Like that'll work. She'll turn me to stone with her ice-ball eyes before I even get close. I'm telling you, she's in a mood. She just told Charlotte to stand up straight, that orangutans moved with more grace. Why are you so late?"

I turn the last corner, backpack slipping off my shoulder, dance bag banging against my hip. I can feel my bun falling out of its knot, hear the tiny metallic pings as bobby pins hit the floor behind me.

"Ugh, Coscoroba kept me after class. He wanted to talk about my term paper. You know how you can never get away from him, right? I mean, he's nice, but God, once he gets going you can't get a word in. Today he had to tell me the entire story of Prometheus and his super-unfortunate liver. I swear he never took a breath the whole time."

"Gross! Okay, look, she sees me out here," Lucas whispers. "I don't want to die a horrible death, so I'm going in. Good luck! If you don't make it, I promise I'll cry real loud at your funeral."

"Stop it, Lucas! I'm running as fast as I can!"

Lucas hangs up, and I shove my phone into my bag. The halls are empty, echoing with the sound of my feet pounding the tile floor, the ragged gasp of my breath. I hate disappointing Madame Levkova. She is my rock star, the sun at the center of my universe. Today she'll give me the look that tells me I've let her down, remind me that people who are late are lazy and inconsiderate, and I'll feel like crap for a week. If I rush in just as she's locking the door, she may not even let me dance today. Depends on how irritated she is.

Juggling books, bag, and backpack, I burst through the massive front doors and breathe the cold winter air into my lungs.

The student parking lot is practically deserted, which would be a little weird for a Thursday, except it's been a tough winter. After the last bell, people scurry home, like rabbits to their burrows. A few cars are left, probably yearbook kids, or people staying late for tutoring. My car is all by itself, in the corner under a huge maple tree, now bare of leaves, empty branches silhouetted against the leaden sky. Some people hate winter in Virginia, but I like how spare it is, cold and clean and uncluttered. I raise my face to the sky. There's snow on the wind.

A car squeals to a stop inches from my left hip. I fall to my knees, dropping everything, spilling notebooks, pens, and all my ballet stuff across the asphalt. I'm so terrified I can't even breathe. I count to nine in my head, trying to slow the panic. When my hands stop shaking and I can breathe again, I look up and see the grille of a huge black Mustang. I smell exhaust, feel the relentless percussion of heavy metal.

I know this car.

Tristan King, white in tooth, blond in hair, rich in parents. Hollins Creek High School's highest deity, star of the track team, lusted after by anyone with a pulse. Delaney and I have been swooning over him since middle school.

"Oh my God, did I hit you? Are you hurt?" He and all his gorgeousness come flying out of the car, wearing the dark gray suit and crimson tie all the athletes had to wear for the awards assembly this morning. He kneels down to help me collect my things.

"No, no, I'm fine," I manage to croak. "I've got this, really. It's okay."

"I am so, so sorry! Oh no! Your knees are bleeding!"

"Really, it's nothing, honestly." I hold my hands out to keep him away. "They don't even hurt." I've torn huge, gaping holes in the knees of my black tights, and the skin underneath is scraped and raw. Blood trickles slowly from the cuts and soaks into the ragged edges.

My pointe shoes, tied into their nerdy mesh bag, are under his car, along with my books and notebooks. But all the truly awful stuff—deodorant, tampons, panty liners, body spray, Dr. Scholl's blister pads and foot powder, even the dryer sheets I stuff into my dance bag so it won't reek of sweat and BO—is right out there in the pale winter sunlight. All the embarrassing, disgusting detritus of my life. My own personal Museum of Mortification.

I pray for a sudden sinkhole to swallow me whole, a bolt of lightning to fry me to ash, an alien abduction. I'm straight up dying of embarrassment. Dying. Like I-can't-breathe-and-my-heart-hurts dying.

Tristan looks at my knees and says, "Hang on a second. I'll be right back, okay? Don't go anywhere."

I stumble around, gathering my things, surreptitiously trying to wipe away the blood. I lied. My knees hurt like a stinker. I give up and sit down on the curb to assess the damage.

Tristan comes back holding a first aid kit. Kneeling down in his perfect suit, paying no attention to the dirt and gravel, he says, "I'm so, so incredibly sorry. At least let me fix you up."

"You actually carry a first aid kit in your car? Do you run over a lot of people?"

He laughs, and the sound is low and sweet, like soft notes rising from a cello. His teeth are dazzling up close, straight and impossibly white, probably representing a small fortune in orthodontics and bleach. Even his eyebrows are gorgeous.

"Nah," he says. "You're my first attempt at roadkill. If you think your knees are messed up, you should see mine. Bruises and scars like you wouldn't believe. I run high hurdles, and sometimes I miss."

He gently wipes the blood from my knees and brushes away stray bits of gravel. He's so close that I can smell his hair. Lavender, I think. Or rosemary. I breathe him in as deeply and quietly as I can while he dabs Neosporin on the scrapes and covers them with Band-Aids.

When he leans forward and kisses each bandage, I have to work hard not to gasp. Once, when I was really, really small, my mother did the same thing, and for a moment I'm lost in the memory. The way her long hair fell like a dark waterfall over her shoulder as she knelt on the bathroom floor in front of me. Her polished fingernails peeling the wrapping from the bandages. The softness of her lips as she kissed my scraped knees. And though I know it's impossible, for a few seconds I swear the fragrance of my mother's lily of the valley perfume dances in the cold air.

"There," Tristan says, looking up at me. "Now you'll heal faster. Kisses always make things better, don't you think?"

I'm not thinking at all, because my brain has stopped working. I should stand up and push him away. I should tell him he's way out of line, and call him a presumptuous Neanderthal. But his strong hands, his lips on my skin, are making me shiver, and I feel all hot and floaty and liquid, like warm honey is flowing through my veins. I don't want him to stop. I want him to do it again.

"Yes," I whisper, mesmerized by the depth of his gray eyes, the color of a mourning dove's wing. "Kisses always help." I wonder if he can hear my heart pounding.

He stands and helps me to my feet, holding on to my hands for longer than seems necessary. Standing so close, I feel the heat of him, how alive he is. I have the completely bizarre urge to rest my head on his chest, wrap my arms around his waist, and draw that warmth, that life, into myself. I shake my head, tell myself to snap out of it. Me: Amoeba. Him: Tristan King.

Still holding my hands, he pulls me a little closer, then reaches out to tuck a stray curl behind my ear. Looking into my eyes, he smiles and says, "Better now? Will you be okay? Want me to drive you home?"

I nod, never taking my eyes from his face. "I'll be fine, really," I whisper.

I don't want him to let go. With my hands in his, I feel safe, as though he's standing between me and the entire rest of the world, like my own personal knight, complete with sword and shield, sworn to protect me. He is so impossibly beautiful.

He gathers up all my books, places them carefully in my backpack, and zips it. Then he crawls under the car for my pointe shoes.

"Your suit," I say, as he wriggles back out. "It's all dirty now."

He shrugs and smiles. "Doesn't matter. Assembly's over, pictures are done." Cradling my pink satin pointe shoes in both hands, he holds them out like an offering, as though he knows how precious they are to me.

"I'm glad I ran into you, Sparrow."

"You're hilarious." I take my shoes from him and stuff them into my dance bag. I feel like I'm moving in slow motion, my heart, my body unwilling to let this end, my brain knowing that it will, and that when he's gone, it will feel like none of it ever happened. I try to fix all the details in my brain, right now, so they'll be there later. So it will be real.

"Thanks. I do what I can."

"So, anyway," I say. "Thanks for not killing me, but I need to run. I'm unbelievably late for ballet."

I head toward the ancient Volvo that my dad lets me drive

to school and ballet but nowhere else. Tristan runs after me and grabs my hand.

"Wait, Sparrow. Don't go. Not yet."

It feels like my heart has jumped straight up into my throat.

"You sure have changed a lot since we were in geography class together," he says.

"That was fifth grade, Tristan. We've all changed. The last time you spoke to me, you said nobody likes ballerinas and ballet was stupid."

His eyes widen and he puts his hand over his heart and staggers backward, like he's had a sudden shock. "Seriously? I said that?"

"You did. I remember every word."

"Wow, I was kind of a jackass, wasn't I?"

"Yeah, you kind of were."

"I was wrong. And ballet is awesome."

I can't help it. I laugh.

"Right. Have you actually been to any of our performances? You don't exactly seem like the kind of person who'd be wild about ballet."

"Okay, totally busted. But my mother's on the conservatory board, and she's always talking about you. She showed me that article that was in the paper last year. She says you're mad talented."

That article is still taped to the refrigerator. My father refuses to take it down. He even highlighted the line about me being "the rising star of the Appalachian Conservatory Ballet" and called me "Superstar" for a week. It was mortifying.

I feel myself blushing, the red stain creeping all the way up my neck and into my cheeks. Now my freckles will look awesome. "You should come see a performance with your mom sometime."

"Maybe I will," he says softly. He reaches out and cups my face in the palm of his hand, stroking my cheek with his thumb. "You're blushing." He's so close I can feel his warm breath on my skin.

My knees go all rubbery, and I picture myself falling down right where I'm standing, fainting like a Victorian maiden in one of my aunt Sophie's romance novels.

When I speak, my voice comes out all shaky and whispery.

"Listen, really, thanks for the Band-Aids and everything. But I've got to go. We get fined five dollars every time we're late for class. I'm sorry I ran out in front of you. Hope I didn't give you a heart attack or anything."

He smiles and pushes his sun-streaked hair out of his eyes. He has deep dimples on both sides of his mouth. "Have dinner with me on Saturday. Please. Let me make up for almost killing you."

Approximately five thousand thoughts rush through my head. Me at dinner with Tristan King, holding his hand at a candlelit table, sharing a dessert. Kissing him at my front door. Wondering why he's bothering with me, when he's had tons of girlfriends, some of them even college girls. How tightly Sophie will hug me, how she'll whisper that she's happy I'm finally getting out of the house and, even better, going on an actual date. Best of all, telling Delaney. She'll completely lose her mind and scream the scream she reserves for all miraculous occurrences.

"Ummm, that would be great, but I can't. I have rehearsal most of the day on Saturdays, and then——"

"And then what? You'll go home and sit by your window, crying sad little ballerina tears and wishing you'd said yes. You have to eat. I'll take you wherever you want to go, even if you want, I don't know, a gluten-free, vegan, pizza-free pizza. Come on, say yes. Please. Otherwise I'll never get over the guilt."

I hesitate. This will require all kinds of explaining and promising to my father. I'll have to get Sophie to run interference. If we start tonight, it's possible that we can get my dad to cave. My heart beats a little faster. This could actually work.

"Sparrow, come on. I'm sorry I was a jerk in fifth grade. I'm sorry I almost ran you over. Let me make things right. It's just dinner, some pasta and bread, maybe a glass of sparkling water if you're feeling fancy. It's not like I'm asking you to donate a kidney."

I melt, fast and gooey, like a marshmallow in a campfire. "Okay, yes. But I eat like a normal person, just so you know. It's a total myth that ballerinas live on celery sticks and bee pollen."

He laughs. "Point taken. We'll have cheesecake and ice cream, too. I'll pick you up at seven."

"Just be prepared for my dad. No way he'll let me walk out the door without grilling you. He's a trial attorney, and he almost always wins."

"Got it. Beware of kick-ass lawyers. I heard about his big murder case."

"Yeah, everybody says he's ferocious in court. And he's going to treat you like a hostile witness, so gird your loins."

"I'll suck up hard-core. Maybe he'll let me off easy."

"I wouldn't count on it."

Laughing, he walks to his car and gets in, gunning the engine and waving as he peels out of the parking lot.

Levkova has definitely locked the door by now. I may as well go straight home and scrape up five bucks to put in the Jar of Shame she keeps on the piano. I'll do an *adagio* barre in my room and give myself corrections. I'll be alone, but maybe it won't suck so much today.

I throw my dance bag on the passenger seat and sit for a minute while the heater groans. My knees hurt, and my hands are so cold I can't even feel them, but I can't stop smiling. I resist the urge to text Delaney about what just happened, because I want to hear her laugh when I tell her how my tampons were scattered all over the parking lot like candy from a piñata. I want to see the look of utter disbelief on her face when I tell her I have an actual date. With Tristan King.

It always surprises me, how life can change in an instant, how everything can turn upside down on an ordinary winter afternoon. In my heart, I feel the cautious flutter of hope.

2

"Oh my God, Dad, I'm begging you. Put on some shoes."

"What? You told me I had beautiful feet! I thought I'd show them off to your date. So we'll get off on the right foot. Get it?"

"I told you that when I was six! Sophie! Come in here! Dad's going to ruin it!"

My father is standing in the living room, holding a double Scotch on the rocks. *Tannhäuser*, the German opera he can sing by heart, is playing softly in the background. He's dressed in cargo pants and a faded blue UVA Law sweatshirt. His long, pale feet are bare.

I've grown up watching him pace back and forth in the dusky twilight, still in his suit and tie, phone pressed to his ear, bare feet sinking into the grass. Unless there's snow on the ground, he does this every weekday when he comes home from work. I've never asked him about it, because it seems private. Maybe it's just a space between work and home, a moment when he can feel the earth beneath him and muffle the drumbeat of his days. I've always loved the barefoot thing. Until tonight.

Sophie rushes in, bracelets and earrings jingling, her red curls falling down her back. She sounds like wind chimes.

"Avery, what the hell? Go put on some shoes for God's sake! I told you not to embarrass her, and Tristan will be here any minute. Move your butt, or I'll spit in your Scotch."

"You women will be the death of me," my father says. "Can't a man be shoeless in his own home?"

"No!" Sophie and I shout.

"All right, all right," he grumbles, walking down the hall toward the back porch.

When the doorbell rings, my stomach drops to my feet. I clench my hands together and tap my right index finger against my left hand, barely moving it so Sophie won't see, but enough so I can still feel it. Nine times, three groups of three. I do it three times, until my breathing slows.

Sophie walks over to where my feet have practically rooted themselves into the hardwood floor. She pats my cheek and smiles. "Your father's just teasing you, honey. And by the way, you look gorgeous."

I'm wearing my favorite skinny jeans, black suede boots, and a high-necked ivory lace shirt under my black bolero jacket. I don't feel gorgeous. I feel queasy. "Really? You think so?"

"I know so, baby girl. Now go answer the door."

Tristan is standing on the front porch in a leather bomber jacket, black jeans, and a cobalt-blue sweater. His long blond hair is brushed back from his face, showing off his widow's peak. He looks like a rock star.

I introduce him to Sophie, who shakes his hand and invites him in.

"Tristan," she says, holding his hand in both of hers. "It's so nice to meet you. Sparrow told me how you guys met the other day. It was like something out of a movie!"

Tristan looks at me and smiles.

"It was a first for me, ma'am, that's for sure," he says. "Kind of an unusual way to get a date, right? Running a girl down with your car? I'm just glad Sparrow gave me a second chance. Though maybe it was a third chance, since apparently I was a real jerk in fifth grade."

Sophie laughs. "Well, you'll have to come have dinner with us sometime soon. I make a killer lasagna."

"I'd love that, Ms. Rose. Thank you."

"Please, call me Sophie. Everyone does."

I'm winding my pink-and-white scarf around my neck when my father comes clomping down the hall. He's put on his lime-green rubber boots, the ones he wears to spread mulch in the garden. He actually winks at me, like I'm in on the joke.

He strolls into the foyer like there's nothing in the world wrong with this picture and shakes Tristan's hand. I can tell that he's crushing it, because his knuckles are white. Tristan doesn't flinch, never breaks eye contact.

"Tristan King," my dad says. "I know your father."

"He knows you, too, sir. He respects your work."

"That's kind of you to say. Where are you taking Sparrow tonight?"

"I thought we'd go to La Serenissima for dinner, then maybe take a walk down Main Street if it's not too cold."

"You are aware that her curfew is ten o'clock?"

"Yes, sir. I'll have her home on time."

"There will be no drinking this evening, am I clear?"

"Of course, sir. My father would kill me."

"A man after my own heart. Good for him."

"Dad, come on," I say. "Enough."

He ignores me.

"There will be nothing else, either, you get me?"

"Loud and clear, sir."

"How old are you, Tristan?"

"I'll be eighteen in September."

"You take care with my daughter tonight. She's seventeen, too, but she's still younger than you."

"I will, sir. I promise."

"Sparrow," says my father. "I'd like to see you a minute before you leave."

I roll my eyes. Tristan grins at me.

"I'll wait right here. Take your time."

I leave him in the foyer with Sophie, who's making small talk about Italian food. My father and I walk into the kitchen, where a pot of chili is simmering on the stove. Sophie's put a pan of cornbread in to bake.

For one panicky minute I think about staying home, right here in this kitchen, where it's warm and safe and I know the pattern of every day, every night. I think about the moment when I step off the front porch with Tristan, walking into the darkness, into everything unknown. I start tapping my finger against my left hand again. Nine. Nine. It's always nine.

"Helloooooo," my father says. "Earth to Sparrow."

Oh right, I forgot. I want to murder my father.

He puts his arm around my shoulders, pulling me close. "Why on earth did you have to pick such a horrible-looking boy for your first date, my love? He's absolutely hideous! Sasquatch in a leather jacket! What were you thinking, child? He's going to horrify all the waiters and patrons of La Serenissima, eating with his hands and chewing with his mouth open.

"Why don't you just go out with Lucas? At least that beast is familiar. Since I don't know much about Tristan, I guess I'll have to turn my private detectives loose as soon as you leave."

I pull away from him. I am not laughing.

"Dad, you are the actual worst."

He smiles and takes out his wallet, pressing a twenty-dollar bill into my hand. I fold it into thirds, unfold it, and fold it again.

"Sweetie, come on. You know I'm just giving you a hard time. I'm happy for you, Tristan's horrifying appearance notwithstanding. Maybe you could get him to wear a paper bag over his head or something."

"Stop it, Dad. So not funny."

"Too much?"

"Way, way too much."

"Okay, love. I really am very happy for you. You've been laser focused on ballet ever since you started lessons, and if you ask me, which you didn't, you've always been a little too content to stay at home on weekends. It gladdens my heart to see you getting out into the world, having some fun with a boy who seems nice and will treat you well. Though if you tell him I said so, I'll ground you for life. Is your phone charged?"

"Yes, Dad. My phone is charged."

"Put that money in your pocket. I'm just going to say this one more obnoxious fatherly thing, so listen hard. You can roll your eyes all you want.

"If you get to feeling nervous or uncomfortable about anything, you call me. I just . . ." He takes a deep breath and looks away, out the window over the sink. When he looks back at me, his eyes are sad. "I just want you to know that I'm here. That's all. Now, pumpkin, you may go in peace."

He kisses the top of my head. "Be careful, be safe, and have a good time. I love you." I give him a quick hug, breathing his bay rum cologne deep into my lungs.

"Love you too. But you look kind of crazy in those boots."

"Hey, let's get out of here. It's only eight thirty, a whole hour and a half before your curfew. Where do you want to go next? Ice cream? Coffee at Nora's?"

The candle on the table sputters, sending flickering light over the dessert plates scraped clean of chocolate lava cake. Tristan is pocketing his debit card and leaving a cash tip for the waiter.

"God, no, thanks," I say. "I'm completely stuffed. This was wonderful, but you didn't have to do it, honestly. I've already totally forgiven you for almost killing me with your car."

He leans across the table and looks into my eyes.

"You're amazing and beautiful and I'm lucky to be here with you tonight, especially given my total lack of driving skills. Are you sure you're ready to go?"

"I think if we sit here any longer, the back of my head's going to burst into flames. People are staring at me."

He laughs, then stands and takes my hand. "People should stare at you. Here, watch your step. It's dark in here."

He guides me through the restaurant, and heads turn as we walk by. Everyone is looking at him, probably wondering what he's doing with the brown-haired ballerina instead of his usual shiny girl. Like Larissa, who modeled for the Anthropologie catalog last year, then moved to New York just months after they started dating. Or Jemma, first violinist with the youth symphony. They broke up this Christmas, after only six weeks. He seems to go through girlfriends the way I go through leotards. But tonight I don't care. Tonight he is with me.

Outside, on the sidewalk, with the winter evening all around us, breathing promises into the night sky, he gathers me into his arms and buries his face in my hair. His mouth moves against my neck, and it feels more intimate than a kiss. I pull away, but he doesn't let me get far, throwing his arm around my shoulders as we walk to his car.

"Your hair smells so good. What is it? Roses? I can't stop thinking about you, Sparrow. I haven't been able to concentrate since Thursday."

I don't know what to say. No one's ever talked to me like this.

"It's honeysuckle. Hey, I know where we can go next. Have you ever been to the Honeysuckle Pond?"

"The what?"

"Its real name is Aubrey's Cove, but I call it the Honeysuckle Pond, because there's wild honeysuckle all over the place, and it smells amazing."

I'm babbling. I can hear myself doing it, and I want to slap my own face. I don't even know how to behave on a date. I should have asked Delaney for advice.

"You want to go to some random pond? Seriously? Like out in nature? Where it will be cold? You sure you don't want me to take you up to Harper's Point? You know, we can look out at the lights, and maybe the windows will get all foggy? I guarantee I'd keep you warm."

He opens my car door, but before I get in, he bends and kisses me lightly on the lips. My whole body trembles. I want him to do it again. I want to run home and hide.

"I'm just kidding, Sparrow. It's too soon for Harper's Point, and I would love to take you to your freezing pond where the honeysuckle grows. I've never been there."

I breathe out a quiet sigh of relief.

"I can't believe you've never been. It's up on the Parkway, not far, maybe fifteen minutes."

A thin crescent moon is rising over the mountains as we arrive. The sound of the waterfall fills the night, and I lead Tristan over the rocks to my favorite spot, the broad, flat boulder in the middle of the creek. Water rushes all around us, the moon reflected in the rippling surface. Even though it's still winter, the faint scent of honeysuckle lingers in the air.

"Wow," Tristan whispers. "This place is gorgeous."

I love that he's whispering, because I do the same thing when I'm here.

"It was my mother's favorite place. You know the story, right?"

"There's a story?"

"Tristan, seriously? I thought everyone in Hollins Creek knew the story. My mother used to tell it to me when she was brushing my hair before bed. When I was little, it was the last thing I heard before I fell asleep, her voice, like music, telling me about Aubrey. Sophie thinks it's super-depressing, but my mother thought it was tragic and romantic. She loved it."

"Your mom was some kind of artist, right? I heard she was a sculptor."

"She was a painter. She and my dad met when he was in law school at UVA. She was an art student, and one day he saw her, sitting on the Lawn, under a tree near the Rotunda. It was spring, and she was sketching. He said he fell in love with her stillness."

"She died in an accident, am I remembering that right? When you were five?"

"Do you want to hear the story or not?"

Tristan smiles and puts his arm around me. "Yes, I want to hear the story."

"Okay, so this all happened before the Civil War. You have heard of the Civil War, right?"

He pulls me closer, so we're hip to hip on the rock. I can feel the warmth of his body, see his breath making clouds in the cold air.

I tell him the way my mother always told it to me.

"Once there was a beautiful young belle named Aubrey O'Meara. She was nineteen years old, and she died here, just under the waterfall. She killed herself, because the married man she loved with all her heart laughed and slammed the door in her face when she told him she was pregnant. He'd lied to her, told her all these sweet things, that he loved her, that he'd always love her, that his wife was cold and cruel, and Aubrey meant everything to him. That day, when she told him she was going to have his baby, he told her she wouldn't get anything from him, that she should go on home and leave him alone.

"She knew she'd bring everlasting shame to her family, so she spared them the only way she knew how."

I stand and pick my way closer to the waterfall, careful not to slip on the mossy rocks. Tristan follows behind me, sure-footed as a mountain goat. The falls are quieter in winter, because the outside edges always turn to ice, but I still have to raise my voice a little.

"One winter morning, Aubrey filled the pockets of her cloak with stones and threw herself into that pool, right there at the base of the falls."

Tristan crouches down and dips his hand into the clear, sparkling water. He winces at the cold and dries his hand on his jeans, looking up at me, waiting for me to continue.

"The thing that always gets me is that before she jumped, she put her shoes right about here, where I'm standing, along with a silver locket that held a picture of her mother and a curl of her own auburn hair. When her mother died the next year, everyone said it was from a broken heart. They buried Aubrey's locket with her."

Tristan stands and wraps his arms around me, holding me

tight. He smooths my hair back from my forehead and kisses my temple. For a second I can't find the story again. His lips are warm and soft, his arms strong and sure around my shoulders. I feel safe here, with him, even though my mouth is filled with my mother's words.

He leads me across the slippery rocks until we're back on the flat boulder in the middle of the creek.

"Is there more?" he says.

"Not much. But it's the saddest part. Aubrey is supposed to haunt this place. People say you can see her sometimes, standing on the bank right there, near the waterfall. And on the anniversary of her death, if you take a sip of the water from the pool, you can taste the salt of her mother's tears."

We're quiet for a while, listening to the water, looking up at the moon.

"Your mom really told you that story when you were little?"

"Yes."

"Kind of creepy."

"I guess. I never really thought about it. She was just my beautiful mother, brushing my hair, telling me a bedtime story. Everyone loves when their mother tells stories."

I'm lying. I thought about Aubrey all the time. She terrified me.

"My mother painted her."

"Who?"

"Aubrey. Just once or twice. She said the story inspired her."

I close my eyes, lost in the memory of the canvases lined up against my father's bookshelves, drying on easels in the dining room, propped up against the windows in the living room, on the cushions of the window seat at the top of the stairs.

Aubrey under the water, her mouth open in a silent scream. Aubrey taking off her shoes. Aubrey's father finding her dead body on the banks of the New River. Aubrey on her knees in front of her lover, begging. Aubrey weeping. Aubrey screaming. Aubrey dying. She was everywhere.

"What happened to the paintings?"

"I don't know. My dad probably put them in the attic after she died."

He burned them. Every last one.

Tristan puts a finger under my chin and tilts my face up to his. His gray eyes fill my sight; with the beautiful night around me, I fall into them.

"Thank you for telling me," he whispers, kissing me softly. "It is definitely the saddest story . . ." Another kiss, longer this time. He puts his hand in my hair.

". . . I've ever heard."

He lays me back on the rock, runs his thumb down my cheek.

"You're so beautiful, Sparrow. My beautiful ballerina." He kisses me again, so long that I'm afraid I'll stop breathing. I want to stop breathing. I want him to kiss me forever.

3

"So what did you have to eat?" Delaney asks. "What did he have? Where did you sit?"

Lucas rolls his eyes and throws down his sandwich. "Oh, sweet tap-dancing Jesus, where did she sit? Are you kidding me, Laney? Who gives a crap?"

"Shut up, Lucas," Delaney says. "Go over and sit with Brandon and his no-neck brobots if you don't want to hear it. You know how the football guys love ballet dancers."

It's a cold, dreary Monday, and I'm at lunch with Lucas and Delaney and a bunch of ballet and theater and music people. Caleb from ballet, who looks like he's flying when he jumps. Israel, tall and lanky, theater nerd and budding playwright. Sam, who loves to sing.

Luis is the last to arrive, squeezing in beside me. His tray is piled high with his usual: onion bagels spread with Cheez

Whiz, three hot dogs, and a mountain of Tater Tots smothered in ketchup.

I scoot over to make room for him, wishing I could hermetically seal my lunch—plain Greek yogurt, almonds and strawberries, sliced chicken, a wedge of smoked Gouda—to keep it safe from the toxic fumes wafting from Luis's tray. It makes me nauseous. The preservatives in the meat tubes. The nuclear orange of processed cheese.

I arrange strawberries and almonds in alternating groups of three, forming a perfect semicircle of nine above my yogurt and chicken.

Luis does a double take when he notices Delaney, who's wearing a camo T-shirt, a hot-pink feather boa, and round wire-rimmed sunglasses.

"What are you supposed to be? A blind saloon girl?"

"Aren't they great? I got them at Lily and Isabelle on Saturday. And look!"

She lifts her leg so he can see her turquoise cowboy boots.

"Check these out. They're my mom's, from when she was a barrel racer in Texas. I'm never taking them off."

Luis shakes his head and pops a Tater Tot into his mouth. "It's going to be kind of hard to do ballet in cowboy boots, unless there's a rodeo version of *Swan Lake*. Which I would totally pay to see."

Delaney laughs and steals one of his Tots. Licking the ketchup from her fingers, she says, "You're just jealous of my fashion sense."

"You're a crime of fashion, Delaney. That's what you are." He picks up a hot dog and looks around the table. "So what are we talking about? My man Lucas here looks like he just ate a bug."

Caleb looks up from *Apollo's Angels,* the history of ballet that Levkova is making us read, because, according to her, we are all "woefully ignorant children with no knowledge or appreciation of the great artistic history that precedes us." He points at Delaney with a forkful of chicken salad. "We're hearing all about where Sparrow sat on her first date with Prince Charmless. They went to the fancy Italian restaurant downtown."

"La Serenissima." Delaney sighs.

"Where she sat?" Luis says, shoving half the hot dog into his face.

"Exactly," Lucas says. "Because who gives a crap, am I right?"

Israel, who wants to direct plays on Broadway, says, "Hey, it's important to set the scene. I give a crap. Y'all shut up and let her talk."

Delaney crows, "Thank you, Iz. 'He is as full of valor as of kindness. Princely in both.'"

"Act four, scene three, Bedford. I claim your brownie as my prize." Israel grabs Delaney's dessert, a brownie the size of her face, and gives half to Luis, who eats it between the Tater Tots and his second hot dog.

Delaney barely notices. "Spill, sister. Every juicy detail. Again."

"We both had fettuccine Alfredo. And we sat at that booth in the back, you know, the one by the fireplace? Dad and Sophie and I sat there for my birthday last year."

"The Crime Boss Booth," Israel says.

Delaney shakes her head. "Iz, what in the name of Sam Houston does that even mean?"

Israel says, "You know, like in *Scarface*? Every single movie where the evil criminal mastermind is having dinner with his minions? They always sit close to the back wall, so they can see who's coming at them."

"Wise choice," says Lucas. "Half the people in town would love to whack Tristan King."

Delaney slides her dark glasses down her nose and glares at him. "What crawled down your throat and died? Tristan King is gorgeous and full of tasty deliciousness. Every day I think about pinning him down in calculus class and licking him. Pretty sure he'll taste like butterscotch."

The smile spreads across my face like a sunrise. "He actually does."

"Oh, sweet mother, my heart." Delaney closes her eyes and leans back in her chair.

Lucas pretends to stick his finger down his throat and makes the puke face.

Delaney gives him another death stare. "Zip it, Skippy. I'm warning you."

I lean in and whisper to Delaney. "He kissed me until I couldn't breathe. We stayed until the stars came out and the moon was way high. He told me I was beautiful, that we'd belong to each other. He said he felt like we were meant to be together, because of the way we met."

Delaney twists her blond hair into a messy bun. "Bird Girl, I swear, if I didn't love you, I'd hate you. Remember how we used to sit in the bleachers after school and watch him run? How you said he looked like a cheetah chasing a zebra? Now he nearly flattens you in the parking lot, and boom. A love story is born."

"Right? I can hardly believe it myself."

"Please, I'm begging you," Lucas says. "Stop talking right now. If you say another word, I swear I'm going to york my breakfast all over your lunch."

Delaney narrows her eyes. "What is wrong with you today? Why can't you let us be happy for our girl here? Why do you have to crap all over something so good?"

Everybody goes quiet. Luis actually stops eating. Israel gets his pen out to take notes.

"Nothing's wrong with me, but you ladies have apparently lost your minds. Y'all aren't thinking with your brains, that's for sure."

Delaney takes off her sunglasses. "Excuse me? What's that supposed to mean?"

"Lucas," I say. "We're sorry. But seriously, you need to shut up right now."

"Nice, Birdbrain. Thanks."

"Wait, Sparrow," Delaney says. "Don't let the little wanker off the hook. What do you mean we're not thinking with our brains? Are you implying that we're thinking with something else?"

"Well," he says, taking a bite of his sandwich and talking with his mouth full, which he knows we hate. "Since you asked, I think your brains have gone south of the border. If you know what I mean."

Delaney throws half a banana at him. It hits him on the shoulder and falls onto the table. He doesn't flinch, just brushes the goo off his sweater, an expression of disgust on his face. "Wow, Laney. Way to keep it classy."

"You sexist turd. If I said something like that to you—"

"You'd probably be right. I can't believe you're talking about Tristan King like he's suddenly turned into someone else! Do you even remember what a jerk he was in middle school, always bullying the smaller kids? Can you possibly forget how his father was at every soccer game, every Little League tournament, trying to pay off coaches, bailing his psycho kid out of trouble? Has all that leaked out of your tiny brains?"

Delaney rolls her eyes. "All you boys were little douchebags in middle school. It was hard to tell you apart."

"Maybe. But he's the only one who actually hurt people. The

rest of us were just morons. He thought about what he did. He planned it. Luis, remember how he slammed your head into the lockers in eighth grade because you wouldn't let him cheat off your science test? Then he got Brandon and all those troglodytes to egg your house that night?"

Luis rubs the bridge of his nose. "Oh man, our house smelled rank for days. That was my first black eye. My only black eye, actually." He flutters his long Bambi eyelashes at Delaney. "I'm a lover, not a fighter."

"But Luis isn't sitting here holding a grudge," I say. "He isn't stewing about it, right, Luis?"

"Yeah. It was a long time ago. I got over it."

"You're the only one who hangs on to stuff like this, Lucas," I say. "Can't you just forget it?"

I try to eat the rest of my lunch, but I've lost my appetite. I rearrange the strawberries and almonds, replacing the ones I've eaten with slices of chicken.

"Oh, come on, Sparrow! No, I can't forget it. I don't believe you guys! Tristan's been calling me all kinds of foul names since we were eight. For some reason, he needs to make sure I never forget that he's the alpha dog around here. I'm supposed to stick to the script—he's the manly jock, I'm the sissy dancer, and oh, by the way, he's also smarter and stronger and richer. I'm not holding a grudge. I don't even hear it anymore. But people don't change overnight. Assholes don't suddenly turn into angels."

I give up on my lunch and stuff what's left into my bag.

"All I know is that he likes me—and I like him. So I'm not sure what your problem is, but I am sure that it's totally none of your business. You need to back off!" I smack the table with the palm of my hand, and everybody jumps. "I don't know why you think you have any say in my life or what I do when we're not dancing, but you're assuming you're more important than you really are. Your opinion doesn't matter, Lucas. Can you please get that through your thick skull? Just this once?"

Lucas's eyes go wide. Caleb, Israel, and Luis look down at their lunches. Sam lets out a long whistle. "Owned," he says.

"Well, it kind of is my business, Sparrow," Lucas says. "You know, since I see you every day and have to dance *Swan Lake* with you. So if you're all of a sudden with a nasty dude who's bound to make you miserable, it's probably going to affect me, too."

"Don't be such a narcissist. This isn't about you. And he's not nasty. He's amazing. Just because you dance with me doesn't give you the right to tell me what to do. You're not my father. You're my dance partner, and I don't care what you think. So just drop it."

Lucas goes white, then pitches what's left of his lunch into the trash and storms out of the cafeteria.

Just before dawn, I dream about my mother. I'm little again, my hair in a high ponytail tied with a blue satin ribbon. Emily, my favorite bear, is in my arms, and I clutch her to my chest.

My mother is in the living room, painting. I love to watch her work, but this time everything is wrong. The brush she's holding is tipped with long black feathers, dripping with crimson paint. She's wound strands of tiny river pearls through her tangled hair, and her lips are chapped and raw, like she's been biting them. The white streak at her temple is gray with grime.

I stand in the doorway, afraid to move, afraid to speak. But she knows I'm there. She can feel me, hear me breathing. She turns slowly toward me, her smile too wide, her teeth too white, her eyes bright and feverish. "Come here, Savannah," she says. "I want to show you my pictures."

And I know, even in my dream, that I do not want to see

those pictures. That once I look at them, I'll never be able to unsee them. I'll never be able to forget. But if I don't go, she'll be angry, and she will scream and scream and scream.

I walk slowly to her side. The living room is filled with canvases. But the pictures are not of Aubrey, weeping and floating and dying. My mother has painted me into the story. I'm the one under the water. I'm the one staring sightlessly up at the night sky. All the paintings. All of them.

They are all of me.

I wake, panicked and sweating, to the sound of my phone buzzing on the nightstand. It's four thirty in the morning. Lucas sends the disco boy in the purple suit. My hands are shaking so hard it takes three tries before I can send back the flamenco dancer. I take three deep breaths, then three more. I swallow three sips of water.

U awake?

> Yep.

Haven't slept all night. Sorry I was such an asshat at lunch yesterday. Like really, really sorry. I feel terrible.

> Me too. I take back everything I said. I didn't mean any of it. Okay, I did at the time, but I was mad at you.

Yeah, I got that part.

> You know I wouldn't hurt you for the world. Are we cool? We forgive each other, just like always?

Always. Forever cool.

Can you sleep now?

I'll try. You too. Levkova's going to make
us hurt this afternoon.

Nothing new.

Truth.

Night. <3

Morning. <3

But I'm too afraid to go back to sleep. I know I will spend the
entire day trying to forget that dream.

4

May

Two hours into Saturday rehearsal, Lucas lifts me and whispers, "I'm begging you, stop farting in my face. You're killing me." He puts his hands on my waist, guiding me in a *pirouette*. "My eyes are watering. What did you even eat last night?"

I snort with laughter, which earns us both the evil eye from Levkova.

Lucas says, "Oh great, see what you did? Now she'll be all over us like cops on a doughnut."

He's right. If we don't pull it together, we'll be cleaning the stage floor on our hands and knees.

Ever since last month, when Levkova announced that we'd be doing the second act of *Swan Lake* for the Winter Gala next March, class and rehearsals have been even tougher than usual. We spent the first three weeks learning the steps, doing them over and over again so they'd become muscle memory, so much a part of our bodies that we don't have to think about them. Now we're working on interpretation.

It's hard. Nothing prepares you for how much strength and stamina it requires. The swan arms are hard to keep going, and my shoulders ache all the time. The balances are tricky. Everything has to be crisp and clean and pure, at the same time conveying the most complicated human emotions. Love. Loss. Betrayal. Fear.

Today, for the first time, Lucas and I are doing the entire White Swan *pas de deux* from the beginning, no stopping for corrections. I'm wearing pink tights, a black camisole leotard, and a rehearsal tutu. These always take some getting used to, because now the only way I can see my feet and legs is in the mirrors that wrap around three sides of the enormous studio. Lucas wears his usual gray fitted shirt and black tights and slippers.

The twenty-four girls in the *corps de ballet*, the cursed swans who share my fate, are taking a break while Lucas and I dance the *pas de deux*. They bend to pull on leg warmers and stretch tired muscles in front of the windows that reach from floor to ceiling. Even sweating and exhausted, they look beautiful in their white tutus and pointe shoes, like a Degas painting. Behind them, the distant mountains are hazy and blue.

Lucas and I begin, standing in a pool of sunlight that falls from the clerestory windows high on the mirrored wall in front of us. The warm light on my shoulders feels like a blessing. The music fills me up, carrying the sun's warmth into my blood and bones. As soon as it starts, my spine straightens. I pull up, holding myself as though someone is pulling a string through my body and out the top of my head, elongating my legs, my torso, my neck.

Madame Levkova can't help herself. We aren't supposed to stop, but that doesn't mean she'll be quiet. "No, Lucas! Sparrow, make sure you have pointe shoe on center, please. Lucas, if you are not one step ahead, you are late, and you are making her late. Other leg, Lucas! Back, Sparrow, back! Abby, begin again, please."

Abby Samuels, Lucas's next-door neighbor, is our rehearsal pianist. She's the only one who's been able to tame the huge Bösendorfer Imperial grand piano, a gift from a wealthy donor. In the hands of some musicians, it can sound harsh and tinny, but Abby makes it sing. She plays like she's one of us, deep inside the music, feeling it in her heart.

At the end, we're breathless and sweating. I know it was ragged. Lucas has tutu rash all over his face and arms. He bends and puts his hands on his knees, breathing hard. I shake out my arms, which are aching and trembling.

Levkova is not pleased. She paces in front of us, her long chiffon dance skirt swirling around her legs. At nearly sixty, she is still every inch the Bolshoi ballerina she was forty years ago.

Finally she stops pacing, and my entire body freezes. I tense up, shoulders rigid, jaw clenched. I clasp my hands together and tap my finger. Nine times. Nine times more. I can see Levkova thinking. Watching. Planning our evisceration.

"You are dancing like good friends."

We sigh with relief. If she weren't right in front of us, we'd high-five each other.

"This is not a compliment, *mes enfants*."

A murmur rises behind us. Even the girls in the *corps* are nervous. I can hear Delaney whispering, the rustle of their tutus, the sound of their pointe shoes on the wood floor as they stretch out their legs and feet. After you've been dancing for hours and hours, it hurts to stand still.

"Lucas, who are you?" When Levkova gets passionate in her coaching, her smoky Russian accent grows thicker. The whispering in the *corps* grows louder. Levkova's face flushes, and she turns to fuss at them. "Ladies, silence, please. Watch and learn."

Under his breath, Lucas says, "Is it me, or is she starting to sound like Chekov in the *Star Trek* movies?" I elbow him in the side. If we laugh, or even smile right now, we are dead.

Levkova repeats her question. "Lucas. Who are you?"

"Ummm, Siegfried? I'm a prince?"

"Your lack of conviction disappoints me."

His shoulders droop, and he stares at his feet.

"Sparrow, who are you?"

"I am Odette, a princess, under the spell of an evil wizard who preys on young women. I'm a swan in the daytime and human at night. My heart is broken."

When Levkova turns to me, Lucas sticks out his tongue and mouths, *Suck-up!* behind her back.

"Yes, but I am not seeing your broken heart. I do not feel it. You are dancing the steps, but you are not dancing the role."

She takes both of us by the wrist and turns us to face each other.

"Lucas. Your mother has told you that you must marry. It is your twenty-first birthday, and you must choose a bride at the ball tonight. You are a prince, but you have lost your way. You are searching for something, but you do not know what it is. You are in love with no one, and no one is in love with you. You have everything, yet you have nothing."

Levkova's sapphire-blue eyes are shining, and when she gestures, it looks as though she's dancing. A wave of love for her washes over me, warming me from the inside out.

"You are all alone on your birthday, in the middle of a dark forest, on the shores of a silver lake. And you see a creature so ravishing, so enchanting that you fall instantly in love with her. But *hélas!* She is cursed!

"You must show this longing, this love, in your whole being. In every gesture, every expression. You must show that you ache to be with her, body and soul. Can you do this?"

Lucas is blushing, but he looks straight into the blue eyes that always make me think of frozen rivers and glittering jewels and snow falling on onion-shaped domes.

He nods and says, "Yes, Madame. I can do this."

"And, Sparrow," Levkova says, turning to me. "You have lost all your hope. You spend your days and nights grieving near a lake that is filled with your mother's tears. But when you see this prince, when he touches you, you dare to believe that your life could be another way. That you might be saved. And when you look at him, when you touch him, you must make the audience believe that you love him. That you have given him your heart. That you have trusted him with your life."

You could hear a pin drop in the studio. We are all enchanted, mesmerized by her voice, by the story and our roles in it, overwhelmed and humbled by the responsibility to dance it well.

"Now, then. This is what I want to see. Love. Hope. Trust. But mostly love. Passionate, heartbreaking love. Again, from the beginning."

She claps her hands and tosses her head, like a diva at a curtain call. Raising her hand to Abby, the signal to begin, she gives Lucas and me one curt nod. She is done indulging us. Back to work.

This time, it feels different. We aren't just dancing roles. We become Siegfried and Odette, both cursed, each in our own way.

Lucas makes it look like he aches for me, as though when I dance away from him, the space where I'd been moments before has gone cold. With my entire body, with all my heart, I dance the panicked fear of never being human again, the agony of imprisonment, of having no power over my body's form or shape.

I dance, my heart breaking open, filling with love. I let myself melt into Lucas, wishing that I could stay safe in his arms forever, hoping that he will shield me and save me from evil. When I look into his eyes, I see a prince. I let my arms linger around his neck, even as I pull away in fear.

This time, it's magic.

When we finish, staring at each other in embarrassment and exhilaration, there's a deep silence all around us. The last notes of the piano float up to the high ceiling, fading away in the afternoon light.

And then Delaney starts to clap. "You guys! You stud muffins! You slayed it!" Abby stands up and joins her. Soon the entire room is filled with the sound of applause, while Lucas and I stand dazed and panting. Caleb lets out an ear-piercing whistle and shouts, "Brava! Bravo!" We don't respond. We stand still, breathing hard, waiting for Levkova. Nothing is real, nothing is good, until she says so.

I tap my finger against the palm of my hand and count all the things I did wrong. My *arabesques* were wobbly. I was off at the end, almost two beats behind. I felt shaky on the lifts. I'm afraid of what Levkova's going to say. I need her approval, her blessing, like I need air and food and water.

She comes gliding over to us. Her cheeks are flushed, and she is smiling, something as rare as an eclipse. Wordlessly, she puts her hands on my shoulders, kisses me on both cheeks, and tucks a sweaty strand of hair behind my ear. She rests the palm of her hand on my face for a long moment, gazing into my eyes like she wants to tell me something, then turns abruptly and kisses Lucas, who has to bend down so she can reach his scruffy face. She smells like lilacs and snow.

"Better. There is much work yet to be done, but today you

have come a little closer to perfection." Then she says the words I live for: "I am proud of you."

Overcome with relief and joy and the sweet ache of tired muscles, I throw my arms around Lucas and hug him close. He lifts me off my feet, burying his face in my neck, spinning me in slow circles. His arms tighten around me.

"Oh my God, Lucas, that was amazing. You were amazing!"

"Sparrow," he whispers, so quietly I can barely hear him. "I wasn't pretending."

Before I can react or think about what to say or feel, I see Tristan's face at the door over Lucas's shoulder.

Lucas's words are lost in the roaring that fills my ears. All I can see is Tristan. Only then do I think to check the clock on the wall. It's three o'clock. Rehearsal has gone on for half an hour past the time he always picks me up.

"Lucas," I say. "Put me down."

He sets me gently on the floor, but keeps his hands on my waist.

I check the window set high in the studio door. Tristan is gone.

"Birdy," he says softly. "What is it? Did I upset you? What's wrong?"

He looks hurt, and I know I should stay and at least acknowledge what he said. But I can't. "I'm sorry, Lucas, I have to go, like, right now. I'll text you later."

I run to grab my dance bag, piled with the others in a corner near the window. Fumbling with the hooks in my tutu, I step out of it, pin it to a skirt hanger, and hang it crookedly on the metal wardrobe rack.

Lucas is still where I left him, frozen in place, watching me.

I forget the customary *révérence* to Levkova and Abby. Levkova calls out, "Savannah Rose, how dare you leave this studio so rudely! Have you forgotten your manners?" I know I'll lie awake tonight kicking myself, that no apology will ever fix what I'm doing right now, but I keep going. All I can think about is getting to the changing room, taking off my pointe shoes, and meeting Tristan in the parking lot. But the girls in the *corps* surround me, smiling, patting my shoulders, giving me one-armed hugs.

"You were wonderful!" Ainsley squeals.

One of the younger girls, Emma, says, "You looked just like Gillian Murphy! Oh my God, your arms are amazing!"

"Thanks, guys, thanks," I say, trying to smile and not be a jerk. "I'm sorry, but I really need to get out of here. Y'all were great! See you Monday!"

Caleb tries to high-five me as I make my way to the door, but I push past him and run down the hall.

"Aw, man, come on!" he calls after me. "Don't leave a brother hanging!"

In the changing room, I pick at the stubborn knots in the ribbons on my shoes, cursing under my breath. The clock keeps ticking.

I hear the door open and the sound of pointe shoes on tile coming in my direction. Delaney plops down beside me, half of her tutu in my lap. She tightens her bun and leans close to me, examining my face like a detective looking for spatter patterns.

"What's going on? No one leaves without Levkova's permission. No one leaves without the *révérence*. Something's up, and you need to tell me. Like, right now."

"It's nothing," I say, finally loosening the knots and wrapping the ribbons around my shoes. I turn away and shove them into my dance bag. "I just need to get out of here. Tristan's been waiting for more than half an hour. I hate making him wait."

She shakes her head. "Nope. That's not it. You've never, ever rushed out of the studio like that. In fact, you always stay late, because you are a masochist."

"Yeah, but that was before I had a boyfriend. Is it so hard to believe that I want to leave on time so I can be with him?"

"Bird Girl, to be honest, you seem a little wigged-out." She points at my face. "Your mouth is saying one thing, but it doesn't square up with the rest of you."

"Jesus, Laney, you're worse than my dad! Stop with the third degree! I'm not wigged-out, okay? It's just that I don't like to keep anybody waiting. Especially Tristan."

"So what if he's waiting? You're doing something that's important to you, and it's his choice to pick you up. It's not like he's out there bleeding to death. By the way, why does he always drive you to and from ballet now? Like, every single freaking day? Isn't that, I don't know, a bit much? What if you and I wanted to go have coffee at Nora's, like we used to before you were in love?"

"If we wanted to have coffee, he'd be fine with it. And actually, no, it isn't a bit much. It's sweet. He says this way he can see me for a few minutes before I disappear into the studio for three hours after school and five hours on Saturday. You're making it seem like some huge thing, and it's not!"

"Right. If you say so, Swan Queen," she says, standing up and adjusting her tutu. "I'm going back now. Levkova gave us five minutes to 'stop acting like hysterical children and behave properly.' You want me to tell her you're sick?"

"Would you? Tell her I felt faint. Or I threw up. I owe you, Laney."

"Oh, you'll pay, trust me," she says, walking to the mirrors.

She leans in and licks her finger, dabbing at the mascara that's smudged under her eyes. She leaves in a rustle of net and tulle.

As soon as she's gone, I pull a short black denim skirt over my tights, shove my feet into the worn Uggs I've had since ninth grade, and shrug on the bolero jacket I wore on my first date with Tristan.

Delaney's right. I need to chill out. I smile to myself, imagining how Tristan's arms will be around me in minutes, how he'll kiss me before he pulls out of the parking lot, just like he always does.

I say Sophie's words, the ones that make me feel instantly calm. "All will be well, all will be well, and all manner of things shall be well." He loves me. Everything is fine.

I run down the hall. Tristan is waiting.

5

Fourth of July

Tristan stomps hard on the gas pedal, making the tires squeal as we turn right onto Main Street. "How come every conversation with your father is like a verbal colonoscopy?"

"I'm so, so sorry. He's completely embarrassing. It's the lawyer in him. He feels a moral obligation to cross-examine you every time he sees you. It's not you, personally. He trusts no man around his daughter."

Tristan's hands tighten on the steering wheel, and he scowls at the windshield. He goes quiet. Quiet is dangerous. At least when someone is screaming, you know where you stand.

"When I was thirteen, my dad told me that if he could get away with it, he'd send me to a convent until I was thirty, then arrange my marriage to the rich, impotent son of some obscure European noble family. He said the Benedictines would be a good choice, because I look nice in black."

Tristan turns to me, still frowning. "You think it's funny,

Savannah? Because I don't. He makes me feel like a freaking criminal, and it's starting to piss me off."

I feel sick, like my stomach is crawling up into my throat, and the palms of my hands are sweating. I wipe them on my skirt.

"No, I don't think it's funny. I promise I'll talk to him, okay? I'll get him to back off."

"Hand me a beer. There's a six-pack on the floor behind you."

"You want a beer while you're driving? Really?"

His voice rises into a high falsetto, mimicking me. "Yes, really, I want a beer while I'm driving."

Suddenly he jerks the car to the right and slams on the brakes. I'm thrown forward, and my seat belt locks, digging into my collarbone. He reaches into the back seat and pulls a sweating bottle of Blue Moon from the stash behind me. He twists it open, tosses the cap out the window, and swallows half of the beer.

Tristan guns the engine, pulls away from the curb, and we tear through the traffic lights down Main Street. My sweet little town passes in a blur. Lily and Isabelle locking up their vintage shop, Sadie the corgi waiting patiently at their feet. Nora's cottony white hair behind her bakery case. The twinkle lights sparkling on the gazebo in the town square. Everything flies by so quickly, like visions from a dream.

I can't stand his silence. I don't know what he's thinking, if he's just irritated about my dad or this is blowing up into something bigger.

"I'm super-excited about tonight, aren't you? I know you were at Delaney's Fourth of July party last year, but it will be so much better this year, for me anyway, because we're together. I love Delaney's house, almost as much as I love mine. When we were kids, we spent every weekend at each other's houses. Mostly at mine, but sometimes I went to hers, and her mom always made me feel like I was another daughter. So tonight's going to be—"

"Shut up, Savannah. I can't stand the sound of your voice right now, okay? Just stop talking. Whatever you have to say, I don't care."

Shut up. Don't tell. Got it. I'm good at being quiet.

Tristan speeds up. He's grinding his teeth. I dig my fingernails into the armrest. He's going so fast I'm afraid he'll lose control of the car.

"Tristan," I say softly. "Please slow down. The police are always out on the Fourth of July. I don't want you to get in trouble."

"I don't ever get in trouble, Savannah. Trust me."

He speeds up, probably going sixty where the speed limit is thirty-five.

"You're scaring me. Could you please slow down? For me?"

"I will if you hand me another beer."

"I can't reach behind me."

"Take off your seat belt."

I unbuckle my seat belt and twist myself around, kneeling on the seat to reach the beer behind me. The hot alcohol smell in the car, on his breath, is making me dizzy and sick. In an instant I am a child again, and my parents are in the kitchen, arguing. I hear the crystal sound of glass bottles thrown hard into the big green trash can next to the back door, the sound of my father's furious whispering, and my mother, crying.

Caro, you can't keep forgetting to pick her up at school! What the hell were you doing?

I was working! I got involved in my art, okay? Savannah was fine!

Jesus, your art. Give me a break. You weren't painting, and she wasn't fine! She'd been crying for hours by the time I got there. We've been over this a thousand times! You can't drink! You can't stop taking your meds! You have to try, love. Sweetheart, you need to do better than this.

I close my eyes and hang on to the back of my seat with both hands. When my head clears, I hand Tristan a beer and buckle myself back in.

He grins at me. "Thanks, babe. You weren't afraid I'd stop real quick and send you flying through the windshield?"

"Why would you do that? You love me."

He takes a long swallow of beer and flies through a light just as it turns red. Horns blare in our wake, and I grab on to the armrest again and bite the insides of my cheeks.

"Tristan, please, please slow down. You're really scaring me."

"We're almost there. I thought you wanted to get to the party, because you just love Delaney's house. I'm only trying to make you happy, baby." He's starting to slur his words, and I wonder how much he had to drink before he picked me up.

I try to count the streetlights whizzing past, starting over after every ninth one. In my head, I say the rhyme I made up when I was six. It's stupid, but it calms me down.

One, two, three, count with me. Four, five, six, almost fixed. Seven, eight, nine, I'll be fine. But it doesn't help tonight.

Tristan screeches to a stop in front of Delaney's house, one of the rambling old Victorians on Glastonbury Court. Her brother, Sean, and his band are tuning up in the backyard, and the sound of mandolins and banjos floats out to me across the soft night air.

Tristan cuts the engine and turns to me, running his hand through my hair. I've left it soft and loose for him, because he hates the bun. He says it makes me look uptight. He leans over and kisses me gently, tracing his thumb down my cheek. I lean my head into his palm, kissing him back. I love him so much when he's like this. He traces softly down my neck to my shoulder then stops. He jerks his head back, and my heart starts to race.

"Where's your necklace?" he asks quietly, enunciating carefully, not slurring like he was before. So I'll understand what I've done. What I've failed to do.

"Tristan, I'm so sorry! I must have forgotten to put it on after ballet yesterday."

Thunderclouds are massing in his gray eyes. "You promised me you'd never take it off, ever. Were you lying to me, Savannah?"

Last month, Tristan took me on a picnic to the Honeysuckle Pond to celebrate our three-month anniversary. He opened a bottle of champagne and handed me a black velvet box. Inside, there was a necklace with a silver heart pendant, a sparkling stone at its center. Blue topaz, the color of a summer sky. He made me promise I'd never take it off, because then it would be like he was always with me.

"I didn't lie to you, Tristan, I promise! I know I said I'd wear it all the time, but we're not allowed to wear jewelry in class. I forgot to put it back on. I'm so, so sorry."

"How do you think that makes me feel?" he says, clenching his jaw. I can see the muscles tighten in his face. "I guess that expensive necklace doesn't mean anything to you. Maybe I don't mean anything to you either."

He reaches out to the hollow in my throat, just above where the heart usually rests, and spreads his fingers so that they're around my neck. His eyes never leave mine. My breath quickens, and he starts to squeeze, just a little, but it hurts and I'm afraid.

"Don't, Tristan," I whisper. "Please." He squeezes again, harder this time, then lets go. My eyes are watering.

I reach out to touch his face, to stroke his hair. He recoils like I'm trying to hand him a snake.

"Tristan," I say softly. "Please don't be like this. I love my necklace, and I love you. I was an airhead and forgot to put it back on, that's all. I was excited about the party, excited to see you tonight. I'll make it up to you, I promise, and I'll put it on as soon as I get home. I'll never take it off again, no matter what Levkova says."

I lean over and press my lips to his. He doesn't kiss me back. "Let's go inside, okay? Delaney's waiting."

I jump when Brandon bangs on Tristan's window, holding up his beer. Tristan's face changes in an instant, morphing from anger to amusement. He holds up his empty bottle. "I'm way ahead of you clowns," he says. "Get me another one. I'll be right there."

Delaney waves at us from the front porch and calls, "Come on, y'all! What are you waiting for? Hurry up and get in here!"

Tristan flips her off. "Your friend needs to mind her own damn business, don't you think?" He gets out and slams the door without looking back. Instantly he's surrounded by all the jocks, laughing and high-fiving. He starts toward Brandon's car, where the trunk is open and a cooler full of alcohol awaits.

I get out of the car and run across the lawn to Delaney. She's reciting the rules to everyone as they walk in. "No cigarettes in the house, no weed, no hard stuff. I smell weed, you're out. Look like you're tripping, you're out, and you'll never be back. Spill something in the house, and Sean's college boys will kick your ass. If you're going to puke, you better do it outside, and then you're out. No discussion, no exceptions. We cool? Good."

She sees me and smiles. "Hey, sweetie," she says, giving me a quick hug. "What in the name of my mama's palomino were you guys doing out there?" We both turn to look at Tristan and his friends. "God, what a bunch of tacky, mouth-breathing morons. It's like they're the poster boys for dumb jocks everywhere. Tristan excepted, of course."

"Where's Justin?" I ask.

"I kicked him to the curb last night. He was so freaking handsy all the time, completely uninterested in, you know, actually talking to me like I was a real person. I always felt like I was on a date with a sea creature. All arms and mouth, small, gelatinous brain. It got boring."

"Totally his loss. And you look amazing, by the way."

Delaney's wearing a short white ruffled skirt with one of her mother's braided leather belts slung low on her narrow hips, her turquoise boots, and a black cowboy hat with chunky bits of turquoise and silver around the crown. Thin silver bangles glitter on both arms.

"Of course I look amazing! Who wouldn't, with all this cowgirl swag?"

I put my arm around her waist. "You are such a piece of work. You know that, right?"

"Yes, I do. It's why I am adored far and wide. But seriously, what about you? I thought you'd never get out of that stupid car. Also, I never thought I'd say this about your smokin' hot boyfriend, but he was a total jerk just now. Nothing says, 'Hey, thanks for inviting me to your party' like flipping off the host. What's his problem?"

I lean my head on her shoulder, breathing in the fragrance of pomegranate juice and Amazing Grace perfume. "I know. I'm really sorry."

"Don't apologize for him, Sparrow. You didn't flip me off. He did."

"He's upset because I forgot to wear the necklace."

"Wait, what? Are you telling me your boyfriend is mad because you aren't wearing some piece of jewelry he gave you? That is textbook douchey behavior, Bird Girl."

"It means a lot to him, Laney, and it's totally my fault he's mad. I can't believe I forgot to put it on."

"Sparrow," she says. "It's his fault he's mad, not yours."

I shove her shoulder with mine.

"One of the things I love about you, besides, you know, the whole Rodeo Queen thing, is that you are such a crazy-fierce friend. But this time, you're so, so wrong."

She looks at me for a long moment, then shoves me back.

"Okay, I'm wrong. But I'm still right."

It's such a relief to laugh. "Come on," I say. "Let's go inside. Tristan will get over it. Everything's fine."

Virginia summers are always thick with heat and humidity, but tonight is cooler than usual. Everything feels fresh and earthy and full of hope. The sky is sprinkled with early stars, and the cicadas are beginning to sing. I feel the blue mountains all around, sheltering us.

Tonight will be like every high-school party in the history of the world, the air suffused with beer and bourbon, cinnamon gum and toothpaste, candles that smell like cookies. Someone will be locked in a bathroom, sobbing about being dumped or their parents' bitter divorce or a friend's terrible betrayal. Charlotte will throw up.

Delaney gives me her searching look, her eyes all squinty and worried. "You really going to be able to shake it off?"

"I already have."

As if he knows we're talking about him, Tristan turns to stare at me. No smile, just the stare. He finishes his beer, drops the bottle, and kicks it down the storm drain. Brandon twists the top off another one and hands it to him. He takes a long pull, then chugs the rest.

"Go for it, bro!" Trevor, Brandon's twin brother, pounds a drumroll on his chest. "That's what I'm talkin' about!"

Tristan wipes his mouth and sways a little on his feet, leaning heavily against Brandon's car. "Wooooo!" he yells, pumping his fist in the air. "Let's get this party started!"

Delaney shakes her head. "They are disgusting pigs from hell. I don't know why I keep inviting them."

Suddenly it feels like I'm floating, looking down at myself from far away. Tristan's back to me again, tight and rigid, anger coming off him in waves, like heat from asphalt. Me, my arm around Delaney's waist, never taking my eyes from him because I always need to know where he is.

I start to go inside the house, but Delaney pulls on my arm. "Hang on a second."

"What now?"

"I have to tell you, I'm just the teensiest bit worried."

I give her an exasperated sigh. "I'm fine, Laney. There's nothing for you to be worried about."

"Maybe. But I saw you looking at him just now, and you did not look like a girl who's in love; you looked scared. Tell me the truth. Are you?"

"Am I what?"

"Scared."

Fireflies are flickering in and out of the tree branches, and suddenly I wish I were completely alone, light-years away from any noise or civilization. No party, no Tristan, no Delaney, nobody talking to me, no endless interrogations.

If only he'd look at me, give me a smile, tell me with his eyes that I'm forgiven, that he loves me, that we are okay. If only I could forget his hand on my throat, the pressure of his fingers, the fury in his eyes.

"You're thinking way too hard tonight, cowgirl. No, I'm not scared, not one bit. Now can we go inside? Please?"

She holds up three fingers in the Girl Scout salute. "Okay. I promise I will shut up now and pull my nose out of your business. 'This the Dauphin speaks.'"

Ever since we read *Henry V* last year, Delaney's been crushing on Shakespeare. She throws out random quotes, badgering us to name the act and scene. We get extra points if we nail the speaker.

"Act one, scene two, the Ambassador. Please let that be the last time."

She pats me on the head, like I'm a good puppy.

"Not a chance, brainiac."

I hear Lucas before I see him, the deep, rumbling voice that makes him sound way older than seventeen. He hasn't been to a party since March, when his father was diagnosed with cancer. My whole heart lifts.

"Yeah, thanks. I appreciate it. I'm okay. Anybody seen Sparrow?"

He walks into the kitchen, and the crowd around us melts away. He holds out his arms, and I walk into them. He bends down and kisses the top of my head. I breathe in his familiar scent, Coast soap and Suave coconut shampoo and wintergreen toothpaste. Tears prickle behind my eyes, and I pull him closer. "I've missed you, Lucas Oliver."

"I missed you, too, Birdy Bird." His arms tighten around me. "I'm sorry I didn't answer any of your texts. I was—"

"Oh, Lucas, don't apologize. I just wanted you to know I was thinking about you. I wanted to visit after the funeral so many times, but I didn't know if you wanted to see anyone. I figured you'd let me know when you were ready." I give him another squeeze and let go. The space between us grows cold.

"I didn't want to see anyone. But I would have liked it if you'd come."

"I'm sorry I didn't, but I'm so glad you came tonight. How are you really?"

Lucas, six foot three, muscles on top of muscles, seems smaller tonight. Dark circles under his eyes, sunken cheeks. I wish I could give him a haircut, then fix him a big plate of spaghetti and warm bread, like Sophie does for me whenever I've had a bad day.

"I'm glad to be here, doing something normal. It feels like nothing's been normal in such a long time."

Delaney's kitchen is all blue and yellow with red accents, like the KitchenAid mixer, the coffee maker, the dish towels folded neatly near the sink and draped over the handle of the stove. Lucas walks around the deep-blue granite-topped island, running his hand over the cool surface. He picks up one of the many candles lined up down the middle, sniffs it, and makes a face. "God, I hate candles that try to smell like food. Pumpkin is the worst."

"You didn't really answer my question," I say softly.

He takes a deep breath, walks over to the fridge, and starts rearranging the magnets holding recipes and family pictures. "Twelve weeks, Birdy. He lasted twelve weeks. We didn't have time to get ready. We kept thinking he could get better, even those last few days. How is that even fair?"

His eyes fill, and he strangles a sob.

"Oh, Lucas, it's not fair at all. I'm so, so sorry." Having him right here in front of me, seeing the naked grief that's taken up residence all over his face, is heartbreaking.

"How's your mom?" I ask. "How's Anna?"

"Anna's still so small, I don't think she really gets that he's gone. She keeps going into his study and curling up in the chair near the window. She's waiting for him to come home. My mother is . . . My mother is not good."

He wipes his eyes with the backs of his hands and gives me a watery smile.

"Sorry. It gets me at the weirdest times. I think maybe I'm doing okay, and then something just punches me in the face. Yesterday I pulled into the garage and saw his tools on the workbench, lined up all neat and organized. I sat in my car and cried like a four-year-old."

In all our lives, I've only seen Lucas cry once, after the funeral. He didn't even cry when I broke his nose two years ago coming down from a lift. I picture him all alone in his garage, weeping for his father, and my own eyes fill up.

"Your dad was such a great guy. We all loved him. I'll never forget that weekend he took us to Colonial Williamsburg and wore that stupid tricornered hat and fake powdered wig the whole time. He kept saying 'ye olde' in front of everything. Like 'I need to visit ye olde crapper.'"

He laughs shakily. "Yeah, he could be a dingus, that's for sure. He took us to lunch at that fancy tavern and made us try peanut soup. Remember how gross it was?"

"Ugh, like hot peanut butter. Totally disgusting. But you know what I'll never forget about him? Remember when we were seven and my cat died?"

Now he laughs for real.

"Oh God, 'Lucy the Most Excellent Cat.' He sang it at her funeral, at the top of his lungs. To the 'SpongeBob' tune! How twisted was that? I remember your dad and Sophie were trying so hard not to crack up. Then he gave you that book, what was it called?"

"*Cat Heaven*. He was such a kind man, Lucas. And a really, really good dad. You're so much like him."

"I hope so. I want to be like him. I hope I grow up that fine." His voice catches in his throat. "I'd like to make him proud of me. This is probably lame, but I've been hoping he's still hanging around, watching over us, making sure we'll be okay before he goes, you know, wherever."

I reach up and touch his cheek. He hasn't shaved in days.

"I believe he is; I really do. It was always so obvious how much he loved you and Anna and your mom. You should talk to him when you feel him close. You know, like talk to him inside your heart. He'll hear you. I know he will."

"Thanks, Birdy. I'm really happy to see you, if I haven't already told you."

"You ready to go face the crowd?"

"Yeah, but stay close, okay?"

"Promise."

Just then, Delaney and Caleb, Israel, Sam, and Luis burst into the kitchen, laughing and joking. "Okay, we gave you guys enough time to be all serious," says Sam, throwing his arm around Lucas's shoulders. "Now come outside and have some fun. Sean and the guys are killing it, and there's food."

Lucas perks up. "Food? Where?"

"Right in front of your face, doofus, over there on the table," Delaney says. She smiles and hugs him. "You know how much we love you, right? And we're here for you, no matter what."

"Thanks, Laney. But right now I'm starving, and I need to snag me some snacks." He strafes the kitchen table, grabs a handful of cheese cubes and two burritos, then heads out the door, tucking a burrito into his T-shirt pocket. "For later," he explains.

He and the guys wander off into the backyard, where Sean's band, Lonesome Biscuit Gang, has started their first set. Tonight it's mostly bluegrass, with some Iron & Wine covers. The window over the sink is open, and the outside smells like freshly mown grass and the sharp tang of tomato plants and marigolds. Three girls are swinging in the hammock strung between two enormous sugar maples, their long hair brushing the ground beneath them. Charlotte, drunk already, is doing *piqué* turns in her bare feet, a red Solo cup in each hand, sloshing rum and Coke on anyone who gets close.

"Look at her," Delaney says, coming to stand beside me at the sink. "She's going to puke all over my mother's lavender in about five minutes. I'm going to go kick her out before she does. I'm done hosing down the garden every time she gets wasted."

Delaney leaves, and I'm alone, the noise of the party swirling around me. I tiptoe down the hall and peek out the living room window. I can't see Tristan anywhere. When I come back to the kitchen, I see them. Lemons. In a blue ceramic bowl, the food artfully arranged all around. I pick up the bowl and dump the whole thing into the trash can under the sink.

"What in the hell were you doing with him?" Tristan is standing in the doorway, dangling a beer between his fingers, his eyes glassy and unfocused.

I grab on to the counter to steady myself. "We were just talking."

"You're lying. I saw you. I bring you to a party, and you hang all over the ballerina boy? Again? You just can't help yourself, can you? You can't wait to rub yourself all up against him, like a trashy little cat begging for attention. And don't even think about giving me that crap about how you dance together and you're just friends and it doesn't mean anything. How many times are we going to have this conversation?"

Now I'm holding on to the counter so hard my arms are starting to shake.

"Tristan, I'm sorry. It was nothing, I promise. We were talking, that's all."

"Liar."

I feel like some huge weight is pressing down on my chest. My breath is coming in ragged little gasps. I need to get out of here. I need to hide. I step away from the counter and make my way toward the door. My legs are trembling. I think maybe he's too drunk to care, too drunk to stop me, too drunk to move.

I am wrong.

Without a word, he grabs my arm and twists, nearly pulling me off my feet. He drags me between the island and the stove. Wrenching me around to face him, he digs his fingers into the soft flesh above my elbow.

"Tristan, stop it! Let go! You're hurting me!" I try to free myself, but he's too strong.

"Don't you dare, Savannah. Don't you dare lie to me. You were all over him. I saw you, with your arms wrapped around him. I saw you! He doesn't get anything from you, do you understand? I'm sorry his father croaked, but that's not my problem, and I won't let it be yours!"

He lets go of my arm and grabs my chin, his fingers digging into my jaw, my cheeks, so hard that I start to cry. I can barely open my mouth. "Yes, Tristan, I promise, I understand! Please let go! You're really hurting me."

He takes me by the shoulders, his face inches from mine, and shakes me, like a toddler with a rag doll.

"You must not give a damn about how I feel or what I think."

"Tristan, I love you! You know I do," I sob. He puts his hand on my throat again, just like before. I twist my head to try to get away, but I can't move. He smells like beer and sweat. His eyes are bloodshot, filled with rage.

"God, you look so ugly when you cry." He lets go of my neck and shakes me again, harder this time. "Stop it." I do the trick he taught me, tilting my head back so the tears won't spill, blinking fast so they'll run back into my eyes. "I mean it, Savannah. You stay the hell away from him. You don't talk to him. He walks into a room, you walk out. You don't even look at him. If I ever see you near him again, outside that stupid ballet studio, I will mess him up so bad he'll never dance again. With you or anybody else. Do you hear me?"

I try to nod, but I'm dizzy. Everything is going dark inside my eyes. I can't talk, can't answer him, can't do anything except wipe my eyes and nose with the back of my free hand. His lip curls in disgust.

"You're so unattractive to me right now, you know that?"

Outside, Sean's high, soulful tenor soars, climbing all the way up to the stars. Tristan lets go of my arm and pushes me. My hip slams into the handle of the oven as my elbow smashes into the grate over the gas burner. My leg gives way beneath me, and I fall hard, landing on my tailbone.

"Pull yourself together, Savannah, and get your things. We're leaving."

Scuttling like a crab to the nearest corner, breathless with crying, I cradle my elbow, pressing my head to my knees so I won't be sick. This is my fault, my fault, all my fault. He loves me. He loves me so much. He tells me all the time. This will pass. We'll be fine. He'll feel terrible in a few minutes, and there will be apologies and tears and promises and kisses. I will forgive him, because I love him.

Huddled on the floor of Delaney's kitchen, I do what I always do when I'm too scared to do anything else.

I count. The tiles on the floor. The pearl buttons on my black camisole. The eight lemons I know are in the trash under the sink. There in the dark, I know they're shining like wicked little suns. I can smell them. I hold my breath to block them out, but it doesn't work.

Seven, eight, nine, I'm not fine.

I wish I could find a little cupboard to hide in, where no one would ever find me. I wish I could make myself disappear.

6

Seventh of July

"You ready?" Lucas asks, his voice clipped and terse. It's three days after Delaney's party.

Dressed in black tights and his favorite gray T-shirt, the one with all the holes at the hem, he finishes stretching at the barre.

He won't look at me.

I take off my thick black leg warmers and adjust the wrapping on my ankle. Though I sprained it years ago, this role has brought the old ache back to life, and I greet it like a long-lost friend. Pain means I'm accomplishing something. Pain means I'm alive.

"Yep. Let's go."

We begin where we always begin.

I arrange myself on the floor, left leg bent under me, right leg extended, foot arched and pointed. I rest my forehead on my knee and concentrate on making my arms look as fluid and boneless as possible, crossing my wrists over my leg so they look like the folded wings of a bird. Lucas is supposed to walk slowly toward me, bending over my arms, lifting one wrist, then the other.

But he doesn't. I can hear him behind me, pacing back and forth.

"I can't do this," he says.

"What are you doing?" I straighten up and look around.

He looks me dead in the eye. "No, Sparrow. What are you doing?"

Sighing, I get up and walk to my dance bag. Pulling my leg warmers back on, I say, "What's your problem? Are we going to rehearse or not? It was hard enough to get permission to be here this early in the morning. You really want to waste time?"

"I can't dance with you, not like this." He walks to the barre, tugging on his sweatshirt.

"Not like what?"

"Sick and tired of watching you pretend everything's fine. That your boyfriend's a prince among men, a real stand-up guy."

I close my eyes and breathe in slowly, trying to center myself.

"He is a stand-up guy. And mine is the only opinion that matters."

"Nope, nope, nope, not anymore. I was at Delaney's. Is your memory that short? I saw you crying, Sparrow, all folded up in the corner. On the floor."

"I slipped."

"You're really going to stick with that lame-ass story?"

"Lucas, I'm not doing this with you. I'm just not. I'm fine, and it's all forgotten. Could we please, please get through the *pas de deux* just once? Come on. Let's forget everything and dance. We can talk later, if you want."

Leaning against the barre with his arms folded across his chest, he scowls at me.

"I don't want to talk later. I want to talk now. And for once, I'm not going to let you weasel your way out of telling the truth."

"And I want to dance, which is why we're here, so why don't you just get a freaking grip and stop lecturing me? I've told you before: my life and my boyfriend are none of your business."

There's a sharp rap on the door, and Levkova peers in. "Was I wrong to give you permission to use the studio this morning? You are here to rehearse, are you not? If you want to lounge about and chat, please go somewhere else and waste your time." She slams the door behind her.

Her words, the slam of the door, echo all around us, and we stare at each other, unwilling to give ground. Finally Lucas sighs and pulls off his sweatshirt, balling it up and tossing it into a corner.

"Okay, Birdbrain, you win this round," he says. "But I'm still pissed, and I'm not letting it go, just so you know."

"Whatever. Dance with me."

"Quit bossing me around."

I rearrange myself on the floor. This time, Lucas is with me. He lifts one wrist, then the other. He unfolds me. At the touch of his hands, I raise my head.

I feel Odette's imprisoned soul deep inside me, frightened, submerged, and inhuman. Erased from the world.

The *pas de deux* takes about ten minutes from start to finish, if we don't stop. But of course we do, to move slowly through the footwork until it feels perfect, to work through the placement of Lucas's hands, the *port de bras* at the end that I still can't get quite right. We look at ourselves in the mirrors with unsparing, critical eyes, trying to figure out which angle is best when I'm *en pointe*, he wraps his arms around me from behind, and I rest my head on his shoulder. That's always been my favorite moment, those few seconds when we're mostly still, and the agony of the curse is written on our faces, in our bodies.

By the end, we're drenched with sweat. I can't feel my calves, and my feet are cramping. Lucas lies on the floor, his arms and legs spread like Da Vinci's *Vitruvian Man*—with a Deathly Hallows tattoo on the inside of one wrist.

"It's like we're two old farts trying to climb a flight of stairs," he says. "I'm going to need an oxygen tank and one of those walkers with the tennis balls on the feet just to get out of the building."

"Come on, old fart," I say, holding out my hand. "You ready for some more?"

He groans. "You really going to pull me up off this floor?"

"No, but I thought I'd make the offer." He takes my hand and springs to his feet, then focuses like a laser on my wrist.

"That's new. From Tristan?"

"Yes," I say, pulling my hand out of his. The bracelet, thin silver links with a heart to match my necklace, glitters in the pale morning light streaming in through the windows. I turn away before he can see the inscription.

Forgive me.

"Is that how it works? He's a massive a-hole, then you get jewelry? Is the bling worth whatever he's putting you through?"

"Lucas, look, I really need you to stop this, okay? I know you're going through a tough time right now, with your dad and your mom and Anna—"

His face flushes and his eyes flare with anger. "Stop right there. I mean it, Sparrow. Don't you dare hide behind my father. Yes, I'm going through a tough time. But that doesn't make me blind or stupid or oblivious to what's going on around me. Something's not right with you and Tristan, and I saw it with my own eyes the other night. I know how you hate talking about stuff, especially anything that's even remotely difficult, but I don't even think you're talking to yourself about this."

"Lucas, please, would you just shut up? All I want to do is dance right now. I'm in my favorite place on the planet, with my favorite partner, and we have music and it's finally going to rain and we are seventeen and the principal freaking dancers in Swan Freaking Lake. Could we please enjoy this moment without having to argue? Because I hate arguing, Lucas. Especially with you. Come on. We have the studio for another half an hour. Let's do something fun."

In the hall, the sound of preschool girls arriving for ballet class fills the air. It's such a sweet, joyful sound, the little girls chattering and laughing, their mothers trying to hush them, telling them to behave themselves.

Lucas cracks his back and his neck.

"Gross! You are beyond disgusting. You know I hate that sound."

"Yep, I do. That's why I did it."

I hit his shoulder with my fist.

"You think I even feel that, Birdy?"

"Shut up. Also, you reek. Just so you know."

"Yeah, you smell like a monkey."

"Rather smell like one than look like one."

Finally. A laugh and a high five.

"Good one. Well played."

The knot in my stomach eases, and I smile at him.

"Just play some music, Lucas. I'm tired of talking. Let's dance, for God's sake."

"What do you feel like?" He always asks, and I always let him pick. Otherwise it would be all ballet music all the time, which makes him nuts.

"Your choice. I'm good with anything."

He syncs his phone with the Bluetooth speaker in the corner and thumbs through his library. Barns Courtney's "Hellfire" pounds into the room, and with a grunt like a feral hog, Lucas takes off, his body soaring into the air. He always needs to go super-hard and fast after the slow precision of the *pas de deux*. He does all of his favorite jumps, *grands jetés, sauts de basque, cabrioles*, and barrel turns.

I pretend to ignore him—he gets all weird and self-conscious if he knows I'm watching—so I work on upping my *fouetté* count. I can do a solid twenty-seven, but I'm trying to get to thirty-six, in case I ever get to dance Odile, the Black Swan. Levkova says seventeen is too young to be that evil, but I don't think evil cares how old you are.

When the music stops, we walk around the room together, gathering the last of our strength, working on slowing our breathing, shaking out our arms and rolling our necks and shoulders. I repair my bun, holding bobby pins between my teeth as we walk. My hair is soaked, and the back of my neck is wet. My lips are red and salty with sweat. Lucas keeps looking at me out of the corner of his eye. His face is flushed.

He walks over to his dance bag and takes out the tennis ball he uses to roll out the tired muscles in his feet. But instead of putting it under his foot, he hurls it, hard, at the door. It bounces back and hits a window, which rattles and shakes in its frame, then rolls to a stop at my foot.

I pick it up and sit down, rolling it between my hands, my back to the mirrors, looking out at the gray clouds hanging low over the smoky blue mountains. "So!" I say into the thick silence. "You think Levkova's going to be in a good mood this week or an I'm-going-to-make-them-all-suffer kind of mood?" My voice comes out all perky and squeaky, like I've swallowed a cheerleader. I tap my finger against my hand, three sets of three, then three more, then all over again, whispering to myself, again and again until I lose count. Lucas sees.

He comes to sit across from me, takes the tennis ball away, and puts his hands over mine. "It's okay, Birdy. Stop. It's okay. I'm sorry." We sit like that for a long moment, my hands in his. I'm still counting in my head.

He gives my hands a squeeze and says, "Do you promise you're okay? Pinky swear, and I'll drop it for good." He holds up his hand, pinky finger crooked and ready. Ever since we were kids, a pinky swear for Lucas is like a blood oath.

"Yeah, of course I am! And I don't need to pinky swear. I'm good, for real. My dad is coming home for dinner tonight for the first time in a long time, and Sophie's making that pasta we love, you know, with the bacon and peas that my dad calls Pasta Carbon Footprint?" I tap the toes of my pointe shoes together, counting.

"You know how it's been so annoying, having all those paralegals and suck-up law clerks at the house ever since the trial started? Like they're the ones who are going to save the perp *du jour*? We haven't been able to eat at the dining room table in months. Every morning, my dad drinks coffee and checks the news standing up at the kitchen counter." I take the bobby pins out of my bun and shove them in again, harder, tighter.

"Sophie finally kicked them all out, told them our house wasn't the suburban branch of the firm."

I'm talking way too fast about nothing, and everything sounds like a question. But Lucas is like a dog with a bone.

"Okay, no pinky swear, so I get one more question. Does Tristan know you're here?"

My stomach lurches. I told him I was sleeping late this morning.

"This is mine, Lucas. My work, my dancing, my time. Tristan knows I have to rehearse."

"Yeah, but he wasn't too happy about it that day in the parking lot."

"Jesus, would you just once and for all stop? I can't take it anymore, Lucas! Your hovering, your constant questions, your nose all up in my life, where it does not belong! Let me say it real slow, real clear, so even you will understand. You are not my father. You are not my brother. You don't own me. You have no say over what I do or who I see or what my life is like when I'm not dancing with you. Got it? You think you can remember a complicated concept like that? What I have with Tristan belongs to me. Not you, not Delaney, me. It's none of your business. It's nobody's business. It's private! So shut up and back off!"

He rolls his eyes so hard he can probably see his own brain. "Right. You guys are so private. Nobody sees how he is. Nobody notices when he gets pissed or hears him when he starts to yell. You want me to back off? How's this? Bet you didn't tell him you're here alone with me."

I feel my face turning crimson, the heat coming into my cheeks from the pit of my stomach. "God, what is your problem today? Okay, no. He doesn't know, and no, he wouldn't like it. Pretty sure you've figured out that he's mad jealous of you."

Even saying this much feels all wrong, especially in this room. Sacrilegious, like spitting in a church. All the fight goes out of me. I'm so tired.

"Yeah, but he gets that we don't really have a choice, right?"

I let out a long breath. "Only in an abstract kind of way. Like when you know in your head that you have to go to the dentist, but actually walking into the office and hearing the drill makes you want to barf."

"You want me to talk to him? I promise I'll be chill. I'd love us to have another little chat. I think we had a real connection the other night."

My mouth goes dry. "No, Lucas. Don't you dare."

I stand up and grab onto the barre, and Lucas stands up beside me, staring into the mirror. My skin is all blotchy and red. He rests his arms on the warm polished wood, and I busy myself with the lukewarm bottle of water I left on the floor. Lucas runs his hands through his damp curls, then stretches his hips out, first one side, then the other. He bends double, touching his nose to his knees, all tucked into himself. He breathes deeply, inhaling for a count of three, holding it for a count of three, then exhaling in a long, whooshing sound, like the night wind rushing through the trees.

He straightens up and gives me a look.

"Lucas," I say, "I'm serious. I swear to God, if you say anything to Tristan, I will never, ever speak to you again. Promise me you won't."

His eyes are super-intense, like he's trying to pull the words he wants to hear out of my throat. When I stay quiet, he throws up his hands. I'm not sure if it's surrender or exasperation.

"Yeah, okay, sure. I promise I will not say a word to your douchebag boyfriend. But that doesn't mean I won't flip him off next time I see him. Just so you know."

The sky has darkened, and rain patters against the windows. Inside, the air still feels charged, but we have to finish.

Lucas takes out his phone and turns up the speaker in the corner. We move to center floor to practice the most difficult, most romantic part of the *pas de deux*. It's hard, because we're both angry dancing, but we manage to get through it.

When we're finished, we're exhausted. Lucas grabs two towels from his bag and throws one to me.

"Look," he says, "I'm sorry. You're right; you guys are none of my business. I'll stop with the interrogations. I don't want you to get hurt, that's all, but I'll stop. I was out of line. I'm sorry. Come on, let's do the Last Thing."

He turns up "Devil's Backbone" by the Civil Wars.

"No."

"You have to. It's fish-dive time."

"I don't feel like it."

"You know it's the law of the land. If we don't do the fish dive, the planet will tilt on its axis, birds will drop out of the sky, and sad little chickens will howl at the moon." He sucks in his cheeks and makes a fish face. "Fish dive, Birdbrain. Fish dive."

I bite my lip, trying not to smile.

"You're a total idiot. You know that, right?"

"Yes, because you keep telling me. Come on. Fish dive."

I toss the towel aside, and stand in front of Lucas, moving slowly into *arabesque*. Lucas lifts me high over his head, counts to three, and lowers me crazy fast, so that my head and arms are only inches from the floor. A fish dive, thrilling and unbelievably beautiful.

I hold on to his hips with my legs, and he opens his arms in triumph. "Look at this, people," he crows. "Are we beasting it or what? Bow down and worship, peasants!"

I can't help it; I laugh. Lucas laughs with me, and I start to fall. He grabs my hips to keep me from hitting the floor.

I gasp and cry out, stepping awkwardly out of the dive and crashing to my knees. I'm breathless with pain. There's a loud roaring in my ears, and I feel like I'm going to pass out. I put my hand on my chest and count my heartbeats. By threes. I make it to twelve before I hear Lucas.

"Oh my God, Birdy! Say something! Please!" His face is stricken, his eyes wide. He's standing completely still, frozen, like he's afraid to move.

I try to steady my breathing. My hip is sending blinding bolts of pain all the way around my back and up to my ribs.

"I'm fine, I promise. It's just a little bruise. Give me a second, okay?"

"Sparrow, you're not fine! Oh my God, why won't you tell me the truth?"

7

Early August, a Saturday

Nora brings my latte in a heavy white ceramic cup, a perfect foam heart in the center, sprinkled with cinnamon. She pauses to watch the rain pounding against the big picture window, the wind lashing the trees in the town square across the street. Today she's wearing my favorite apron over her denim wraparound skirt, the pale green one embroidered with strawberries.

"It is a vile and wretched day, my love," she says in her lilting Scottish accent. "It reminds me of Scotland. And not in a good way. It has rained every day for nearly a month!"

She bustles away as the door opens and Sophie blows in, laughing, along with a shrieking gust of wind and rain. The mirrors on the wall rattle. She hangs her dripping raincoat on the rack near the cash register and makes her way over to our table in front of the window. "Nora! I'm sorry I'm dripping all over your floor! Give me a mop, and I'll clean up after myself!"

"Oh, hush," Nora says. "Nobody mops my floor but me. Go sit down, and I'll bring you a towel."

Sophie blows her a kiss and scoots into the booth across from me. Her jasmine perfume wafts over me like a benediction. Nora returns and sets a steaming cup of green tea in front of Sophie, along with two laminated menus and a fresh tea towel for her hair.

"You are an angel, Nora. Thank you!"

"You're welcome, darling. I made split-pea-and-ham soup to-day. It's delicious, if I do say so myself!"

She heads back to the kitchen, stopping to chat at every table along the way.

"I'm so sorry I'm late, sweetie," Sophie says. "It was murder finding a parking space. She squints her eyes at me and leans closer. "Honey, you're so pale! Are you getting sick?"

"No, I'm just exhausted. My feet won't stop cramping. Also, the swan arms are killing me. And you know, the whole thing with Lucas."

"What whole thing with Lucas?"

"Remember I told you we had an argument? After the Fourth of July?"

"You guys still haven't patched things up?"

"No. We're barely talking to each other."

"That's so unlike Lucas. I mean, that boy could talk the ears off an elephant. He's always so open and honest about everything. And he hates for people to be upset with him. Especially you."

"Yeah, well, not so much lately. I mean, we talk about danc-ing when we're in the studio, but that's it. And because he's not talking about anything else, and I feel so terrible about the nasty, ugly things I said to him, we're dancing like crap. Levkova is to-tally pissed off at both of us. Like today, in front of everybody, she told us if we couldn't stop acting like 'petulant children,' she'd find two other dancers who were worthy of *Swan Lake*. So that sucked."

I unwrap my silverware and put the spoon in my coffee cup, dead center, careful not to touch the sides. I wreck the heart, stirring the foam three times clockwise, three times counterclockwise. If I touch the sides, I have to start again.

Sophie reaches out and takes hold of my wrist. "Sparrow, honey," she says quietly. "Enough. Stop. Tell me more about Lucas. Tell me how I can help."

"I wish you could, but you can't. I mean, we don't even text each other anymore, and I know it's stupid, but I miss that most of all. I texted more with him than I do with Delaney. Every day he'd send me funny cat videos and pictures of baby goats, and if I was in a crappy mood, he was always the one who could make me laugh."

Sophie squeezes my hand. "Oh, sweetie. You really are having a bad day."

I sigh. "The whole thing is just this huge nasty ball of suck. It's not just today; it's everything right now. Lucas, *Swan Lake*, everything. I just want to eat and go home and take a hot bath. I'll get over it. I always do."

"Well," she says, scanning her menu. "You stop talking about it, which isn't exactly the same thing, but okay. When we get home, I'll find you some lavender to put in your bath. It will help you relax. Come on, let's eat. You must be starving, and I know I am."

Nora comes back to take our order. My stomach feels like I've swallowed jagged rocks, but I'll get unending grief if I only order toast and a boiled egg.

"How about the chicken salad sandwich? And could I please have some sliced tomato instead of potato salad?"

"You got it, Missy. Soph?"

"I'll do the split-pea soup and the flatbread, please. And I'd like some sweet tea, too, now that I'm all warmed up. With lime, please." Nora finishes writing on her little pad and grins at me.

"I'm coming to the gala in March. I already bought my ticket and paid for the sixth row, center orchestra. Be sure to wave at me."

"Nora, are you kidding? Levkova would kill me."

She chuckles and heads back to the kitchen.

I dig my phone out of my purse and set it carefully on the windowsill, beside the planters filled with bright yellow calla lilies and African violets. Two seconds later I change my mind and tuck it under my right thigh, so I'll be sure to feel it vibrate.

Sophie is not amused. "Do we not have a rule about phones during meals?"

"Yes, we do, Sophie, but I don't want to miss Tristan."

As if he can hear me talking about him, my phone buzzes. Sophie gives me a dark look. "Don't you even think about it."

"Sophie, I have to. It'll just be a second."

Where are u?

> Lunch with Sophie. <3

Where?

> Nora's.

K. Call me when you're done.

When I look up, Sophie's playing with her favorite bracelet, twisting it around her wrist and fingering the charms like beads on a rosary. A lighthouse, a dinosaur, a star. An angel, a paintbrush, a key. She does this when she's thinking. Or when she's irritated. "Are you done now?"

"Yes. I'm sorry. I just hate to miss him, especially when I've been at ballet all morning."

"Dancing is your passion, your gift. At this point, it can hardly be a surprise to your boyfriend that you have to work hard at it."

Nora comes with our food, and the air is filled with the warm fragrance of basil and cheese, tomatoes and red peppers. Maybe now Sophie will stop talking.

I peel the bread off my sandwich and scrape the chicken salad onto the plate. My stomach turns over. I cannot possibly eat this. The grapes look like eyeballs.

Sophie watches me silently, then takes my hand in hers. "Honey, can we talk about something?"

Under my thigh, my phone vibrates, buzzing like a wasp.

"Don't, Sparrow. Turn it off if it's going to distract you, because I would seriously like to have all your attention right now. Tristan can wait until we're done with lunch."

I put my phone back on the windowsill. I do not turn it off.

I take a sip of water and cut a slice of tomato with my fork. It bleeds onto the plate. "Okay. You have all my attention. But could you please not talk to me about ballet or Lucas or school starting soon? I'm wigged-out enough about that stuff. Wig me out about something else."

She gives me a faint smile. "I'm not trying to wig you out, honey. But I need to say something, and I need you to hear me."

My phone vibrates again, and I put my hand over it. Maybe he'll feel me reaching out to him. Maybe he'll know that I'm trapped. That I'm sorry.

Sophie swallows a bite of flatbread and takes a sip of sweet tea. She pushes her damp curls off her forehead and adjusts her long, dangly earrings. "Here's the thing. I'm wondering—and honestly, I'm really not trying to intrude here—but I'm a little concerned that this thing with Tristan has gotten way too serious, way too fast."

I roll my eyes. "Oh my God, Sophie, don't even start."

"Don't you roll your eyes at me, Miss Crabbypants. It's unkind, and it makes me feel that you think what I'm saying is stupid."

"I'm sorry, Sophie. I don't think you're stupid. But I love Tristan. He loves me. We want to be together as much as we can. That doesn't make us too serious. That just means that what we have is, you know . . . real."

Sophie squeezes more lime into her tea and stirs in two fake sugars. Sweet tea is never sweet enough for Sophie. "I hear you, and I understand what you're saying. I still remember Jesse, my first boyfriend. I was fifteen, and he was all I could think about, every minute of every day."

I smash the chicken salad with the back of my fork and look out the window at the rain. It just will not quit.

"But I want to make sure that things are okay, that there's nothing bothering you."

My phone buzzes seven times. A phone call. It stops, then starts again.

I rest my hand on the phone, willing it to stop. Sophie sees.

"Are you okay, Sparrow?"

I'm so tired. All the way down in my bones. It exhausts me, walking around filled up with words I cannot, will not speak. Sometimes I imagine them overflowing, leaking out of my eyes and ears, lifting the skin from the palms of my hands, roaring out of my mouth like a tsunami, muddy and filled with debris.

"Sophie, yes, I promise. Everything is still good. Tristan is a wonderful boyfriend. You know how sweet he's been to me. It's like I told you, everything right now is kind of crazy. I'm super-stressed about *Swan Lake*. Learning the White Swan is hard, and everybody's on edge. Plus, I'm nervous about senior year and all those AP classes and, you know, if I'm really good enough to be a professional dancer. Tristan's applying to colleges, so that's no fun. It's just a lot right now."

Sophie doesn't respond, just steeples her fingers and looks at me thoughtfully. Though this always makes me nervous, I've learned to wait her out. It's like she believes her silence will eventually make me spill my guts. It never does.

She sighs. "Honey, I know it's a stressful time for you both, but something's changed since March. You're so quiet. The only time I know you're in the house for sure is when I hear you banging out *fouettés* in the middle of the night."

"I can't get them fast enough for Levkova. And I'm still traveling a little. If I do them over and over again, I'll get better."

"Not if you're losing sleep doing them in the middle of the night. You're not eating, either. Something is going on. I love you, and I'm worried about you."

"Sophie, I'm telling you. It's all good."

My phone buzzes.

"For the love of all that is good and holy, will you please turn off your phone while I'm trying to talk to you?"

"Sophie, I can't. Please don't make me. He gets really— itchy—when we're not together."

Her eyebrows rise almost to her hairline, like startled little caterpillars.

"Sweetheart," she says. "You realize how controlling that is, right?"

I can't answer. All my energy is focused on staying calm, not showing her the panic that's coming at me like a dark wave.

"Sparrow," Sophie says quietly. "Honey. I wish you could see your face right now. You're kind of proving my point here."

"You're kind of making a big deal out of nothing. I can handle Tristan."

"Can you?" she says, pushing her plate away.

"Look." I hold up my phone and grab my purse. "See? I'm putting my phone in my purse. He's not controlling. I didn't realize I was committing some godawful crime by wanting to stay in touch with my boyfriend, but if it bothers you so much, I'm putting my phone away, and I'll pretend he doesn't exist. Okay? Happy now?"

I throw my phone in my purse and put it beside me so it's touching my hip. I turn and look out the window.

Sophie takes my hands in hers, running her thumbs gently over mine, like she used to do when I was little. "Oh, sweetheart," she says softly. "Please don't be angry with me. Do you remember the first words I said to you when I moved in with you and your dad?"

"Of course I do."

"Tell them to me."

I don't want to go back there. I try so hard not to remember.

The harsh sound of my father's weeping on the last day. The wintry echo of glass shattering as he threw every picture of her into a box and carried it to the attic. The crackling of her paintings, burning in the backyard. Seven night-lights to banish the nightmares. And Sophie's voice, reading to me every morning just before dawn, for two years.

My eyes fill, and my voice cracks. "You said, 'Fear not, little bird. All will be well, all will be well, and all manner of things shall be well. I am here now. I'll always be here.'"

My aunt Sophie squeezes my hands. "I'm going to tell you something, Sparrow, and I want you to listen, okay?"

"Okay."

She smiles at me, and I feel her love all around me, enveloping me like a warm cocoon.

"Here it is. Sometimes in a relationship, especially one that's so new and intense, it helps to take a step back . . . and it's okay to walk away if you feel uncomfortable or anxious or disappointed.

"But, sweetheart, here's the most important thing. It's also okay to walk away just because you want to. You don't need to explain or justify anything. You don't have to have a reason. You can just want out."

My phone vibrates inside my purse. I can feel it against my hip. Fear rises in my throat.

I know Sophie's talking to me, because I see her lips moving, but all I can feel is the vibration against my hip, traveling up to my rib cage and into my chest. Sophie's voice fades away. I look down on my body from far away, frozen in this booth, the roof above me, the walls around me disappearing, the rain pouring into my eyes, my nose, my mouth, while my phone vibrates on and on.

The crash of a plate shattering on the floor brings me back. I take a deep breath and focus on Sophie's face. "Sophie, I swear, you're totally overreacting. There's nothing wrong, nothing I can't handle. Tristan and I are just figuring stuff out. You know, relationship stuff. I promise, if I get worried, I'll talk to you. But I'll handle things my own way. I'm an adult."

"Oh, honey." She sighs. "No, you're not. You're only seventeen, my sweet baby girl, and I don't want you to get hurt."

"I won't. I promise." I try to eat a bite of chicken salad just to make her happy, but I spit it into my napkin when she's not looking. Outside, the rain has stopped, and there are patches of deep blue sky over the lush green mountains.

Nora brings the check, along with a white box filled with pumpkin muffins.

"These are on the house," she says, handing them to me. She gives me a peck on the cheek.

While Sophie pays, I check my phone. There are fifteen new texts, six missed calls, and four voicemails. All from him.

> **Where are you? Why is lunch taking so long?**
>
> **Can't wait to see you tonight. Wear that pink sweater I love, okay?**
>
> **Why aren't you answering? I worry about you when we're apart.**
>
> **You're not with him, are you?**
>
> **I need you to answer me now.**
>
> **Right now.**

He loves me, I tell myself. He loves me more than anything. He tells me every day. It's okay for him to go a little nuts when we're not together. I'm lucky that he wants to be with me all the time, that he worries about me, that he feels bad when his temper flares. He would never hurt me. Not really.

Fear not. I pull my necklace out from under my leotard, adjust the bracelet so that the charm sparkles in the growing sunlight.

Everything will be okay, I tell myself. All will be well, all will be well, and all manner of things shall be well.

"You aren't seeing Tristan tonight? Has the Earth stopped spinning? Has Mercury entered retrograde? What terrible cosmic forces have conspired to keep you lovebirds apart?"

My dad is sitting in his favorite Adirondack chair, reading glasses perched on his nose, yellow legal pad in his lap. He's wearing a faded Jethro Tull T-shirt and baggy jeans that have grass stains on the knees. His feet are bare.

"No cosmic forces. We had a date, but his father's making him stay home and work on his college essays."

"Having to write those things in the first place is bad enough. Being forced to do it practically guarantees lousy work."

"For real. He texted me a few minutes ago. He wanted to know if writing about running as a metaphor for life would be stupid."

"What did you tell him?"

"What he wanted to hear. That it was a brilliant idea."

He laughs. "And so original. I'm sure no admissions officer anywhere on the planet has ever read an essay comparing athletics to life."

"Well, he's a good writer. Maybe he can pull it off."

"What's his dad like? I know he's a neurosurgeon, and I see him every now and then at school board meetings, but that's about it."

"I've only talked to him a couple of times, but he's kind of scary, to be honest. I mean, he's nice enough to me, but he's super-hard on Tristan. Like when he shows up at track meets with a clipboard and a stopwatch and yells at Tristan from the sidelines if his time is off by even half a second. It makes me so sad, the look on Tristan's face when that happens, like he knows he's disappointing his dad, even when he's doing his absolute best. It makes me just want to hug him close and tell him how wonderful he is."

I nudge my dad's leg with my foot.

"But I guess we all can't have awesome dads like you, right?"

He switches off the lamp on the table beside him. It's almost full dark, and for a second all I can see is the gray at his temples that makes him look so distinguished, the streaks of silver in his dark brown hair. When I was little, I'd sit on his lap on summer nights, and we'd watch the fireflies flit through the yard. He told me they were fairies, and if he wasn't around to protect me, they always would. I wish I still believed it.

"Sparrow, my love," he says, so quietly I have to lean forward to hear him. "I think we both know that I'm pretty far from an awesome dad."

Not going there. Not now, not ever.

"Dad, you're probably the only person in the world who sits around barefoot, in dirty jeans and a T-shirt, writing with a Montblanc fountain pen."

He clears his throat. "You know me, sugar bear. Always trying to keep it classy."

"What are you writing?"

"Just some notes. Closing arguments are coming up, and you know how I love to be eloquent."

"Do you think you'll win this one?"

He sighs, takes off his glasses, and rubs the bridge of his nose.

"Well, court is always a crapshoot, especially when a jury's involved. You've heard me say that all your life. But I think we've presented a good, strong case. It doesn't hurt that the prosecutor is an arrogant, pompous ass who has pissed off the judge a few times. We may prevail."

"Did your guy do it?"

I can feel him smiling at me.

"Haven't we had this conversation before?" He caps his pen and sets it and the legal pad on the table beside him. "Whether he did it or not, my job is to defend him to the best of my ability and see that he gets a fair trial. But in this case, I will tell you that

I believe he is a young man who has been falsely accused. At this point, we have to trust that the jury will see it that way, too."

My dad. Defender of some of the worst criminals on the planet. His commitment to justice and due process is something I've admired all my life. It's corny, but I've always thought of him as a modern-day Atticus Finch.

But tonight I'm tired, and the old, familiar grief comes at me like a runaway train. The way my father reads people is kind of scary. He told me once that he could hear what people were thinking in the silent spaces between their spoken words. That he could tell what someone was feeling just by looking into their eyes.

So I wonder, as I have so many times since I was small, why he couldn't see the terror in my eyes. Why he couldn't defend me, the way he defends his bad guys now. But it doesn't bear thinking about for long. It's too late. What's done is done.

We're quiet for a while, waiting for the fireflies to light their way into the darkness. Even after so many nights with my father on this porch, I still think fireflies are beautiful. They never get old.

"Here," I say. "I came out to give you these." I stand up and tuck a spare pair of reading glasses into the neck of his shirt. "For when you lose the ones you're wearing."

"Thanks, pumpkin. You are a prince among daughters."

"Yes, I am. And now I'm going to bed. I'm wiped out."

"It's exhausting work, being Queen of the Swans."

I bend down to hug my father good night, breathing in the familiar smell of bay rum and freshly mown grass and the red wine he had with dinner. "I love you to pieces, sweet girl."

"I love you too, Dad."

Pausing with my hand on the screen door, I say softly, "You know, Daddy, you don't have to work all the time. I know you're in the middle of a trial and everything, but it's nice when you're home. I miss having you around."

"I know, sweetheart, and I'm trying. I don't want to work so much, but I always end up, you know, working so much. Keep calling me out on it, would you please? I'd appreciate the reminders. You know how we old farts are. Can't remember a damn thing."

"That will never happen to you. Good night, Daddy."

"Good night, pumpkin. Angels all around you."

I wake at three twenty, twisted in sweaty sheets, shaking so hard my teeth are chattering. I stuff my pillow in my mouth so I won't scream, so Sophie won't hear me crying. Another nightmare. I try to forget, but all I can do is remember.

I am in the White Swan costume—white tutu, feathered headdress, jeweled tiara—dancing on the rock at the Honeysuckle Pond. My mother is near the waterfall, standing in front of an easel. Her sleeveless white shirt sparkles with rubies. She is painting Aubrey, whose pale face is just barely above the water, her skirts billowed around her. Her eyes are wide and frightened, her lips blue with cold. Instead of arms, my mother has given Aubrey great white wings.

As I watch, unable to move, my mother turns slowly to me and smiles, her dark red lips stretching across her face, wide, wide, too wide. She blows me a kiss, and the rubies on her shirt rise into the air and turn into drops of blood. They land on my white tutu and run in rivulets down my arms and face.

When I look up, horrified, black feathers drift from my mother's raven hair, floating gently over the water and swirling in the pool beneath the waterfall until they disappear.

I pull the sheets from around my legs and slip out of bed,

lighting the candle I keep on my nightstand. I focus on breathing deeply, watch the candle flickering in the dark. The flame calms and centers me. In my bare feet, I do my *fouettés*, the fiendishly difficult whiplash turns I've been trying to perfect for months, propelling myself around and around with a raised leg that never touches the ground. I focus on not traveling, staying in one spot, but because I'm barefoot and not *en pointe*, the foot on the floor begins to burn. I manage twenty-six before I stop, breathless and sweating. But it worked. The nightmare is starting to fade. I dry my face with my pajama sleeve and crawl back into bed.

Just before I fall asleep, I hear Sophie's voice in my head.

It's okay to walk away just because you want to. You don't have to have a reason.

Oh God, I can't leave him. I love him, for a million reasons. The way he's so tender with me, draping his coat over my shoulders when I'm cold, pulling out my chair when we go out to dinner, opening my car door like some courtly, old-school gentleman. The way he holds me so gently in his arms when he knows I've had a bad day, the way he makes me feel safe and beloved and precious to him. I love him for how sorry he is when we fight, when he hurts me, the way he cries and cries and tells me he doesn't deserve me. How fiercely he promises never to hurt me again.

Oh God, I can't leave him. Can I?

8

Last Saturday in August

"Tristan, I've been thinking."

"Uh-oh. Never a good thing."

I force a laugh. "No, seriously, I need to talk to you about something."

My voice is shaky, and I almost tell him to turn the car around, that I don't want to go to Vittorio's for pizza or the jazz concert on the town square. I almost tell him that I don't feel well, that I have a miserable headache. Anything to get me back to the warmth and safety of my house, where my father is busy losing his glasses and staining his shirts with fountain pen ink, and Sophie is in her attic studio, working on the stained-glass seascape she started last week.

I hold my hands tightly together and take a deep breath. *Fear not.* He's my boyfriend. He loves me. He hates fighting. He's ashamed of his temper. He promised he would never, ever hurt me again.

"I know what it is. You want my smokin' body, right? Tell the truth." He smiles at me, almost too gorgeous to look at in his white T-shirt and gray Hollister shorts. He's in such a good mood, and that sweet crooked smile always makes me a little weak in the knees, even with his chipped bottom tooth. Maybe especially because of that tiny imperfection. I know the story, how his father made him play catch in the front yard when all Tristan wanted to do was go swimming with his friends, how the baseball caught him in the mouth, splitting his lip and chipping that tooth. He told everybody he got it playing football, but when I asked why he never got it fixed, he told me the truth. He kept it to remind himself never to defy his dad. It broke my heart.

He smiles again, and I almost lose my nerve.

"Well, no. I mean, yes, but it's something else."

He turns to me, a puzzled look on his face. "Okay, I'm listening."

"I was thinking maybe we need to take a break."

He punches on the stereo, finds Chemical Autopsy on his phone, and the air fills with the sound of death metal. We turn onto Main Street, where the traffic is heavy. People are jockeying to find parking spaces and walking the six blocks toward the gazebo, armed with picnic baskets and blankets, strollers and lawn chairs. Tristan leans on the horn and guns the engine.

"A break? What are you talking about, Savannah?"

"I think it might be good if we took a breather. From each other. Just for a little while. School is starting soon, and I'm taking four AP classes. Ballet is getting more intense every day, and you've already started training for track. You have all those college essays to write. We're both so busy right now, and it's only going to get worse."

I'm talking too fast. I try to slow myself down. Count the streetlights. Count the mailboxes. Count the seconds until he speaks again. I look at him out of the corner of my eye and see the muscle in his jaw clenching and unclenching. He's so handsome, beautiful, really, but now he's gone cold. He's drumming his fingers on the steering wheel, harder and harder, in time to the music. When he turns to look at me, there's nothing but anger in his eyes.

"What you're really saying is you want to be with someone else, am I right? Who is it, Savannah? Your ballerina boyfriend? I've seen the way you love to crawl all over him. Twice now, actually. What is it with him? Is there something you're trying to tell me here?"

"Tristan," I say, my voice high and thin. "It's nothing like that. I keep telling you there's no one else. I just need more time to focus on dancing and school. And I want you to be able to focus on your life, too. We've been so intense for the last five months, and I think it would be good for us to just, you know, cool things down for a while."

"You want to cool things down?"

"Yes, I do. Just for a while, not forever."

"You're breaking up with me, you lying little tramp."

"No!" I cry, gripping the armrest. The tires squeal as he makes a sharp turn down an alley, away from all the traffic. Away from all the people. "I'm not breaking up with you, Tristan, I swear!"

He grabs my phone, opens his window, and throws it hard. I hear it bang against a metal trash can. Then he floors the gas.

"Tristan! Stop! I need my phone!"

"No, you don't."

We turn onto Jefferson Drive, flying past Vittorio's and a row of tiny shops with blue twinkle lights in their windows. "Wait! Aren't we going to dinner?"

"Shut up. I'm sick of the sound of your voice."

I feel the rage boiling out of his pores, incandescent and dangerous.

"Savannah," he says quietly. "You want a break?"

I don't answer.

"That is never going to happen. Ever."

He turns the music up so loud that I feel the percussion in my stomach, the growling vocals at the back of my throat.

My phone is gone. I'm all alone. My breaths are coming too fast, ragged and shallow. I can't get enough air, and I feel like I'm going to be sick. Count the houses. Count the streetlights. Count the minutes until Tristan turns back into the boy I love.

He's grinding his teeth now, fuming as he races down the quiet streets faster and faster, until we're squealing around the curves, running red lights and stop signs. I look out the window at the pavement rushing by and wonder how messed up I'd get if I jumped out.

We tear through another red light. Cars skid to avoid us. Drivers lean on their horns.

The muscle in his jaw is clenched, like stone beneath his skin. Sweat is beading at his temple, and he's gripping the steering wheel so tightly that I can't believe it hasn't broken into pieces.

He reaches to turn down the music and says incredulously, "Did you really think I'd let you walk away from me? That I would ever let you be with someone else?"

"Oh God, Tristan, please, please look at the road. I don't want to be with anyone else. I'm sorry! I didn't realize you'd get so upset. Please turn around, and we can talk!"

He reaches out and grabs my hair. Twisting it around his fist, he jerks my head back. "It's too late for talking, Savannah. Way too late." My eyes fill with tears, but I don't dare let them spill.

When he speaks, his voice is tight and controlled, all coiled up on itself like a rattlesnake. "I am so sick of you putting me last in your pathetic little life. Who do you think you are, telling me how things are going to be?"

I focus on blinking the tears back into my eyes. I try to calm myself with thoughts of Sophie, her long red curls and dangly earrings, the smile that lights her up from the inside. I think of my father, his legal pads, his lame jokes, his wavy dark hair threaded with silver. They're waiting for me at home, probably having a glass of wine together before dinner.

"Look, Tristan, I'm sorry. I was stupid. I thought maybe we were getting too intense, but I made a mistake. I was wrong, okay? I don't want anyone but you. Forget I said anything. I'll make it up to you, I promise."

"Liar," he says. He pulls my hair harder, banging my head back against the seat, over and over again, sounding another ominous drumbeat inside the speeding car.

The streets are deserted. Where are all the old couples out walking their dogs, the cranky ones who would recognize Tristan's car and call the police to rat him out for speeding? Where are the actual police, who are always everywhere on summer nights, hoping for a little mischief to relieve the boredom?

"It's not over until I say it's over, Savannah. I'm the one who makes that decision, not you."

"Tristan, please let go of me! I'm not breaking up with you, I promise!"

We're going at least seventy-five now, flying away from everything that's safe, headed toward the outskirts of town. All the warm, golden porch lights disappear behind us. When we jounce across the railroad tracks, I bite my tongue and taste blood. The engine roars and roars, like some huge and starving beast.

Past the feed store and the lumberyard, past the Methodist church, where the cheesy sign for the last two weeks has been *God Always Answers Knee-Mail*. Tristan veers sharply onto Sweetbriar Road, tires shrieking, then fishtails crazily onto the ramp that leads to the Blue Ridge Parkway.

He hasn't let go of my hair, and I put my hands on the sides of my head, trying to ease the pain. I start praying softly, under my breath, something I haven't done since I was little.

> *In you, O Lord, I have taken refuge,*
> *Let me never be put to shame.*
> *In your righteousness deliver me.*
> *Incline your ear to me;*
> *Rescue me quickly.*
> *Be a rock of refuge for me,*
> *A strong fortress to save me.*

But there's no answer, nothing but the dusky night closing all around us, the cold moon and indifferent stars, the lights of Hollins Creek far below us, growing fainter as we climb, until everything goes dark.

"Tristan," I sob. "Please, please don't be like this. I'm so sorry. I shouldn't have upset you, I know that. I take it all back. Please let's go home. We can sit on the porch swing and talk, like we used to. Please turn around. I love you. I'll do whatever you want me to do, whatever it will take for you to stop being mad at me."

"You don't love me," he snarls. "You don't love anyone but yourself."

He swerves sharply onto the shoulder of the road and slams

the brakes. Gravel sprays into the grass. Even in the dark, I know where we are. A few feet beyond my door is the head of the trail that leads to the Honeysuckle Pond.

Tristan finally lets me go. Long strands of hair are stuck to his fingers. In small, quiet movements, I rub my temples and the back of my neck. "I'm sorry, Tristan," I say softly, not looking at him. "I'm sorry I've made you so angry. Tell me what I can do to make it right. I'll do anything. Just, please, let's go home."

He's silent, staring out the windshield, breathing hard through his nose, the blue vein in his temple throbbing, as though there's something alive crawling under his skin. He cuts the engine, and we're plunged into thick, suffocating darkness. Suddenly he grabs my chin, forcing me to meet his gaze, squeezing so hard there are bound to be bruises.

"Did you honestly believe I'd let you break up with me? If you won't be with me, Savannah, then I'll make damn sure you won't be with anyone."

He hauls himself out of the car, wrenches my door open, and pulls me into the night. I try to breathe deeply, forcing the sweet mountain air into my lungs. I try to gather my strength. I hear the raspy song of cicadas, the soft whisper of the wind high in the trees, the sharp snap of twigs beneath my stumbling feet. Tristan's hand on my arm is like a vise. I trip and fall to my knees, but he doesn't let me get up, dragging me over roots and sharp rocks until I cry out. Finally he jerks me roughly to my feet. I struggle to keep up with his long, angry strides.

"Tristan, please. Please!" I cry. "We can work this out. Just talk to me!"

"Walk. Shut up and walk."

There is a desert in his voice, parched and empty.

I smell honeysuckle and cold creek water. I hear the waterfall, see the white birch trees shimmering in the pale moonlight, the flat rock in the middle of the creek, where I told him about Aubrey. The place where he first kissed me, where he told me we belonged to each other.

It's almost a relief when he hits me.

Everything comes back to me, all of it. I remember to tighten my body so I won't fall, how to pull up, just like in ballet, every muscle taut and prepared. I know how to protect my face, where to hold my arms to keep the first, the strongest blows from reaching the softest parts of my body.

But I'm weak and out of practice. I've forgotten how much it hurts, how the pain takes me out of my head until I can't think at all, every muscle, every bone, eyes and mouth, blood, brain and sinew bracing for the next blow, which always, always comes. His fists, his curses raining down on me. How much he loved me. How I've betrayed and disappointed him, over and over again. He is only giving me what I've asked for. I don't deserve it, but he is willing to teach me one last lesson, one I'll never forget. I have no one to blame but myself. I've forced him to do this. I shouldn't have made him angry. It's all my fault. The old prayer slips into my mind, and I try to speak the words. So he will hear. So he will stop.

Through my fault, through my fault, through my most grievous fault.

Half a moon, silver bright, diamond stars glittering on a black velvet sky, cool wet leaves like a pillow under my cheek.

The earth tilts beneath me.

My hand falls into the rushing water, blood spooling out from my fingers, dark ribbons in the moonlit stream. The stars flare and disappear.

I float away on a sea of mercies.

Paper snow falling on my upturned face, slow *pirouettes* in white chiffon. Lucas lifting me soaring above the stage, my arms arched like a cathedral window.

I love you, Daddy.

I love you, Sophie.

I'm sorry.

At the end of everything, a fish dive.

Lucas

When sorrows come, they come not single spies, but in battalions.

WILLIAM SHAKESPEARE, *Hamlet*

9

After Lunch, March

I'm walking so fast I feel like I'm about to jump out of my own skin. Tristan King. What is she thinking? I swear, her brain has turned to Jell-O and leaked out of her ears.

I pound a random locker with my fist, wishing I knew some magic spell that would erase the last twenty minutes of my life.

"Wait, Lucas! Hold up!"

Israel, with his Ichabod Crane legs, catches up first, Caleb, Luis, and Sam close behind.

"Hey," Israel says quietly, "I don't want to get all up your business or anything, but what the hell was that back there? What's chewing on you?"

I'm so pissed I'm afraid what will come out of my mouth won't even be words, just incoherent noise. "I'm cool, Iz. Just, you know. Freaking Tristan King. Kissing Sparrow."

"Okay, but you were a big old shiny turd just now, and no one likes a turd, shiny or otherwise. Especially at lunch. I mean this in the nicest possible way." He claps his hand on my shoulder. "What's up? Anything else you want to share with Uncle Israel?"

"Nah. I'm just tired, I guess. My dad was up puking all night. Said he'd had too much junk food out on the road. So I didn't sleep much, because my father is not exactly a quiet hurler. Sounded like he was ralphing up his socks."

"I feel you, man. I hate all things vomit related."

"Word."

We take our usual seats for study hall, in the back of the chemistry lab. We're supposed to work quietly, sitting on high stools at scratched-up counters covered with test tubes and Bunsen burners and vials of nasty-smelling chemicals. The chairs are hard, the tables are sticky, and the whole room smells like burned eggs.

I hate chemistry, and I'm definitely not a fan of Dr. Holcomb, who was born without a sense of humor. If he were a Muppet, he'd be Oscar the Grouch, but with way less charm. Permanently sour expression, reading glasses sliding down his nose, seersucker suits even in the winter, wispy white hair like dandelion fluff. He wears bow ties, a different color for each day of the week. Monday is always muddy green, so today his Oscar game is strong. My dad says you can never trust a man who wears a bow tie.

He's up at the board, writing equations.

"Ladies and gentlemen," he says without turning around. "You know the drill. Study quietly. Books, not phones. And I do not want to hear any talking."

So we whisper.

Caleb picks up a test tube, opens it, and sniffs the innards. "Smells like my cat's litter box. This room sucks hard-core."

Luis opens his history book and draws a mustache and goatee on Mother Teresa. "So, for real, what was all that at lunch?" he asks, adding sunglasses and a fedora.

Sam says, "Yeah, honestly, you were kind of acting like a jerk."

"That's what I told him," Israel says.

"Come on! Did you see him back there?" I fume. "Did you see how he put his mouth on her like it was his job? Did you see his face?"

"Nah, man," says Luis. "I couldn't watch. Mushy crap makes me sick. My mama would smack the fire out of me if I ever acted like that in public." Israel and Sam nod in agreement.

Caleb says, "Yeah, but oh baby, Charlotte sure would like to suck your face off."

"Shut up, idiot," Luis says.

"You know, Luis," Israel chimes in. "For a guy who's supposed to be such a genius, sometimes you're dumb as a sack of hammers."

"You guys missed it, then," I say. "The whole time, he was looking straight at me. Like he was saying, 'This is mine, and don't you forget it.'"

"Tristan's always had a problem with you, bro," Caleb says. "You're taller than he is, and you got seriously jacked in middle school. Tristan does not like that. He needs everyone to understand that he's the big dog around here, not some prancing dancer. But, hey, look on the bright side. It could have been worse. He could have peed on Sparrow. You know, marking his territory."

"He might as well have," I say, unable to keep the bitterness out of my voice.

"Yeah, okay, truth. It was disgusting," Israel says. "I mean, nobody likes to watch that stuff play out in front of them, unless it's like in a movie or something. But it was just a jackass being a jackass. Shake it off, man."

"I can't."

"Because . . . ?" says Luis.

"I don't know. I just can't."

But I do know. I can't forget Tristan slamming me up against the lockers when I was nine, calling me a queer because I'd started taking ballet lessons. I didn't even know what a queer was. Tristan tripping me at soccer practice when I was eleven and kicking me with his cleats while I was down. Tristan and his buddies letting the air out of my tires in the conservatory parking lot last year. He hurts people. It's what he does.

"Okay, okay," I say. "First of all, I don't understand why she's all of a sudden so blind about a guy we've pretty much hated all our lives. He was a bully when we were kids, and he's a bully now. He just hides it better."

My voice is getting louder, and Caleb motions for me to keep it down, looking over his shoulder at Dr. Holcomb. Caleb talks big, like a rule-breaking badass, but he folds like a cheap lawn chair when he gets caught. He says that his first solid food was Catholic guilt and tears. He hates being in trouble.

"Yeah, but here's the thing, Lucas. You've hated him all your life. The rest of us just think he's a bigger-than-average turd. Okay, yeah, he used to tease us when we were kids, but he teased everybody. Nobody escaped. It was like— Luis, what's that thing when you have to go through something crappy to grow yourself up?"

"Rite of passage."

"That's it. Putting up with Tristan was our rite of passage. We got over it, but you still hate him. Why is that?"

"Guys," I say, exasperated. "What's wrong with you? He has a bad temper and a mean streak a mile wide. I hate him because he never lets anything go. Once you're in his crosshairs, you stay there forever, trust me. And now he's got his sights set on Sparrow."

Dr. Holcomb turns around and surveys his domain. We all

put our heads down, pretending to read *Anna Karenina*, which we're doing for AP English and is about to kill us all. It's almost a thousand pages long, there are at least a million characters with unpronounceable Russian names who are straight-up awful to each other, and word is there's a suicide by train at the end. Super-festive.

When the chalk begins to scratch out equations again, Israel says, "That's what's bugging you? He just now noticed Sparrow turned out awesome? Come on, man! She has a boyfriend. She's happy. Why is that not a good thing?"

"Really, Iz? Tristan King and Sparrow? It's freaking unnatural, like watching a hermit crab trying to hook up with a wildebeest. They're completely different species. It's never going to work. Because she's, you know, Sparrow, and he is the Mighty King of Douchebags."

"Yeah, but that's not yours to worry about," Caleb says. "She gets to make decisions for herself, even if you don't like them."

"I know, I know. But I'm worried she'll get hurt. He's just— he's too much for her. She needs someone who's not so all about himself, you know?"

Luis squints and gives me his genius look, the one that tells everyone he knows way more than he's letting on, that he always has, he's just been messing with you. Luis loves to be underestimated.

"You mean someone like you?"

"Shut the hell up, Luis."

Sam, who's been quiet up until now, studying German verbs and humming under his breath, gives his trademark low whistle. "Watch out, people. Somebody just hit a nerve."

Israel does an exaggerated facepalm. "Holy Unrequited Love, Batman! I'm thick as a brick. That's what this is about. You have a thing for Sparrow."

"What? No! I don't have a thing for Sparrow. It's just, I'm worried for her."

"Why? Has he done anything crappy?"

"Well, no. I mean, it's only been five days. He hasn't had time."

Luis and Sam roll their eyes.

"Do you guys remember Chloe Arsenault?" I ask.

"That girl who was valedictorian last year?"

"Yeah. She went on to study, I don't know, like astrophysics or nuclear engineering at Virginia Tech."

"So?"

"Remember how Tristan was dating her last spring? It only lasted about three weeks, but everybody said they were all hot and heavy. Anyway, I saw them arguing in the hall just before finals. He grabbed her cell phone out of her hand and smashed it on the floor, right in front of her locker. She just about lost her mind. He laughed and said he was only kidding, that he didn't mean to throw it so hard, but I saw the look on his face. He meant it. She told him to get lost, that she was done, and he said something that I couldn't hear. But it must have been crazy ugly, because it made her cry."

"Okay," Sam says. "So he's a doucheburger. But you think if you keep talking smack about him, Sparrow will suddenly see the light? You saw her back there. She's got it bad. And trust me, man, you do not want to get all up in that. It will blow up in your face, and you'll be the bad guy, not him. Just be cool and let her handle herself. You're worrying about nothing."

I'm getting nowhere with these guys.

"Okay, okay, this is me, giving up. I get it. I'm an idiot. But just so you know, I don't have a thing for Sparrow. I love dancing with her, that's all. And she's a friend. I don't want her to get hurt."

Israel grins and raises his eyebrows. "'The lady doth protest too much, methinks.'"

"Knock it off, Iz. I can't stand it from Delaney, so don't you start. Besides, that's *Hamlet*, not *Henry V.* You should know better, drama dork."

Caleb busts out laughing. Dr. Holcomb turns around, scowling behind his reading glasses, and points his chalk at us.

"Gentlemen in the back, five hundred words on the merits of silence. On my desk by homeroom tomorrow."

I've learned my lesson. You can't count on anything. Nothing lasts, especially the good stuff.

She has Tristan now.

10

After Rehearsal, May

I'm sorry, Lucas, I have to go, like, right now. I'll text you later.

Everybody watches as Sparrow pushes me away, then runs across the room, fumbling with her tutu. She runs the gauntlet of the *corps*, mouth frozen in a smile that never reaches her eyes. Delaney chases after her.

I can't believe the way we danced just now, the way she felt in my arms, the way she looked at me. The way I finally let myself look at her. For ten minutes I let the truth show. *Sparrow, I wasn't pretending.*

What was I thinking? I want to smack myself in the face. I blew it; she bolted. End of story.

The whole room is buzzing, chewing over what just happened. Now there will be something extra delicious to savor at lunch, to dissect and analyze before class, over coffee at Nora's.

Levkova claps her hands together, trying to regain control.

"Ladies and gentlemen, you are acting like a pack of hyenas.

Please remember who and where you are, and retrieve your manners. This minute, please."

I wait as long as I can stand it for everyone to make it back to center floor, still chattering softly. "Madame," I say, shifting from one foot to the other, running my hands through my sweaty hair. "Madame, please—"

She looks at me with such compassion and understanding that I almost lose it.

"Go."

I grab my bag and tear out of there like my hair is on fire, still in my tights and slippers. I can smell her honeysuckle shampoo on my skin, taste the salt of her sweat on my lips, feel her damp curls under my chin.

Outside, where the air is filled with the sound of birds and the sun is warm and bright, Tristan King is pacing in front of his car like a caged tiger. "What the hell did I just see, Savannah?" he shouts. "You were hanging on to him like you wanted to crawl inside his clothes!"

"Tristan," she says. "Please calm down. Stop shouting at me."

"I saw what you were doing! His hands were all over you!"

He grabs her arm and jerks her to him. She twists away without making a sound. Opening the passenger door, he snarls, "Get in the car."

My heart starts to race, and I break into a run. He's parked at the back of the lot, and I feel like I'm in one of those nightmares where you're running as fast as you can but you never get anywhere.

She sees me before he does.

I reach out and pull her behind me. Her entire body is shaking.

"Back off, asshole. She's not getting in the car with you."

Tristan's voice is icy, filled with contempt. "Hell yes, she is. You think you're going to stop me? You? A dude wearing tights?"

People have started to leave, standing in small groups to chat, tossing dance bags into their cars, laughing and joking around.

"I know I'm going to stop you. You really want to make a scene here, Tristan? You want to prove to all these people that you're still the same douchebag you've always been?"

Sparrow says, "Tristan, please stop. You're scaring me."

"I'll take you home, Birdy. Go get in my car. Go now, okay?" I hand her my car keys, which I'm grateful I had the brains to dig out while I was flying down the hall.

She clutches the keys so tightly that her knuckles turn white. "Tristan, please," she says. "I love you so much. Please don't be like this. We were just dancing. It didn't mean anything. It's work to us, that's all."

Ouch. Her words are like a kick in the teeth, but I'll chew on them later. When I know she's safe.

"You know what?" Tristan says, slamming the passenger door shut and walking to the driver's side. He doesn't look at Sparrow. He keeps his eyes on me. "Go ahead and go home with your ballerina boyfriend, Savannah. I don't give a crap what you do. He's obviously the one you really want. I'm out of here." She runs to my Jeep.

He flips me off and peels out, blaring Plague Pyre from his speakers. I take a minute to visualize his tires blowing out all at once, that shiny black car wrapped around a tree, his face planted in the airbag. It makes me feel a little lighter.

When I open my car door, Sparrow is sitting with her knees drawn up to her face, rocking back and forth. I get in and start the engine.

"What did he say to you?" she asks.

"The usual. He's not exactly an original thinker."

"What did you say to him?"

"Are you okay?"

"You asked him if he was okay?"

"No, Birdbrain, I'm asking you."

I'm trying to keep it light, make her laugh, but she is in my car, surrounded by the stench of mildewed tights, the memories of burritos past, and the sour ghost of the chocolate cherry milkshake I spilled all over the floor two weeks ago.

"Okay, no joking," I say softly. "I told him that you're way out of his league. I told him that he doesn't deserve you. And then I encouraged him to have romantic relations with a farm animal."

She closes her eyes and leans against the window. "I'm so tired," she says.

I pull out of the parking lot and turn on some music. *Swan Lake*.

"No," she says, her eyes still closed. "Anything but that. I can't stand it right now. The oboe breaks my heart."

She presses her face against her knees. I rest my hand between her shoulder blades and rub slow, gentle circles down her back, feeling the knots in her muscles, the knobs of her spine. I do this for her in the wings before every performance, when she's so nervous she's afraid she'll throw up. She says it makes her feel calm.

"Look, Birdy," I say quietly. "I'm sorry I said what I said when we finished the *pas de deux*. I was out of line, and I know I probably freaked you out. I just . . . well, I don't seem to have much of a filter right now. So I'm sorry, and we can talk about it or not."

"Oh, Lucas, you didn't freak me out. Okay, maybe a little. Let's talk about it later, okay? I don't have the juice right now."

"You got it. Whatever you want."

We're quiet for a while. She stares out the window, then turns to me.

"Are you okay? When you said you didn't have much of a filter, you sounded funny for a second."

Oh God, how I want to tell her, to tell someone. I've been carrying it around with me for weeks now, like a stone in my heart. It never goes away.

"Well, no, actually. I'm kind of not okay, but I don't want to unload any more crappy crap on you right now. Seems like you have your hands full."

"Lucas. Tell me. If there's something wrong, I want to know. Maybe I can help?"

"I wish you could, Birdy. I sure do wish you could."

"Tell me."

"Okay, but it's just between you and me, okay? I don't want it getting out all over school, and my mom wants to keep it quiet."

"Promise. I won't tell a soul."

I give her a weak smile. "Yeah. You're freakishly good at keeping secrets."

"Don't start."

"Okay. So, remember when my dad got home in March, after he'd been away for three weeks?"

"Yeah. That was a long time. Your mom was really missing him."

"We all were. Anyway, he had a good trip. He'd sold three of those machines that blast kidney stones and stuff with, I don't know, death rays from outer space. So my mom made him this awesome dinner, all his favorites, like glazed ham and scalloped potatoes."

"And baked apples and that chocolate pecan pie. I was there on his birthday last year. Super-delicious, right?"

"Right. Except when he walked in, he looked like death on toast. Vampire pale, big dark circles under his eyes. He said he was feeling kind of puny, probably because he ate too much junk food while he was traveling. He went straight to bed, then puked all night long. The next day I actually complained to the guys that I couldn't sleep because he was hurling. I feel terrible about that now."

"Lucas, what is it?"

I pull over on Main Street, near the gazebo. I don't trust myself to say this next part without driving us into a ditch.

"So, when he didn't get better after a couple of days, my mom took him to the emergency room. She was afraid he was getting dehydrated, because he couldn't stop barfing. Turns out it wasn't too many Big Macs. It's pancreatic cancer."

Her hand flies to her mouth, and her eyes go wide and fill with tears.

"Sparrow, please, please don't cry. I can take it from anybody but you."

"Oh, Lucas," she says, the tears spilling down her cheeks. "Oh my God, no, no, no!" My face feels like it's about to cave in on itself. I am one nanosecond away from losing it.

"Okay, I'm sorry. I'll stop. Hang on."

She fishes in her purse for a Kleenex, blows her nose, wipes her eyes hard, then looks at me, not quite dry-eyed, but completely focused. Her chin is trembling.

"So, what, does he have to have chemotherapy or surgery or something?"

"The doctor says they can do some chemo to try to shrink the tumor, but it's super-aggressive, and the chemo will only buy him some time. It's too far gone. It's in his liver, too."

"Oh my God, Lucas. I don't know what to say. I'm so freaking sorry."

She unbuckles her seat belt, kneels on her seat, then leans over the console and puts her arms around me. She rocks back and forth, holding on all tight and fierce. I wrap my arms around her.

"What can I do? Can I tell Sophie? She'll want to cook

dinners for you guys so you don't have to worry about food. My dad will want to help, too."

I'm quiet, remembering my mom telling me how she didn't want it all over Hollins Creek. But this is Sophie and Mr. Rose. I need somebody to know what's happening. I need one place to go that hasn't turned into a shrieking nightmare.

"Okay, yeah, you can tell Sophie and your dad, but they have to keep it on the down-low, okay? Seriously, I don't want the entire town gossiping about our family."

"Don't worry about that. They'll keep it quiet. But, Lucas, how come you didn't tell me? All this time, keeping something like that to yourself? Pretending like everything is okay? It must have been so hard."

I stare out the windshield at everybody else's lives going on just like they always do. People getting takeout from Thai One On, having coffee and pie at Nora's, picking up their clothes at the dry cleaner's. Laughing. It feels wrong, like nobody should be happy. Like everyone should be falling to their knees and screaming and tearing out their hair.

"I didn't tell anybody because I thought maybe if I didn't say the words out loud, then they wouldn't be true. If nobody knew, then I could go to school and dance with you and hang out with the guys, and nothing would change. Except I didn't know that I'd carry it around with me, all the time. It's like grief walks with you, sits beside you in calculus class, asks you to pass the salt at the dinner table."

"How's your dad now? How's your mom? Anna?"

"Well, that's the hell of it. He's doing the chemo, and the doctor gave him a bunch of other medicine. He's lost a lot of weight, and he looks like somebody kneed him in the nuts, like he just can't believe this is happening to him. But he's still smiling and joking around. Trying, you know, to still be himself. When his hair started falling out, he put on that stupid hat from Williamsburg. He wears it all the time, so it's like living with a bald minuteman. My mother, on the other hand, is completely destroyed. She keeps disappearing into the nearest bathroom and running the shower so we won't hear her crying. I want to help her, but I'm afraid if I go in there with her, I'll start crying, too. And if I do, I'll never stop. Anna doesn't know anything, only that Dad's sick and has to take some medicine. She's still so little."

"Do you know—oh, this is such a terrible thing to ask—do you know—"

"How long he has?"

"Yes."

"The doctor said anywhere from six weeks to nine months, best case."

"Oh my God. Lucas."

She hugs me tighter, and I can feel her hot tears slipping down the side of my neck and into my shirt. I pull her closer. I don't have any more words.

She rests her forehead against mine. "You call me, text me, come banging on our door any time of the day or night if you need to talk or get out of the house. I mean it, Lucas. Don't go dark on me. I will come dance with you whenever you need to work it out that way. Sophie will feed you and won't make you talk. My dad will take you fishing. Even if you want to come over and yell and scream and break things, you do it with us, okay? Anything you need. We are all here. Me, most of all. You got it?"

I breathe her in deep, smelling her shampoo, her sweat, the fabric softener she uses on her leotards. I have to think quickly about stupid crap, like Monty Python movies and Luis cramming hot dogs into his face, because if I don't, I will lose my mind right here, and I don't know what I'll do if I have to feel everything all at once. I don't know how to *be* anymore.

"Thanks, Birdy," I say into her hair. "I will definitely talk to you if I need help. But right now, put your seat belt back on and let me get you home. Sitting here in my smelly Jeep isn't going to make anything better."

She puts her head down, rooting through her purse for more Kleenex. I pretend not to see her crying.

Sparrow's house is on Larkspur Way, at the top of the cul-de-sac. It's a bungalow with a deep, wide porch, thick square columns on stone bases, and bay windows on the second floor that let in the afternoon light. Her room looks out across the foothills to Mount Aberdeen.

When I turn into her driveway, the stone in my heart gains ten pounds, and my eyes blur. It all looks so freaking normal. The mailbox is shaped like a fish, and Sophie paints it every spring. This year, it's midnight blue, with stars for eyes and constellations on the fins and tail. Purple and pink wisteria wind around the porch columns, and peonies bloom in the beds in front of the house. Sparrow's father is outside, watering the hanging baskets. Pruning shears are sticking out of his back pocket. When he sees us, he grins and waves.

When I left for the conservatory this morning, my father was asleep on the couch, his tricornered hat askew on his bald head. His skin is a weird shade of gray, and his cheekbones are so sharp it's like you can see the skull underneath his skin. But he woke up and smiled at me. Walking out of the house, I noticed the dead geraniums in the flowerpots, my mother's car thick with dirt and pollen, the green dumpster packed with pizza boxes. There is no wisteria where I live. No carefully tended grass. No father outside, singing "Bungle in the Jungle" at the top of his lungs and watering the plants.

I stop the car behind Sophie's bright red Subaru, covered in bumper stickers. *Got Books?* and *Blessed Be*, and my personal favorite, *When I Want Your Opinion, I'll Read It in Your Entrails.*

Sparrow makes no move to get out of the car.

"You going to be okay?" I ask.

"Are you?"

"No. I don't think I'll be okay for a long time, but I'll try like a champ to fake it."

"Not with me, though, right?"

"Never with you. How about you? You going to keep pretending everything's okay with your boyfriend?"

"Everything is okay with my boyfriend, Lucas. He already feels terrible, I promise you. He'll come over tonight with flowers. He'll apologize. He'll be his normal sweet self, and we'll talk it all out. Trust me, everything will be fine."

She forces a weak little smile.

"All will be well, all will be well, and all manner of things shall be well."

She blanches a little, realizing what she just said.

"Oh God, I'm sorry. All will not be well. I'm sorry, Lucas. I'm a nitwit."

"It's okay, Birdy. I know what you meant."

Her father looks over at us, probably wondering why we're still in the car, why we aren't laughing and joking around.

She leans over the console again and gives me an awkward one-armed hug.

"Bye," she says. "Thank you for rescuing me. I'm glad you were there. And I'm glad you told me, Lucas. You call me, okay? I'll keep my phone on all the time. I don't want you to go through this alone. If you let me, I'll be your person, the one you can talk to. I'll walk with you. All the way, Lucas, every step. Okay?"

"Right," I say.

She kisses me on the cheek. "You really are a prince, Lucas Oliver Henry."

I hate hearing my entire constipated preacher name.

"Yeah, yeah, that's what all the ladies say."

She walks up to the front porch, where her dad is waiting. She puts her hand in his and leans against him. They both wave to me as I back out of the driveway.

Terrible news spilled like a dark stain into the world. Check.

Ballerina delivered safely home. Check.

I head to my house, where I'll cut the grass and wash my mother's car. Maybe I'll even go to the nursery and buy something to replace the dead geraniums.

Anything to keep from going inside.

11

June, After the Funeral

"There's no such thing as a beautiful funeral, sweetie. They all suck. I made you a coconut cake."

With the June sun shining down bright and fierce on our brown front lawn, Sophie wraps her arms around me and hugs me hard. Sparrow makes her way from the car, holding an enormous cake carrier, while Mr. Rose juggles a vase of his prized white roses. I look over Sophie's shoulder through the big picture window in the living room.

The house is packed. People are drinking beers and balancing plates filled with food. I see my mom, walking through the living room like a ghost, wearing a shapeless green dress and the pearls my dad gave her when they got married. Her hair is pulled back off her face into a messy ponytail, and she's not wearing any makeup. She looks so pale. I watch her stop when people talk to her, nodding, maybe saying a word or two, but I can tell that she's not hearing anything. Her eyes are faraway, and she walks like she's floating through a dream. She's not even halfway here.

Near the fireplace, Anna is curled up in my dad's big leather chair. When anyone tries to talk to her, she covers her ears. All these people in our house, eating and drinking, talking and laughing. It's the biggest party we've ever had, but underneath all the noise, the house feels abandoned. Like there should be white sheets on the furniture and cobwebs in the corners and mice scuttling through all the empty rooms.

Sophie lets go of me, and Sparrow's father shakes my hand, then pulls me into the one-armed bro hug. "You know you're part of our family, right?" he says quietly. "Stay close, Lucas, you hear me? The hardest part starts tomorrow, when all this crazy noise and activity go away. Then you have to figure out how to get through the days. We're here to help you, any way we can. I hope you'll let us."

"Thanks, Mr. Rose. I appreciate that. You guys are the only ones who tell it straight. You should hear some of the things people are saying."

"Let me guess. 'God needed another angel. God never gives you more than you can handle. Your father is in a better place. At least he's not suffering anymore.' You want to punch them in the face, am I right?"

"How did you know?"

"Trust me, I've heard it all before, the meaningless things people say without thinking, because they have to say something and need to make themselves feel better. Frankly, if God is going around cutting down good, loving, decent men like your dad just because he's lonely up there, because he wants to punish us for being strong, then I'm not sure I like him very much."

I reach out to shake his hand again. "Thank you, sir."

"You hang in there, Lucas. Fight the good fight. We're with you all the way."

Sparrow gives Sophie the cake carrier.

"Lucas," says Sophie. "Should I just put this in the kitchen?"

"Sure, but be careful. My granny Deirdre is in there washing dishes. She's been in there for two hours. She won't come out, and she won't let anyone help her."

"She's your father's mother?"

"Yes, ma'am. No one can get her to budge. She says she doesn't feel like talking to strangers."

Sophie heads to the kitchen. "I don't blame her one bit. I'll be quick."

"Mr. Rose," I say. "There's beer and wine and a ton of food in the dining room, if you can make it through the crowd. My mom's in the living room. I know she'd be glad to see you."

"Where's little Anna?"

"In the big chair in front of the fireplace."

"I'll visit with them both, Lucas. Remember what I said, okay?"

"I will, sir. Thank you for coming."

Sparrow is standing quietly near the front door. She's wearing a pale purple dress covered with white lace, and her hair is in a soft bun low on the back of her neck. My mom didn't want everyone dressed in black and asked me to spread the word for people to wear my dad's favorite colors. Purple. Citadel blue. Forest green. Sparrow looks beautiful, even though she's been crying and her eyes are all swollen and red.

"Tristan's not here?"

"No. He didn't think you'd want him to come."

"Was he at least at the funeral? To be there for you? You loved my dad crazy-hard."

"He doesn't like funerals. He thinks they're depressing."

"Right. Because most people think they're a real laugh riot. What a guy."

"Lucas," she says softly. "Maybe give it a rest today."

I sling my arm around her shoulders. "You're right. Come on, let's go out back. I can't breathe in there."

We walk around the house to the patio, where Delaney and Luis, Israel, Caleb, and Sam are sitting in a circle, drinking beers from the ice-filled tub near the grill. I grab one and hand Sparrow a Sprite. Some of the adults give us the stink eye, clearly disapproving of our underage drinking. But I'm the dude with the dead father. They wisely choose to remain silent.

"How long have you guys been out here?" I ask.

Delaney says, "I was the first one out. This sweet old lady started telling me about how she contacted her dead husband with a Ouija board. She was super-calm, like she was talking about what she had for breakfast. A Ouija board! I mean, hello, nice lady? Have you ever seen *The Exorcist*? Everybody knows that's how you end up with your head doing a three-sixty and spewing green puke on a priest. I came out here to get some air."

"It's so sad and weird," Caleb says. "Like some people are crying and talking about how great your dad was, and other people are having totally normal conversations about work and their kids and where they went to dinner last night. I don't get it." He grabs another sweating beer from the tub.

"I don't even know who half those people are," I say. I pull out a chair for Sparrow and squeeze her in between Delaney and Sam, then sit on Delaney's other side, perching on one of the low teak tables. I loosen my tie and take a deep breath. All day long, I've felt like I was choking.

"For real, man," says Sam. "It's bizarre. People are totally chowing down in there. And getting super-drunk, too. Strangest social gathering I've ever been to in my life. Like 'Hey, somebody died, let's party.'"

"Truth," says Israel. "You know what would have been way better?"

I take a long swallow of my beer, suddenly remembering how my dad loved to have a couple of cold ones after he'd worked up a sweat cutting the grass. I wonder if this is how it's going to be for the rest of my life, gut-smacked by memories every minute of every day.

"No, Iz, what would have been way better?" Delaney asks.

"A Viking funeral."

Sparrow says, "Israel, come on, don't."

"No, seriously, man," Luis says. "Instead of us all packed like sweaty sardines into Blessed Sacrament, we'd be standing outside. On the riverbank, in the sun. Everybody who loved your dad would have gotten together when he passed to build him a sweet raft out of logs, like in *Huckleberry Finn*. He'd be all stretched out under the big blue sky, wearing shorts and a Citadel T-shirt, or maybe his Marine uniform, looking up at the mountains. He loved outdoorsy stuff, right?"

"Yeah," I say. "He did."

Delaney snorts with laughter, then covers her mouth with both hands, eyes wide, shoulders shaking. The sound is so unexpected, so happy, so normal, that a smile tugs at my mouth. It feels weird, like my face is broken.

She wipes her eyes and takes a sip of her beer, then points the bottle at Luis. "Which one of you clowns would shoot the flaming arrow? You can barely walk and chew gum at the same time. And all y'all have that little problem with your knuckles dragging on the ground."

"Hey, that's not fair," says Sam. "We learned archery in Boy Scouts."

"When you were what, ten? You think maybe those skills might have gotten a little rusty over the years? I'm just saying."

"Well, maybe," says Luis. "But I'll bet Lucas's dad would have picked the Viking funeral option if he'd had the choice. Way to go out in a blaze of glory, right, Lucas? Everybody would remember a funeral like that."

"He was definitely not the most subtle guy." I picture a flaming wooden barge floating down the New River, everything burning to ash, my father carried on the wind all the way to the sea. He would have loved it.

"So," Delaney asks, fiddling with the beads around the neck of her navy-blue dress. "How are you doing, for real? And don't say you're fine, because there's no possible way."

I finish my beer and set it down beside me. Caleb hands me another one. I don't want to get drunk, but I want to get drunk. I want to pass out cold and wake up in some other universe. One where my dad is holding a huge mug of coffee and scrambling eggs on a Sunday morning, my mom is asking him for the millionth time if he'd please fix the stair that creaks, and Anna is at the kitchen table, completely lost in a new box of crayons, drawing pictures of dolphins.

"I don't know, Laney, to be honest. I mean, sometimes I think I'm doing okay. And then suddenly I'm not. I mean, how am I supposed to do this, live the whole rest of my life without a dad? Without *my* dad? Last night I started counting up all the things he'll never see. My graduation. Me dancing Siegfried. Anna playing in the soccer tournament next week. He'll never terrify her first boyfriend or walk her down the aisle when she gets married. It's like a hundred million nevers stretching out in a long line in front of me, so far that I can't see where it ends."

Delaney says quietly, "None of us can even imagine what you're feeling, Lucas, but we're all here for you. We love you."

"Thanks, Laney. But the truth is, nobody can help me, not really. I don't mean to be a jerk about it, but I'm the only one who can figure out a way to do normal stuff like go to school and dance and help Anna with her homework, when the whole time it feels like something with sharp claws has reached down my throat and yanked out all my guts."

"That sucks," says Luis. "If you want to lose it right now, there's no one here to see but us. If I were you, I'd be curled up on the floor like a pill bug, crying my face off."

"That's the weird thing. I can't. It's like I'm all dried up and empty, you know, like those cicada husks you see in the grass every summer? Sometimes I think maybe I'm going to lose it, and then I just . . . don't. You know what our dentist said to me after the funeral?" I say. "Dr. Burch?"

"Oh man, dentists scare me so bad," says Sam. "What did he say?"

"He said now I'm the man of the house. What does that even mean? My dad was the man of the house. He played football for the Citadel. He fought in the Gulf War way before I was born. I was so lucky to be his son. I mean, sure, I want to be like him someday, but I can't just take over where he left off; it's probably the lamest thing anyone's ever said to me."

My voice cracks and I swallow hard, forcing down the lump in my throat.

"Lucas," Sparrow says. "Nobody expects you to be your dad. It's like my father told you. Dr. Burch just couldn't think of anything else to say. Forget about him. And you're already like your dad. Look what you did for me in the parking lot last month. You were a hero."

I can't let her go on thinking that. It's a lie. I'm nobody's hero.

"So, can I tell you guys something? Promise you won't think I'm disgusting or weird or seriously twisted?"

Relief blooms all over their faces. Finally, something they can do. They jump at the chance.

Sparrow says quietly, "Lucas, you can tell us anything. Nothing will change."

"Besides, we already think you're disgusting and weird and seriously twisted," Delaney adds. "How can it possibly get worse?"

· "I don't know, guys. I think maybe this is kind of bad."

"Spill it," Delaney orders.

I take a couple of shaky breaths and crack my neck.

Sparrow says, "Gross, Lucas."

"I haven't told this to anyone, so keep it to yourselves. I haven't even told my mom, and I don't plan to. Like, ever."

"Dude," says Sam. "You know you can trust us. Just spit it out, for God's sake."

"Okay. The last day, the day he died, we were all with him. My mom and Granny Deirdre, and Anna and me. Y'all know he was in the hospital, because he'd gotten an infection, right? We kept talking to each other like he was going to wake up any minute, like he'd recognize us and say something, something big that we could hold on to after he was gone. Like he saw a bright light at the end of a long tunnel, or his dead father showed up to bring him the rest of the way, you know, that kind of woo-woo stuff."

I still can't get the smell out of my nose. Bleach and bandages and coffee and blood. As long as I live, I'll never be able to walk into another hospital, even if I'm the one who's sick. There's no way I could get past the front doors. I'd rather lie out on the sidewalk and die all by myself, looking up at the mountains.

Everyone is quiet, waiting for me to go on.

"It's so strange, what I remember. My mom was wearing the diamond earrings Dad gave her for Christmas. They sparkled, even in those awful hospital lights, and I couldn't stop looking at them. Anna had just announced she wasn't going to talk to anyone ever again, and Granny Deirdre was humming 'Danny Boy' real softly, under her breath."

Luis hands me another beer, and I take a long swallow. I feel dried out, like I'd crumble into little pieces and blow away if the wind rose.

"Anyway, my dad had been asleep for three days. He hadn't opened his eyes once, in all that time. Don't know if you ever noticed, but they're green, the way the mountains look in the summer. My mom was holding one of his hands. Granny Deirdre was holding the other." My voice cracks again. Another swig of beer.

"This next part is hard," I whisper.

Sparrow says, "Take your time. We're not going anywhere."

"Nobody tells you how quiet it is at the end. I thought he'd breathe out real noisy and his head would fall to the side. You know, the way people die in the movies. But it wasn't like that. He breathed out once, and we waited and waited for him to breathe in, but there was nothing. He was gone. We'd never see them again, those eyes that always seemed to be laughing at something, remember? I got so scared, terrified that I'd already started forgetting things about him, things that were important.

"Anyway, his doctor came in and was real sweet to us. She said to take our time, to stay as long as we wanted. My mom thought it would be a good idea if we each said our goodbyes privately. When it was my turn, I walked over to the bed and took down the railing. I put my hand on his head; he'd lost every single bit of his hair, even his eyebrows and eyelashes. His skin was warm, and it felt like he was still there, still with us. I kissed him on the forehead, and I said, 'Dad, come back. Please come back.' But of course he didn't."

I feel sick, like I have a fever, like everything in the world is upside down.

"Then—then—damn. Hang on. This is the bad part."

Another lump in my throat, another long swallow of beer.

"I know how awful this sounds. I—I lifted up one of his eyelids. Because I couldn't stand to think I'd forget the color of my father's eyes. That's totally sick, right?"

Delaney is crying so hard she sounds like she's choking. Sparrow's shoulders are heaving. Caleb and Luis wipe their eyes. Israel and Sam are looking down at their shoes.

"No, Lucas," Delaney says, her voice thick with tears. "It's not sick, not at all. It's actually kind of beautiful. Now you'll always remember. You were right to do it."

Just then my granny Deirdre opens the porch door and stands on the top step. She's holding a nearly empty glass of white wine.

"Do you young people mind if I come out and sit with you?" she says in her Irish brogue.

"No, no, Granny," I say. "We don't mind at all. Come on out here."

Israel, who's closest to the door, leaps up and offers her his arm, escorting her gently down the stairs, like she's made of glass. Caleb pulls up another chair, and Delaney and I move to make room between us. When Granny is settled in, she says, "I'd much rather be here with you than in there trying to talk to people I don't know. They all want to tell me stories about Liam, and I couldn't listen for another minute."

"That's why we're all out here. Where's Anna?" I ask.

"She's on your mother's lap, asleep. She won't let anyone carry her up to bed."

She swallows the last sip of her wine. Delaney takes the glass from her and puts it on the picnic table behind us.

Inside, my dad's Marine buddies have started singing "The Parting Glass." They do it at every funeral, but there's no way I can go inside. That song destroys me on a good day.

My granny reaches out to me and says, "Hold my hand, Lucas? Otherwise I think I might float right off this earth." Delaney takes her other hand, then wordlessly reaches out to Sparrow, who reaches out to Sam, who grabs Israel's hand, until we're all linked together. If anybody had ever told me that I'd be sitting in a circle one day, holding hands with my friends and my grandmother, I would have laughed. But it's not funny. Or stupid. It's actually the only thing that's felt right all day.

When the song is finished, Delaney looks up and says softly, "'And, when he shall die, take him and cut him out in little stars, and he will make the face of heaven so fine that all the world will be in love with night.'"

My grandmother looks up at the darkening sky. A few stars are sprinkled among the clouds. "Yes, he will," she says. Tears are streaming down her soft, wrinkled cheeks. "Oh, Liam, my darling boy," she whispers. "My sweet, sweet child."

And there in the growing dark, holding my granny's hand, with all my friends around me, I bow my head and cry.

12

Party, Fourth of July

I mean it, Savannah. You stay the hell away from him!

Standing on Delaney's back deck, my hand on the doorknob, I can hear him, his voice low, the words slurred and running together. He's completely hammered. And Sparrow is sobbing.

I slam the door open.

As long as I live, I'll never get this picture out of my head. Sparrow on the floor, crying, pressed into a corner, trying to make herself invisible. Tristan standing over her with his fists clenched.

"You should have told me he'd be here," he snarls. "First the necklace, then all that crap I saw in the studio, and now this? Acting like a slut as soon as my back is turned? You were all over him! You let him put his hands on you! Are you trying to piss me off? What do I have to do to get you to take me seriously, Savannah?"

Everything inside my eyes turns red, and my face gets hot. It's official. I will destroy him.

I reach out and yank him off his feet, pulling him away from her. He stumbles and catches himself on the counter.

"Get away from her!"

Tristan straightens up, instantly sober, his face dark with rage. He jabs his finger into my chest. "Turn yourself around right now and get the hell out of here." I smack his hand away.

"Back off, jackass," I say, trying to get to Sparrow. He blocks me.

"You do not want to get in my face right now," he hisses through clenched teeth. He shoves me toward the door. I shove him back.

"Get your hands off me, Tristan. I'm not going anywhere."

Sparrow tries to get up. She holds her hand out, like she's trying to ward me off. "I slipped, Lucas. That's all. Somebody spilled a beer, and I hit the stove. I'm okay. Please go back to the party. Please."

Tristan grins. "She's right. For a ballerina, this is one clumsy chick! Must have hurt like hell. But she's okay now. Right, honey? Right, baby?"

She doesn't look up.

"That's crap, and you know it," I say, elbowing my way past him. I kneel down in front of Sparrow. She shakes her head at me, telling me to play it cool. But I can't.

I put my arms around her shoulders and help her stand. "Come on, Birdy," I say. "Let's get out of here."

She hangs on to me for the smallest second, then pushes me away.

"Lucas, don't. I'm fine."

"Did you hear what she said?" Tristan says. "She's fine. So get your damn hands off my girlfriend." He takes Sparrow's hand and pulls her to him. Outside, the music has stopped, and the sound of Israel's laughter drifts in through the open window over the sink. Charlotte is crying. Delaney's telling her to go home, that she's tired of hosing puke out of the bushes.

Sparrow tears off a paper towel from the roll on the counter, then wipes her eyes and blows her nose.

"Tristan's right, Lucas. I'm fine; I just slipped. I banged my leg, but it's okay now. It doesn't even hurt."

She's lying. I cannot take this for one more second.

"Birdy, are you freaking kidding me right now?"

Sparrow stares at me, her face suddenly scoured clean of any emotion. Like a blank canvas, waiting for her to paint on a feeling that looks real.

"I told you, I slipped. Somebody spilled a beer. I'm fine. Let it go."

"Really? You slipped in some beer? Then how come your skirt is dry? How come I don't smell any beer? How come the floor isn't wet? He hurt you. You know it, I know it, and he knows it. You're really going to stand there and lie to my face?"

"I told you already, he didn't hurt me." she says evenly.

"Sorry. I'm not buying it."

Tristan pushes her out of the way. "You know, I've been wanting to ask you something. What's it like being the man of the house, without, you know, actually being a man?"

Sparrow's face blanches. "Tristan, don't. That's a terrible thing to say."

"Shut up, Savannah," he says. "I didn't ask for your opinion."

My dad. My stomach flips, and my eyes burn. There's the essence of Tristan King right there, going straight for the jugular, savoring the kill shot. I miss my dad so much right now that I can't breathe.

But I will be damned if I will let this douchebag see. "You're so freaking predictable, Tristan, going straight for the dead dad.

That the best you got? At least my dad was a normal guy. He didn't show up everywhere with his wallet out, buying his kid out of all the messes he made, paying his way into places he couldn't get into by himself. Is that how college is going to work, too? No one will even need to read your applications? I guess they're just for peasants like the rest of us. Everybody knows rich Daddy King will just make a big, fat donation to the Ivy of your choice."

His face goes purple. "I will kill you for that. I will beat you so hard even your mama won't recognize you."

"You really want to do this, bro?" I say, planting my feet. "You want to bring it right now? Right here? Go ahead. Give me a reason. I've been dying to kick your ass for years."

"You don't have the stones."

"Try me."

Sparrow ducks between us, arms outstretched, pulled up, trying to make herself look tall. "Lucas, walk away. Tristan, baby, come on. Let's go."

Tristan smiles at her, a real smile, like whatever nasty wind just blew through here is all gone now, and everything is all kittens and unicorns again. He wraps his arms around her, kisses her on the cheek, runs his fingers through her curls.

"I'm sorry I yelled just now. Your dancer friend here just pissed me off." He kisses her on the mouth.

She looks up at him with a mixture of love and relief and fear. I can't watch them; it makes me sick.

"You okay now, babe? Your leg hurt?"

"I'm fine, really," she says, smiling shakily. "Let's just go, okay?"

Tristan actually has the balls to wink at me. "Well, it's been a kick chatting with a real prince, but we're going to make like a baby and head out. You go on back to the party, have a juice box or something. We got us some window fogging to do. Fourth of July, right? We're going to make our own fireworks, if you know what I mean."

Neither one of them looks back, and in a few seconds I hear the deafening roar of his muscle car, the shrieking sound of industrial metal pounding from the oversized speakers, shaking the ground beneath my feet.

Hours later, when the only people left are passed out on the back lawn, I stand at the kitchen sink, helping Delaney clean up. The cicadas are loud tonight, singing the theme music of summer in Virginia. Usually I love the sound, but tonight everything feels itchy, like the world is one big, scratchy wool sweater. I can't stop thinking about how she's in that shiny black car, how his hands are probably all over her. She's alone. With him.

Delaney passes me a platter to dry, and I stand there, looking out the window, holding it in my hands.

"Lucas! Dry the plate. I'm exhausted, and you need to go home."

She scoots me out of the way and opens the cabinet door under the sink to tie up the trash. "What in the world?"

Someone has thrown her mother's favorite blue bowl in the garbage. There are lemons everywhere, under the disposal, in the totes holding the cleaning supplies.

"Laney?"

She's on her knees, head under the sink, gathering up the lemons and cursing while she shoves them into the trash bag. "What?"

"So there was a thing. With Sparrow. Earlier."

She backs out so quickly she bangs her head on the cupboard

door and releases a string of profanity deeply impressive in its scope and creativity. I tell her what happened, leaving out the stuff Tristan said about my dad. She leans against the sink next to me while I dry the plate and put it away.

"Oh my God," she whispers. "I thought I heard yelling. Do you think she was lying? About how she slipped?"

"They were both lying. There was no beer on the floor, and her skirt was dry. I didn't see it, but I think he pushed her, or hit her. He did something. She was terrified."

"But you don't know. Not for sure."

"Laney, I need you to be on my side here."

"I am on your side, Lucas! I'm not arguing. I'm just saying, you can't be sure. We all know Tristan can be a monumental jerk. He actually flipped me off when they got here. He was all pissy because Sparrow forgot to wear that necklace. I don't trust him. But he really has been sweet to her. Even though you don't want to hear it, it's true. Besides, you can't just go around accusing a person of something you think might have happened. If you do, you can bet Tristan's father will sue you for slander."

"She was on the floor, Delaney. He yelled at her and held her way too tight. I wanted to put her in my car and drive her to a galaxy far, far away."

"Yeah, I feel you. But what can we do? She said she slipped. And here's the thing: she's in love with him, and she's never been in love before."

I fight the urge to gag.

"So what?"

"Maybe we need to let her be in love, to figure things out on her own. Do I think something is going on? I don't know. Maybe. I've only seen the thing with the necklace, and when I tried to talk to her about it, she shut me down hard. But she's strong and brave, and if she's in over her head, she'll ask for help. Until she does, we have to stay out of it."

Delaney slides to the floor and sits cross-legged against the whirring dishwasher. She leans her head back and closes her eyes. I slide down next to her. The smell of the lemons in the trash is overpowering. My nose hairs are frying.

"Do you believe what just came out of your mouth?"

"No."

"When has she ever asked for help? When has she ever told anybody anything about what she's thinking? Or feeling?"

"That would be never."

"Do you remember that summer we were ten? When we were climbing the sweet gum tree in your backyard and daring each other to see who could climb highest? You, because you are an obnoxious overachiever, were way high up. I stopped when I got scared, and Sparrow was between us."

"Yeah. She slipped and fell and got the wind knocked out of her. Remember how she was so still for a minute we thought she was dead?"

"We totally lost our minds and almost fell out of the tree ourselves."

She laughs. "We were such little morons. But she hurt her wrist and didn't tell a soul. Not even us. She went to the drugstore all by herself, bought an Ace bandage, and wrapped it up. She told everyone it didn't hurt. For, like, five days! But her arm turned black up to the elbow, remember? And when Sophie ran her to the ER, sure enough, her wrist was broken."

"She drives me nuts, the way she clams up. My granny would say, 'She keeps herself to herself.' She keeps everything, especially the important things, all locked up inside. I just wonder what it's going to take for her to blow."

I bump her shoulder with mine.

"So what do we do?"

"I don't know. Watch and wait and see how it plays out?"

"I can't do that, Laney. I just can't sit around waiting for something terrible to happen."

"And you can't stick your nose in where she doesn't want you, so where does that leave us?"

I turn to her, holding up my pinky.

"What, Lucas? Are we eight years old again?"

"Do it, Laney. Do it. We need to make a pact."

It's time for a blood oath. Without the actual blood.

She rolls her eyes, but holds up her pinky.

"What are we swearing to?"

"That we're going to try to get her to tell us the truth. Both of us. If we both corner her, she'll have nowhere to go. She has to spill sometime."

"Actually, no, she doesn't."

"Hang on, there's more."

I take a deep breath. Here's the thing we'll never be able to undo.

"This is the hard part, but we have to promise each other. We have to swear. No backing out."

"Just say it."

"If Sparrow doesn't talk, if she refuses to tell the truth, then we tell Sophie and Mr. Rose. No matter what. Even though she'll probably never speak to us again and hate us for the rest of our lives. But at least she'll be away from that douchebag."

I hold out my hand, waiting for hers. She hesitates.

"Lucas, she'll never forgive us."

"I know. When you swear a blood oath, there's always a price. We have to do it, Laney. We have to."

She hooks my pinky with hers, gives it a little tug. "Okay, I swear. But I hate you."

"I hate myself. But we're doing the right thing."

I hand her my dish towel and she wipes her eyes. "Doing the right thing blows."

"Word. In the meantime, we text each other right away if we see anything weird. We stay on her like stink on a skunk, but we play it like ninjas, right? All stealthy and quiet-like. We'll spook her if she knows we're watching. Deal?"

"Deal. Now go away so I can go to bed."

The house is dark and silent when I get home. Not surprising, since it's after one in the morning. But I won't be able to sleep if I don't make my rounds.

I tiptoe up the front stairs, avoiding the creaky third step, the one my dad never did get around to fixing. Ever since he died, Anna refuses to turn her bedroom lamps off, even in the daytime. She also sleeps with three night-lights, just in case her lamps ever burn out. Last week she asked me if I could teach her to sleep with her eyes open.

Tonight she's like a human burrito, all wrapped up in her sheets and blankets, with her head at the foot of her bed and her little feet pushed up against the headboard. She says no stupid angels can take her to Heaven if she goes to sleep upside down, because she'll be invisible and they won't know which part to grab. I don't tell her this makes no sense. She's only eight. She's allowed.

I pick her up and turn her right side up, and a picture falls out of her hand. Anna and my dad at the Outer Banks three years ago. She's sitting on his lap, her cheeks sunburned and freckled, the wind blowing her dark hair into the enormous strawberry ice cream cone melting in rivers down her arm. My dad is wearing a Red Sox cap and laughing into the camera. The St. Michael the Archangel medal Granny Deirdre gave him when he was deployed gleams in the sun. I tuck the blankets tightly around my little sister.

She stirs, and I kiss her sweaty hair. "Night, Anna Banana," I whisper. She turns over and mumbles, "Night, Lucas Pukas. Don't steal my picture."

I prop it against her ladybug lamp so she'll see it when she wakes up.

My mother's room smells like unwashed pajamas and my father's cologne. She still sleeps on her side of the bed, leaving his side smooth and untouched except for his plaid bathrobe, which she keeps draped over his pillow. Tonight she's wearing one of his Citadel T-shirts and the ridiculously enormous watch he always wore on dive trips. Her long auburn hair is matted and dirty, in braids she hasn't undone for days. She's tied the ends with Anna's dinosaur elastics. They make her look crazy.

I don't touch her, don't speak, just quietly pick up the bottle of sleeping pills on the nightstand and tuck it into my pocket. Sometimes she wakes up just before dawn and can't remember how many she's taken, so she takes more. I keep them with me now, ever since the day she slept so long she forgot to meet Anna's school bus. Every night she pretends she's misplaced them. Every night I pretend to find them in the medicine cabinet.

Just before I drift off to sleep, Sparrow's face floats into my head, her eyes filling with the tears she couldn't wipe away fast enough.

I fumble on the nightstand for my phone and type in the dancer emoji I always use, the only one there is, the disco guy in the purple suit. I wait, hoping to see the flamenco dancer that's her signature, but there's nothing.

Birdy, you there?

Birdy?

Let me know you're okay.

You okay?

I'm here if you need me.

I always will be. Just so you know.

Her silence is deafening.

13

The Fight, Three Days Later

I'm fine, I promise. It's just a little bruise. Give me a second, okay?

Sparrow, you're not fine! Oh my God, why won't you tell me the truth?

She's still on the floor, her hand pressed against her hip.

"If you don't talk to me right now, I swear on my grandmother's grave I'm calling an ambulance."

I run for my dance bag and dig out my phone, holding it up so she can see. She raises her head and looks at me, but it's like I'm not even there. Her eyes are distant and faraway. I wish I knew where she went when she gets like this. I'd go with her so she wouldn't be alone.

"Birdy, I'm calling 9–1–1."

She takes a deep, shuddering breath, and the color starts to come back to her face.

"Lucas, would you stop being such a drama queen? And your

grandmother isn't dead, you idiot. She sat with us on the patio after your dad's funeral."

"Yeah, I was talking about the other one, wiseass."

I hold up my phone and punch the nine. "If you don't tell me what's going on, the ones are coming next."

"All right! Will you just stop?"

I put the phone down and cross my arms, waiting.

"I'm okay, really. I twisted something when I came down, and it hurt like a mother."

She rummages in her bag, finds her hairbrush, then shakes out what looks like an entire handful of Advil, chugging them down with half a bottle of water.

I'm so fed up with pretending that everything is awesome. I am bone tired of looking the other way, sick of letting her call the shots. I give her exactly one minute, then plop myself down beside her and her ginormous bottle of Advil.

"Birdy Bird," I say. I can't keep the irritation out of my voice. "For God's sake, when are you going to come clean?"

She undoes her bun and starts brushing it out like she's angry at her own hair. She won't look at me. The sky is filled with pink and gold clouds, and there's a daylight moon disappearing as the light grows. We are the only ones here, except for one of the youth symphony violinists, who comes here to practice in the early mornings because his house is too noisy.

"Lucas, I don't even know what you're talking about."

"You know exactly what I'm talking about. Do you think I'm stupid?"

She doesn't answer me, but moves her legs into splits, hissing between her teeth at the pain. She never stops brushing her hair.

"Because I'm not blind. I saw your face at Delaney's. You were hurt, and you were scared. And the only person in the room who could have made you that way was your boyfriend. So tell me again how nothing happened."

She slams the brush down on the floor and glares at me, eyes blazing.

"I'm not going to do this again with you. I've told you and told you and told you, and you just will not listen. Go ahead and believe whatever you want to believe. I don't care anymore."

"You know what really gets me, Sparrow? This is me you're talking to. Me. We've grown up together. You have your own place at our kitchen table, and there's one for me at your house. All our lives, I've told you things I haven't told anyone else. But when I ask you anything about, you know, you, oh no, that's not allowed. You just push me away, again and again. You tell me a whole lot of nothing. Why is that?"

"That's not true. I tell you stuff."

"No, you don't, Birdface. Talking about your father's trials doesn't count. That's his life, not yours."

She won't make eye contact. She's distracted and spooked and keeps staring out the huge arched windows. Like she's afraid someone will be looking back at her, though the windows are so high you'd have to be on stilts to see inside.

"Sparrow."

She touches her head to the floor, which has to hurt like Satan if her hip is badly bruised. Which I totally think it is. But she's playing the game again. The one where I'm always wrong, always imagining things, and she's cool. Perfectly fine. Right as freaking rain.

"Sparrow. Look at me."

She straightens up and squares her shoulders. Her face is flushed and sweaty. Even now, when I'm frustrated and mad, I can't help thinking about how she is straight-up beautiful and doesn't even know it.

"God, Lucas! What do you want me to say?"

I stand up and start pacing. I can't sit still and be angry at the same time, and I want to be angry right now. I want to feel it coursing through my veins. I want her to see how completely messed up this whole thing is.

"I want you to tell me why you look so scared all the time. I want you to tell me what really happened at Delaney's. I want you to tell me why we just blew the fish dive. I want to know why you almost passed out when I touched your hip. And I want to know if your steaming turd of a boyfriend is hurting you. That's what I want you to say."

She looks away, out the window again. She's gone so far away, it's like I haven't even spoken. I kneel down in front of her and put my hands on her shoulders. She almost jumps out of her skin.

"Don't scare me like that!" she hisses. "Stop touching me!"

"Stop touching you? Are you kidding me right now?"

"No, I'm not kidding! Can you please, just for one second, quit hounding me? It's nothing! I'm fine! I've told you until I'm blue in the face. I slipped!"

She's a pro, I'll give her that. But I'm not smelling what she's selling. Good liars are still liars.

"Because if he is, if he's hurting you, I will wreck him. Then I'm going to tell Sophie, because she'll hold my coat and lie to the cops for me. And then I'll tell your dad so he can mess him up all legal-like."

So much for the blood oath with Delaney. So much for being all stealthy and quiet, like ninjas. I just threw it right out there, like some hairy, stinking carcass.

Her eyes fill with panic. Then she shoves it all the way down, deep inside herself. I watch her do it. I've watched her do it all our lives. She swallows hard, then turns it all into fury. She turns it on me.

"Are you actually asking if my boyfriend is hitting me? Are you hoping it's true, because, oh my God, maybe you're jealous of him? I'm in love for the first time and you can't stand that it isn't with you, so you're creating this sick little fantasy? So you can rush in and save me and be my hero forever? Is that what's going on? Is it, Lucas?"

I draw in a sharp breath. This here is some cruel juice. We are never ugly to each other. Obnoxious, irritating, snarky, hell to the yes. But never, ever truly mean.

"Do you have anything you want to add before I tell you the truth? Anything else you want to get off your chest?" She's all up in my face, fists clenched at her sides, eyes wide with fury.

"You're on a roll. Go for it." I try to act like it makes no difference to me, but I've never been good at hiding things. Unlike Birdy McBirdface here.

Outside, gray clouds are scudding across the sky. A flash of lightning burns white through the windows. Thunder rumbles. I feel it in the pit of my stomach.

"For your information, I slipped in the kitchen a couple of nights ago. Sophie spazzed out loading the dishwasher, and there was water on the floor. I bashed into the corner of the counter and bruised my hip. So when I slid in the beer at Delaney's and I hit the stove, it was like the same thing all over again. You know how I bruise if someone even looks at me cross-eyed. Now I have bruises on bruises. And yes. They hurt."

"What about the marks around your wrists?"

She tugs down the sleeves of her shrug. "I have no idea what you're talking about."

"It's too late for that. I saw those the week before the party."

"They're nothing. Just from all the rehearsals and extra classes."

"Those marks aren't from dancing, Sparrow, so don't even

try to go there. I know what bruises from ballet look like; I have them myself. Those look like somebody held you down."

"I don't even remember where I got them, Lucas."

It makes my blood run cold, not that she's lying, but that she's lying about this.

"Sorry, Birdy. Not buying it. Although maybe you should stay out of kitchens for a while."

"You don't believe me because you hate my boyfriend."

"I don't believe you because of what happened at Delaney's. I don't believe you because he's got serious anger issues. I don't believe you because you haven't answered any of my texts since then. You're acting weird. So yeah, you're right. I seriously don't believe you. And yes, I hate your boyfriend."

"Nothing happened at Delaney's, except you totally lost your mind! You got it all wrong."

"Oh, right. Nothing happened. I see how he is, Sparrow, pretending to be such a great guy, taking his girlfriend out to fancy dinners, buying her flowers and jewelry. Next thing you'll tell me is that he comes to your house at night and serenades you in the moonlight. But underneath all that fake shine, he's still the same old Tristan King, mean as a snake."

"You don't know him the way I do, Lucas. He's kind and thoughtful and brings me little presents that he knows I'll love. He listens to me when I've had a bad day, he's learning about ballet, and he makes me laugh. He's not mean. He's sweet."

She takes off her pointe shoes and crams them into her dance bag without wrapping the ribbons around the shanks. She's upset, but I don't care, not this time. Everything I've kept bottled up inside comes flying out of my mouth. Every word I haven't spoken, every thought I've been afraid to voice for weeks. For months. Righteous anger, friends and neighbors. It's better than

Taco Bell and a couple of tequila shots with Caleb and Israel and Sam on a Friday night.

"I'm closer to you, literally, than anyone else, unless you and Captain Douchemuffin are doing it, which I doubt, because you'd never give that much of yourself away."

Her face goes white, like someone's dusted her with chalk. "You pig!" She leaps to her feet, tears off her rehearsal tutu, and throws it in my face, then starts shoving the rest of her stuff into her bag. Water bottle, the huge container of Advil, ratty leg warmers. But I've developed a severe case of verbal diarrhea. The words pour out of me like an intestinal virus.

"You can throw sweaty tutus at me all day long. Doesn't bother me. I know you, Birdy. I know how you always start humming five beats before you jump. I know when your ankle aches, when your blisters sting, when your head hurts, even when you have cramps. Not because you tell me, but because of the way you hold your body.

"So do you really expect me to believe everything's okay? You're always looking over your shoulder, like you're afraid of something. I wish I could put you in the Witness Protection Program, but you'd have to want to go. And honestly? That's what scares me the most. Because there's no way anyone can protect you from yourself!"

Even her lips have gone pale. "Shut up, Lucas!" She shoves her feet into her Uggs, grabs her bag, and marches out the door. I catch up with her before she makes it outside.

"You're lying to me," I say to the back of her head. "You're lying to Delaney and Levkova and your dad and Sophie and all the people who care about you. You're scared, Sparrow. You're scared of Tristan."

She wheels around and walks back to me.

"I. Said. Shut. Up!" she cries, shoving against my chest with both hands. Her fingernails are bitten bloody, worse than usual. "Who the hell do you think you are, Lucas? It's not your job to protect me. I never asked you to care, and I don't need you sticking your nose into my life! Tristan and I are none of your business, so back off!"

She crashes out the door.

For a second I can't catch my breath. I can't move. Then I run after her.

"Sparrow! Wait! Stop! I'm sorry! I'm sorry!"

I watch as she screeches out of the parking lot, fishtailing and spraying water when she hits the potholes. She flies through the yellow light at the intersection half a block away. I stand shivering in the rain until her taillights disappear.

Walking back to the studio, soaked to the skin, I tell myself I was right to call her out. I was right to tell her I know something bad is going down. That she's not as good at keeping secrets as she thinks she is. Pretty sure she's the one who threw the lemons in the trash at Delaney's. I know about the Aubrey paintings and her bad dreams, and I know she does *fouettés* in the middle of the night when she needs to stop remembering her mother.

I was right, and it makes me feel like one of those guys who bashes baby seals in the head for a living.

I just blew up the last thing in my life that was good.

Sparrow

For I have sworn thee fair and thought thee bright,
Who art as black as hell, as dark as night.

WILLIAM SHAKESPEARE, "Sonnet 147"

14

August, After

I lie at the bottom of a deep, silent sea. My bones have turned to ice. My eyes are frozen shut. I am so cold.

Far above me, flashing lights spin, burning red and blue, blue and red. A wild screaming noise fills my head, building to a crescendo, falling and rising again, over and over. I know there are people up there, but I can't see them. I know I need to fight, to swim hard and strong up to where they are. I know I should shout, "I'm here! I'm still me!"

But I can't do it. It is too hard, and I am too tired.

I'm not going up there. Down here I'm cold, but I'm safe.

I rock gently in the current.

Soon there are stars.

People running. Bright lights stab into my eyes. Inside the running there is shouting and a man, whispering. *Yea, though I walk through the valley of the shadow of death, I will fear no evil: for thou art with me; thy rod and thy staff they comfort me.* The stars and the words bear me up, into the light and the noise.

Shoes pound on the floor, heavy, loud, and clumsy, not light and graceful like pointe shoes. Though I try to hold on to the man's voice, to ride it like a wave back into the silent dark, I am pulled back again and again until I surrender.

A thousand thousand people are talking at once, over and around and below each other. The voices are outside and inside me. They won't go away. They won't leave me alone.

I try to say hush, please hush, but I can't feel my mouth or my throat. I don't know if there's anything left of me.

"On my count. One. Two. Three."

"We lost her twice on the way."

"Give it to me fast, Mike. Angela, I need that intubation tray, quick. Quick!"

"They found her at Aubrey's Cove. Looks like she was out there most of the night. Multiple maxillofacial injuries, at least five broken ribs. Both pupils reactive to light. Injuries inside the mouth, four missing teeth, and it looks like she bit through her bottom lip. Petechiae in and around both eyes, scratches and abrasions on her neck. Defense wounds on both forearms. Right ankle is bruised and swollen."

"Do we have ID?"

"Avery Rose's daughter."

"Sparrow?"

"Yeah."

"Lord have mercy."

"I didn't even know it was her until we checked her pockets and found her license."

"What about consent? Who's here?"

"Her father's right outside, with Sophie. They're both hanging on by their fingernails."

"Angela, could you go out and make sure those consent forms get signed? Just ask for consent right now. I'll talk to them as soon as we get her stable. Mike, do they know who did it? Did they get him?"

"They've brought the boyfriend, that King kid, in for questioning. Tommy's hanging around, hoping he can talk to her."

"Nope. Not going to happen."

"He knows. Also, you didn't hear this from me, but he's looking a little shaky. You might want to have someone check him out. He's the one who got to her first. She's going to be okay, right?"

"Hush, Mikey. She can hear you. We'll know more in a few hours."

"Yeah, but damn it, Mags. She's had more bad stuff in her life than most kids her age. You'd think she'd catch a break."

"I know, sweetie. Go on now. You did amazing out there. Now let us do what we do."

"Sparrow? Can you hear me? Can you open your eyes for me? Try to open your eyes, Sparrow.

"Okay then. You rest for now. Hang on to the sound of my voice. My name is Maggie. I'm the doctor who's taking care of you. You're safe now, in the emergency room at Saint Germaine's. Only good people are here, people who care about you.

"Can you squeeze my hand a little? Squeeze if you can hear me.

"Okay, no worries, sweetie. I'm not going to lie, Sparrow, you're pretty banged up, but we're going to do everything we can to help you get better. I know you're scared and hurting, but don't be afraid. We won't leave you. You're safe, I promise.

"Sparrow, while I'm talking, you'll feel me touching you. I need to find all the places where you're hurt, and we need to take some pictures, so you might see some bright flashes. We also need to get some X-rays and a CT scan to see what's hurt on the inside. David, hang on a second. Help me hold her so I can see her back. There, right there, that's good.

"You know, Sparrow, I saw you dance last year. I took Hannah, my little girl, to see you in *The Nutcracker*. You were such a wonderful Clara. We came backstage to see you after. You pulled a rose out of that huge bouquet, and you gave it to Hannah and curtsied to her, just like she was a princess. She's never forgotten it. She's only seven, but she says she wants to be a ballerina, just like you.

"Stay with me, Sparrow. You stay with me. You're a fighter. Fight now, honey. Fight hard.

"We'll let your daddy come in after a little while, and your aunt, too. Rest now, and when you're ready, you come back to us. You come on back, you hear me?"

"Sweet Jesus, Mary, and Joseph. Oh, my baby, I'm so sorry. I'm going to find who did this and when I do, I promise you, I'm going to . . ."

"Avery. Not now. Keep it together."

"Look at her, Soph! Holy God, look what he's done to her!"

"I am looking at her. She's still our Sparrow. She can hear you, little brother. Talk to her. Tell her you love her."

A long, trembling breath.

"Baby, it's Daddy. I love you so much, and I'm right here, my sweetheart. Open your eyes, honey. Oh God, please, don't do this to me. Don't leave me, Sparrow. Please, honey."

A strangled cry.

"Oh, Sparrow, my sweet baby. I've failed you in the worst way, in every way. I'm so sorry, for not seeing, for not knowing. I'm so sorry! You're the most precious thing in the world to me, and I should have known! I've been so blind! I couldn't see anything, not now, not then, even when you were four and stopped smiling and laughing. I was always so worried about her, and all the time you were the one who was suffering. Oh dear God, forgive me! Open your eyes, sweetheart, please. I promise, I'll do anything. Please, baby girl. Come back to me."

My father, sobbing.

Jasmine perfume. Silvery wind chime sounds. Bracelets. Soft hair on my face, warm breath in my ear.

"Sparrow, my little bird. Wake up, love. Let me see your beautiful eyes. Wake up, sweetheart. There are angels all around you, Sparrow. Nothing can hurt you here. You're safe now. Come back, love. We're all here, waiting."

"Hey, Birdy Bird. Hey."

Quick footsteps, walking away. A whisper, barely there. *Help me, Dad, help me.*

"Sophie, I can't do this. I can't even tell it's her. What happened to her hair?"

"Lucas, take a breath, love. It's scary, I know, and it's so brave of you to be here. I know this must be awful after everything you went through with your dad. If it's too much, I totally understand.

It's a lot to ask. It's just—we think she hears us, so we're trying to get the people she loves to come talk to her. To see if we can bring her back."

A shallow breath, then another.

Slow footsteps, coming back.

"No, no, it's okay. I just freaked out for a second. I'm good. I'll stay."

"Okay, honey. They had to shave her head so they could stitch her scalp. As soon as the swelling goes down, they'll take the tube out of her throat. Do you want me to step out? Would that make things easier?"

"You wouldn't mind?"

"Not at all. Come hug me goodbye when you're done. Five minutes, that's all, okay?"

A chair dragged across the floor.

"Birdy, it's Lucas. I'm holding your hand. Can you feel me? Come back and dance with me, Birdface. We can do fish dives all day long if you want."

My hand turned over, my fist opened, warm breath on my fingers. A scratchy kiss in my palm.

"Wake up, Sparrow. Wake up so I can tell you how sorry I am for all the terrible things I said to you. Come back and tell me you hate my guts. I don't care what you say as long as you come back. I just—I can't lose you."

Light footsteps. Amazing Grace perfume. Fingers stroking my forehead. Soft voice drifting down through the dark of an endless tunnel, where no light has ever been.

"Oh, Sparrow." Quick, shallow, shaking breaths.

"Why couldn't you talk to me? Why couldn't you tell me how bad it was? You must have been so scared.

"I don't know what to say, except I'm sorry. I'm so sorry I wasn't there for you. I should have known. I should have listened to Lucas. I should have done something. You're my best friend, and it kills me that you were alone with all that, with him, for so long.

"Remember how when we were little, Sophie and my mom took us to *Nutcracker* every Christmas? We'd get all dressed up and have a fancy dinner before? Remember how when we were nine we decided that the sound of pointe shoes on the stage floor was the most beautiful sound in the world? When you dance, Sparrow, you have something none of the rest of us will ever have. It's like you're all filled up with magic or, I don't know, light from the stars.

"I brought my lucky pointe shoes with me. I'm tucking them underneath your blanket. I wore them for my audition at the conservatory when we were in sixth grade. Remember how terrified we were? Maybe they'll help you find your way home.

"I promise I won't miss anything ever again. Please come back, Bird Girl. I can't let you go. Not like this."

Lilacs and snow. Footsteps whispering, gliding.

A voice, aching, full of sadness.

"My little bird, my beautiful dancer."

Soft cheek pressed against mine.

"I have never borne a child, but I love you as though you were my own. Oh, my dearest child, how I wish I had told you this before."

A kiss on each cheek.

"You must live. You must. This is all that is left to us in the face of evil and suffering and grief. Live, darling Sparrow. Live to dance again. Live for your papa, for your aunt Sophie. Live for Lucas and Delaney and everyone who loves you.

"Live for me.

"Please. Live for me."

Levkova, weeping.

All the stars have gone away. Only the dark remains, and the voices that come to me from far away, telling me to come back.

But I don't know how anymore. I feel myself fading, bleeding softly into the dark, everything I once was slipping away, like smoke into shadow.

15

In the Valley of the Shadow

Insubstantial as air, I float near the ceiling of the hospital room, looking down at the wreckage that used to be me. The girl in the bed doesn't even look human. Her eyes are black and swollen shut. Both arms are in casts to her elbows. There's a tube down her throat, and her right foot is bandaged, the toes purple and black. Bloody stitches march across her forehead and her scalp. She has no hair.

Staring at his folded hands, my father whispers magic words to himself, over and over again. "All will be well, all will be well, and all manner of things shall be well."

Sophie stands at the window, arms crossed tightly across her body, swaying from side to side. She hums tunelessly and wipes her eyes with a balled-up tissue.

I've come to say goodbye. I'm not going back to that body. I won't live in her skin again. I don't know where I'll go next. I don't care. I only know I don't want this.

I drift softly down to the bed and hover over the broken girl, a breath, a whisper away. She smells like chemicals, like blood and sweat. There's shiny ointment on her eyes and her cracked lips. Her chest rises and falls, like her insides have turned to clockwork.

I whisper in her ear, telling her that she doesn't have to suffer any longer. I touch her face with my hand, which has become transparent. I can see the veins glowing inside, like tiny blue roads. She is not me. I am not her.

Come on, I say. *Let's go. It won't hurt anymore, I promise. Nothing hurts here.* My father stands up so quickly that his chair tips over. It makes a loud, metallic noise that echoes in the silent room. His eyes are wide, and his hands are trembling. He lowers the railing on the bed and leans over the ruined girl. With his face inches from hers, he whispers, "Sparrow?" He strokes her swollen cheek.

Instantly, Sophie is beside him.

"Did she move?"

"No. I just thought—never mind. It was nothing."

"You felt her, didn't you, Avery? Something happened."

"Maybe. I don't know. I thought I heard her voice, but that's impossible. I hoped—never mind. I was half asleep. Just a dream."

"What did she say?"

"What does it matter?"

Sophie returns to her post at the window. My father closes his eyes.

Come, girl in the bed. Come with me. It's time.

Nothing hurts. I am whole. There are no casts, no bruises, no bloody stitches. My hands are filled with golden light; it pours from my fingertips. I'm wearing an ivory lace camisole and a fluttering chiffon skirt. My pointe shoes gleam softly in the sunlight.

The Honeysuckle Pond is the same, but different. The landscape is familiar and impossible at the same time, like being inside a fairy tale. Climbing roses and honeysuckle twine around the trunks and fall gracefully from the branches of towering tulip poplars. The forest floor is carpeted with bluebells and forget-me-nots. White rhododendrons, in full flower, bloom from crevices in the rocks. Bright red cardinals dive and swoop around me, trilling their songs. The waterfall is bigger and higher, roaring with summer rain. I am standing on the flat, sun-warmed rock in the middle of the creek. Cold, clear water rushes all around me.

I do a perfect *arabesque* on my rock, then a deep, heartfelt *révérence* to the waterfall. My arms feel like liquid, fluid and strong. I will dance here forever. Inside the rushing water, the rocks and roaring waterfall, around and between the singing birds and the wind sighing through the trees, an oboe weeps and grieves. I begin to dance the fourth act of *Swan Lake*, which I've never danced before, but somehow know by heart. I am filled with sorrow and loss. Siegfried has betrayed me, promising himself to another. Now I am doomed to be a swan forever, my heart filled with love that has nowhere to go.

I dance and dance, my body mirroring the depth of my despair, the love I will carry with me until my dying day, the pain of his betrayal. My feet float over the sparkling creek. My arms bend in supplication, pleading with the waterfall, the trees and the flowers. My heart cries out to the earth and the sky. Please let it not be true, that I am lost. I surrender to an anguish so deep, I know it will consume me.

Across the water lies a place where the sun does not reach. It shimmers with heat and malevolence. I shiver. Something bad happened there. I turn away and concentrate on the water, the wavering light, the riot of flowers, my beautiful shoes. If I don't look at the darkness, I can't be afraid. If I don't look, I can't remember.

Someone is calling.

"Savannah."

Before I can think, before I can run away, I find myself on the creek bank. The cold seeps through the thin soles of my shoes. Everything has gone silent.

"Come to me, Savannah."

Wrapped in darkness, my mother waits for me.

16

Mama

Her jet-black hair drifts slowly around her face in a breeze I cannot feel. The wide white streak at her temple shimmers. She's dressed in the outfit she wore the last time I saw her, white capri pants and a sleeveless flowered blouse. We were baking cookies together. The smell of butter and chocolate, sugar and vanilla wafts over me. I close my eyes and let the memory wrap around me. She laughed that morning, and I laughed with her. She let me lick the batter from the mixing bowl.

I step toward her, and when she smiles, I take another step, then another, until I'm standing in front of her.

"Savannah," she whispers, reaching out her arms. "My girl." I step into her embrace, and her smile grows wider and wider until it stretches across her face, a rictus of mirth.

I try to back away, but it is too late. My feet are rooted to the ground. My mother smiles and smiles. The capri pants and flowered blouse are gone, replaced with a trailing gown, black as a moonless night, glittering with rubies scattered like constellations across the bodice and hem. Sleek black feathers begin to cover her throat, her bare shoulders and arms, growing to points over her hands. They are so dark they look blue in the dusky light. I hear them, whispering over her skin.

The white streak at her temple is no longer hair, but feathers that lift and tremble, as though they have a life of their own. A tiara appears on her head, a high arch of needle-sharp points, sparkling with dark jewels. Milky, opalescent pearls twine around her feathered throat and weave themselves into her hair. As I watch, unable to tear my eyes away, unable to move, enormous black wings unfurl behind her, raising themselves high over her head with a sound like a thousand birds taking off at once.

Black stones rain from her eyes.

"Go away, Mama. Go away. I don't want you here."

She smiles, deep red lips parting to reveal perfect white teeth, sharpened to points. Near her feet, green shoots are pushing their way out of the damp earth, growing taller and taller, limbs and branches forming before my eyes.

A lemon tree blooms beside her.

I close my eyes, praying that this is only another nightmare, that I'll wake up back on my sun-warmed rock, surrounded by flowers and sunlight and the smell of honeysuckle. That she will not be my eternity.

"Go away, Mama," I whisper again. "Go away. I hate you."

She doesn't answer, just stands there, the feathers on those terrible wings moving, shivering, the stones falling from her eyes. They make an icy sound, like sleet, when they hit the ground.

"I have a message for you, Savannah."

The smell of lemons is overpowering, and I press my hands to my face, trying to keep it away. Her dark eyes glitter like a bird's.

"I don't care. I don't want to listen to you. I don't want to

look at you. Whatever you have to tell me, it's too late. You're too
late."

"It will never be too late, Savannah."

I try to clap my hands over my ears, but I'm paralyzed. My
arms hang uselessly at my sides.

"You're dead, Mama. I won't listen to you."

"What have I always told you, Savannah? What are you
never, ever supposed to forget?"

My heart aches, heavy in my chest. "Oh, Mama," I whisper,
wishing with everything that's left of me that I'd had a mother
who would wrap her arms around me when I was frightened. Who
would comfort me now and tell me that I'm only dreaming. That
I am not broken and dying, but whole and alive. A mother who
would smile gently, tell me that she loves me more than the moon
and the stars, that yes, yes, of course I will dance again.

"You want my arms around you, Savannah?"

She steps toward me and enfolds me in her dark wings, pressing me so close I feel them trembling, growing tighter and tighter
until everything goes dark in my eyes. An agonizing pain flares
deep in my chest.

Trapped in my mother's embrace, I am once again hiding
in the suffocating darkness of the closet under the stairs. I feel
the spiders crawling on my legs, their webs in my hair and on
my face. I smell the stinging pine scent of the floor mop, see the
shadowy bucket, the big bottle of Lysol. Curled into a ball, in
the farthest corner away from the tiny door, I hear her outside.
Raging. Laughing. Screaming my name over and over. When she
comes for me, I will tell her. When she pulls my hair and shouts
at me, I will tell her I haven't forgotten. I know little girls should
be quiet. Wicked little girls must never say a word.

"I remember, Mama," I say, voice gone lisping and high,
like it was when I was four. "Never tell anyone, not even Daddy.

Especially not Daddy. That's what I need to remember. I'll never tell, I promise. Please go away. Please let me go."

"I can't let you go. Not when I've been without you for so long."

She pulls away from me. Her wings rise. She smiles and smiles and smiles. The lemons gleam with yellow light.

As I watch, all her sharp edges, the wings, the shimmering tiara, her teeth, begin to blur, until only her eyes are left, still weeping stones. I hear her voice, as from a great distance. "What is your haunted name, the secret name of your deepest self?"

And I answer, "Sorrow."

The air around me is charged with my mother's presence, the way it feels before a thunderstorm. Threatening. Dangerous. I can't see her, but I know she is still here, somewhere. Watching me, waiting for me with her black wings. I can still feel them folded tight around me, moving against my skin, suffocating and close. I close my eyes, but she is with me. She will always be with me.

The sharp pain flares in my chest again, like someone is squeezing my heart inside an iron fist. I lie down carefully on the damp earth, my arms and legs outstretched, like a starfish. The fallen leaves and flowers are fragrant and cool beneath me. From far, far away, I hear the sound of a machine beeping, and then one long, endless note, discordant and piercing, the period at the end of a long sentence. Gradually it grows silent.

I try hard to breathe, and then I remember. Dead girls can't breathe.

I stare up through the trees at the starlit sky. The pain grows smaller and smaller until it is gone. I feel nothing but emptiness and relief.

I find myself lying on the sun-warmed rock again. The clear

blue water swirls and eddies all around me, holding me safe. My hair smells like honeysuckle, and my pointe shoes bear no trace of the mud and the dirt and the dark; the pink satin shines. I laugh out loud, because I taste pound cake. And coffee with cinnamon and sugar.

But as I sit up and lift my face to the warmth and the light, another voice, a soft voice, calls to me. Gentle and familiar, like warm honey poured from a sparkling crystal jar, the voice pulls at me, an invisible thread anchored at my core. It is everywhere all at once, floating out to me from inside the waterfall, from the water beside me rushing over the smooth gray stones, from the sweetly scented air. A whisper at first, it quickly becomes a lilting song that refuses to let me go. I cover my ears, but I can still hear it.

Sophie.

I close my eyes, remembering all the nights I woke up screaming, my head and my heart full of nightmares. I remember Sophie's soft arms around me, her jasmine perfume floating on the air, telling me even before I opened my terrified eyes that I was safe, because she was with me. Because she loved me.

Sophie.

"Oh, no, no, no, please. Don't leave us, honey. Please don't go, Sparrow. Come back, my love. Wake up, sweetheart. Wake up. Remember the lullaby I used to sing to you? I am here, little bird. Don't be afraid. We are right here."

Sleep my child and peace attend thee, all through the night.
Guardian angels God will send thee, all through the night.

I remember.

My father coming home from work on soft spring evenings, tossing his polished wing tips and dark socks onto the front porch steps, the sound of his joyful sigh as his bare feet touched the cool grass.

The lush green heat of the countless summer nights Delaney slept over at my house, how we'd crawl out my bay window and lie on the warm roof, talking about everything and nothing.

Lucas rehearsing by himself in the small studio, brow furrowed in concentration, jumping over and over and over again until his hair dripped with sweat. The smile in his eyes when he caught me spying on him.

Levkova in the big studio, sunlight pooled at her feet.

Abby playing the enormous piano.

Sophie baking brownies, stirring soup, sneaking into my room to leave little presents on my pillow. A book of poems. A sparkling stone. A gardenia blossom. *All will be well.*

"Oh God, please come back, Sparrow. Please, sweetheart, please. We are all waiting for you with our arms open wide. We love you so much. Come home, baby girl. Come back to us. We love you, Sparrow. We love you."

I hear her anguish, feel all the voices rising inside me, a chorus of fear and grief and longing.

Come back, come back, come back.

I open my eyes.

Lucas

Woe to the hand that shed this costly blood!

<small>WILLIAM SHAKESPEARE,</small> *Julius Caesar*

17

Last Sunday in August

"Lucas, honey, wake up. Wake up, love."

It's five thirty on Sunday morning, and my mother is shaking me.

I groan and burrow deeper into the covers, pulling them over my head. "Mom, geez! Stop!"

I hear her walk across the room and pull up the blinds. She turns on the lamps beside my bed, along with the overhead lights and the wonky ceiling fan.

"It's the only day I get to sleep in! Go away."

"I can't, sweetie. I need you to wake up now." She perches on the side of my bed. "Come on, Lucas."

I sit up slowly and run my hands through my hair, wincing at the light pouring into my eyes. I am not a morning person. Unless I'm dancing. Which I am not.

"Mom, you are freaking relentless."

When I stop squinting, it's hard to believe what I'm seeing.

I actually blink, in case I'm seeing a mirage. My mother is dressed in a flowered skirt and a clean white T-shirt. Her hair is washed and tied back with a green scarf. She's wearing gold hoop earrings and clear lip gloss. She smells like she used to, Dove soap and Olay lotion and vanilla. Her eyes are clear and focused. She looks like the mom I was trying to make myself forget, in case I never saw her again.

"Mom? Am I dreaming? You're dressed?"

She looks so sad when she answers. "Yes, honey. I'm dressed and my hair is clean and I have even brushed my teeth. I'm sorry I woke you up, but I have something hard to tell you. Are you awake enough to listen?"

"Is Anna okay? You aren't sick, are you? Mom? Are you sick?"

Her face softens, and she takes my hand.

"No, honey, I'm not sick. Anna's fine, snoring away."

I don't want to hear whatever she has to tell me. So I stall.

"Is she upside down?"

"No, I turned her around before I went to bed."

Outside, the sky has turned a pale and smoky gray, the mountains still dark silhouettes all around us. I stare out the window, wishing I were high above Hollins Creek, hiking to the top of Mount Aberdeen, where it's fresh and cool, even in the hottest part of the summer. I'd stay up there forever.

I'm still looking at the hills, wishing myself away, when my mother says, "Honey, something's happened to Sparrow."

My heart pounds so hard I feel dizzy. I want to tell her to take it back.

"She's at Saint Germaine's. Someone—someone attacked her last night. They found her at Aubrey's Cove. Sophie just called me."

"How bad?" My voice sounds foreign. Strangled.

My mother's eyes fill. "Sweetie, it's bad."

"Mom! How bad?"

"She's unconscious and they had to put a tube down her throat to help her breathe. She has broken ribs and some deep cuts and her foot is hurt. She's lost a lot of blood. They think she was out there most of the night. The doctors aren't sure—" She coughs a little, like the words are hurting her throat. "They'll know more later, but right now it's touch and go, honey. They're working hard to help her, but Sophie said that there's a possibility—"

"What, Mom? What? Are you telling me she could die?"

My mother's eyes fill. She takes my hands in hers. I pull them away.

"Yes. It's possible. Oh, Lucas, sweetheart, I'm so sorry to have to tell you this."

I throw the covers back and grab a pair of sweatpants off the floor. Pulling them on over my boxers, I run into the hall and tear down the stairs to the front door.

"Lucas, no! Wait!"

I fumble for my car keys in the bowl on the foyer table, sending it crashing to the tile floor, and run out the door. My mom catches up with me before I get to my Jeep, grabbing my T-shirt and jerking me backward. I whirl around to face her. The grass is cool and damp on my bare feet.

"Damn it, Mom! Let go of me." I tear my shirt out of her grasp. I yank open the door and slide into the driver's seat, but my mother steps between the door and me. She grabs both of my shoulders and turns me to face her.

"Lucas, I need you to listen to me."

"Mom, I'm backing this car out of the driveway. I'm going to the hospital. You can come with me if you want, but I'm going. With or without you."

Her eyes are sad and fierce and scared all at the same time.

"Sweetheart, no. You can't."

"Hell yes, I can, Mom. You can't stop me."

"No, I can't, but listen to me for a second." I start prying her hands off, but she's got a death grip on me. "One second, Lucas, that's all I'm asking."

I put the car into reverse, but keep my foot on the brake.

"Honey, the ambulance just brought her in a little while ago; she's still in the emergency room. Mr. Rose and Sophie are there. The police are there, too. If you go running into all that, you'll distract everyone from doing what they need to do. You won't mean to, but you will. Give them some time to figure out where things stand. Sophie will let us know when we can come, and then I promise, we'll go together. Okay?"

I turn the car off and my mother moves away. I push past her and walk quickly down the driveway, stopping when my legs give out. It's like they've turned to water, refusing to hold me up anymore. I sink to my knees, pressing my forehead to the ground. Bits of gravel and dirt dig into my skin. I want it to hurt. I hope it makes me bleed.

My mother comes up behind me and gathers me into her arms, rocking me like she used to when I fell off my bike or caught a soccer ball with my face.

"Oh my God, Mom, no, no, no. Not Sparrow, please. I can't stand it." I pound my fists on the ground. My mother rubs my shoulders, smooths my hair back from my forehead. "Hush, sweetheart. Hush now. I know I haven't been here for you since your father died, and I'm sorrier than you'll ever know. I'm so sorry, Lucas. I let you down, and I let Anna down. But I'm here now, honey, and I promise we will face this together. Everything is going to be all right."

"Mom, are you nuts? How can you even say that? Nothing is all right. Nothing's ever going to be all right."

By now, lights are beginning to come on in the houses around us. Across the street, nosy Mrs. Peterson pulls aside her living room curtains and peers out at my mom and me kneeling in the driveway. Everyone will hear about this before they've finished their first cup of coffee.

My mother takes my face in her hands. "I know, sweetheart. But I say it anyway, because maybe someday it will be true. Because I want to believe it. I'm saying it because Sparrow is a fighter and a survivor. I say it, love, to get you up off this driveway and into the house so we can figure out how to help Sparrow and Avery and Sophie. And so you can tell me how I can help you."

She stands up and holds out her hand. "Come on. I'll fix breakfast."

"I can't eat."

"Me neither, but let's try, okay? I'll make pancakes."

I wipe my nose and eyes on the hem of my shirt. "Pancakes," I say dully. "You think they fix everything."

"No, honey. I think it's the only thing I know to do."

We walk slowly across the lawn and up the steps to the front door, my mother's arm around my waist.

Where are you now, Birdy Bird? If you can hear me, please don't die. Please don't leave me.

"Mom, wait." She pauses, holding open the screen door. "Tristan did it."

"Oh, Lucas. No one is thinking about that right now, except maybe the police."

"I know he did."

"How do you know this, Lucas?"

"They had a huge fight in the parking lot at the conservatory. Like, he was screaming at her. And he shoved her or something at Delaney's Fourth of July party."

"You saw him?"

"I came in right after. She was on the floor, crying. And when I saw her at rehearsal, she had bruises."

"You think he was getting violent with her?"

"I don't think. I know."

We walk into the kitchen, where my mother busies herself with wire whisks and buttermilk and flour, chocolate chips and strawberries for me, blueberries and bananas for Anna, who's beginning to stir upstairs. I can hear her singing.

"Lucas, I want you to be really careful about saying anything against Tristan. If you saw him hurting her, then we need to tell the police. But if it's just a suspicion, you shouldn't jump to any conclusions. Certainly you should tell them what you saw, but it's up to them to figure this out. It is not up to you."

I look out the window at the sun, just beginning to climb over the highest ridge. Warm light floods the kitchen.

"Lucas? Are you hearing me?"

"Yeah, Mom, I hear you. Delaney said the same thing."

"Delaney is right, honey. You can't accuse someone of a crime just because he's a rotten little creep. Which Tristan King most certainly is."

She hands me a tall glass of milk and a cinnamon roll to tide me over until the pancakes are ready. Cinnamon. The smell reminds me of Sparrow, and I want to run out of here, all the way to Saint Germaine's. I want to kneel in the front yard and tear at my hair and howl like a wolf.

I should have told Sophie. I should have told Mr. Rose. I was a fool for listening to Sparrow, for keeping my mouth shut, for playing by her rules.

This is all my fault.

18

Aubrey's Cove, Ten Days Later

I hear a car door slam, the rustling sound of footsteps on fallen leaves, the sharp snap of twigs breaking as Delaney makes her way to our rock. I'm trying to skip stones over the water, but I've completely lost my touch, and they just sink quietly into the pond. When Delaney gets to the yellow crime scene tape, she stands there with her head bowed, like a pilgrim at a woodland shrine.

After a moment she drops her backpack onto the ground and starts tearing the tape away, bunching it angrily into a ball as she pulls it from the tree trunks, picking at the knot where it's tied around a tulip poplar.

"I hate this ugly crap!" she yells. "I don't care if they arrest me and send me to prison and feed me moldy pig slop for the rest of my life! This mess has got to go!"

I wish I'd thought to do it.

She shoves the whole wad into her pack and slings it over her shoulder, hopping over the rocks. I stand up to meet her. Droplets of water splash onto her turquoise boots, sparkling like little diamonds. It's early September, still hot and humid, but the nights are turning a little cooler. In a few weeks, the leaves will begin to turn. Sparrow's favorite season.

"Hey, you," Delaney says, wrapping her arms tight around my waist. "I stopped by your house to hug your mom. She sent sustenance; it's in my pack. She seems so much better! She smiled and hugged me back, just like always."

In the middle of the creek, smooth gray boulders rise out of the water, like the backs of prehistoric tortoises, close enough together that it's possible to cross from one side of the creek to the other without getting soaked. In the summer and early fall, everyone comes here to swim and sunbathe and hang out, but today it's deserted. People are spooked.

"Yeah," I say, sitting down cross-legged on the biggest rock, still warm from the sun. "She's better, all right."

Delaney sits down beside me, pulling off her boots and hitching up her long skirt to dangle her legs in the icy water. She gasps at the cold, letting out a little squeal, then looks at me over her round sunglasses.

"Why are you saying it all sarcastic?"

She reaches into her backpack and takes out my dented green thermos from Cub Scouts and two Styrofoam cups. She pours out my mother's tomato bisque and unwraps two grilled cheese sandwiches with bacon.

"She yelled at me big-time last night."

The sandwiches are still warm. Since I was a kid, these have been my mom's secret weapon, the meal she makes whenever we argue. She's smart. Like a fox.

"Your mom? No way. I've never heard her yell. She's, like,

the sweetest mom on the planet. You must have done something heinous."

"Well, yeah, I guess I had it coming."

"Tell me, and don't leave anything out."

Delaney takes a bite of grilled cheese. "Oh, yum. Bacon rules. I don't care if your mom yelled at you. She's still a boss, and I love her."

I stick my feet in the water next to hers. They go instantly numb.

"Whatever. So, you know I can get angry sometimes."

"You? Angry? Say it isn't so!"

"Shut up. Anyway. It feels like I have ants crawling under my skin. Ever since they found her. You know that feeling?"

She takes her sunglasses off and sets them beside her.

"I do know that feeling. For me it's like I've swallowed something really nasty, and I can't get the taste out."

"So what do you do when you feel like that? Does it go away after a while?"

She takes another bite of her sandwich and stares out at the waterfall. There's so much mist in the air, when she turns back to me, her hair has started to curl around her face. "No, not by itself. I have to do something. I've tried a whole bunch of things over the years. First I started working out extra-hard. Didn't even make a dent. Then one weekend after I flunked a trig test, I baked nonstop. Muffins. It was always muffins, so many that my mom made me stop. She said she knew I was upset, but she and my dad were going to go bankrupt keeping me in flour and nuts and sugar and also they'd pork out and die from clogged arteries."

I lie back on the rock, the warmth sinking into my back. I still can't feel my feet.

"I've known you all my life and have never seen you bake anything. Not even a frozen pizza."

"Truth. I liked it, but it didn't help. I tried it again, for a couple days after they found Sparrow. But the whole time I was baking muffins, I couldn't stop thinking about her, all beat-up, lying in that hospital bed. In a freaking coma. My mouth tasted like that smell from biology class, you know, the juice they keep the frogs in before they get dissected?"

"Formaldehyde."

"Yeah, that's it. I brushed my teeth twenty times a day and drank grapefruit juice and it still wouldn't go away."

She takes the last sip of her soup, rinses her cup in the creek, and tucks it into her pack. She lies down beside me and takes my hand, kicking her feet so drops of water arc and fall in the sunlight.

"So now what do you do?"

"I'm writing poems again. I sort of quit when we started *Swan Lake*, because I was so wiped out all the time. But when I'm writing, trying to find the right words, I can't think about anything else. It's peaceful. It makes me feel calm, helps me believe that she'll be okay, that she'll wake up and dance again. And my mouth doesn't taste like it's full of poison."

"I like your poems. Except that one about your dog. That was kind of lame."

"I know, but it's one of my favorites. I wrote it one night when my parents were arguing in the kitchen. My mom was slamming pots and pans and cabinet doors, and my dad was talking real loud. So I went up to my room and took out that old leather notebook, remember? The one I carried around all the time in middle school? And it was like as soon as I started writing, this super-soft quiet wrapped itself all around me. I just thought about Molly and her sweet ears and her big brown eyes, and I couldn't hear my parents anymore. That's why I write poems. To get to that quiet place. To get that bad taste out of my mouth. It doesn't really matter if they're any good.

"Anyway, sorry. I got off track. Why's your mom all mad?"

"Last night I slammed my fist through my bedroom wall. I pretended it was Tristan's face." I hold up my hand so she'll notice the bandage.

Delaney sits up, takes her feet out of the water, and pulls me with her. Her eyes go all wide and she covers her mouth. I sit facing her, rubbing my frozen feet.

"Oh, Lucas, no. Did you break anything?"

"Just the wall. I busted my knuckles pretty good. They bled like crazy. Doesn't hurt anymore, though."

"Levkova's going to be pissed."

"She's got nothing on my mom."

"So she really yelled at you?"

"It wasn't really yelling, more like super-intense fussing. She said we needed to have a conversation, then she did all the talking. Told me that money was tight and she didn't have a whole lot of extra funds right now to support my systematic destruction of our house. She's making me pay for it."

"Why'd you do it?"

"I felt like if I didn't, my head was going to explode. I mean, all the stuff in the news about how he's denying everything, how he says he left her up there because they had a fight and she wouldn't let him take her home, how he played video games the rest of the night with his bros. How can anybody possibly believe him?"

"I know; it's ridiculous. So, did it help? Punching a hole in the wall?"

"No."

"I feel you, Lucas. I really do."

A red-tailed hawk circles over the pool, lower and lower, until he's skimming the water with his wings. Delaney, who sees omens and portents in the weather, the cream clouds in her coffee, the way shadows fall across the mountains, doesn't even notice.

She unbraids her hair, then braids it again, her brand-new nervous habit. When she finishes, she digs in her pack and holds out her phone.

"Okay, promise you won't, you know, punch a rock or anything, but have you seen the latest?"

"What, that crap on Instagram? I've seen it. I don't need to see it again."

"Look anyway. This is new."

I take her phone like it's a live scorpion. There's a picture of a swan on a moonlit lake. The caption says, *If she dies, she'll be a Swan Queen forever. #swansong #sparrow*

I shake my head in disgust. "Why can't they just leave her alone?"

Delaney starts to cry. "You know what I can't stand? I mean, the thing that keeps me awake at night, besides the total terror that she's going to die and I won't ever see her again?"

I put my arm around her and pull her close. "What?"

"I can't stand that he went home. He just beat her and left her, and he went home. Like he knew everyone would believe him and someone would clean up the mess he left, just like they've done all his life. And his parents and Brandon and all those pigs are lying for him. If—when—she wakes up, she'll have to talk. She'll have to tell them. She'll have to say his name."

"I know, Laney. Please stop crying; I can't stand it. It's all going to be okay."

"How can you even say that? Nothing is ever going to be okay again."

"My mom says it all the time. She says it makes her feel hope-ful. Maybe if I say it enough, I'll start believing it."

She wipes her eyes and says, "I want him to pay, Lucas. I want him to die. I've never wished anybody dead before, but I'm making an exception in his case."

"I'll go you one better. I want to be the one to take him out."

"I'll hold your coat."

Just then her phone, which I'm still holding, buzzes with a text. Without looking, I hand it to her.

She looks at the screen, then up at me, like she doesn't want to tell me.

"It's Charlotte. She says she was driving by Tristan's house and saw two police cruisers. They brought him out and took him away."

I stand up so quickly that I trip on my backpack and step on what's left of Delaney's grilled cheese. My skin itches. I can't stand still.

"Lucas, what are you doing? What's wrong?"

I pace back and forth on the rock, running my hands through my hair. If I leave now, I can get there in time. If I leave now, I'll be doing something instead of just sitting around waiting for the next terrible thing.

"Lucas? Are you okay?"

"No," I say, wrapping up her sandwich and stuffing it in her pack. I pull my socks over my wet feet and cram my shoes back on. I need do something. Anything.

"Lucas, you're freaking me out a little. Talk to me!"

"I need to go, Laney. Right now."

"Where?"

"I don't know. The police station."

"Why? What do you think you're going to do there?"

"I'm not sure. Something."

"Oh my God, Lucas, everybody knows what you're doing. That you're looking for Tristan. You haven't exactly made it a secret that you want to beat the crap out of him."

"Don't worry about me, Delaney. I'll be cool, promise. But I'm going."

Delaney starts pulling on her boots. I start making my way back over the rocks. "Wait!" she calls. "I'm coming with you!"

"No, you're not!" I shout over my shoulder. "Go on home; I'll text you later."

"Lucas! Don't do this! You aren't helping! You have to stop!"

But I can't wait. I can't stop.

I start running.

I park across the street from the police station. Everything is quiet, no hordes of reporters, no flashing lights, no drama, nothing. But I know Tristan is inside. I can feel the evil leaking out of the bricks.

My knee jitters up and down. I'm chewing the inside of my cheek, drumming my hands on the steering wheel, imagining what it would feel like to pound the condescending smirk off his face. I want him to be the one who's afraid. I want him to know what it feels like to be on the receiving end of vicious.

My phone buzzes. A text from Israel.

Did you hear? Cops took TK away.

I heard. At the police station now.

Seriously?

In my car. Across the street.

You have a plan?

How about I wreck him?

Don't think that will end well. You know,
what with it being the freaking POLICE
STATION, you MASSIVE moron!

Haha. His dad just pulled up. Later.

Don't get arrested.

Dr. Magnus King pulls up in his gleaming black Jaguar. He parks right in front, in the space marked *Officer of the Month*.

He gets out of the car. He's wearing a long-sleeved white shirt that looks like it just came from the dry cleaner's. Sharp creases in the sleeves, French cuffs. Red-and-blue striped tie, shiny black shoes. He reaches into the back seat, pulls out a suit jacket and shrugs it on, tugging down the sleeves and brushing off the lapels. His gold cufflinks flare in the sunlight. He jogs up the steps to the station and disappears behind the glass doors.

A cruiser pulls in across the street, and Tommy Bayliss gets out. I slide down in my seat, but it's too late. He sees me and waves, then walks over. I roll down the window. "Hey, Tommy. How's it going?"

Tommy's wearing aviator sunglasses and his Smokey Bear hat. The handcuffs at his waist jingle when he moves. "What are you doing here, Lucas?"

"Oh, not much. Just hanging out."

I can feel the muscles in my legs and arms thrumming with adrenaline. I grab the steering wheel to still my hands. "Is Tristan inside?"

"You know I can't tell you that."

"Come on, man. I just saw his father. I know he's in there."

"Then why are you asking me? Look, we're all sick about what happened to Sparrow. And we are investigating the case with rigor and determination, at least as much as we can without actually hearing anything from the victim herself."

I stare out the windshield, trying to make something happen through sheer force of will. Anything. My knee pumps up and down like a piston. The ants crawl under my skin.

"Please don't call her a victim. It makes it sound like she's not a real person."

Tommy's voice softens.

"Look, Lucas, I know you're upset. Everybody's upset. Believe me, I know how hard this is, how powerless you feel, how you want someone to pay for what happened to her. I know you want to help."

I nod, unable to speak.

"So I'm telling you this for your own good, and you can pass it along to all your friends. The best thing you can do is to stay out of the way. Let us do our jobs. Don't do anything to make things harder. If we have questions, we'll ask. So go on home now. You aren't accomplishing anything by being here, and your mom and Anna need you. You hear me?"

I don't say anything.

"Lucas? You got me?"

I hold out my fist. He bumps it and smiles.

"Good man. I'm going inside now, and when I look out the window in five minutes, I don't want to see this piece-of-crap car still here."

"Yeah, Tommy. Okay."

He walks slowly back across the street and runs up the red-brick steps. At the door, he turns and points his index finger at me and mouths, *Go home!*

I give him a thumbs-up.

I do not go home.

Fifteen minutes later Tristan and his father emerge. They're both laughing.

Laughing, while Sparrow lies in a coma for the tenth day in a row. Laughing, while Sophie and Mr. Rose slowly lose their minds. Laughing, while the doctors say every day that they don't know why she hasn't woken up yet.

I'm not stupid enough to try something here. But I'm watching. Maybe not today, maybe not tomorrow, but someday, somewhere, Tristan will find himself all alone. And when that day comes, I'll be there.

I'm going to fucking kill him.

19

Back to School

I walk past Sparrow's locker on the way to first period, trying not to see all the bright notes decorated with glitter. It's only the third day of school, but somebody's already taped twinkle lights all over her locker. There are plastic flowers stuffed into the vents, pictures and other crap all over the floor. A blue bear in a pink tutu, a stuffed swan wearing a crown, a rotting red rose next to a coffee-ringed program from last year's *Nutcracker*. It's open to the cast list—Clara: Savannah Darcy Rose—with her name circled in black. I stop, even though I know it's going to make me nuts. Luis comes up behind me.

"Man, this is unbelievable. Who has this much freaking glitter? It looks like a fairy puked."

"Word."

"If I were you, man, I'd keep walking. This is beyond sick, and it's not helping you to hang out and look at it. You want me to walk to class with you?"

"No, thanks. I'm cool."

"Doubtful, but okay. Catch you later." He pounds my shoulder and heads down the hall. I can't go to class. I'm stuck, like my feet are glued to the floor. I can't look away.

The notes are nauseating, from people who never knew her, who never cared enough to try. The popular kids who acted like she was invisible. The mean girls, who laughed whenever Brandon yelled at her to eat a cheeseburger. Now they're all kicking themselves, wishing they'd paid more attention, because she's all anyone can talk about.

Get better, Sparrow! Thoughts and prayers!
I know you'll dance again, Swan Queen.
My heart is breaking for you.
I can't stop crying. Please don't die.

Do they actually believe she's reading any of this? That she can see it from her hospital bed, through her swollen black eyes? Do they think their crocodile tears will bring her back? They don't want her back. They're hoping she dies. Then they can look hot in black dresses and sob at her funeral.

I pitch the bear and the swan into the trash, followed by the wilted rose, which smells rancid and foul. When I start tearing the notes off her locker, the shiny girls clustered in a tight little knot near the bathroom yell at me to stop. "Lucas!" shrieks Tahlia Jones, last year's homecoming queen. "You're ruining her memorial!"

"Memorials are for dead people, you idiot, and she's not dead!" I snarl.

"At least not yet." Willow Burke, a spray-tanned cheerleader, yawns and examines her French manicure. Last year she told everyone that Sparrow was anorexic and her father was sending her to a mental hospital in California. When that didn't stick, she started a rumor that Sophie was a recovering cocaine addict. Sparrow hates her.

I pound the locker with my fist, which makes Willow nearly jump out of her snow-white Nikes. But it's not enough to make them leave. I walk over, get all up in their false eyelashes and yell, "Shut up and get out of here, you freaking ghouls!"

They give me filthy looks, but book it down the hall.

I finish tearing the notes off the locker until all that's left are scraps of tape and stray glitter. Leaning my head against the cool metal, I try to summon her, remembering the feel of her hand in mine, the way her eyes shine when we nail a fish dive. But I can't do it. There's a hole in my heart where she used to be.

The first bell rings, but I ignore it. No way I'm going to physics. I tried to do the homework last night, and the numbers swam on the page like evil little tadpoles.

I feel a hand on my shoulder, smell pomegranate juice and apricot shampoo.

"Oh my God, Lucas, what are you doing?" Delaney stares at the glitter on the floor, the tangle of twinkle lights sticking out of the trash bin, along with the stuffed swan's crowned head.

"I'm cleaning up, Laney. What does it look like?"

"It looks like you're losing your mind, if you want to know the truth."

"I don't, actually. I've had enough truth to last me for the rest of my life. But thanks, anyway."

She punches me on the arm. Hard. "I'm so mad at you. How's that for some truth?"

"Lots of people are mad at me. You should get in line."

"Lucas," she says. "Come on, look at me. I'm not the enemy here."

I turn to look at her. She's wearing a fringed leather vest over an Alabama Shakes T-shirt, a pink chiffon dance skirt, black leggings, and the ever-present turquoise boots. A silver sheriff's star is pinned to the vest. Her hair is tied back with a beaded piece of rawhide, and there's a turkey feather tucked into her braid.

"Mixed signals today, Laney. Are you Wyatt Earp or Sacagawea?"

"Shut up. How come you won't answer my texts? I don't even know what happened at the police station, and that was, like, almost a week ago. It's been total radio silence from you ever since the Honeysuckle Pond, and that is not fair, dude. I thought we were in this together."

I sigh and pitch the last of the crap across the hall into the bin. "We are. I'm sorry. I'm just—I don't know. Messed up."

"You're not the only one."

"I know, Laney. I just can't seem to figure myself out. One minute I'm crazy angry, and the next, I'm so scared I can't even see straight. I'd rather be mad, to be honest."

"Mad's always better than sad. So tell me what happened."

"Nothing to tell. Tommy Bayliss told me to beat feet. I saw Tristan, though. Yukking it up with his dad. That was special."

"Douchebag passes from father to son. It's a biological fact."

"Damn, I love science."

She smacks my arm again. "Don't shut me out anymore, Lucas. I can't take it. I've been writing lots of poems about what a turd you are."

"I'm sorry, Laney. Really."

"You suck. But I forgive you."

Just then, Mr. Freeman, the principal and one of my dad's diving buddies, comes walking down the hall.

"You guys going to class this morning?"

"Yes, sir," says Delaney, at the same time I say, "No, sir."

He smiles. "You might want to get your stories straight."

"We were just talking," I say, not meeting his eyes. "I guess we didn't hear the bell."

"It's okay, guys. I'm not going to bust you."

His eyes are full of kindness. Right now he doesn't look like a principal. He looks like a dad.

"Here's the deal," he says, taking out the pad of yellow passes he carries in the pocket of his blue blazer. "I'm going to give you both a pass for the rest of the week. I want you to show up every morning. Go to homeroom, let your teachers know you're here. But if you need to miss class and take some time to hang out with each other, or any of Sparrow's friends, you have my permission. Just don't leave campus. Also—"

He hesitates, seeing that the décor is gone from Sparrow's locker.

"Also, I know you'd probably rather talk to each other instead of any of us, but you can always come talk to me. I'm a pretty decent listener. Dr. Ramirez and her counseling staff are available to you and anyone else who feels like they could use an ear. Or a shoulder. This is tough stuff for everybody, and we're here for you."

"Yes, sir," we say. Delaney gives him a watery smile. "Thanks, Mr. Freeman. For, you know, understanding."

"You're welcome, Ms. Spenser," he says. "But maybe it would be a good idea to go to the commons or the cafeteria instead of hanging out at Sparrow's locker. This can't be helping. And next week I'll expect you in class, participating, showing leadership, and making excellent grades. Understood?"

We nod. "Yes, sir. Understood," Delaney says.

He gives us a little wave as he walks down the hall, tucking the passes back in his pocket. "Stay out of trouble," he calls over his shoulder.

"'So shines a good deed in a weary world,'" Delaney says.

For once, I don't roll my eyes.

"I'm going to go write in the library," she says. "You want to come with me?"

"Thanks, but I think I'll go get something to eat. I didn't have any breakfast."

"Will you be okay?"

If I can find Tristan and make him pay, I'll be freaking awesome.

"Yeah, I'm fine, Laney. See you at lunch."

When class lets out, I'm still sitting on the floor in front of Sparrow's locker. How can I talk to Dr. Ramirez? How can I talk to anyone? How could they possibly understand that I'm drowning in guilt? I knew Tristan was evil to the core, but I let her convince me not to tell. I wanted to believe her, but I knew. And now she could die without hearing me say I'm sorry.

Without knowing that I love her.

20

One Week Later

"Are you seriously cutting class? Again?" Sam asks. "Freeman's going to be on you like a donkey on a waffle."

"We're already busted because of yesterday. I thought he was going to have a heart attack."

"But he understood, right?"

"He said he did, but he yelled at us anyway."

When Sophie texted out of the blue that Sparrow was awake, Delaney and I flew out of the cafeteria, racing to the hospital without a word to anyone. But it was all for nothing. The doctors wouldn't let us see her. Everybody told us to go back to school, that it was too soon. Sophie said Sparrow won't talk to anyone, not even her. Not even Mr. Rose. If anyone touches her, she freaks out.

"It sucks you got in so much trouble and didn't even get to see her."

"Truth," I say wearily. "You'd better get to class. If I go down in flames, I don't want to drag you with me."

"Okay, later. Lucas—I don't want to get all sloppy on you or anything, but you know we're all here, right? I mean, we'd do anything—"

"Sam, I know. Thanks. Go learn something."

I can't think about anything else but Sparrow, awake and afraid and silent. I can't think at all. I can't sit still. It's like the ants under my skin have set themselves on fire. My brain is like a hamster in a wheel, whirring around and around, never getting anywhere. If I could just see her face. If I could say "I love you" just once, even if she told me she never wanted to see me again.

I find a place behind the boxwood hedge in the courtyard and press myself against the branches, trying to make myself invisible. I close my eyes, resting my head on my knees. I figure I can live for the next couple of days without AP English and Dr. Lipton gushing about the brilliance of Joseph Conrad. We've started *Heart of Darkness*, and on Monday I got in big trouble for asking if it was the autobiography of Tristan King. Now it's Wednesday, and Delaney and I have to start a week of detention for leaving school grounds without permission. This makes us late for ballet. This means Levkova is also mad at us.

I chill against the bushes for half an hour or so, but then I get antsy. I need to get out of here. Even these shrubs smell like school, and it feels like all the windows are eyes, watching me. I shoulder my backpack and dig in my pocket for car keys.

My phone buzzes with a text. Caleb.

> TK sighting. In the parking lot. Be chill.
> Wherever you are, stay there.

> What's he doing?

I walk faster.

> Word is he's getting tutored after school.
> His parents are making him stay home,
> and Freeman thinks it's better if he's not
> around other humans.

> > Shoulda started that plan in
> > kindergarten.

> Looks like he's waiting until everybody
> leaves. Be cool, bro. Do not mess with
> this. I am serious. Stay away.

I'm typing as I run through the halls.

> > I am always cool.

> Hahahaha, no.

I haul ass to the east entrance, busting through the doors into the light of the outside world. The sky is bright blue, the air warm and still thick with what's left of summer. His black car glowers way in the back, a stain against the redbrick wall of the field house. He's leaning against the hood, texting. He is all alone.

I don't think. My lizard brain takes over, moving my feet for me, clenching my fists, gritting my teeth. A loud roaring in my ears deadens everything around me, the sound of bells ringing, the rising cacophony of voices behind me, the metallic clang of lockers slamming.

Tristan looks up, surprised.

I grab him by the front of his shirt and slam him hard against the wall. The breath whooshes out of him. Mouthwash and coffee.

"You sick, lying, evil bastard," I say. "You beat her up and left her to die. You left her there!"

His eyes darken. "Get your hands off me, ballerina. You don't have the chops for this. You know it, I know it. Walk away before you get hurt."

He tries to push me away, but he doesn't have any leverage. I am all up in his face. I slam him against the wall, harder this time. "You're a monster. You know that, right?"

"I didn't leave anyone anywhere," he says. "You need to be real careful who you go around accusing, asshole."

"You don't scare me, Tristan. You never have."

I don't plan it; I'm not even thinking. I haul off and punch him in the face. Twice. I hear a sickening crunch, and his nose erupts in a fountain of blood. My barely healed hand screams in agony, but I don't care.

From a distance, I hear somebody yell, "Fight! Fight!"

I punch him again and again. I can't stop. He goes down like a sack of bricks, the front of his white T-shirt spattered with blood. He raises his hands to ward off the blows, but I do not stop. I couldn't, even if I tried, which I do not want to do.

"How does it feel, Tristan? How does it feel to have your face bashed in by a *ballerina*?" I'm gasping, my breath harsh and ragged. He's saying something through his split lip. His nose is weirdly askew on his face. His eyes are puffy, beginning to swell shut. He turns over and rises to all fours, retching.

"I'll kill you for this," he slurs, spitting blood onto the asphalt.

Strong arms pull me away, locking around my chest. Caleb. And Israel.

"Lucas. Lucas! Stop! Jesus, enough! You're going to kill him!"

"That's the whole point! Let me go," I wheeze. "Come on, let me go!"

Tristan lies motionless, breathing wetly through his bloody mouth. I don't think his nose works right anymore.

The crowd around us parts, and Mr. Freeman stands in front of me, shaking with fury. "Lucas!" he shouts. "What the hell did I say to you just last week? How is this staying out of trouble?" He kneels down beside Tristan and takes out his phone.

"Take him to my office, guys," he says to Israel and Caleb. "Make sure he stays put until I get there."

Kids I've known all my life are looking at me like they've never seen me before. Like I've gone crazy. Iz and Caleb half carry, half drag me to Mr. Freeman's office.

Soon there are sirens.

While we wait for my mom, Mr. Freeman brings ice for my hand, which is already swollen and turning purple.

"It's probably broken, Lucas. Most guys who've never thrown a punch before don't do it right and screw up their fourth metacarpal. And no, I'm not going to tell you how I came by that information."

I don't know what I broke, only that it hurts like hell.

"You want to tell me what that was back there?"

"I don't know. I guess I lost my mind when I saw him."

"You think? That would be the understatement of the century."

"He should be in jail."

"Lucas, he hasn't been charged with a crime. He's denying everything, and his father has him all lawyered up. It's his word against—well, basically no one's, since Sparrow isn't talking."

"Everyone knows he did it."

"That may be true, but it's for the police and the legal system to figure out, certainly not you or any of your friends. In the meantime, you've really stepped in it. Please tell me he threw the first punch. Did he do anything to provoke you?"

"What, besides beat up Sparrow and leave her for dead?"

"Watch the tone, Lucas. You need to be careful about saying things like that. I meant just now."

"No. He called me a ballerina, but he's been doing that since we were kids."

"Well, that's one way to make a guy take a swing, though it doesn't excuse you. You know about the zero-tolerance policy for fighting, so you'll be cooling your heels at home for two weeks."

He runs his hand through his hair, then takes off his glasses and rubs his eyes. "Of all the kids in this school, Lucas, I never thought I'd be having this conversation with you."

"Lucas?"

My mom is standing at the door, pale and worried, but also super-fierce, the way she always gets when anyone messes with her kids.

"What happened to your hand? You got in a fight? Doug, are you sure? Are you sure it was him?"

"Colleen, yes, I'm sure," Mr. Freeman says. "I saw it with my own eyes. He beat the ever-loving bejesus out of Tristan King."

I see the light dawning across my mother's face.

"Ahhh," she says. "Not exactly a surprise."

"I'm sorry, but I'm going to need you to take him home. Doesn't matter who started the fight or who finished it—all participants are suspended immediately. I'll make sure to have one of his buddies bring his work by the house so he won't get behind."

"Is Tristan okay?"

I roll my eyes, and my mother gives me the Look. Like she's shooting poison darts out of her eyeballs.

"He's a mess. EMTs brought him to Saint Germaine's. I

think his nose is broken, and he may have a couple of cracked ribs. Lucas got him pretty good."

"Great." She closes her eyes, shakes her head, takes a deep breath. "Just great. Come on, Lucas. Let's go home. Thanks, Doug. I am so sorry about all this. Let me know how Tristan's doing, if you wouldn't mind."

"Will do. And, Lucas, one more thing. I know you're hurting. But you have got to pull yourself together, or you're going to do something that will affect the rest of your life, something you can't walk away from. I sure would hate to see that. And so would your dad."

I nod, pretending that I heard him, that his words made a difference, and walk outside again, into the beautiful day.

My mom stares out the windshield, her expression grim.

"Mom? How pissed off are you, on a scale of one to apoplexy?"

She drives her red pickup out of the parking lot and stops at the traffic light in front of the school. Fumbling in the console for her sunglasses, she glances at me as she turns onto the parkway that leads to Main Street.

"I'd say maybe seven, approaching eight. But I'm not the one with the anger issue here. What were you even thinking, Lucas, getting into a fight? What is wrong with you?"

"Nothing's wrong with me, Mom."

"I beg to differ. Honestly, if someone had told me a year ago that my son would beat the snot out of Tristan King the second week of his senior year—my sweet, kind, gentle boy, who can't stand the sight of blood and cringes when his little sister loses a tooth—I'd have called them a liar."

"Mom, please. Stop. I can't take a lecture right now."

"Oh, I'm just getting warmed up. This is the first of many lectures, so you'd better strap in, kiddo. You have really, really screwed things up for yourself. I don't think you even realize what you've set in motion. This is bad, Lucas. Maybe it felt good to give Tristan a taste of his own medicine, but it sure isn't going to feel good from here on out."

She sighs the way only moms can sigh. None of the words, all of the guilt.

"I'm in so far over my head here. I don't know what to do about you. I don't know what to do for you."

"You can't do anything for me, Mom. Unless you can go to Sparrow's hospital room and wave a magic wand to make her all better."

"Right now, Lucas, Sparrow is not the person I'm worried about. She's getting all the help she needs. But you won't let anyone help you. You won't talk to me, and you won't see a counselor. You have got to control this anger. You walk around the house slamming doors, pounding walls, snapping at me and Anna. I don't know who this is, sitting here in my truck, suspended for beating up another kid. I don't think you know who he is either."

We're on Shenandoah Street now, just a few blocks from home, but she slows down and pulls into the Kroger parking lot. She takes off her sunglasses and tosses them onto the dash. I pretend to fool with the air conditioning so I won't have to look at her eyes.

"I want to say something to you before we get home, while I have the chance and it's just you and me. Anna has already had to deal with way more than she should. Losing your dad was terrible enough, but now she feels like she's losing you, too, and it's breaking her heart.

"You're hurting, I get that, Lucas. You're grieving your father, and then this horrific thing happens to a girl you adore. But you can't keep lashing out at everyone around you, especially your sister. You can't expect us to keep swallowing your anger. I am an adult, and I'll cut you some slack. But she's still a little girl, and she's just so——bewildered.

"All you've done since Sparrow got hurt is yell at us and sit in your room listening to Johnny Cash over and over again. I'm gently suggesting, honey, that playing 'Hurt' five hundred times a day is not the most constructive way to spend your time."

I look out the window and see Caleb's mom pushing a grocery cart with a wonky wheel packed with huge containers of the mint chocolate chip protein powder he loves. She gives us a little wave.

"Mom. Stop. I get it, okay? I promise I won't beat anyone else up."

"Don't you dare smart-mouth me, Lucas Oliver. There are going to be serious consequences from what you did today."

"I know, I know."

"No, you don't. You don't have the first clue. Everything depends on how you handle yourself from here on out. Everything. If you keep this up, the person you'll hurt most is not me or Anna or Tristan. The person you'll hurt most is you. And I can't bear to watch that happen. I won't. Do you understand?"

"I guess so. I'll do better, Mom. I'll try."

She looks at me for a long moment, then puts the truck in gear. "Okay. Let's go home and wait for the nuclear fallout. I should probably take away your phone and your laptop, drop some serious punishment on you, but I can't see how that's going to help anything. I'll make pancakes."

She loves me, but she doesn't believe me.

I don't even believe myself.

Sparrow

My stars shine darkly over me. . . . Therefore shall I crave of you your leave that I may bear my evils alone.

WILLIAM SHAKESPEARE, *Twelfth Night*

21

Day Eighteen

I open my eyes.

Sophie is standing at the window, whispering prayers.

My father sees me and stops pacing. He runs to my side. "Sophie! Soph! Get a nurse! Now, Sophie, now! Oh, sweet Jesus. Hurry!"

Sophie runs, and then people come in, one after the other. They are doing things to the machines. They are doing things to me.

Everything is too much, the lights, the noise, all the people talking to me and to each other. I feel so heavy, like there is iron ore in my veins instead of blood. If I could, I would sink through this bed, into the floor, down, down, all the way down into the dark and silent earth.

My throat hurts.

A woman in a white coat smiles at me, then shines a light so bright, so painful, into my eyes that I squeeze them shut, hoping she'll be gone when I open them again. I smell horrible things. Blood. Bleach. Sweat. Urine. The way my father smells when he comes home from the prison. Except this time it is coming from me. Tears leak from the corners of my eyes. They turn cold and drip into my ears.

My father's face, a century older, fills my sight. His hair is dirty and he has a scruffy beard. His breath is bad, coffee and something new and stale. Cigarettes.

"Sparrow? Can you hear me? Sparrow, baby, move your fingers if you can hear me." He touches my hand.

The feel of his skin on mine makes me want to scream. He's too close. I try to pull my hand from his, but I can't lift my arms. They are both in casts from my hands to my elbows.

Something is hurting me, binding me.

I am tied down.

I am tied to the bed, I am tied to the bed, I am tied to the bed.

A scream rises in my throat, desperate, horrified, but I can't open my mouth to let it out. I can only whimper. Like an animal.

I thrash and pound my hands weakly against the bed. I try to kick my feet, but only one will move. The other is in a cast that pokes out from beneath a thin blue blanket. My toes are black. I kick the mattress again and again with my good foot, struggling to escape, struggling to scream. I arch my back. I try to get away.

The woman in white takes my father's place. There's a stethoscope around her neck. Her nose is pierced on one side with a tiny, sparkling jewel.

"Sparrow, be still now. Listen to me. I am Dr. Sharma. Do not be afraid. I am taking the restraints off right now. When you began to wake up, you were very agitated, and we did not want you to hurt yourself."

I hear the harsh, tearing sound of Velcro. Everything is too bright, too loud.

"Please, Sparrow, be still. There is a tube in your throat that was helping you to breathe. You do not need it any longer, and we will take it out very soon. This is why you cannot speak. Two of the bones in your foot are broken. After they heal, we will take the cast off."

She looks over her shoulder at the door and shakes her head.

"Absolutely not, Detectives. No questions today. Lucas and Delaney, just family now. Go back to school."

She motions to another woman, who's wearing bright pink scrubs. She stands beside me and pushes the plunger of a syringe into a tube that snakes from my chest to a bag above my head.

She smiles at me. "You'll feel better soon, sweetheart."

My father paces back and forth in front of the window. The blinds are crooked. He holds his hands behind his back and stoops forward a little, the way he does when he's practicing an argument. "Sparrow, honey, please let the doctors help you." I turn away. I don't want to look at him.

Sophie is crying. She kisses me gently on each cheek. "Welcome back, baby girl," she whispers. "Welcome back, sweetheart. You're safe now, my love. You've come back to us. No one can hurt you now."

Even her hand on mine, her lips on my cheeks, are too much to bear. I shrink back into the pillows, trying to get away from the touching, from the feel of other people's skin, but there's nowhere to go. I tell her with my eyes to go away, to leave me alone. She doesn't listen.

Sleep is coming quickly. Everything blurs and sounds faraway, like the ocean on some distant shore.

I am not safe. I will never be safe.

I float away on a sea of despair.

Inside my eyes, my mother waits for me. Down, down, down in the shadows, I see the feathers trembling at her throat, the pearls twisted in her hair, the sharp points of her dark tiara reaching up to the moonless night.

I hear the beat and murmur of her terrible wings.

22

Day Nineteen

"Five minutes, that's all. Are we clear?"

"Got it, Doc. We won't be long."

My father and Sophie are sitting in plastic chairs, in a corner near the window. My father's knee pumps up and down. Sophie is braiding the fringe on her paisley shawl.

I can hear Dr. Sharma through the closed door. "She hasn't said a word since she woke up. Not to me or the nurses. Not even to her family. Take it slowly, please. Do not upset her."

"We'll do our best."

Dr. Sharma opens my door and stands aside as Tommy Bayliss comes in, along with a woman in a pale gray suit and a man with a dark mustache. They hang back while Tommy comes to stand beside my bed. He tries to speak softly, gently, but his eyes betray him. He wants something.

I squeeze my eyes shut, willing him to disappear.

"Hey, kid," says Tommy. "You scared the crap out of us. How are you doing?"

I breathe slowly, keeping my eyes closed. If I don't see him, he isn't here. If I don't see him, I will not hear him.

"We need you to tell us who did this to you, Sparrow. Who hurt you?"

One beat. Then another. A long, long pause. I hear the leather of his shoes creak as he shifts his weight. After a while he walks away. The three of them whisper urgently together near the door. The men leave. The woman stays.

My throat is on fire from where the tube used to be, from throwing up in my lap when my father tried to wrap his arms around me. I'm so filled up with pain that I feel it leaking out of my pores, filling the room with its raw, animal power.

I open my eyes again. The woman walks over to my bed.

"Sparrow," she says. "My name is Violet Bell, and the gentleman out there with Officer Bayliss is Daniel Gutierrez. We're both detectives, and we work with young women just like you. Please, it's important that you tell me who did this. Can you remember anything at all? Even the smallest detail would help us."

If there was any part of me that was still alive, the faintest flicker of life left at my core, it goes dark now. I feel her passing, the girl I was before. All that I ever was or could be is gone. This is the girl I am now, battered and empty. Unrecognizable, even to myself. Especially to myself.

"Just say his name," says Violet Bell. "That will be enough for now."

Tears spill down my cheeks, but I don't make a sound. I'll never say his name again.

I promise, Mama. I'll be quiet. I'll be good.

I am not the kind of girl who tells.

Lucas

Affliction is enamored of thy parts, and thou art wedded to calamity.

WILLIAM SHAKESPEARE, *Romeo and Juliet*

23

Ashes, Ashes, We All Fall Down

It's only November, but it already seems like winter, so freaking cold in Delaney's car that I can't feel my nose or my feet. It's like we skipped right over fall and went straight to February.

Sparrow has been home for a month. She refuses to see anyone, nobody from ballet, nobody from school. If people show up unannounced, Sophie and Mr. Rose turn them away. Yesterday they called in the cavalry, which is basically me and Delaney, without the horses.

In spite of the hot chocolate and bagels we brought from Nora's and the Taco Bell chili cheese burritos I made Delaney stop for on the way, I don't see how this is going to end well. We went to the hospital five times, hanging around outside her door like faithful dogs, enduring the pitying glances of the nurses, the whispered apologies from Sophie and Mr. Rose. She was having a bad day. She was asleep. She didn't want to see anyone. She didn't want to see us.

We pull up in front of Sparrow's house, but Delaney speeds up and drives past, turning out of the cul-de-sac and back down Larkspur Way.

"Laney," I say, pitching a burrito wrapper into the back seat. "What are you doing? We said we'd be there at four. That's five minutes from now."

She parks across from Mr. Chastain's house, three doors down from Sparrow's. Bundled in hat, scarf, blue down parka, and fingerless gloves, she looks like a Smurf about to harness up some sled dogs and run the Iditarod.

"Can we please just sit here for a minute?" she says. "I need to get my guts up."

"Yeah, sure."

Mr. Chastain comes out onto his front porch with a glass of red wine, and we wave at him. He's done this every day since his wife died last year, even when it's cold, even when it's raining. He wears a heavy corduroy coat and a green fedora with a feather in the brim. When he sits down in his white wicker rocker, he puts one hand on the chair beside him, where Mrs. Chastain used to sit. He rocks for them both.

Delaney unwraps her cinnamon raisin bagel and takes a bite. As she stares out the windshield, she wipes cream cheese from the corners of her mouth and says, "My Swan Queen blows."

"No, it doesn't," I say automatically, though she's mostly right. She's only been dancing Sparrow's role for a few weeks, but she can't get out of her own way. She's tentative and nervous and stressed, so she makes mistakes. What little patience Levkova had is starting to wear thin with both of us. I can't hide that I'm uncomfortable partnering with Delaney. And it's not her fault, so I feel like a jerk.

"Yes, it does, and you know it. But thank you for lying. I

know Levkova's saying I'm learning it just in case Sparrow can't do it, but I still have to learn it, you know?"

"You'll get the hang of it."

"Maybe," she says glumly. "But I'm never going to nail those turns in the *Variation*. They make me dizzy as crap. And the footwork in the *Coda* is killing me. Sparrow did it like she had springs in her feet and barely broke a sweat. And her arms were boneless! I'm so seriously screwed."

We started rehearsing with Levkova, just the two of us, at six thirty this morning, almost three hours before everyone else arrived. We're not clicking because we dance like Sparrow's shadow is between us.

It doesn't help that Levkova's been acting super-weird lately, distant and distracted. Just after we began this morning, she stopped watching us and stared at the place where Sparrow always stands at the barre. She was crying. Like really crying, tears streaming down her face. We pretended not to notice.

When we were done, she didn't give me any corrections, focusing completely on Delaney. I'm good, but I'm not that good. Something's up.

We're both quiet, finishing our hot chocolate, trying to stay warm in the frigid car.

"So why's your mom so mad at you today?" she asks.

"Change the subject, please."

"Tell me or I'll put cream cheese in your hair."

Lately Delaney's the only person I can stand to be around. Caleb and Iz and Luis and Sam all want to hang out and pretend everything is the same. Which it isn't, especially now that it looks like I won't be going back to school for the foreseeable future.

"It would be best for all concerned . . ." is how the email to my mother began. Dr. Freeman explained that Tristan's father had "retained counsel," and threatened to sue the school if I were not kept away from his son. He said he'd get a restraining order against me if I got anywhere near his golden boy. Not sure he could actually do it, but he's friends with three judges, so let's just say that the odds are not in my favor. Mr. Freeman wants me to "lie low" for the rest of the semester. My mom's working a deal with him and my teachers that would let me graduate on time. I can't make myself care.

"Laney, my mom's mad at me all the time. Nothing special about today."

"Nah, she was really smoked when I picked you up. She had the crazy eyes. What was it this time?"

"You are like a freaking badger. You know that, right?"

She grins, but it doesn't go all the way to her eyes.

"It's one of my many charms."

"Okay, so she's trying to get me to write this letter of apology to Tristan and his parents. I pointed out that this may seem slightly insincere, since the beatdown happened almost two months ago."

"Definitely cruel and unusual punishment."

"I know, right? But she thinks if I act all sorry and ashamed of myself, Dr. King will calm down and stop screaming for my head on a pike."

"You know what I think?" she says, flipping down the mirror on her visor and checking her teeth for bagel remnants. "I think his father's all hat and no cattle. He's just yelling because he likes the sound of his own voice. So you broke Tristan's stupid nose. It's not like you killed him, or you know, put him in one of those wheelchairs you move by blowing through a straw."

"He had a couple of cracked ribs, too. And both eyes were black."

"Oh, boo frickin' hoo. Cry me a river. He so had it coming.

I'll bet at least half the people who saw that fight wished they'd been the one to rain down the fisticuffs."

"Yeah, well. I'm not sorry, and that makes it kind of hard to write an apology. My mom told me to suck it up and fake it. She wants me to say whatever will get them off my case and let me go back to school in January. So I tried. I really did. Sat in front of my laptop for an hour, trying to come up with the perfect apology. She did not approve of the result."

"I can't wait. What did you say?"

"'Dear Tristan, I'm sorry you're a douchebag. Very truly yours, Lucas.'"

She throws back her head and laughs, the old Delaney laugh I haven't heard in a long time, an earsplitting combination of snorts, gasps, and braying donkey.

"Oh my God, that's why your mom's so chafed."

"Yep. She says she can't help me if I won't help myself. I told her 'whatever.' That didn't go over so well."

"She loves you, though her reasons escape me."

"Yeah," I say. "Me too."

"What time is it?"

"Ten after four. We're late." I'm so nervous about seeing Sparrow that I feel sick.

"Do you think she'll be happy to see us?" Delaney asks softly.

"I don't know. I don't see how she could be happy about anything right now."

"You're right. This is going to suck. Sophie says she hasn't said a word since she woke up, that she cries so hard when those detectives try to get her to talk they have to give her drugs to calm her down."

"I'm afraid she's going to hate me, after all the terrible things I said to her. What if she thinks I'm just like him? Especially after what I did? What if I am just like him? You know, a bully who hurts people?"

She puts her icy fingers on either side of my face, forcing me to look at her.

"Are you out of your mind? Listen to me, Lucas Oliver, and listen good. You're nothing like him. He's a monster, and you're, like, I don't know, a cocker spaniel. A really screwed-up cocker spaniel who should be in therapy right now, but still. You were standing up for someone you love. Maybe it wasn't the right way to do it, and maybe there's trouble in your future, but nobody seriously faults you. I, for one, am glad you broke his perfect nose." She opens her car door, puts one foot out onto the pavement.

"Let's leave the car here and walk back. I need the cold to clear the cobwebs out of my brain."

As we walk up the middle of the street, I take her hand. It seems like such a small thing, holding her hand in mine, walking up Sparrow's driveway. But right now it feels huge, bigger and deeper than the cold sky above us. It's the only thing that keeps me from running.

Sophie's waiting for us at the door, looking exhausted and sick, like she's had the flu for a couple of years. "I'm so glad to see you guys," she says, hugging us. "So, so glad."

"We miss you, Sophie," Delaney says, hugging her tight. "Has she said anything?"

"Not a word, to us or the police. Madame Levkova's been here three times, and Sparrow wouldn't even talk to her, which I never thought I'd live to see. Her body's broken, but her heart is broken way worse. I know I'm putting so much pressure on you, but please, see if you can get her to say something. Anything. At this point, I'd be happy with a string of curse words." Her voice catches. "It's like she's just . . . gone."

"Oh, Sophie, don't cry. We'll do our best, promise. Lucas, you ready?"

I want a massive crater to open in the floor and swallow me whole.

"You bet. Let's do it."

Sparrow is in the living room, lying on the enormous white couch. She's wearing her favorite blue plaid pajamas, which seems familiar at first, but then feels jarring and wrong, like some discordant echo of who she used to be. Her hair is starting to grow in a little, and she looks like a prison camp escapee. The stitches on her head aren't as livid and red as they were in the hospital, but they look painful, like a row of scabby little ants marching across her skull. Her face is still bruised, her busted lip still slightly swollen and raw. She's wearing a hard plastic boot, and her foot is resting on a pillow, the toes blackish purple.

It's hard to look at her.

When Delaney bends down to hug her, she pulls away, shrinking back against the pillows, furiously shaking her head. Delaney backs off but doesn't miss a beat, pretending like everything's cool.

"We've missed you so much!" she says brightly. "Ballet isn't the same without you. We suck so hard; Lucas can attest. You need to get better so you can dance Swan Queen. I can't do it, but you were born for that role, right, Lucas?"

"Truth."

Sparrow turns and stares out the window. I can feel this—this force—coming from her, like something vicious and cold is putting its bony fingers on the back of my neck.

It's not her. Not anymore. The compassionate friend who talked me off the ledge when my dad got sick and again after he died, the joyful dancer all filled up with light and grace, is gone.

Whatever lives inside her now is dark and ravenous. It's consuming her, piece by piece, and I wonder if we're too late, if this is the Sparrow who'll walk the earth with us now.

Standing here, helpless, in her living room, I know now that death isn't the only way you can lose someone you love. She's gone, but she's here. And somehow that seems worse than dying, savage and cruel and pointless.

Delaney looks at me, her eyes filled with panic. She's about to lose it.

"We miss you, Sparrow," I say. "I miss being your Siegfried."

She turns to me, her eyes filled with venom and something so terrible it doesn't even have a name. She looks at both of us, and her mouth begins to move. It takes a while for the sound to come out.

"No," she says. *"No."*

Her voice is like a graveyard, full of ruin.

Delaney takes a step back, shocked.

"Sweetie," she says, her voice trembling. "It's just Lucas and me. Come on, you can talk to us. We love you."

"No," Sparrow says, in that moldering, dusty voice. "Get out."

"Birdy," I say, desperate for some recognition, some familiar light in those poisonous eyes. "We were both there before you woke up. In the hospital. We talked to you. Did you hear us?"

She lifts her face to the ceiling. I can see the muscles in her throat working, hear the terrible gasping sounds she makes trying to breathe, trying to speak. She puts her hands over her ears and howls, a bloody, guttural sound, like she's swallowed knives.

"I didn't hear *anything*! Get *out of here*!" she screams. "Get *away* from me! I *hate* you! I hate you *all*! *Get out!*"

My voice dies in my throat. I can't move. It's like I've turned to stone. Everything goes quiet. It feels like the world has come to a full stop, like the sun should go dark, like clocks should stop ticking. I'm holding my breath, afraid to let it out, afraid to move. Because if I do, maybe something worse will happen.

Delaney starts to cry, gulping, breathless sounds, breaking the spell. I pull her to me as Sophie rushes in. Delaney buries her face in my shoulder, but I can't stop looking at Sparrow, who's still holding her hands to her ears, her mouth open in a silent scream.

Sophie rushes in and tries to gather Sparrow into her arms, but Sparrow thrashes and slaps her hands away. Delaney and I are paralyzed.

"Sophie, we're sorry," Delaney sobs. "We're so sorry. Oh my God, we didn't mean to upset her. We're so, so sorry!"

As she kneels at Sparrow's side, Sophie looks at us like she's surprised we're still there. "Guys," she says. "I need to help her calm down now. Probably best for everyone if you go on home. I love you both so much for coming and for trying. We'll talk later, okay?"

I don't have any words left. They've all flown out of my brain, like songbirds heading south for the winter. Delaney cries harder, and I unlock my legs, still holding her, and turn to leave. Just before we reach the front door, I look back. Sophie reaches out to Sparrow again. One flailing arm, heavy in its cast, hits Sophie in the face.

Delaney's sobbing fades to hiccups as we walk back down the driveway. I open her car door and she slides behind the wheel. Her face is raw and blotchy. When I make no move to get in with her, she says, "Aren't you coming?"

"No," I whisper. "I'll walk."

"Lucas, it's three miles. And it's cold."

"I know."

"You'll freeze."

"I'll be okay."

"You sure you don't want a ride?"

"I can't—I can't be with anybody right now."

She stares at me for a second, then nods and drives slowly away.

It's so much worse than I thought.

She hates us.

She hates me.

24

Consequences

When I get home, long after the sun has set and the dinner dishes have been washed and put away, my mom is standing at the kitchen sink, staring out the window at the dark. She's holding her cell phone. Anna's sitting at the kitchen table, coloring a map of the United States. She's made Virginia purple, her favorite color.

I take off my jacket and toss it on a kitchen chair, then rub my frozen ears to get some feeling back. They ache with cold.

"I just talked to Mr. Freeman," my mom says without turning around.

"So what? Not much else they can do to me, unless there's a blindfold and a firing squad in my future."

"What's a firing squad?" says Anna.

No one answers her.

"I saw Sparrow today. Does anybody give a damn about how she's doing?"

Anna stops coloring.

"Don't say bad words, Lucas," she chirps.

"Shut up, dork."

"Lucas," says my mother, turning to face me. "Do you want to know what Mr. Freeman said?"

"No, I don't. Because it won't change shit."

Anna's eyes widen. "That's a really bad word, isn't it, Mommy?"

"Yes, it is, sweetheart. Why don't you finish your map in your room? I'll come up and check on you in a few minutes."

"Yeah, Anna. Why don't you go upstairs? And you're eight. You should be able to stay inside the lines by now, twerp."

Anna gathers up her crayons and her map, then turns to me, her mouth trembling, her big blue eyes filled with tears. "You didn't used to be so mean, Lucas. I like the old Lucas way better than the one you are now. You're nasty. Don't talk to me anymore."

Her little shoulders shake as she leaves the kitchen, but she holds her head high. I don't hear her crying until after she slams her door.

"Nice work, son. Have you made sure to hurt everyone in your world today? Do you check us off on a list every night? I'm sure you're not finished with me, so go ahead. Take a shot." She leans back against the sink, folding her arms across her chest.

I'm suddenly so freaking tired I could crawl under the table and fall asleep on the floor.

"You don't seem interested in what Mr. Freeman had to say, so I'll fill you in. Magnus King is suing the school because the fight happened on campus. He's claiming 'negligent supervision.' I'm also named in the suit, because you're a minor, so I'm being held responsible for your 'willful misconduct.'"

"What does that mean?"

I wish she would smile at me, maybe take a foil-covered plate out of the oven, tell me she saved some dinner for me. Maybe that's happening in my parallel universe, where all the good stuff lives. It is definitely not happening here.

"It means that because of what you did, I am going to end up paying Tristan's medical bills, for as long as his father cares to drag it out. I'll also be paying his psychiatrist's fees, since his father is screaming about emotional damage and PTSD. I don't have the money for this, Lucas."

Tristan King. The gift that keeps on taking.

"What happens when they finally figure out he's the one who hurt Sparrow? What happens when he goes to jail?"

"I don't have the luxury of playing the what-if game, kiddo. I have to deal with what's happening right now. And right now I'm terrified that this will put us in a real financial bind. I've got some job interviews lined up next week, but substitute English teachers don't exactly make big bucks."

"Mom—"

"Lucas, I can't talk to you anymore. Our lives are falling apart here, but hey, I'll figure it out. I don't really have a choice, do I? In the meantime, you need to go upstairs and tell your sister you're sorry. Shame on you for speaking to her like that. Right this minute I'm more angry at you for hurting Anna than for beating up Tristan King."

I leave her in the kitchen, making a cup of tea, looking small and alone. Walking up the stairs, I take inventory.

Sparrow hates me. My mother is in trouble because of me. Delaney's a wreck, and I've been a total jerk to the one person who believes I hung the moon. When I walk past Anna's bedroom door, I hear her crying, her face buried in a pillow so no one will hear. That's when I know I'm a coward. I can't even face my eight-year-old sister.

Three days later, I get a text from Levkova, asking if I can come to her office in the late afternoon, after her annual daylong meeting with the board of directors. A text from her is like a royal summons. You don't say no unless you want to lose your head or some other vital body part.

After Anna left for school, my mother went off to meet with the attorney who handled everything when my dad died. Anna told me I was the worst brother on the planet, and she didn't need me to name her stuffed animals or read her stories before bed. She even put a sign on her door. It says, *Go away, Lucas Pukas. You aren't my brother anymore.*

When I get to the conservatory, Levkova isn't in her office. The tall leather chair behind the antique table that serves as her desk is pushed neatly in, and the collection of glass inkwells she keeps in a corner sparkles in the light. Not one thing is out of order, the rose brocade pillows on the love seat neatly plumped and placed, a pot of yellow-and-purple orchids on the credenza behind the desk.

I find her in the big studio, sitting at the piano, listening to the *Swan Lake* score with her eyes closed. It's so loud that she doesn't hear me until I'm standing beside her.

"Madame," I say. No response. I clear my throat and she jumps about a mile.

"Oh, Lucas, you startled me," she says, turning down the music. "I am sorry. I have lost track of the time. We can talk here, if that is all right with you."

I'm instantly nervous and on guard. On the Chekov scale of one to ten, she's already at a solid twelve.

"Yes, Madame. I'm sorry Delaney and I are taking so long to figure things out. We'll get there, I promise. We're practicing on our own, and I think we're a little better this week."

Her frosty blue eyes freak me out. If she told me to shave my head and bark like a dog, I'd do it, just to make her stop looking at me.

"Lucas," she says, standing up and taking both of my hands in hers. Oh God, this is going to be bad. "I did not ask you here to talk about your dancing. I have something very difficult to tell you."

My stomach drops into my shoes.

"You know that it is a requirement for all conservatory students to remain in good standing at school and in the community. This is in the contract you signed when you were accepted. You have seen many dancers leave because they were failing in their coursework. Or because they were in trouble."

No, no, no, please. Not this. "Madame, I—"

She shakes her head, silencing me.

"I'm afraid, Lucas, that you cannot remain a student here until your issues are resolved. You have assaulted another student. You have caused your school to become involved in a lawsuit, and you have received much attention—much notoriety—in our community and even beyond. Until this dies down, until Dr. King is no longer upset, until your name is cleared, I cannot allow you to dance here. This is not my decision. If it were up to me, I would let you stay. This comes from the board, and they are adamant."

"Tristan's mother is on the board."

"She is. She abstained from the vote. But even without her, this decision, it was unanimous. You have been given an indefinite leave of absence. Your place will be held for one year, and then we must offer it to another student. I am so sorry, Lucas."

I'm so dizzy that I bend over, my hands on my knees. When she speaks again, her voice sounds like it's coming from far away. I feel her cool hand on my shoulder.

"Lucas, it makes me so sad to tell you this. You are such a gifted, promising young dancer. It is my hope that your troubles will soon be behind you, and you will return to us. But these are the rules, and I cannot break them. Not even for you. And—"

"And what, Madame?" There's an edge in my voice. Even I can hear it.

"You must know that you are not helping Sparrow. You are causing great harm to yourself, though I suspect you cannot see this. This anger—everyone can feel it. There is no room for that here. I cannot have you in class. I know, believe me, what it is to be powerless, to watch the suffering of one you love. It is best that you take some time away—for you and for us. You must decide how—if—you can calm yourself enough to dance well again, to be part of this company."

When I straighten up, those icy blue eyes are filled with anguish. And pity. Anguish I can take, but the pity feels like a kick in the 'nads. Before she can make me feel any worse, I walk away.

Back at home, I find every single heavy object in my room and line them all up on my bed, in order of weight and importance.

The sea-creature paperweight I got for my birthday when I was seven, the year I wanted to be a marine biologist and train killer whales at SeaWorld.

The baseball I caught when I was ten and my dad took me to Richmond to see the Flying Squirrels play at the Diamond. Back then I couldn't decide whether I loved Little League or ballet more.

Three cheesy soccer trophies with marble bases.

My thirty-pound dumbbells.

A photo in a heavy silver frame, me with Sparrow right after *Nutcracker* last year. She's holding a huge bouquet of red roses, and I'm grinning like a baboon. My arm is around her shoulders, and she's beaming, dressed in the long white nightgown that Clara wears through most of the performance. I'm in the Russian costume, blousy black pants and boots, long white shirt, red-and-gold sash knotted at my waist.

The paperweight goes first, sailing across the room and out the closed window like a champ. The echo of shattering glass is sweet and cold, the way ice would sound if it could sing. The baseball is next, followed by the soccer trophies. When every pane of glass is broken, the jagged edges sparkling viciously in the last rays of the setting sun, I heave the dumbbells at the wall, hitting the spot that was just repaired from the damage I did weeks ago. Fine dust drifts onto my bed, my desk, my orange lava lamp, the beat-up beanbag chair from fourth grade. I save the photo for last. I don't see the glass break when it lands, but I hear it, and that's good enough.

I pause, panting, looking for other missiles to launch. Suddenly the door flies open, and my mother stands there, dressed in her black suit and pearls, her hair in a French twist. Her non-mom look.

Horrified, she looks at the window, the twice-ruined wall, then the ruin that is me.

"Lucas, what—"

"It's all my fault, Mom! Everything! I knew! And I kept quiet! What kind of a person does that? I could have done something. I could have taken her away. I could have stopped him! If I hadn't been such a coward, she wouldn't be—she'd still—she wouldn't be broken."

I half sit, half fall down beside the bed. My bones feel so

heavy inside my skin. My mother kneels on the floor beside me and puts her arms around me. She kisses the top of my head, whispers "Hush," and then all the meaningless words moms use to try to make everything better. "We'll fix this, love. I'm right here with you. I won't let anything bad happen. This too shall pass."

But those words have lost all the power they had when I was a kid. Now they're empty, full of air and impossible promises.

"Lucas, my sweetheart, what happened to Sparrow wasn't your fault. Nobody could have stopped it. Not even you, honey. You have got to stop blaming yourself."

I will never stop blaming myself. I've only just begun.

I look over her shoulder and see what I've done like I'm seeing it for the first time. Like I'm seeing it through her eyes.

"Oh God, Mom. I'm sorry. I'm so sorry."

"I know you are, baby," she says, smoothing my hair, holding me tight. Her voice is thick with unshed tears. "But we can't go on like this. You need to get away from here. I'm sending you to Granny Deirdre."

Sparrow

I will encounter darkness as a bride,
And hug it in mine arms.

WILLIAM SHAKESPEARE, *Measure for Measure*

25

Nightmare

My mother's bare feet float just above the dead leaves on the forest floor. She drifts closer and closer as I crouch on the flat rock in the middle of the creek. Her wings are unfurled. The white feathers in her hair lift and settle, lift and settle, though there's no wind. The black stones pour from her eyes, rolling off the rock into the water, turning to deep obsidian pools that swirl in the current.

Come to me, Savannah. Come down in the dark. You belong to me.

You'd think that after all these weeks I'd be used to the nightmare, that I'd be able to wake up and shrug it off, to remain unmoved by something that has grown so familiar. But I'm not. Most nights, I wake up screaming. Sophie always comes, dependable as a kitchen timer. At first she tried to hold me, but I never let her. Now she brings me a glass of water and sits in the chair near my bed, reading *A Tree Grows in Brooklyn* out loud until I can fall asleep again. Some nights it takes a long time.

"Sparrow," she whispers, careful not to touch me. "Baby girl, stop. It was only a dream."

No, Sophie, I say in my head. *It was not only a dream. I let my mother back in, and now she won't go away.*

Today I'm not even in my bed when the dream comes. I've fallen asleep in the living room, under two blankets, which I've learned to arrange so I won't have to look at any part of myself.

This time I don't scream. I wake up and swallow it all back down so no one will come. So no one will touch me.

Sophie wanders in anyway, wearing a black Williams-Sonoma apron dusted with flour. I pretend I don't see her, turning to look out the window at the last of the gold and scarlet leaves drifting gently to the earth from the maple tree in the front yard. She's been baking pumpkin muffins, just for me. The smell makes me sick. She smiles and says, "Thanksgiving's next week. Should we invite the Spensers and the Henrys, like last year?"

When I don't answer, she changes the subject.

"I bought you something, honey, but I've been waiting to give it to you until you were a little stronger."

I stare at her, willing her to go away.

"Oh, baby girl," she says softly. "Remember we talked about this the other night? That you'd try to speak a little more?"

There was no "we." You did all the talking.

"Honey, please?"

"Great," I say, in my new raspy voice, the one that sounds like my throat is lined with sandpaper.

She pulls a book from her apron pocket and holds it out to me like it contains all the collected wisdom of the world.

Back from Violence: Five Inspiring Stories from Women Who Survived.

"I've read it, sweetheart, and I think it might really help you. Sometimes hearing about other people who've gone through similar experiences can help you find the tools you need to heal your-self."

"Thanks," I croak.

I take the book, then struggle to my feet, limp across the room, and toss it into the fireplace. I don't turn around to see the expression on Sophie's face, but I hear her gasp. "Sparrow!"

Ignoring her, I grab the heavy poker and give the book a savage jab, shoving it back as far as it will go, so the flames will eat it fast. It blazes like a torch before finally turning to ember and ash. I watch it burn.

The doorbell rings, and Sophie leaves to answer it, her shoulders drooping. Back on the couch, blankets carefully arranged over my boot, my arms hidden from view, I see Mrs. Cranston from next door, holding a couple of foil-covered dishes. Another casserole, another plate of cookies. She cranes her neck and gives me a smile and a wave. I close my eyes.

If I could tell the truth, I'd tell all the people fluttering around me like demented moths that the thing lying on the living room couch isn't me; it's a breathing carcass. Sentient carrion. I'd beg them to put me out in the cold, let me drift away on an ice floe, leave me to the wolves.

The harder I try to disappear, the more everyone hovers. No matter how many times I beg them, no matter how many times I whisper, "Please, please, leave me alone," they refuse. Every-one—my dad, Sophie, and a score of other people—insist on coming "to talk." To bring me food and books, to "sit with" me, to make sure I'm never alone long enough to "dwell on" what's happened to me. They say I should move forward. But I don't want to move anywhere at all.

It started in the hospital, the day after I woke up. First there was a priest. I pretended to be asleep. After a while he went away.

The next few days brought a psychologist in a tweed jacket

and a bolo tie, a gum-chewing social worker with a tattoo of a spider on her neck, and a physical therapist who smelled like tuna fish and Listerine.

Dr. Sharma was the only one who was never bothered by my silence. She just smiled at me and spoke softly. She didn't want anything. Sometimes she'd sit in the chair beside my bed and make notes in my chart. Her presence was like the beacon from a lighthouse, silent and calm, reaching out across a dark and stormy sea.

The police officers and Detectives Gutierrez and Bell have been to see me almost every day since I got home, begging me to tell them everything about what happened that night. They want me to say his name.

In the rare moments when I'm actually alone, I explore my room like an archaeologist excavating a lost civilization. Three pairs of pointe shoes lined up neatly on the flowered armchair in the corner, toes out, ribbons wrapped tightly around the shanks. The textbooks on my desk gathering dust, the pink-and-white comforter embroidered with swans, the earrings and braided bracelets tangled together on my dresser, the absence of Tristan's gifts like a splinter buried deep under my skin, always with me, impossible to ignore.

I always save the best for last, the painting over my bed. It's the thing I love most, my most prized possession for the last three years. My father gave it to me for my fourteenth birthday. Me as Odette, the tragic Swan Queen. It's like he knew. The card is still tucked into the gilt frame. "Someday, my Sparrow!" Delaney and I spent hours staring at that girl in the painting, hoping, wishing, planning.

Now it's nothing but a lie.

This time when the nightmare comes, I'm ready. There's a brand-new candle on my nightstand, along with a pack of matches.

After I've calmed myself down, after I've banished my winged, floating mother to the box I keep stuffed deep inside myself, after I chain her up again and turn the key in the heavy padlock, I sit up and undo the straps of the boot, slowly, so the sound of Velcro doesn't wake Sophie.

When it's off, I stand and limp to the barre across from my bed, the barre my father installed when I was eight and raised every year as I grew taller. The mirrored wall shows my shadow approaching, backlit by the glow of my night-lights. I look away quickly so I won't see myself. I don't look in mirrors anymore.

I turn to light the candle, inhaling the soft fragrance of peony and jasmine, then rest my left hand on the barre's worn smoothness. Inside the boot, my foot has gone all pale and pruny, except for where it's still bruised. It looks disgusting and smells even worse.

I can't pretend that *fouettés* are still possible, but I am determined to do one thing that reminds me I am a dancer.

That I *was* a dancer.

I breathe in and close my eyes, then pull up and raise my right leg in an *extension à la seconde*.

Unconsciously, reflexively, muscle memory kicks in, and I point my toes.

Instant, white-hot agony travels up my leg and into my stomach like a lit fuse. The pain comes in waves, so savage that bright spots dance in front of my eyes. Bile rises, burning in my throat, and I fall to my knees.

I forget not to look in the mirror.

Oh, sweet Jesus, I forget. Now I see what my father and Sophie have noticed over the last few weeks, what's caused them to look at each other in barely concealed alarm. Now I know why they've been smiling those fake, toothy smiles that people use to mask their shock.

I've lost so much weight that my cheekbones rise like razor blades underneath my skin.

Before, my hair was brown, with auburn highlights. Now it's jet-black, dark as the inside of a cave.

At my left temple, there's a brand-new streak of pure, snowy white. I reach a trembling hand to my head and touch it. Softer than the rest of my hair.

I look just like my mother.

Come to me, Savannah. Come down, down, down in the dark. We can be together forever.

I do not scream or cry. My breathing is calm and even, my movements slow and sure as I strap the boot back on. The candle flares and sputters, directing me to look up, to rest my eyes on the Swan Queen above my bed.

I'm holding my huge sewing scissors, climbing up on my pillows, before I realize what I'm about to do.

My father made a mistake. And Levkova was wrong.

I've never been the white swan, the pure, innocent princess cursed by an evil sorcerer. I do not have Swan Queen blood.

My father, more than anyone, should have known. I'm the Black Swan. Curses swirl in my blood. Wickedness is buried in my bones, bound to make everyone who loves me suffer. I'm a black hole, a night without stars, drawing pain and grief and heartbreak to me like a magnet. Destined to make no one happy, ever.

I am my mother's daughter.

I'm eye to eye with the ballerina in my painting, the perfect dancer who looks exactly like me. Odette, Queen of the Swans, her feathered headdress anchored with a sparkling tiara, her snow-white tutu covered with sequins and feathers, her face—my face—grave and sad, because she is pure and good and powerless to be her true self.

Reverently, I touch her long eyelashes, her beautiful mouth, her chestnut hair, her gleaming shoulders and fragile collarbones. She gives a little beneath my fingers. I kiss her painted cheek. I tell her goodbye.

When I plunge the scissors into the canvas, I smell oil paint.

I cut out her face first, then her tiara, then her pointe shoes. Holding the scissors open, I slash the white feathered tutu, her graceful arms, her strong muscled legs, the lake that shimmers in the background, the soft, moonlit sky. I tear apart all her swan sisters, arranged in perfect rows behind her.

When I'm finished, I bend to rest my head on the white velvet headboard, then gather what's left of my strength to lift the canvas off the wall and lay it on my bed. I cut the rest of it to ribbons, then gouge the frame until my hands are covered with flecks of gold. The painting lies in shreds. The Swan Queen is dead.

All will be well, all will be well, and all manner of things shall be well.

When the door to my room flies open, I'm running ribbons of shredded canvas through my fingers. I've dusted gold flecks into my hair. They catch the candlelight and sparkle on my hands. My father's face goes white, and he runs for his phone.

I smile. *There's nothing to worry about. All will be well. It's done now. I'm all better. See?*

Sophie stands in the doorway, her eyes wide with shock. She comes in and takes the scissors away.

"Oh, sweetheart. What have you done, baby girl?"

I've gotten rid of the lie, Sophie. I am not sweet and pure. I never have been. You should have told me long ago, so I wouldn't have wasted so much time trying. I'm tainted. Spoiled meat. I've been that way since I was small. That's what people smell on me. Poison. That's what breathes out of my pores. That's what makes me prey.

My father's voice floats out to me, insistent, frightened. I hear him say, "Emergency."

Sophie puts her hand to her head and sways a little, then falls into my desk chair and buries her face in her hands. "Divine mother of us all," she whispers. "Give heed to the voice of my cry, hear my prayer. Oh God. Please, please help us."

Oh, Sophie, don't be silly. Trust me, no one's listening. No one cares.

I hold my candle up and look in the mirror. The gold paint in my hair glitters, and I turn my head from side to side, admiring the dark and the light, the white streak that wasn't there before.

It's soft. Like feathers.

Lucas

There is some soul of goodness in things evil.

WILLIAM SHAKESPEARE, *Henry V*

26

Exile

I pitch my luggage into the back seat of my Jeep, along with my backpack and dance bag, though I won't need it where I'm going. I thought about leaving it behind, but I can't. I've had this one—a black Puma duffel—since I was fourteen, and right now it's the only thing that makes me feel like I'm still me. Packed with black tights and sweatpants, ballet slippers and protein powder, resistance bands and clean T-shirts, it holds what used to be the best thing in my life, the one thing I was good at.

Folded carefully on top is the shirt I wore the day we danced the *pas de deux* and I picked her up after and held her in my arms. It still smells faintly of honeysuckle shampoo and lavender soap, and if I hold it to my face and close my eyes, I can make myself believe she'll come back to me. When I sling this bag over my shoulder, I'm still a dancer, still back in the time when I could make her laugh, when we're alone in the big studio, nailing the hell out of fish dives.

My mom comes outside wearing one of my dad's Marine

Corps sweatshirts over a pair of black yoga pants. It's gray and cold and starting to spit rain, but she's barefoot, juggling a box of groceries for Granny Deirdre and leftovers from Thanksgiving. Store-bought pies for the first time ever, sliced turkey and sides from Kroger. Like Granny will get within a mile of that crap. She makes her own mayonnaise, for God's sake.

Without a word, I take the groceries and the food from my mom, shove it all in the back, and slam the door. The car is filthy, still grimy with the salt that covered the roads after the surprise snowfall we had last week. I wipe my hand on my jeans, cursing under my breath. My mom opens the passenger door, pushes the seat forward, and starts mucking out the back seat, tossing old tights, Taco Bell wrappers, milkshake cups, and a half-full bottle of Mountain Dew onto the lawn. She doesn't look at me when she speaks.

"Make sure Granny gets some rest and stays off that ankle." She slams the seat back into place and shuts the door, which takes two tries, because the handle is hanging by a thread. "Anna and I will come at Christmas, like we talked about."

I zip my heavy blue fleece all the way and cram my Sherpa hat down over my ears. My hair's too long and sticks out from underneath. It's freezing out here. I ignore my mother, trying not to hear the sound of her voice.

She runs into the house and comes back wearing my dad's slippers. Standing in front of me, she looks up into my face and says softly, "I know you don't want to go, and I know you're really angry at me, but I think you need some time away. We talked about this."

"No," I say, practically spitting the words. "You talked about it."

I get in the driver's seat, but she does that thing where she scoots in between me and the door so I can't slam it in her face. She has tears in her eyes, but I'm too angry to care. She doesn't get to own this scene. I'm the one she's sending away.

"Lucas, please, try to find a way forward. And keep up with

your schoolwork. Mr. Freeman is doing you a huge favor, letting you work from Granny's. And remember, if nothing changes, you will be seeing a therapist when you get home."

The tears are running down her cheeks now, and she wipes them away with the sleeves of my dad's sweatshirt.

I glare out the windshield and start the car.

"Lucas, wait."

She reaches underneath the sweatshirt and pulls a long silver chain over her head. My father's St. Michael medal. She lets the chain waterfall into the palm of her hand and holds it out to me.

"Mom, no way. I can't take that."

"He'd want you to have it, Lucas."

I take the chain and straighten it out, looking at the medal my dad wore every day of my life. St. Michael the Archangel, patron saint of warriors, circumscribed in a shining silver circle, sword upraised, wings spread, foot planted firmly on Lucifer's neck. *St. Michael, Defend Us in Battle* is inscribed around the edge. Wordlessly, I slip it over my head.

"Thank you."

"You're welcome."

She moves away and I close the door hard. I still can't look at her. When she taps on the window, I wait a beat before I roll it down.

"I can't believe you're making me do this, Mom."

She pulls my father's sleeves down over her hands, crossing her arms in front of her, like she's hugging herself. Even though I'm so angry I could chew nails, sadness for her washes over me like a tidal wave. My dad isn't here to wrap his arms around her or dance with her in the kitchen or rest his chin on top of her head and make her laugh with his stupid jokes. When he died, he took part of her with him.

"Sweetheart, I'm doing it because I'm afraid for you. Please don't leave like this. Please don't let anger be the last thing you feel for me when you drive away. I love you so much, and if you think this is easy for me, you're wrong. Maybe when you stop being so angry, you'll realize that I'm doing this out of love. It isn't punishment."

I roll my eyes. "Could have fooled me."

She lays her hand on my arm. I jerk it away.

"You aren't even going to hug me?"

"Nope."

"Did you tell Anna goodbye?"

"She wouldn't talk to me."

She sighs. "Lucas, her heart is broken. This is uncharted territory for all of us. I wish I had the map that would get us through, but I don't. I'm flying blind here."

I roll up the window while she's still talking, shift into reverse, and back slowly down the driveway. I look up at Anna's bedroom window and see her standing there with Mr. Feathers, her ratty stuffed owl. I stop, roll down the window, stick my head out, and yell, "Bye, Anna Banana! I love you, and I love all your freckles!" She yells something back and disappears.

I shift into park and get out of the car.

Anna tears out of the house, crying, Mr. Feathers clutched tight in one hand. She leaps into my arms, wrapping her legs round my waist, pressing her wet face into my neck.

"Lucas, don't go. Please don't go. I'll miss you too much."

"I have to, Anna Banana. I keep getting myself in trouble, and I need to go away so I can stop and be a good person again. I'll call you every day, and I'll write you letters, and I'll take funny pictures of Beau the Most Excellent Dog. Okay?"

She sobs harder, her little shoulders heaving against my chest.

"I didn't mean it when I said you were a bad brother. I was just mad. I love you, Lucas. I don't want you to go."

"I know, Banana Face. I love you, too. I'll see you at Christmas, okay?"

"You promise? You promise you won't leave forever? Like Daddy?"

"Oh, baby sister." My voice catches in my throat. "No, you little Froot Loop. I'm not leaving forever, and yes, I promise. I'll be back before you know it. And I will get you an awesome Christmas present. Maybe I'll ask Granny to sew some clothes for Mr. Feathers."

She pulls away, puts one hand on my face, and holds up Mr. Feathers with the other hand. "Lucas, you dummy," she says. "Look at him. He's an owl. He doesn't wear clothes."

I fake a laugh, and she gives me a tiny smile. "Fair point, Anna Banana. I'll come up with something else. Something amazing. How about a unicorn?" She rolls her eyes, but I get a real Anna grin this time.

I set her down gently, bending to kiss her cheek. She winds her arms around my neck and whispers, "Every day. Call me every day. I love you, Lucas Pukas."

She turns and runs into the house, holding Mr. Feathers by one tattered wing. My mother stands in the driveway, shivering.

"Bye, Mom," I whisper. I don't think she can hear me, but as I pull away, she calls, "Goodbye, my sweetheart. Text me when you get there."

On the way out of town, I pull into the Dairy Queen parking lot and text Sparrow one last time before I leave. I know it's useless, but I do it anyway. Delaney and I tried to visit her again the day before Thanksgiving, but she wouldn't see us.

I send the disco boy first. Even though my life is a raging dumpster fire, traditions must be upheld.

> Hey, Birdy Bird. Just wanted to tell you bye.

Nothing.

> I'm leaving for Ruby Grove, the rectal end of NC.

Nothing.

> I never stop thinking about you. I hope someday you won't hate me. Wish we were in the studio right now, doing fish dives. Miss you.

Nothing.

> Okay. Bye for real.

I wait for a beat.
Nothing.
Delaney's next.

> I'm outta here. Going where the banjos play all the livelong day.

Noooooo! Don't go!

> No choice. It's this or sitting in a dark room where some musty old fart picks lint off his pants and makes me talk about my FEELINGS. My mom's right, but don't tell her I said so. Nothing good will happen if I stay.

You stay close and text me every day, K?
Miss your face already. Love you.

> Love you back. Let me know if anything changes. You know. With her.

Will do, sweetie. Take care of you. <3

And that's it. There's nobody else I want to tell goodbye. I point the car toward the interstate and turn on the radio. Lady Gaga, "A Million Reasons."

Awesome.

27

Granny Deirdre

I pull into Ruby Grove an hour before sunset, flying off the I-40 exit ramp and turning right to drive through town. At the stoplight, a faded blue sign with paint peeling off the wooden letters reads, *Welcome to Ruby Grove, Crown Jewel of the Blue Ridge*. My dad used to joke about that sign every single time we drove past it. He said they should have made a sign that said, *Run! There's Nothing for You Here!* Even in its heyday, which was, like, a hundred years ago, Ruby Grove has never been more than a wide spot in the road.

I drive through town, which is like a sad and faded version of Hollins Creek. Main Street is only five blocks long, and everything feels old and decrepit. There are three dark and dusty stores that sell tchotchkes to the tourists, who still trickle through to see the fall foliage. Bears with clocks in their stomachs. Enormous purple geodes that probably come from China and have been on the shelves since I was a kid. Dish towels with stupid sayings like *I Love You More than Biscuits and Gravy.*

There's a tiny, dark gallery called Appalachian Mist, filled with enormous framed photos of fuzzy mountain sunsets, jewelry made out of rocks, and baskets of books about local ghosts. My dad loved those. Every year, he'd buy one, then build a fire in Granny's backyard and read them out loud in this voice that was supposed to be scary, but made him sound like an old guy with bowel issues.

My all-time favorite is Uncle Deacon's Taxidermy and Clock Shoppe. I told Sparrow about it when we were in middle school, and she didn't believe me. But even I couldn't make this place up. First of all, it's been closed my entire life, and no one could ever tell me who Uncle Deacon was or what he looked like. I like to picture a big dude with a potbelly and a cheek full of chewing tobacco, watery blue eyes and red suspenders. My dad fully supported this vision. Inside the shop, a long glass counter lines the walls, the entire surface piled two feet high with broken clocks and their innards, rusty tools, and gadgets that look like they came out of a steampunk novel. Best of all, there's a stuffed raccoon in the window, standing on its hind legs, mouth open in an eternal snarl, red glass eyes staring at the ceiling. When I was a kid, I could not get enough of that thing. I named him Spike.

My grandmother lives alone at the top of a mountain, eight miles up Highway 18, a long, winding road with switchbacks and hairpin turns that make you puke if you're not the one driving. Whenever we spent Christmas or Thanksgiving here, my dad always had to pull over so Anna and I could york. He joked that it was his favorite part of the journey, a cherished family tradition.

As I pass one of the places we always stopped, near the entrance to a gravel road lined with rusting, dented mailboxes, I remember how he always packed thick white washcloths in the ice chest, along with the cans of Mountain Dew and Barq's root beer he loved. When we were done barfing, he'd hand one of the cloths to me and one to Anna, both of us still kneeling in the dirt by the side of the road, emptied out and dizzy. They smelled like mint and Irish Spring soap. They smelled like him.

Today I creep around the switchbacks, pulling as far away as possible from the yawning ravines on my right. I've never driven this road by myself, and while it helps with the carsick portion of the program, it's a real sphincter check otherwise. There are no guardrails, just a faded white stripe between me and the abyss.

I turn down my grandmother's driveway just in time to watch the sun slip behind the hills. Her rambling old house looks out over Pisgah National Forest, and mountain ridges undulate like ocean waves for miles and miles into the distance. When the sun goes down, the mountains turn into bluish-gray shadows, and sometimes the valleys are filled with clouds. At night there are no lights anywhere, except for the moon and the stars, no sign that there's anyone else out there in the wide world. My dad told me once that when he was in Kuwait, the thing he missed most was this silent sky. I thought he was nuts; the quiet used to creep me out crazy-hard, especially during my zombie apocalypse years. But I get it now.

I step out of the car and crack my back, roll my shoulders. Everything smells cold and fresh. It's dead quiet, not a sound, no frogs, no crickets, no owls calling softly to each other. Even the trees are still. Just beyond the gravel driveway, where the ground falls away in a wicked steep slope covered with scrubby pine trees and rhododendron, I curl my toes over the edge and wonder how much air I'd grab before I hit the ground. The clouds glow pink and gold, turning the trees to fire.

"Lucas? Is that you?"

My grandmother is holding open the screen door, backlit by

the warm light coming from the lamps in the foyer. She's leaning on a cane, her left ankle bandaged almost halfway up her leg. She looks down and smiles as Beau, her golden retriever, tears down the front steps, tongue hanging out, tail wagging furiously, little whimpers of joy coming from his throat when I fall to my knees and hug his neck.

"Beau, you good old dog!" I whisper into his fur, scratching the sweet spot between his velvety ears, letting him slobber all over my face. "How you doing, boy? How's everything in Puppy Town? You keeping Granny out of trouble? Bet she's giving you fits, am I right, dog?"

"Beau! You come back here and stop mauling my grandson! Beau!"

My grandmother, in her sensible shoes, green tartan skirt, and the gold locket Grandpa Finn gave her when my dad was born, raises her thumb and index finger to her mouth and whistles like a boss. Instantly Beau returns to the front porch, arranging himself primly beside her, like he has no idea what just came over him.

I can't do this.

I imagine getting back in the car and peeling out of here, gravel spraying in my wake. I wouldn't say goodbye. I wouldn't even look back. I could drive anywhere, end up in some town in, like, Iowa, where it's flat and boring and corn grows everywhere. I could wait tables in a greasy diner and live in a crappy apartment and read books. I'd keep to myself. I wouldn't talk to anyone about anything, and nobody would care. I could start over.

I grab my backpack and suitcase from the back seat, leaving the dance bag. I can't look at it right now. It reminds me of everything I've lost.

I slam the door and trudge up the driveway, breathing in the cold, crisp air, wondering how I'm going to play the role of good grandson. I've already screwed up brother, son, friend, dancer. This is all I've got left, and I don't think I can do it.

"Come in, child," Granny calls, "before you catch your death. I've made some supper." She looks smaller since the funeral, diminished. Her hair looks a couple of shades whiter, and there are dark circles under her cornflower-blue eyes, like she hasn't slept in a while. She's wearing a wide belt around her skirt, but I can see the fabric underneath, all bunched up at the waist. She doesn't want me to see how much weight she's lost.

She's tough, my granny Deirdre, definitely not a Hallmark Channel grandmother. She and Grandpa Finn came to America from Northern Ireland in the sixties to escape the Troubles. She was pregnant with my dad and told her family she refused to raise her child to the sound of gunfire and explosions. Two years after they left, her youngest brother, Diarmuid, was killed in a bombing in Belfast. His name meant "without enemy." She never talks about him.

I walk up the three steps to where she's standing and wrap my arms around her.

"Oh, darling boy. I'm so happy to see you."

Even though she's been in this country for nearly fifty years, she hasn't lost her Irish accent. All my friends love listening to her. That soft brogue fools people into thinking that she's all mushy and sweet on the inside, like a jelly doughnut.

I have to bend nearly in half to hug her, and she pats my shoulders awkwardly, the cane banging against the backs of my legs. I kiss her cheek, breathing in her old-lady face powder and the violet-scented lotion she's worn ever since I can remember. I guess she still looks pretty good for a seventy-two-year-old lady.

"Hi, Granny. Mom sent some groceries."

"That was lovely of her. Go ahead and bring them in so they won't spoil in that filthy car of yours."

"My car isn't filthy, Granny."

"Don't lie to me the first five minutes you're here, Lucas Henry. I have eyes. That thing is an abomination in the eyes of the Lord. I can practically smell it from here."

I snicker and walk back to the car, Beau trotting happily behind me. When I grab the box of groceries and the bags of Thanksgiving leftovers, Beau sits down and looks expectantly at the passenger door, wagging his tail. He smiles at me, pink tongue hanging out. I know what he wants.

"You think I should bring in the dance bag, Beau-Butt?"

He wags his tail harder, but sits up all straight and dignified, like he's trying to boss me around with his doggy mind.

"Okay, okay. If you say so. I'm trusting you here, buddy."

I grab the bag and sling it over my shoulder, juggling the box and the leftovers. My grandmother has wheeled my suitcase into the foyer, and Beau noses open the screen door like the gentleman he is.

I shrug off the dance bag, settling it and my backpack in the small alcove beside the stairs. I'm hoping I can find some time to rehearse while I'm here. Maybe while I'm away and out of sight, people will forgive me. Maybe Levkova will relent and let me dance Siegfried.

To boost my chances of such a miracle, I make a small sacrifice. While Granny's puttering around, rearranging the throw pillows on the sofa, I dig all the way to the bottom of my bag and toss Beau a dirty sock. He goes nuts over anything that stinks. He takes it in his mouth and crawls under the coffee table, tail thumping against the floor.

"Okay if I leave my stuff here for now?"

"Of course it is, sweetheart." Granny's voice goes all soft. "I've given you the big guest room, if that's all right. Unless you'd like to be in your father's old room?"

No possible way can I stay in my dad's room, with all the high-school and Citadel football trophies lining the shelves, the heavy yearbooks arranged chronologically in the walnut bookcases my grandpa Finn made by hand, the framed picture of my father in dress blues, standing beside my mom at the Marine Ball. And my favorite, the photo of him wearing combat gear and grinning with his buddies, their eyes hidden behind dark sunglasses.

"No, thanks, Granny. The guest room is fine."

She pats me on the arm. "You can hang your jacket in the hall closet, and please, for the love of all the saints in Heaven, take off that hat. You look like a goatherd."

I do as she says, opening the cedar-lined closet where Grandpa Finn used to keep his stash of gray fedoras and the scarves Granny crocheted for him every fall. His favorite hat is still there.

She waits until I've hung my coat neatly beside her ancient down parka, then says, "Come bring those groceries into the kitchen, and let me feed you, you great, hulking beast. There's some space in the icebox, and you can just set the rest on the counter."

The house looks the same as it always has, red-and-blue braided rugs under the sofas and dining room table, the enormous Belleek vase filled with bittersweet perfectly centered on the baby grand piano Granny used to play before her arthritis got bad.

"So, Granny, how did you sprain your ankle?" I ask, trailing behind her as she makes her way into the kitchen. I watch how she steadies herself against the door frame, how she seems so small and frail. She opens a cupboard and reaches for plates and bowls. I nudge her gently out of the way.

"Granny, stop. I'm here to help, remember?"

"Sure, you are, Lucas, but you're like a bull in a china shop. Get down the nice plates, if you can manage not to shatter them all to pieces. We'll have a little celebration, just the two of us."

"So, your ankle? How'd you manage to mess yourself up? I heard Louisa Fairfax ratted you out. Was she here when it happened?"

I set down the ivory china with the shamrock clusters around the edges and place two dinner plates carefully on the huge round oak table, centering them on the pale yellow placemats. Every time my dad set the table with these dishes, he'd sing all the verses of "I'll Tell Me Ma" and waltz Granny around the kitchen until they were both breathless and red faced, laughing their brains out.

"No, she wasn't here, but she found out anyway, that old busybody," Granny says. "She has a face on her like a plate of mortal sin. And a big mouth, to go along with her big behind."

"Granny, geez! You'll have to go to confession for that."

"I won't, because it's not a lie. If you want to know the truth, I was out in the garden just before dark, trying to get in the last of the persimmons. I missed the last two steps on the blessed ladder. It was stupid; I should have waited until the morning, but I wanted to make the preserves, like I do every year. So I picked myself up and drove to the hospital in Asheville. I thought maybe my ankle was broken, because it hurt like the very devil. But they took X-rays and fixed me right up."

"Wait, you drove all the way to Asheville with a busted ankle?"

"I certainly did."

"Granny Deirdre, you are awesome."

She smiles and smacks me on the arm.

"Sure, I wasn't going to call Louisa to help me. She would have lived on it for months. Besides, it was all over the mountain by the time I got home, the great yammering blabbermouth. Now be a love, and go get the candles off the mantel. We may as well do things up right."

"The ones beside the Blessed Mother?"

"She won't mind."

I walk back into the living room to the huge fireplace that always smells like woodsmoke, even in the summer. A statue of the Virgin Mary, flanked by magnolia leaves and birds' nests and two tall white tapers in crystal holders, stands on the mantel. Framed pictures cover every surface, my dad and Grandpa Finn in a canoe on Smith Mountain Lake, my mother and me grilling hot dogs in our backyard, all of us at the family reunion six years ago, when Anna was just a baby and nobody was sick or dead.

I bring the candles to Granny, who places them on either side of a pale green glass bowl filled with yellow gourds and tiny pumpkins. She hands me a box of long matches, and I strike one and hold the flame to the wicks. When the table is ready and she's directed me where to put the roast pork and baked apples, the scalloped potatoes and cornbread and green beans from her garden, I pull out her chair and take her cane, sliding it under the table beside me. Beau sits between us, looking up at me with his soft brown eyes, obviously expecting to join us for dinner.

"Thank you, *A leanbh*. That cane is humiliating. It makes me feel like a withered old crone."

"No way, Granny. You'll never be old. Or a crone. You still got some serious mojo."

"Oh, go on with you," she says, but I can tell she's pleased.

We eat in silence for a while. I'm starving, but Granny's not really eating, just pushing her food around her plate, every now and then taking a birdlike bite of something. When she's not looking, I slip Beau a bite of roast pork. He takes it delicately from my fingers and chews quietly. His table manners are impeccable. Granny looks up as I break off a piece of cornbread, so I put it on my leg, under the table. I feel his warm breath and slobbery tongue on my jeans.

"I saw that, Lucas," Granny says, trying not to smile. "He likes butter on his cornbread, in case you're planning to give him any more. But just a little. Too much rich food will make him fat and give him bad dreams."

I hear Beau's tail swishing against the wood floor, his soft sigh of contentment as he rests his head on my feet.

"So, darling, tell me all the news from home. How is your mother?"

I chew thoughtfully, choosing my words. I don't want to sound as pissed off as I really am. I don't want to raise my voice. I don't want to lose it. Looking into those vivid blue eyes, I swallow the anger down with a sip of sweet tea.

"She's good, actually. Better. I mean, she's really, really sad, obviously. She's still wearing dad's clothes and his dive watch, and every night she sleeps with his bathrobe. She cries a lot, when she thinks we can't see, but she wakes up in the morning and gets dressed and fixes breakfast and drives Anna to school, and last week she went to a Friends of the Library meeting, so yeah. She's doing okay. As well as can be expected, I guess."

"That's good to hear. When your grandpa Finn died, I couldn't clean out his side of the closet for more than a year. I still wear his favorite sweater sometimes, especially when it feels like snow."

"The green one with the leather on the elbows?"

"The very one."

"Mom wears a lot of Dad's Citadel stuff. It's way too big on her, but she does it anyway."

"She needs to work through things in her own way, in her own time. We do what we have to do to keep breathing, to put one foot in front of the other. And little Anna? How is she holding up?"

I think of my baby sister, crying in the driveway this morning, terrified that I'd never come back, and I wonder if any of us will ever be whole again. I feel like a dish that's been shattered on the floor and glued back together. Falling apart along the cracks.

"She's okay, I guess. I mean, she's so little, she doesn't really understand that he's never coming back. For a long time she'd sit on the front porch at six o'clock every night, waiting for him to come home from work. She'd ask if he was coming to her soccer games. Even though his car was still parked in the driveway, even though she was with us in the hospital when he passed, even though she said goodbye. She doesn't get it."

Granny sighs and puts her fork down. She's barely touched a thing. Under the table, Beau snores gently.

"That's the blessing of being young. The little ones still have so much hope, even when there's no hope left to be had. That's how they survive. That's how they bear their sorrows."

"So it's a good thing?"

"I've always thought so."

I stand up and clear the dishes from the table, put on the kettle to make her some tea. There's a picture taped to the refrigerator. Just one. I've been trying not to look at it straight on. My father, on the day he graduated from the Citadel. He's standing tall and proud in his uniform, one arm around Grandpa Finn and the other around Granny, who's wearing a huge corsage. Someone has scrawled *Beloved* across the bottom.

We need to talk about something else. Fast.

"What can I help you with while I'm here, Granny?"

I scoop Irish breakfast tea into the silver tea ball, hang it from the lip of Granny's blue china teapot, and pour in the boiling water. While it steeps, I nuke the little pitcher of milk. Granny taught me how to make legit tea when I was nine. She said tea bags were "the work of the Antichrist," and only lazy people used them.

"It's hard for me to go to Harris Teeter for the messages."

For a second I think maybe she's losing her mind, but then I remember. "The messages" are Irish-speak for "groceries."

"I'll make a list, and maybe you could pick up a few things."

"Sure, no problem."

I bring the teapot and her sunflower-yellow mug to her, along with the milk and the sugar bowl. She busies herself with the tea business.

"And you, Lucas? Your mother told me you're in trouble. She said you hurt a boy at school."

And *bam*. Here we go.

"He's not some random 'boy at school,' Granny," I say. "He's a terrible person, and he almost killed Savannah Rose. Sparrow. You met her at dad's funeral. She was sitting out on the patio with the rest of us. You probably don't remember."

"Don't insult me, child. I may be old, but I am in possession of all my faculties, thank you very much. I remember your Sparrow quite well. Tiny little slip of a thing. Beautiful hair, remarkable eyes. Graceful in bearing and expression. I thought she was lovely."

My Sparrow.

"Get out! I hate you! Get out and leave me alone!"

I fold my napkin, then shake it out and fold it again. I can't take her eyes, staring at me, seeing everything.

"Did Mom tell you what happened to her? Did she tell you how he beat her up? How she almost died?"

"She did. Not in so many words, but she told me Sparrow was badly hurt."

"He did it, Granny."

"She also said he's not been charged with a crime."

"Not yet, anyway."

"And that's why you attacked him? Because you felt you were the one to deliver justice? Or was it vengeance you were after?"

My face flushes, not so much because I'm angry, but because for the first time since September, faced with my granny's piercing eyes and quiet insight, I'm ashamed of myself. Beau puts his head on my knee, whimpering a little, trying to make me feel better. I reach down and stroke his soft ears. "Granny, are you going to fuss at me?"

"Not at all. I imagine you've had your fill of lectures and punishments and guilt. I doubt that I could add anything that would make a difference. But, Lucas, I've known so many good, sweet boys just like you who've gotten themselves caught up in dreadful things, things that were bigger and more complicated than they could possibly understand. They convinced themselves they were doing good in the world, righting terrible wrongs, and maybe they were. It was hard to tell, because they left so much destruction behind. Somewhere along the way, they stopped seeing any humanity in the people they called their enemies. And when that happens, when you don't see a human being on the other side, you give yourself permission to do great harm. That's when you start losing pieces of your soul. You tell yourself all the reasons why you're right, that it's the others who are evil and must be stopped, by any means. But the truth is, you're both wrong."

She smiles gently, the corners of her eyes crinkling. She reaches out and covers my hand with hers, giving it a little squeeze. "Now I've gone and given you a lecture after all."

"It's okay, Granny. But this guy is totally evil. I mean, there's not one good thing about him. He's rotten to the core. You've never met him, so you don't know."

Beau wanders out from under the table with my sock in his mouth, turns in circles, then curls up in his cushy dog bed beside the door to the pantry. He smiles at me before he closes his eyes, his smelly treasure between his paws.

"Oh, darling," Granny says, stirring her tea, "I haven't met him, it's true. Still, it's hard for me to believe anyone is purely evil. Some people become kinder, gentler when their troubles come. Others harden their hearts and harm the innocent. Yes, he did a terrible, evil thing, and he should pay for it. But perhaps someday, a long time from now, you'll be able to think of this boy with more compassion than hatred. Neither you nor I know what's happened in his life to make him the way he is. And now I've gone and said my piece. We'll speak no more of it. Give me that horrid cane, please."

I pull it out from under the table and hand it to her, then help her up out of her chair. She hobbles her way to the sink and turns on the faucet, squirting in dish soap until the sink is filled with suds. Steam rises, clouding the window that overlooks her garden.

"I don't know if I'll ever feel sorry for him, Granny, even if I live to be a hundred. But right now I'll man up and do the dishes. Why don't you chill and finish your tea?"

There's a perfectly good dishwasher in Granny's kitchen, but she's never used it. She says she doesn't trust a machine to clean her dishes properly. She sits down again, wincing a little when she bends her ankle. "Ah, that's a grand idea. But please, for the love of all the angels and saints, be careful with my china, will you?"

When I glance over my shoulder, she's staring off into space, her eyes tired and sad. I know she's remembering Ireland. And her brother.

"Yes, ma'am," I say, fighting the urge to drop the f-bomb when I plunge my hands into the scalding water. "So, what else do you need me to do around here? Going for groceries can't be the only thing. Want me to plow the back forty? Milk some cows? Slaughter the chickens? Pick the cotton?"

She pokes me in the butt with her cane. "You know good and well there's no plow or cows or chickens or cotton, you ridiculous thing. But we will need some more firewood, if you wouldn't mind splitting some logs. Young Colin from town stocked me up in August before he left for college, but it never hurts to be extra prepared. Just in case we get snowed in and the power goes out."

"Granny, I'm a dancer, not a lumberjack. I'm totally game to go out there and give it a shot, but just so you know, I'm going to suck. I'll probably lose some fingers, maybe even a whole arm. Dad was a log-splitting beast, but I've never done it before. It may be unwise to trust me around sharp objects."

"It's not complicated, Lucas. You're a big, strapping lad. I'm sure you'll figure it out. I'll help you."

"Ummm, no, that's not going to happen. You can sit outside in a lawn chair and boss me around, maybe sew my severed limbs back on."

Another poke in the butt.

"Also, the screen door needs to come off and go out to the shed, and we'll need the storm door put on before it gets much colder. The wind is fierce in the winter, as you well know. And the gutters need to be cleaned out before it snows. Do you think you can manage that, or do I need to call Colin's father?"

I picture myself high up on a ladder in a raging windstorm, leaves and snow swirling around me as I throw handfuls of soggy, slimy gutter slop to the ground. I remember Tristan doubled over in the parking lot, bleeding and bruised. I hear Sparrow screaming that she hates me. And I think maybe it would be okay if I fell off that ladder. Maybe it would be okay if I bashed my head on the ground and never remembered another terrible thing, if I weren't around to cause any more trouble for anyone. I find these thoughts oddly comforting.

Suddenly my arms and legs feel too heavy to hold me up anymore. The charade of acting like I'm okay, joking around with my grandmother, is freaking exhausting. We can pretend all day long that I'm here to help her chop wood and clean gutters and switch out the screen door, but the truth is that my own mother has kicked me out of my own house because I'm a live grenade. She doesn't want me around.

I put the last of the plates in the dish drainer and fold the dish towel, draping it over the lip of the sink. Granny's fallen asleep in her chair, her hand still wrapped around her teacup, her chin on her chest.

How am I supposed to help her, when I can't even help myself?

After midnight, when the sound of my grandmother's soft snoring and the ticking of the grandfather clock in the dining room are the only sounds in the house, I tiptoe downstairs to the kitchen. I'm not really hungry, but I'm mad itchy, and I can't sleep.

I flip on the small lamp tucked into the corner beside the fridge, then pour a glass of milk and cut a slice of Granny's Criminally Delicious Caramel Apple Pound Cake. Dad's the one who named it, because she only ever made it at Christmas when he was a kid. But after he came home from overseas, she made it every single time she saw him. She serves it warm, with this kick-ass sauce she makes from butter and milk and brown sugar and vanilla. I'd screw that up hard-core if I even tried, so I just slather the cake with soft butter and stick it in the microwave for a few seconds.

Beau stirs in his bed when the microwave beeps, opening his mouth in a huge yawn and stretching his long legs out in front of him. When he comes to sit beside me, I break off a little piece of cake for him, blowing on it first so it won't burn his mouth. He wags his tail, scarfs the cake, then pads back to his bed and falls asleep.

It's pitch-black outside, and I catch my reflection in the window over the sink. My hair is sticking up all over the place, and there are dark circles under my eyes. I've lost weight, just like Granny. A gust of wind rattles the trees, and the barred owls that live nearby call softly to each other, like they're asking, "Who cooks for you? Who cooks for you?" In the middle of the night, it's a haunting, lonely sound.

I can't face going back upstairs to the guest room, so I plop myself down on the floor beside Beau's bed and reach over to stroke his soft yellow fur. Even when he sleeps, he looks happy.

I pull my phone out and check it for the millionth time. Nothing from Sparrow.

> Laney, you awake?

Yep. Can't sleep.

> Me neither. What happened at rehearsal?

Ugh. Swan Queen with Caleb. So awful I can't even.

> Did you talk to her? Does she answer your texts?

No. Tried to see her again after ballet. Mr. Rose was home in the middle of the day, and tbh, he looks like poo on a pancake. They're going to see a shrink. You know she wrecked her painting, right?

Sophie told me. That's messed up.

She's still not talking much. She won't
see anyone. Not even me.

Don't cry, Laney.

How do you know I'm crying?

I just do.

Go to sleep, you. I have an English test in
the morning.

Okay. Talk tomorrow?

You bet. Night.

I give Beau a final scratch between the ears, rinse my plate and glass, and put them in the dish rack. When I put the milk back in the fridge, I stop to look at the picture of my dad.

Beloved.

All the hearts around me, once so big and filled with joy. And now look.

They're broken all to pieces.

Sparrow

*Give sorrow words; the grief that does not speak knits
up the o'er wrought heart and bids it break.*

WILLIAM SHAKESPEARE, *Macbeth*

28

The Sound of Silence

"Sparrow, welcome. It's good to see you. Congratulations on getting your casts off! You must feel so much lighter, having all that plaster gone."

I'm sorry, lady, I don't mean to be rude, but how could you possibly know what I feel? We've never had a conversation. And we never will.

Dr. Gray stands at the door that opens from the waiting room into her office. When I stand, my leg bangs into the coffee table, jostling the cheerful cornucopia in the center, the go-to fall decoration of waiting rooms everywhere. It's artfully spilling fake gourds and grapes, plastic apples, and fall leaves made out of paper. A tastefully lettered card is tented next to the plastic bounty. *Practice Gratitude.* I wonder what, exactly, crazy people are supposed to be grateful for.

My father, Sophie, and I stand and file past Dr. Gray silently, like we're walking into a church. Or a funeral home. She's a tall woman, taller than my dad, with smooth dark skin and hundreds of tiny braids pulled into a loose coil at the back of her neck. Her brown almond-shaped eyes regard me solemnly. She's wearing deep red lipstick and gold hoops in her ears. I don't know what I was expecting, an old white guy, maybe, with little round glasses and a pointy beard. Definitely not someone like Seraphina Gray.

"Where do you want us to sit?" Sophie asks.

"Please, make yourselves comfortable wherever you like."

The cornucopia in the waiting room is lame, but Dr. Gray's office is not. It's beautiful, actually, though it pains me to admit it. I want to hate it. I want to hate her.

The walls are painted a warm, buttery ivory, and lamps with red and blue shades glow on the desk and side tables. I head for the far end of a long powder-blue sofa, moving aside a tasseled throw pillow so I can squeeze myself all the way into the corner, as far away from my father as possible. He sits at the other end, nervous and jittery. It's been two days since I trashed the painting, but he's still wigged-out.

Sophie picks up the pillow I've tossed aside and hugs it to her chest, perching on a wing chair next to my dad. Dr. Gray picks up a leather notebook and a fountain pen from her desk and takes the chair across from me. It's upholstered in shades of yellow and blue and red, and there are little jewel-colored birds with their wings spread gliding through the yellow parts.

My father clears his throat and puts his reading glasses on, which is stupid, since he won't be reading anything. Sophie starts braiding all the tassels on the pillow she's kept on her lap, her hands working while her eyes dart around the room. I try to wedge myself deeper into the corner of the sofa, tucking my legs under me, folding my hands and pressing them between my knees. Pretty sure all three of us look completely insane right about now.

Dr. Gray looks at each of us, her mouth turned up in what I'm sure she hopes is a reassuring smile. It isn't, but it doesn't matter to me. I'm not planning to say a word.

"What I'd like to do for these first couple of sessions is talk with Sparrow alone, so that we can get to know each other a little. As she and I progress, I'll want to speak with each of you individually and then all three of you as a family. We may do several of those sessions, depending on how Sparrow is feeling and what comes up during our one-on-one time."

Nothing's going to come up. Absolutely nothing.

"So why don't the two of you go get some coffee and come back in about forty-five minutes?"

Sophie places the pillow gently on the chair, all the tassels neatly braided. My father can't hide his relief and stands up so quickly I'm afraid he'll get a nosebleed from the sudden change in altitude. I refuse to look at either one of them. I hate them for dragging me here.

When they're gone, Dr. Gray trains her eyes on me. We sit in silence for a while, but it doesn't seem to make her uncomfortable. After a few minutes she stands and puts her notebook and pen down on the table beside her chair. She walks to where Sophie was sitting, picks up the white throw folded neatly over the back of the chair, and sets it gently beside me.

"If you're cold, Sparrow, feel free to wrap yourself up in that. It's soft, and it's warm." I rest my hand on the blanket. And though I don't want to give this woman anything, I am cold. And tired. And scared. I pull it over my knees, then tuck my hands underneath.

She takes her seat again, but doesn't pick up her notebook and pen.

"I know you don't feel much like talking, Sparrow, and that's fine. So I'll talk for now, and maybe later, if you feel more comfortable, speaking will be a little easier."

Nope, lady. Not going to happen. I'm not the kind of girl who tells. You won't get anything from me, but this blanket is super-toasty. I don't trust you, and I'm still going to hate you, but thanks.

"I think the most important thing I'd like you to know right now is that you're safe. You are safe with me, and you are safe in this room. I can't know for sure, not until you tell me, but right now I suspect you might be feeling a little scared, and maybe a lot angry. It's not my intention to put words into your mouth, or feelings into your heart, so please forgive me if I've gotten it wrong."

I look out the casement windows at the perfectly circular silver lake, the fountain in the middle with the icicles hanging from its base. I wonder if she chose this office so all her crazy people could have something pretty to look at, something to soothe them into believing that she'll be the one to get the darkness and the screaming out of their heads. I wonder if any of them ever get better.

Dr. Gray crosses her long legs and folds her hands in her lap. I can feel her eyes on me, trying to see past my freaky hair, through my skull, into my brain.

"Your aunt Sophie told me that you're reading *A Tree Grows in Brooklyn*."

I look up, surprised. This, I was not expecting.

She smiles. "It was my favorite book when I was in middle school. I grew up in Odessa, Texas. My father worked as a rough-neck, in the oil fields. It's hard, dangerous work, and my mother, my brother, and I were always worried that my dad would get hurt. So I'd go to the library every Saturday afternoon and bring home a huge stack of books. Reading helped me feel less anxious, less afraid. I read *A Tree Grows in Brooklyn* three times in a row the summer I was thirteen. At first, I loved it for the descriptions of life in New York. City life was so far from what I knew that it was like reading about another planet. West Texas is brown and flat and hot and even on a good day, Odessa smelled like rotten eggs."

Outside, two women are walking around the lake. The wind is making ripples on its surface, and the water looks like it's dancing. The women have their heads close together, and they're both holding Starbucks cups. Even though they're wearing coats and hats and scarves, I can see that one of them, the taller one, has long blond hair. It's woven into a golden braid down her back and reminds me of Delaney.

Dr. Gray keeps talking, like we're actually having a conversation, like having a silent zombie girl in her office is perfectly fine with her, just another day in the life.

"But later I read it because I fell in love with Francie Nolan, and I realized it wasn't just a book about one girl's life in Brooklyn. It was a book about love and family and hope, and what it means to be human, trying to make a life for yourself. I think it's as true and rich and beautiful today as it was years ago. And now I'll stop with the literary lecture."

She chuckles and gives me a warm smile. I keep staring out the window.

The Starbucks ladies head up one of the paths to the office building across the lake. I wonder what they do inside. Maybe they're scientists who sit at long lab tables trying to find cures for terrible diseases. Maybe they're engineers or social workers or writers or lawyers. In my head, I wish them a good rest of the day. I hope they're friends.

"Let's see," Dr. Gray says, playing with the clasp on a heavy gold bracelet. "What else can I tell you? I have three cats, and I am unapologetic about how much I spoil them. They're called Portia, Miranda, and Hamlet, because I adore Shakespeare. I'm picky about food, and can't stand kale, eggplant, or lima beans. And I don't care how deep you fry it, okra is disgusting. I love museums and Renaissance music and thunderstorms. Every Christmas I make my entire family watch *It's a Wonderful Life*, and I always cry at the end."

She can smile at me all day, I'm still not talking to her.

I count the books on the shelves beside the window.

One, two, three, count with me. Four, five, six, almost fixed. Seven, eight, nine, I am fine.

On the wall behind the desk, there's an enormous painting. It's a winter scene, in shades of white and gray, black and brown. A snow-covered path leads between two high stone walls, which are capped with drifts of snow. Behind the walls, snow-dusted trees reach their heavy limbs up to a low gray sky. At the very center of the painting, there's a small figure in a long black coat and a tall black hat. It's impossible to tell whether it's a man or a woman. I feel an instant kinship with this person, rendered so simply, with a few brushstrokes. In that wide expanse of snow and sky, in all the cold gray and white, he—or she—seems so alone.

Dr. Gray watches me studying the painting. I can feel her eyes on me.

"Are you afraid, Sparrow? Is that why you're not speaking?" Dr. Gray asks quietly. "Are you afraid to talk about Tristan King?"

His name lingers in the air between us.

"You flinched just now, when I said his name. You may not be saying anything with your voice, Sparrow," she says gently, "but you are speaking volumes, whether you mean to or not. You've curled yourself into a little ball in the corner of that couch, but I can see the pain in your eyes. I am so sorry for everything you've suffered, for everything you continue to suffer. I hope I can earn your trust. Before we finish today, I'd like to ask you to please think about speaking with me. I believe I can help you, whenever you're ready."

I hear voices in the waiting room, along with the churning sound of the Keurig. My father and Sophie are back, and I know Sophie's making a cup of hot chocolate with extra sugar.

"Just one more thing," says Dr. Gray softly. "Your father and your aunt are not going to stop bringing you here. They are both patient and persistent and determined to help you. You can choose to speak to me or not, Sparrow. That's entirely up to you. I hope that next Tuesday, when we meet again, you'll feel a little more comfortable.

"Now, why don't you go out into the waiting room and send in your father and your aunt. I'll look forward to seeing you next week. And if you change your mind and want to talk, you have all my contact information. You can call me anytime, either here at the office or on my cell. Be well."

As I leave, I take another look at the painting I think I'm starting to love.

And I know one thing, deep in my bones. Seraphina Gray is going to be impossible to hate.

November 16
9:30 a.m.
Savannah Darcy Rose ("Sparrow")

Subjective:

Savannah Rose (Sparrow) is a seventeen-year-old young woman who is recovering from a brutal assault. (See attached medical report.) She is a ballet dancer. Before the attack, she studied with Valentina Levkova at the Appalachian Conservatory and was slated to dance the role of Odette in the Winter Gala in March, a role that her father says was "a dream come true." It is unclear whether or not she will be able to dance this role—or any other—given the extent of her injuries and the long course of physical therapy that will be necessary to help rebuild her strength and stamina.

Sparrow's father, Avery Rose (a criminal defense attorney), and her aunt Sophie Rose (an artist), who have cared for Sparrow since her mother's death, asked me to see her on an emergency basis after she destroyed a much-cherished gift from her father, a painting of her as Odette. Since she regained consciousness at St. Germaine's Hospital approximately two months ago, she has refused to speak more than a few words at a time, with the exception of an incident where she became agitated and angry at two close friends who visited with her in her home. Despite numerous attempts on the part of her family, friends, and the police officers and detectives investigating the crime, Sparrow steadfastly refuses to talk to anyone about the assault or anything else.

Objective:

Appearance: Sparrow is a petite young woman, and her athleticism is evident despite the fact that she has not danced since the assault. She moves with grace, even though she most certainly is in pain. She has clearly lost weight over the past few months. Her clothes, while stylish and well cared for, are ill fitting. She wore a sweater that seemed several sizes too big, and her jeans were baggy. Her face remains bruised, though her father tells me that has markedly improved over the last three weeks. Casts were removed from her arms yesterday (November 15); her aunt reports that her arms are thinner than they used to be. Sparrow is pale, and her hair is extremely short. According to her aunt, Sparrow's hair changed color when it grew back after her hospital stay. There is a streak of white at her left temple; the rest of her hair is deep black. Sparrow's father tells me that she bears a striking resemblance to her late mother. From his tone, it would appear that this is alarming to him.

General Behavior: Sparrow rarely made eye contact with me. When she did, her eyes were alert and attentive. She is engaged, though she tries to maintain an affect of boredom. She sat in the corner of a sofa, with her hands tightly folded and pressed between her knees. No mannerisms, gestures observed. She barely moved. Sparrow refused to speak for the duration of the session. She observed—intently—her surroundings, staring out the window, at the bookshelves, the painting behind my desk, the furniture.

Attitude: Vigilant, alert, hostile at times. Though she did not speak, she appeared frightened and angry. Emotions are difficult to assess in any comprehensive way, as she refused to answer my questions.

Speech: Unable to assess.

Mood: Unable to assess.

Affect: Superficial boredom. Body language indicated fear, anger, discomfort. Difficult to assess.

Thought process: Unable to assess.

November 21
10:30 a.m.
Savannah Darcy Rose

Sparrow refused to speak during this session. Unable to assess.

November 27
1:00 p.m.
Savannah Darcy Rose

Sparrow refused to speak during this session. Unable to assess.

December 4
9:30 a.m.
Savannah Darcy Rose

Sparrow refused to speak during this session. Unable to assess. Avery Rose and his sister are increasingly frustrated and upset.

29

A Painting

I walk around Dr. Gray's office, running my hand along the soft throw on the back of an oversized red chair, smelling the fragrant candles she's placed on her desk and along the bookshelves. I pick up the carved ebony figurines she brought back from a trip to Africa, mothers cradling children, women carrying baskets on their heads, warriors. They're beautiful, and I love the feel of the smooth, dark wood, the way it smells so warm and spicy.

I can't stand being at home. Inside those walls are all the things that remind me of everything I've lost. Here I am wrapped up in warmth, safe and hidden away from the world.

Lamps glow in every corner, and icy sunlight streams through the windows. Photographs crowd the credenza behind the desk, two little girls with beaded braids—Dr. Gray's granddaughters—building a sandcastle at the beach, her smiling husband in front of the Christmas tree at Rockefeller Center, her drop-dead gorgeous daughter, laughing into the camera, tight curls framing her heart-shaped face.

Dr. Gray sits quietly behind her desk, watching me.

The dark figure in the snow painting is still alone.

DECEMBER 13

I pick up the jewelry box that has quickly become one of my favorite things, a silver filigreed rectangle with a red velvet interior. When I open the lid, a tiny ballerina in a white net tutu pops up. If I wind the key on the bottom, she twirls to the tinny music-box version of the swan theme. I only did that once.

"My mother gave that to me when I was six," Dr. Gray says. "She wanted me to be a ballerina, but that was never going to happen. She was in serious denial, my poor mother. I kept growing and growing until I was taller than most of the boys and all of the girls in my class."

I raise my eyebrows at her, questioning.

"No, it didn't bother me, not becoming a ballerina. Well, yes, and then no. I got good at other things."

I smile and put the box back on the shelf. Curling up in the red chair, I wrap the white afghan around me. It makes me think of clouds, how they always look so soft, and I raise my eyes to gaze at the painting. The sky is still gray, and I think it might snow again in that world. The figure in black stands starkly outlined against all the white and the pale stone of the wall. It is still cold. But today she doesn't look so alone.

DECEMBER 19

Outside, the snow flurries have turned thick and heavy, falling in fat white flakes past the window. I am in my usual place, looking at the painting. Dr. Gray is writing in her notebook. Her fountain pen makes a comforting scratchy sound. She sees me looking and puts her pen down. She turns around and looks up at the painting behind her.

"I love that painting," she says quietly. "What do you think of it?"

I clear my throat, once. Twice. The third time makes me cough, and Dr. Gray pours me a glass of water and brings it to me, sitting down in the chair across from me.

"I've always thought you can feel winter when you look at it," she says.

I take a sip of water.

"So much snow," I say. The words feel strange in my mouth. My voice is hoarse and rusty. Dr. Gray doesn't bat an eye. No joyful shrieking, no crying, no high-fiving. She doesn't try to hug me. There's only quiet acceptance.

"I'm glad you like the painting. I see something different every time I look at it."

"Me too. First I saw the snow, then the person in black. Then I saw the sky. I love it."

She leans toward me.

"Sparrow, I'm so happy to hear your voice."

I pull the afghan more tightly around me.

"I'm going to ask you a question. Would that be okay?"

I nod.

"Can you tell me why you won't let Sophie hug you?"

"I don't like how it feels."

"How what feels?"

"Skin. I don't like how other people's skin feels on mine."

"Why do you think that is?"

I shake my head.

"Take your time, Sparrow. This isn't a test. There's no wrong answer."

"I feel sick when I think about it."

"Do you want to take a break? Do you want to stop?"

"No. I can try."

She's quiet, listening.

"When people touch me, when I feel other people's skin, it makes me want to scream and cry and run away. It makes me . . ." I take another sip of water. "It makes me remember him. And I don't want to. I want to forget. And if I don't let anybody touch me, then I don't have to remember. I can shut it all out, stuff it all away where I don't have to think about it."

"You're protecting yourself."

"Yes."

"What you're doing is absolutely normal, totally understandable. But let me ask you something. Is it possible that pushing away the people who love you might actually make you feel more isolated? More alone?"

I look out the window at the snow, then at the figure in the painting.

"I *am* alone," I whisper.

"Tell me about that, about feeling alone."

"Nobody understands how I feel. Nobody. I don't think they're even trying. Everybody—my father, Sophie—everybody talks about how I should focus on healing and moving forward. They don't get it. They can't, and they never, ever will. I think about what happened—about him—all the time. I can't stop. It's like a movie that plays in my head, over and over and over again."

"So, the problem isn't so much that you can't forget. The problem is you can't stop remembering. Is that right?"

"Yes," I say softly. "I'm so scared. I can't stop being scared. I feel like I've been afraid all my life."

She comes to sit beside me, leaving her notebook and pen on the chair. Her eyes are filled with such honest compassion that I can't make myself turn away.

I can't stop smelling honeysuckle, the warm sweetness all around me, the honeyed taste on my tongue when we'd squeeze the blossoms bright in the summer sun, the way it twined all around the fresh fragrance of the water running over the smooth gray rocks. I can't get the red, salty iron smell off my skin, the taste of blood out of my mouth. I still feel the cool leaves, the rocks and earth, underneath my cheek.

I slide out of the chair and onto the floor, pressing my face to my knees. Dr. Gray sits down beside me. She doesn't touch me. I've tried so hard to hate her, but I can't. She smells like my father's white roses after it rains.

"Sparrow, you will get through this. There's a long, hard road ahead of you, but I'm not telling you anything you don't already know. I will stay with you every step of the way, I promise. You are not alone, Sparrow."

I want to push her away, tell her she's lying, that nobody can help me.

Instead I rest my head on her shoulder and close my eyes.

30

A Memory

It's the middle of January, and all the outside looks like the world in Dr. Gray's painting. Snow, endless pewter skies, people huddled into themselves against the cold. I've been coming here for more than two months. Today I'm afraid. I can't get warm.

"I keep having dreams about my mother."

I look up at the painting, wishing I could vanish into that winter, maybe walk beside the girl in black. She could tell me her secrets, and I would be quiet. I would listen.

"Do you want to tell me about them?" Dr. Gray asks.

"Not the dreams so much, at least not yet. I feel like I want to tell you about what happened that last day, but I don't know if I can get through it. I've never talked about it. Ever. To anyone." My mouth is dry. My hands are like ice. I pull the white afghan around me.

"Then we'll do what we always do. Go ahead and begin, and

if it feels overwhelming or too frightening, we'll stop and talk about something else."

I look out the window at the heavy gray clouds massing over the mountains.

I close my eyes, and I am five years old again.

I tell.

"It was summer. I remember, because it smelled green. You know that smell? Like grass and flowers and blue sky, all at the same time.

"But I can't go outside to play on my swings, because my mother is mad at me, and I have to hide. I never know what I do to make her mad, because she never tells me with her words.

"When I'm bad, she comes looking for me. I try to switch my hiding places around, and sometimes I find a new one, a good place that takes her a long time to find. Sometimes I use an old one that she doesn't remember. Those are the best days, when I hide so long and so hard that my daddy comes home before she can hurt me.

"Some days aren't very bad, and she only pulls my hair or slaps my face or hits the backs of my legs with her big wooden spoon.

"But other days she thinks for a long time before she comes for me, and those are the days that make me cry very hard, even though I try hard not to make a sound. When I cry, it lasts longer.

"Once she scraped the cheese grater on my knees and told my daddy I fell on the playground. They bled and bled, and I had to put five Grover Band-Aids on one knee and three Elmo ones on the other. Daddy kissed them when he came home.

"On the last day, I am hiding in my best, most favorite hiding place, the tiny cupboard under the stairs, where the bleach and the vacuum cleaner and the mops live. Sometimes there are spiders in the cupboard, but I don't mind. Their legs are soft and tickly. They like the dark, same as me.

"I can hear my mother screaming, 'Savannah! Savannah Darcy Rose! You come here this minute!'

"When she opens the door under the stairs, she grabs me by my hair and twists my ponytail in her fist so I can't get away. My favorite blue hair ribbon falls to the floor, and my mother kicks it away. I fight as hard as I can. I always fight. But I am little, and she is strong.

"She pulls me into the kitchen and puts me on the floor. She pins my arms down with her knees. They are bony and sharp, and I am afraid that my arms will break right in half.

"She is screaming and I am screaming.

"My mother screams, 'Open your eyes, goddamn you! Open your evil eyes!'

"And I do, I do open my eyes, because I'm too afraid not to. She holds them open with her long fingernails. They're pointy and pink.

"She takes the bright plastic lemon from her apron pocket and squirts the cold lemon juice into my eyes. First the left, then the right, back and forth until the lemon is empty.

"It burns like bees. Stinging and stinging and stinging.

"'I'm sorry, Mama!' I scream. 'I'm sorry I made you mad!'"

When I finish, my eyes are dry. Telling it in the daylight has been easier than dreaming it in the dark. I feel hollowed, emptied out, strangely calm.

"Oh, Sparrow," says Dr. Gray, her eyes wide and sad. "Is there more?"

"Not really. That was the last time my mother touched me.

My father came home early, because he had a bad cold and a big brief due the next day. He found us there, on the kitchen floor. My mother was screaming that I was a demon from Hell. He pulled her off me. I don't remember much after that. We went to the emergency room. Two days later my father told me that my mother had died, that she'd been in a car accident. When I was twelve, maybe thirteen, I asked Sophie if that's what really happened."

I pause, looking up at the painting. Dr. Gray waits silently for me to continue.

"She told me that my mother had been walking in the middle of the interstate, near Roanoke. It was night, and there was fog. She was hit by three cars, one right after the other. She died looking up at Tinker Mountain.

"Anyway, Dr. Gray, you probably already knew all this. Pretty sure everyone in town knows."

She stands up and pours me a glass of water from the pitcher on her desk.

"Let me ask you this. Do you see any connection between what happened with your mother and what happened with Tristan? Any similarities in those two relationships?"

I can't help it. I snort with laughter.

"Dr. Gray, I may be a hot mess right now, but I'm not brain-dead. They didn't give me a lobotomy in the hospital, so yes, I see a connection. My mother was a monster, and Tristan was—is—a monster."

"Are they different? The same?"

I can't help it. I roll my eyes.

"I must have done something awful to deserve what my mother did to me. I know she was sick and troubled, but if she couldn't love her own child, it must have been my fault, some-thing terrible she saw in me that pushed her away, made her want to punish me. I just never knew what it was, or how to be different. I couldn't figure out how to make her stop. I was too little.

"But I was all grown up when I fell in love with Tristan. I knew what I was doing. I knew he had a temper, but I made him mad anyway. I pushed him. I provoked him. I was a horrible girlfriend. I was selfish and self-centered. I'm not saying that I deserved what he did to me, but I share the blame. If I hadn't made him so angry, none of this would have happened."

I take a sip of the icy water, feeling it slide all the way down, cooling my parched throat. Outside, snow is falling.

"Sparrow," Dr. Gray says gently. "You did nothing to deserve what your mother or that boy did to you. People get angry every day, but most of them don't hurt their children, or beat up their girlfriends or their spouses, their boyfriends or partners. Most people handle their anger without physical violence. You share none of the blame for any of it, Sparrow, not then, not now, not ever. None of it. Do you hear me?"

I shake my head. I hear her, but she's wrong.

"Listen to me. Your mother was troubled and ill, but it doesn't excuse her. She set a pattern for you when you were very young, and your experience with her taught you that love is all twisted up with pain. But that's not love, Sparrow. Violence has no place between two people who love each other. Violence has no place, ever, in any relationship. What happened to you was not your fault. Not even close. Say it."

My head feels all swimmy, like at the party that night, when I felt like I was looking down at Tristan from far away. I say it, just to make her stop. I say it because I wonder what the words will taste like.

"What happened was not my fault."

"Say it again."

"What happened was not my fault."

I choke on the words, so unfamiliar, so strange.

"How do you feel, saying those words?"

I look up at my friend in the painting, still standing between the cold stone walls, underneath the snowy branches, still alone. But maybe she's walking somewhere. Maybe she's walking away from something, happy to be going to another place, a place where she can be warm. Where she can breathe. Where something good is waiting for her.

"Like part of me is lying to myself, but another part is hoping it could be true."

"Why are you hoping it's true?"

"Because then I could lay it down. Then I'd stop blaming myself, telling myself all day, every day, that I'm a terrible person who deserves what she got. That I was a bad child who deserved to be punished. That I hurt him first, and I had it coming. That he was right and I was wrong."

"Nobody deserves to be hurt, Sparrow. Not little girls and not grown women. Not boys or men. No one ever 'has it coming,' no matter what they say or do. On some level you know this. It's why you fought and survived your mother. And it's why you're fighting so hard now to make yourself whole. Can you see that?"

Across the room, I feel the girl in the painting smile. In her world, maybe spring is coming and the snow will melt soon. She will take off her heavy dark coat and her tall hat and walk between the stone walls in a bright yellow dress sprinkled with tiny jewel-colored birds. She will turn her face up to the sun and breathe in the perfume of melting snow, the flowers waiting beneath the earth.

"I think I can. I'm not sure, not yet, but maybe I'll get there soon."

She smiles softly. "I know you will, Sparrow. I'm certain of it."

What happened was not my fault. What happened was not my fault.

I ask myself if this could possibly be true. And my heart answers with joy and love and sorrow for the girl I used to be.

You are innocent. You are beloved.

Deep inside me, in the dark place where I keep all the things that frighten and haunt me, a small light glimmers.

I think maybe it's hope.

31

My First Funeral

"There's a big, old elephant in this room," Dr. Gray says. "And her name is Carolina Jane Rose."

It's Valentine's Day, and I'm spending it with my shrink. Dr. Gray hands me the silver jewelry box and settles the white afghan around me, resting her hands on my shoulders. I lean back into her warmth, closing my eyes and breathing in the heady fragrance of the red roses on her desk.

At the sound of my mother's name, my father recoils, as though someone's just slapped him. His face flushes, and he takes off his glasses and leans forward, like he always does when he wants you to feel the full force of his Steely Lawyer Glare. Dr. Gray looks calmly into his eyes, waiting.

My father stands up, because there's no way he's going to say his piece sitting in a comfy chair. He's used to commanding any room he happens to be in, and I know he's feeling out of place and wrong-footed here. Dr. Gray makes him nervous. Still, that doesn't stop him from trying.

"Dr. Gray, I know you're only trying to help here, but we don't talk about her. I don't see what good it will do, bringing her up. It was a long time ago. We've gotten over it.

"Besides, don't you think it would be a more productive use of our time to try to make Sparrow see that she needs to talk to the police?"

Sophie bites her lip and starts braiding the fringe on the hem of her sweater.

"Avery," she says, so softly that I barely hear her. She clears her throat and says it again, louder. Stronger. "Avery." Her fingers move faster, and she looks up at her brother. "Avery, don't. Please. You aren't in charge here, so deal with it and stop acting like a wounded bear. If this session is awful, let it be awful. It won't be the first time. We'll survive. We need to do all the hard things now. For Sparrow. And for us."

"We don't need to talk about her, Sophie, and I won't."

"Could we please let Dr. Gray decide? Come on, sit down and let's get on with it."

Dr. Gray takes her place in the chair across from me. She runs her eyes over my hideous hair, the scar under my lower lip, my thin arms, and my foot, still slightly swollen at the ankle. If I look at it hard when I'm in the shower, I can still see some of the bruises. She motions for my father to take a seat. I'm kind of astonished when he does. And I realize, in one of those sudden flashes of insight, that my father isn't angry. He's terrified.

"Sophie, thank you," Dr. Gray says. "I hope today won't be awful, but if it is, we will deal with it, okay?"

Sophie nods. Her fingers haven't stopped. Now she's braiding the braids.

When Dr. Gray turns to my father, her voice is soft. Gentle.

"I don't want to make Sparrow see anything, Avery. She will come to her own decisions and conclusions in her own time. But here's my question for you: Have you really gotten over it? Do you think Sparrow's gotten over it? How well has it worked for this family, not talking about terrible things, pretending they never happened?"

My father doesn't respond, but I can tell he's getting more and more upset. His brow is furrowed and he's breathing hard, through his nose. He's twisting his grandfather's heavy gold signet ring, the only jewelry he wears besides his watch, around and around his finger. I've never seen him do that before.

"I know you expected that all of our sessions would deal with Sparrow's relationship with Tristan, and Sparrow and I have begun to do that. You can be sure that we will be talking about him in greater depth as we proceed. But first we need to go further back, and I think all three of you know it. There are patterns here. Everything is connected."

My father closes his eyes and shakes his head. He runs his fingers through his hair, then rubs his eyes. He leans forward again, resting his elbows on his knees. He folds his hands and looks down at his shoes. He's a wreck.

"Connected?" he says wearily. "That's ridiculous. How could something that happened so long ago have anything to do with what that—that monster—did to my daughter?"

His voice breaks. He sits up and faces us again. He looks exhausted. When the going gets tough, facts come before emotions on Planet Avery. It's easier to hide yourself behind a barricade of details and data, building it high, fortifying it a little more every day against a world of feeling. And that's why he hates this so much. Because it's what we're here to do. Feel.

"Dad," I say. "She's right, so please stop. You're making it worse. And honestly? If I have to do crappy stuff in here, you do, too. You don't get a pass."

My father is shocked.

"Sparrow, no. Stop right there."

"No, Dad. I won't stop." I take a deep breath.

"Look, I know you feel super-guilty about what happened to me, and I don't want you to be sad, but oh my freaking God, you think maybe we should finally, finally talk about her? I know she was sick, that she heard voices sometimes. I've always known that, Daddy, but you would never talk to me about it. I also know she drank way too much, and she swore she'd stopped. Everyone thought she'd be fine as long as she quit drinking and took her meds. But she didn't. And you know what? I don't give one single crap that she was sick or alcoholic; it doesn't matter. Not to me. She was a nightmare. She was my nightmare, and she still is.

"I'm not blaming you, Daddy. I never have. I know you loved her and tried to help her. But sometimes I wonder why a super-smart lawyer like you didn't notice that I was terrified all the time. I wonder why you weren't there for me, why you didn't save me. I love you, Daddy. But could we please, please throw it all out into the middle of the room and look at it? For once?"

It's the scariest, most honest thing I've ever said to my father, and I totally expect him to lose his mind. I wait for his eyes to blaze, for him to stand up again and pace around the room and tell me very calmly all the reasons why I'm wrong.

But he doesn't. He bursts into tears.

Dr. Gray hands him the box of Kleenex she keeps on the coffee table.

"I think what happened long ago has a great deal to do with what happened last August," she says quietly. "For that reason, I am going to ask Sparrow to talk about her mother, Avery. She'll never be whole if we don't, and you have to be strong enough to hear her. But as I've told her often, it's safe here. It's safe for all of you."

Sophie starts to cry. "I knew it, Avery," she sobs. "We should have talked about it! We should have gotten therapy for her when she was little. We let it go too long, and now look where we are!"

"Sophie," says Dr. Gray. "It's not going to help Sparrow or you to second-guess the decisions you made years ago. Let's hear what she has to say today, and move forward from there."

She turns to me and says, "I know how hard these conversations are, Sparrow, believe me. You've come such a long way since the days you sat in my office and didn't speak a word. You've already talked to me about your mother, and we've discussed that last day. Today I'd like to go back to those last days again, all of us, together."

She stands up and cracks the window behind her desk. "You can do this, Sparrow. Remember the hope you told me you're beginning to feel. Look how far you've come. I'm right here. And just like always, if it's too much, we'll stop."

I breathe in the cold. In and out. Three times. Three times more. Nine in all.

One, two, three, count with me.

Dr. Gray returns to her seat. "I'd like to begin with Carolina's funeral."

I am wearing a new dress. White with pale blue flowers that look happy, because their insides are bright pink, my favorite color. My sandals are new too, shiny and white. My toes can feel the sunshine. My father bought me new things yesterday, to wear for my mother's funeral. There are lots of people at our house, and everybody is bringing food. Food that nobody eats. Everybody downstairs looks sad, but I can tell some of them are only pretending.

Sophie sits behind me on my bed and braids my hair. Her eyes are all red. She's good at braiding, and I like the way her soft fingers tickle my neck. She ties a wide blue ribbon on the end of my braid, but I don't like it.

"No, Sophie, a red one."

"Sweetie, red doesn't go with your dress. Don't you like the blue ribbon? I thought it was your favorite."

I feel my lip start to quiver, the way it does when I'm trying not to cry. "No, I don't like blue ribbons anymore. I hate them."

She looks at me funny, then wraps me up in her arms and kisses the top of my head. Her freckles are like cinnamon sprinkled on milk. I love Sophie. I love her so much. She smells good, and she's safe. Nothing can hurt me when she's here.

"Okay, baby girl. We'll do red."

She finds the ribbon and ties it in a bow, then takes my hand. "Are you ready, sweetheart?"

"For what?"

"We're going to St. Monica's now, to say some prayers for your mama."

"I don't want to say prayers for Mama."

"You don't have to say a single one, my darling. But maybe other people would like to. So we'll go for them, and I'll bring your new crayons. You can color until we're all finished, and then we'll come home. How's that?"

"Can I have *Beauty and the Beast*? And will you bring *A Little Princess*, so I can look at the pictures?"

"Whatever you want, love. Whatever you want."

When we go downstairs, there are lots of ladies from church in the kitchen. Sophie calls them the St. Monica Meddlers. The ladies stop talking when we come in, but I hear some of them whisper, "Poor little thing."

One lady, who's at the sink washing dishes, doesn't see us. She hands another lady a plate to dry and says, "You can't really tell anything happened, not to look at her. I heard Carolina was crazy even when he married her, that she had to go to a mental hospital. Twice! Can you imagine? All that liquor can't have helped either. Did you even see all the empty bottles in the trash? Bless her heart."

Sophie clears her throat and sounds very mad, like she was when she came to visit us and called me Sparrow for the first time. She said I was quick, like a little bird. One night my mama grabbed my arm hard, because I wanted to stay downstairs with Sophie and Mama wanted me to go to bed. Sophie pulled me away, wrapped me in her soft freckly arms, and carried me into the living room. She called my mama a witch and held me on her lap for a long time. We read fairy tales and looked at all the pictures. There are lots of witches in fairy tales, but none of them looked like my mama. She was pretty, even though she was mean sometimes. Even though she hurt me. It would have been better if she'd been ugly, with green skin and a wart on her nose. Then I would have known.

Sophie says, "She's not deaf, ladies, so I'll thank you to watch what you say around my niece and keep your opinions to yourself. We're leaving for the church now. Thank you for all you've done, but I think we're in good shape. We'll be back in a couple of hours."

A tall, skinny lady with white hair, who looks like one of those birds that stand on one leg says, "Sophie, are you sure? We're happy to come back and help serve, after they get that woman in the ground."

Sophie covers my ears, but I can hear her anyway. "Hush,

Madolyn! It's hard enough, so try to have some decency. If you can't do it for me, do it for this sweet baby girl. We'll welcome you as guests when we get home. I'll serve. Avery will help."

"Avery? He needs to rest!"

"Trust me, he needs to stay busy. Lock up when you leave, please, and put the key under the pot of geraniums on the porch rail. Thank you again."

In front of our house, a long black car is waiting. It's the biggest car I've ever seen. My father picks me up and kisses me, then buckles me into my booster seat. A man in a dark suit with nice sparkly eyes says, "Hello there, young lady!" I smile at him, and he gives me a little bear with a pink ribbon around her neck.

"My little girl has one just like it. She named hers Stella. I thought you'd like to have one, too."

"Oh, thank you," I say, hugging her to my chest. "I'm going to call her Emily. That's my favorite name."

He winks at me, then gets in the driver's seat. We pull away from the house, and all the church ladies stand on the front porch and watch us. Nobody talks on the way to St. Monica's, but my daddy holds my hand. He looks out the window the whole time. I think he is sad. And afraid. Sophie wipes her eyes with one of his big white handkerchiefs.

I love the way St. Monica's smells, like candle wax and the smoky thing Sophie calls incense, and the perfume of all the ladies mixed together. And I always like the prayers, because the words sound like music. But I don't like any of it today. It smells like too many flowers, too sweet, like the smell is trying to crawl down my throat. And sad music is coming from the organ.

There's a big, long box in front of the altar. It's made out of shiny wood, and there are golden handles on both sides. Everybody stands up and stares when we walk in behind Father Hammond. I'm between my father and Sophie, and I look down at my new shoes, squeezing Emily tight. I don't like the way all the eyes feel on my skin.

When we slide into the front pew, I tug on my father's sleeve.

"Daddy, what's that box for, and why are there so many flowers?"

"It's called a casket, sweetheart, remember?" he whispers. "We talked about this last night. And people send the flowers because it's a nice thing to do."

"And Mama's in the box?"

"Your mama's body is in there, honey. She died, remember? She had an accident, and she's gone to Heaven."

Under her breath, Sophie says, "Doubt it."

"Sophie, hush!" my daddy says.

The priests are saying some prayers in front of the box. One of them walks around it, swinging the gold incense thing. I can see pictures in the smoke as it climbs all the way up to the high ceiling. A horse, a bird, a lady's face.

"Daddy, are you sure Mama's in there?"

He looks down at me. His face is so sad.

"I'm sure, little Sparrow. I'm sure."

"And she can't get out?"

Two tears slip down my daddy's face and his voice is soft and shaky.

"She can't get out, honey."

"Not ever?"

"Not ever."

"Do you promise?"

He pulls me onto his lap and wraps his arms around me real tight.

"I promise."

At the end, the organ plays another sad song, and the choir

sings. Some grown-up boys carry the box with my dead mother outside. They push her into the back of a big car.

"Tell them to lock the doors, Daddy."

"It's okay, pumpkin. You're safe now."

"No, I'm not. Tell them to lock the doors."

We get in our long black car again, and I hold Emily close.

When the car stops, we get out and walk up a big hill. There are white chairs under a tent. The box is there, still covered with the white flowers that smell bad. Father Hammond says more prayers. My father's knee moves up and down, up and down. He doesn't like being here. I sit on Sophie's lap and breathe in her sweet perfume. She holds me close and rocks me gently from side to side.

Father Hammond says, "Avery, Sophie, would you like to say anything?"

"No," says my father.

Sophie whispers, "No." Her arms tighten around me.

Behind us, the tall bird lady from our kitchen taps Sophie on the shoulder. When we both turn around, she says, "Doesn't little Sparrow want to go up and kiss her mother goodbye?" Her mouth is mean.

Sophie's whisper is fast and sharp, like a knife.

"You hush your nasty mouth, Madolyn. This little girl isn't getting near that woman ever again."

Father Hammond says another prayer, and we leave. People come up to Sophie and my daddy and hug them. They say thank you, but we go around all the people as fast as bunnies and get back into our black car.

"Don't you want to talk to the people, Daddy?"

"I do not, sweetheart. Not today."

When we are home inside our yellow kitchen, Sophie fixes

me dinosaur-shaped chicken nuggets and a big bowl of macaroni and cheese. She doesn't make me eat any vegetables.

Afterward, when the people start to come and our house is filled with strangers, Emily and I walk up the stairs and crawl into my toy box. It's just big enough for me, if I curl myself up into a little ball.

When my mother gets out of her box, she won't be able to find me.

When I finish, nobody says anything. I can't look at my father. Dr. Gray looks straight into my eyes. She does not look away.

"Oh God, honey," cries Sophie. "You remembered everything. All this time you've been carrying those terrible memories around with you."

My father is crying. As in sobbing. He doesn't even try to wipe the tears away. "I'm sorry," he whispers. "I'm so, so sorry, sweetheart. For everything. For all of it." The box of Kleenex is empty.

Dr. Gray asks, "Sparrow, how are you feeling?"

How am I feeling? I have no idea, so I pick the loudest, most familiar one, the feeling that's with me most of the time.

"I'm afraid."

"What are you afraid of?" she asks gently.

"I'm afraid of my mother. I'm always afraid of her. I don't know how to stop."

"Honey, she's gone," my father says. "She can't hurt you anymore."

"When was the last time you had a dream about her?" Dr. Gray asks.

"Night before last."

"Can you share it with us?"

"It's always the same. She has . . . black feathers. And wings. She says, 'Come to me.'"

Sophie cries harder. My father wipes his eyes.

Dr. Gray says, "Why do you think you're still afraid of her?"

"I don't know; I haven't really thought about why. I'm just always scared, like part of me never really believed she was dead. I mean, I was so little then, I didn't know what dying meant, that it was forever. So when I was a kid, I was always terrified that she'd show up in the backyard one day and pull me off the swings, or be sitting in the parking lot at school, waiting for me, or just appear in the kitchen at breakfast time, holding a plastic lemon in each hand. I used to hide from her, for years after she died, until I was too big to fit in that cupboard under the stairs. Then I switched to my closet, behind all the pointe shoe boxes."

"Oh God," my father whispers. "Oh my God."

"Go on, Sparrow," Dr. Gray says.

"There's not much more, just that by the time I was old enough to know that dead really was forever, it was too late to stop being afraid. It's not like a switch I could flip, you know? It was part of me, that fear, that terror. When I was in middle school, it changed. It got bigger. It went inside, which was way worse. Instead of always being afraid that I'd actually see her again, it was like I carried her with me all the time, like every minute of every day. Sometimes I feel like I'm so filled up with fear that there's no room for anything else."

Dr. Gray is quiet for a while. Then she comes and sits beside me. She takes my hands in hers.

"Sparrow," she says softly, "you are a remarkable young woman. You articulated your feelings, your fear, so powerfully just now. Honestly, you just did amazing work, and it was really, really brave of you to dig so deep and bring those fears out into the open."

My father blows his nose. Sophie collects all the balled-up tissues into her lap and mashes them into one huge wad.

"Is there anything else you'd like to say?" Dr. Gray says.

There's more, so much more. It's like I've taken a teaspoon of water out of an impossibly deep well. I am empty and exhausted. But I feel clean, the way it feels when you're caught outside in a summer shower, the soft rain falling while the blazing sun shines. Whenever that happened on blistering afternoons when the heat was so thick it hurt to breathe, I always saw a rainbow. I'd stand completely still, soaked to the skin, my face turned up to the sky, and wait for the bright arc to appear. It always did. Always.

"I don't think so. I'm kind of wiped out, to be honest."

"You've done hard work today. I'm proud of you."

Sophie and my dad are sitting on the edges of their chairs, ready to bolt. I'm still curled up in the red chair, clutching the afghan around me. I wish I could sleep here.

"But let's all think about something before we meet next time. First I want you to know that I really do understand the instinct that made you—that still makes you—want to repress the memories of Sparrow's mother. But what Sparrow just shared is powerful evidence that those memories are still there, whether you acknowledge them or not. They're not going away. Painful memories rarely do, especially when you don't look at them or talk about them. They clamor and they scream, because they're determined to get your attention one way or another.

"By not talking about Carolina, you haven't been able to move on, at least not in a way that's healthy, in a way you can live with. She haunts you. If Sparrow is going to heal, truly heal, not just from the assault, but also from her experience with her mother and her toxic relationship with Tristan, she's going to have to look at all those dark things. And you both are going to have to look with her, to acknowledge them and talk about them. And then you can begin—separately and together—to fashion a way to move on, not just to live, but to thrive."

I'm not sure yet. I can't be sure of anything. But maybe, here in Dr. Gray's beautiful office, the air still ringing with terrible words, heavy with years of fear and dread and horror, maybe it's like a summer rain just stopped. Maybe I'm standing outside, drenched and clean, and the sun is shining in the sparkling world.

And maybe, just maybe, I've caught the smallest glimpse of a rainbow.

That afternoon, just as the sun is sinking behind the mountains, Levkova comes to see me. It's been quiet since we got home from Dr. Gray's office, but the air feels thick, filled with all the things we've never said out loud, all the words we have yet to speak. My father has escaped to his study, nursing a double Scotch, and Sophie's in the kitchen, chopping vegetables for spaghetti sauce. She always cooks when she's upset.

When the doorbell rings, I yell that I'll get it, but nobody responds. I figure it's probably Mrs. Cranston, with yet another tuna casserole, so I try to plaster a pleasant smile on my face. But when I open the door, Madame Levkova is standing on the doorstep in the fading light, a lavender scarf draped artfully over her snow-white hair. She's holding a box wrapped in silver paper and tied with a white ribbon.

"Hello, little bird. Is this a good time for a visit? I can come back another time—I don't want to interrupt your dinner or disturb your family."

"Oh, no, no, Madame," I stammer. "I mean, yes, please, come in."

I take her coat and scarf and hang them in the hall closet. She follows me into the living room, and we sit on the sofa, in front of the fire. February is the most miserable month of winter, if you ask me, and I am so tired I could sink to the floor and sleep for a year.

"How are you, my dear?" she asks. "How is your foot?"

"It's much better, Madame. Thank you for asking. It aches when I'm tired, and if I'm on my feet for a long time, it swells a little."

"May I see?"

We're all so used to Levkova staring at our bodies, touching us, adjusting the tilt of our hips, stretching our arms and legs, examining all our many injuries, that without question I take off my shoe and sock and prop my foot on the couch. She picks it up tenderly and cradles it in her lap. Moving it from side to side, she looks at my face. "Does this hurt?" she asks softly.

"No, Madame. It only feels a little stiff."

She runs her thumb along the tops of my toes.

"And your toes? They were not damaged?"

"No, Madame. Just the bones in my foot."

She bends her head and strokes my foot, from my ankle to my toes, again and again.

"I came to see you in the hospital. Do you remember?"

Live for me. Please. Live for me.

"Yes, Madame. I thought I was dreaming, but Sophie told me you were really there."

She looks up and smiles. "I am glad. I have been worried that you would not remember, so I came here today to tell you again, in person, what I said that afternoon." She pauses, like she's centering herself.

"My darling little bird, I came to tell you that I love you very, very much, as though you were my own child. And I came to tell you that you will dance again. Because I am going to help you."

She rests her hands on my foot, which is still in her lap. There is a huge lump in my throat. I can't take my eyes off her.

"You have heard the stories of great dancers who have come back from terrible injuries, yes? Beautiful, brave dancers like Misty Copeland and David Hallberg?"

I nod, and she takes my hands in hers.

"We know how they struggled because they had the courage to share their pain, their suffering, their grief," Levkova continues. "Like them, you will have to work very hard, but you are no stranger to hard work. And when you fear that you can do no more, you will think of these dancers and how they triumphed over their injuries. Their stories will help you strengthen your will and your heart. Together, you and I will bring you back to what you love."

She hands me the box. "I have also brought you a gift. A symbol, perhaps, of a new beginning."

I untie the white ribbon and tear the paper away, revealing a box from the London company that creates handmade pointe shoes for some of the most famous ballerinas in the world. Each pair is marked with the personal symbol of the maker who crafted them.

Inside are the most exquisite pointe shoes I have ever seen.

"Oh, Madame, thank you! They're beautiful!"

"I chose the maker myself and spoke to him several times. He knows your story and asked me to tell you it was an honor to make your shoes."

My eyes fill, and I close the box so my tears won't drip onto the beautiful shoes. Leaning forward, I wrap my arms around Madame Levkova and hug her close. "I love you too," I whisper. "So much."

She holds me in her arms and rocks back and forth. "We are going to work hard," she says. "Very hard, indeed. You will dance again, little bird. This, I know."

"I will work hard, Madame, I promise."

At the front door, she clasps my hands in hers and kisses me on both cheeks. "Tomorrow morning, at seven thirty, you will come to the studio. And so we will begin."

"Yes, Madame. I'll be there." I wave as she drives away.

You are innocent. You are beloved.

And in this moment, I begin to believe.

Lucas

To weep is to make less the depth of grief.

WILLIAM SHAKESPEARE, *Henry VI*, Part 3

32

A Walk in the Woods

"Granny! I'm taking Beau for a walk!"

It's the week before Christmas, and my mom and Anna will be here in two days. I can't decide if I'll be happy to see them or wish they'd stayed home, so I could have this quiet and peace and Granny and Beau to myself for a little longer.

Granny walks out onto the screened back porch, pulling on her favorite Christmas sweater, the nuclear-green one with the creepy dancing elves.

"My ankle feels so much better without that wretched bandage. It's nice to wear a proper pair of shoes again. Now, why were you shouting at me, you brazen article?"

"Granny, that Irish stuff makes no sense whatsoever. I wasn't shouting at you. I was just letting you know that I'm going to take Beau for a walk. He says it's going to snow later, and he wants to go sniff around in the woods before it covers up all his favorite places."

She smiles, her face creasing into a thousand soft wrinkles, especially around her eyes and her mouth. "He told you all that now, did he?"

"Yes, ma'am. He's a smart dog. He's also good at predicting the weather."

"He's a right coward, that's what he is. You've seen him shaking in his shoes when there's a thunderstorm."

She opens the door all the way, and Beau leaps from the top step and lands in the hydrangea bushes, which are pretty much only sticks this time of year. He yelps once, so we'll feel sorry for him, then tears around the yard like his tail is on fire.

Granny shakes her head. "Look at him. Six years old, and he thinks he's still a puppy."

We stand there watching Beau act like a moron for a while, until Granny shivers and looks up at the sky.

"It is most certainly going to snow, Lucas. Will you be warm enough?"

"Yes, Granny. I'm plenty warm."

"Are you hungry? Do you want to take along some of the cookies your mother sent?"

"No, ma'am. But thank you."

"You can't stay mad at her forever."

"Maybe not, but that's my current plan."

"Is it so terrible, being here with an old lady?"

"Oh, Granny, no. It's not you. It's that my own mother sent me away. Not cool."

"If you ask me, she was wise to do it. Go have your walk. And don't lose my dog."

I call Beau and set off, promising Granny I won't be more than half an hour. Beau trots happily beside me, looking up every now and then with adoration. I don't read much into those big chocolate eyes. He'd adore a serial killer if the dude took him for a walk.

When I'm out of sight of the house, just before we reach the dense boundary of trees that divides my grandmother's property from the deep woods beyond, I sit down on a lichen-covered log and pull out my phone. Beau whines in frustration.

"Chill out, dog. I have important human business to conduct."

He walks away in a huff, pushing his nose into fallen leaves and pine needles, lifting his head to breathe the wind.

I send the disco boy and wait for her flamenco dancer. I'd be happy with anything, to be honest. The waving hand. The middle finger. Even the smiling turd.

Hey, Birdy.

It's cold up here. Snow on the way.

I wait. And wait. And wait.

Nothing.

I shove my phone back in my pocket and whistle for Beau.

My head aches. My heart hurts. Yesterday I tried to dance a little in the backyard, some fast turns, a couple of *tours jetés*, but it was all wrong. It made me feel too much, want too much. It made me remember that day in the studio, when *Swan Lake* finally clicked, when I was a prince and she was the Swan Queen. It made me remember that perfect round mole on the underside of her left arm, her hair, her river-green eyes. It made me remember, when all I want to do is forget.

Beau runs ahead, pausing to pee on trees along the way, then trots back to me with a stick. I pull it out of his mouth and throw it as hard as I can, but he just stands there, wagging his tail, looking at me expectantly. Like I'm the one who's supposed to go fetch it.

"Look, Doggy McDogface," I say, throwing another stick. "I throw, you fetch. That's how it's done, you dumb dog."

He runs ahead, past the place where the stick landed. I can't see him anymore.

"Beau!" I call. Granny will kill me if her dog runs off. "Beau, get your furry butt back here!"

Nothing.

I trudge on, deeper and deeper into the woods, where the path grows fainter, then disappears completely. The trees grow so closely together that they block out the cold winter light, and it suddenly feels spooky, too dark and claustrophobic. Up ahead, I see a flash of yellow, and I start running.

"Beau, don't you dare move, you mangy mutt! Stay! Stay right there!"

I find him at the edge of a clearing. Tall tulip poplars reach their spindly arms up to the sky, which is thick with low gray clouds. A few snowflakes drift past, settling on the wet brown leaves before they melt away.

Beau is sniffing at something under a tree, whining and looking back at me. If he's killed another rabbit like he did last week, leaving its eviscerated carcass next to my boots, I will throw up on his head.

But it's not a rabbit. It's a bird.

"Move, Beau. It's okay, buddy. Come on, move over."

I nudge him gently out of the way, and he whines, telling me that he got there first and I am not being fair. "Yeah, yeah, I know. Go pee on something."

I kneel down on the carpet of leaves, careful not to get too close, in case it's something that wants to peck out my eyeballs.

It's small and bright yellow, with black-and-white wings. Its beak is smashed, and one of its wings is bent at a weird angle, folded in half right down the middle. There's a little blood on the top of its head. I can see it breathing, fast and hard. One glittering black eye looks at me, like it recognizes me, like it's asking me for something. Its chest heaves up and down, and it opens its beak and lets out a little sound.

She sounds like she's crying.

I slide my hands underneath her body and pick her up, holding her close to my chest. She's trembling so hard that I can feel the vibrations in my wrists and elbows. She tries to flap her wings, and her head moves frantically back and forth. She's terrified, unable to fly away, to do the only thing that keeps her safe.

"Come on, bird," I say. "Not on my watch. I'll stay with you until you feel better. Until you can fly again." I run my finger along her downy breast, and she makes that little cry again. Her beak opens and closes, like she's telling me something. *It hurts. I'm afraid.*

I blow warm air over her so she won't be cold, and she shudders. I stroke her chest some more, the black spot on the top of her head. I cup my palms around her a little more tightly and blow another warm breath onto her bright feathers. Gradually, her breathing slows. Her beak opens once, then closes, and opens again.

I watch the light leak out of her eyes. I breathe on her, over and over again. I tell her what a beautiful bird she is, how soon her wing won't hurt anymore and she'll be flying somewhere peaceful and warm, where there's music in the clouds and plenty of food and it's always summer and there are no cats.

She shudders and lets out a tiny cry. She tries again to flap her wings. Then her eyes close, and she goes still. She dies in my hands.

She dies.

"Oh, no, no, no. Don't go, bird. Birdy Bird, don't leave me. Please don't leave me alone."

The sobs come up from the soles of my feet. I put my forehead on the wet carpet of leaves and I cry and cry and cry, with no one to hear me but Beau. He whimpers and lies beside me, resting his head on my thigh. I rock back and forth, holding the bird, my tears falling onto her feathers as her body grows cold in my hands. The light starts to fade, and it begins to snow in earnest. I cry until my throat is raw, until my eyes burn, until I choke and can't breathe. Big white flakes drift down and land in Beau's fur, in my hair, on the back of my neck.

I close my hands so she'll stay warm.

"Let her go, Lucas."

I feel my grandmother's hand between my shoulders. She kneels down beside me on the cold ground.

"Let me see," she says.

I open my hands and show her the bird. I can't stop crying. My shoulders heave, and I close my eyes so I won't have to see anything, the dog, my grandmother, the snow.

The little bird.

Granny doesn't say anything, just waits until I stop, her gloved hand still on my back, her thin shoulder pressed up against my arm. The snow is falling fast and thick, covering my grandmother's silver-white hair like a lace veil.

"You couldn't have saved her, Lucas."

"I could have brought her home. I could have set her wing. I could have helped her. I could have fixed her."

Granny doesn't answer right away. When she does, she isn't talking about the bird. Her eyes are faraway, seeing things that aren't there.

"Oh, child. There are some things that can't be fixed, not by you, not by me, not by anyone. There was nothing you could have done for that poor creature. It was her time. You couldn't have changed that, and if you'd tried, you would have hurt her and frightened her and only put off what was going to happen anyway. You were kind. You stayed with her. She wasn't alone. Sometimes all we can do is watch and grieve. And that has to be enough."

"It isn't."

"No," she agrees. "It isn't."

"We should bury her."

"Give her to me."

I open my hands, and she takes the bird and sets her down on a bed of leaves.

"We can't just leave her here! We need to bury her, Granny."

"No, darling," she says gently. "She wouldn't want to be under the dark earth, when all she's ever known is the sunlight on the trees and the sweet air all around her. We'll lay her down and let her be. Come on, now. It's getting dark. You held her and spoke to her, and that's all you could have done. Let's go home."

I stand up and help my grandmother to her feet.

"What kind of bird is she?"

"A goldfinch. They love the winter woods."

She takes my arm and calls softly to Beau, and we walk down the path toward home. We hold on to each other all the way.

33

Epiphany

I pull the stairs to the attic down from the ceiling in the upstairs hallway and carry the box of old photo albums up, stair by steep stair. My grandmother has approximately eleventy thousand pictures, carefully pasted into thick leather albums, all captioned in her perfect Catholic school penmanship. We've been looking at them every night after dinner, making our way from her wedding day in Belfast to last year's *Nutcracker*. When Dad was still here. The problem is that she keeps them all in one huge box, which weighs as much as a Volkswagen. Inside the attic, the smell of cedar makes me feel like I'm in a giant hamster cage.

After breakfast this morning, I finally chopped up the nine-foot Fraser fir Christmas tree, which I took down after New Year's, and dragged all the pieces into the woods so they can do that whole circle-of-life thing. Beau helped me pull some of the branches, holding them in his mouth and tripping over them with his big muddy feet.

It's the third week in February, and I'm going home in a couple of days. At Christmas I told my mother I wasn't ready to go back to school, and Granny faked a cough and said she'd been feeling poorly lately, that she could use my help just a little longer. We worked it out ahead of time. She was lying. I was not. My mom talked to Mr. Freeman, who said that since I've been keeping up with the work and turning assignments in on time, he'd see what he could do about extending my Beatdown Leave. Though it's doubtful those were his exact words.

"Lucas," Granny calls up the stairs. "What in the name of all the saints is taking you so long? Come down and have your lunch!"

I hear Beau's panting and see his big yellow head peek up over the top of the stairs. He smiles his slobbery smile and climbs the rest of the way, trotting over to sit beside me, his wagging tail sending dust motes into the dim light.

"I'll be right there, Granny!"

I shove the box in the corner with the holiday decorations. If I stand in front of the octagonal window at the far end of the attic, I can get a decent signal.

I send the disco boy emoji first.

> Hey, Birdy. Just wanted to say hi. Granny has me chopping up trees and hauling boxes. Beau is helping me. Not with the boxes or the chopping, obvs, just tons of moral support. Like a furry cheerleader, with the most revolting breath on the planet.

Nothing. Then three dots.
I wait. And wait. And wait.

> Beau sounds like a great dog.

My heart pounds into my throat, and my hands start to shake. I tap her picture, the one I took at the Honeysuckle Pond two summers ago, when she'd just come up out of the water and her hair was wet and tangled and she was squinting and smiling into the sun. Her contact information comes up. My thumb hovers over her phone number.

I need to hear her voice. I need to tell her everything, all of it, right this minute. I need to know how she's doing, if she's okay. If she's dancing, even a little. If she still hates me. She's so close right now, and I need to talk to her so badly. I need to tell her about the goldfinch.

I put my phone down and walk away, so I won't do something stupid. What I need isn't important. This is about what she needs. A friend. Somebody who isn't selfish. Somebody who won't scare her away.

I shake out my hands and pick up the phone.

> He's the best dog ever. He thinks he's human. How are you?

I'm okay. Some days better than others.
I'm talking to a doctor about stuff.
My mother. Everything.

> That's good, right?

It's awful. Crazy-hard. But also good.

> I'm glad, Birdy.

I need to run. Have fun with Beau.

> I will. Take care.

You too.

Two beats later, three more dots. She sends the flamenco dancer emoji.

I swear to God, I almost lose it. A small conversation, big as the starry firmament that arches over me at night. Beau sits up and wags his tail. I bury my face in his neck, and he makes little doggy sounds of joy.

"Oh, Beau, you wonderdog. She talked to me. She talked to me!"

Beau licks my ear, like he's saying, *You ridiculous human. I told you so.*

"Lucas! Come down from there! The soup will get cold!"

Beau looks at me, alarm in his sweet brown eyes.

"I know, buddy. Granny's going to throw an embolism if we don't book it downstairs. Come on, let's go."

In the kitchen, my grandmother is ladling thick corn chowder into her blue ceramic bowls, the ones with the yellow and red flowers around the edges.

"Thank you for chopping up the tree, Lucas. Was it dry enough? It wasn't too heavy?"

"It was dry as a bone. No problem. Not for these manly arms."

She smiles and hands me a bowl of chowder. I set napkins and spoons at our places.

"It gladdens my heart that we were all together, especially this Christmas. It was grand to see your mother again. I didn't realize how much I'd missed her. And Anna is such a darling. I'm happy you got the stick out of your behind and spoke kindly to her. And to your mother."

"Haha, Granny. You're hilarious."

She sets a huge ham sandwich in front of me, then sits down with her own lunch, a small cup of soup and three soda crackers. Old people eat like birds.

"This was Grandpa Finn's favorite lunch, wasn't it?"

"Your grandfather never met a ham he didn't like. That's why he loved you so much."

"Wow, Granny. You're on fire today."

She chuckles.

"I'm just happy to have had you with me all this time. I'll be very sorry to see you go. I was dreading the holidays, but you made them happier than I thought they could ever be."

I look at my grandmother like she's a real person and not just my grandmother. When I was a kid, I thought she was kind of magical, though maybe that was just the whole Irish thing. It seemed like she was made up of earth and fire. Now she's all air and water, fragile and small. Like she's getting tired of carrying the weight of her own bones.

"Granny," I say, stirring the soup with my spoon. "Are you okay?"

"Of course, child. I'm just fine. I've had my strong, handsome grandson all to myself for a good, long while, and that's made me a happy old Irishwoman. How are you feeling about going home? Have you sorted things out?"

"I don't know, to be honest. Sparrow just texted me back for, like, the first time since it happened. Maybe someday she'll forgive me."

"What on earth does she have to forgive you for?"

"For about a thousand things. I said some really ugly stuff to her. Things about Tristan."

"Were they true?"

"Yeah. They were true."

"Then you have nothing to be sorry for, Lucas."

"But see, Granny, I do. I could have told someone. I could have done something to stop him."

"Oh, Lucas." She sighs.

She hasn't touched her soup, but gets up to put the kettle on. She always busies herself with the tea-making ritual whenever she has something she wants to tell me. Usually it's something I don't want to hear.

She stands at the kitchen sink, looking out at the lilac bushes in the backyard, the bare branches heavy with snow.

"Do you know who I'm named for?" she asks, without turning around.

"A saint?"

"No. It's an old name, from the Ulster Cycle, a group of legends that go back way before Christianity. Deirdre was a beautiful young woman who defied a king to run away with the man she loved. The king had his men search all over the country for them, and when they were found far away from their home, he promised that no harm would come to them if they returned. They trusted him. And of course, as Irish legends so often go, it did not end well.

"As soon as they arrived, Deirdre's lover and his men were slaughtered on the spot. Deirdre died of a broken heart. Ever since, she's been called Deirdre of the Sorrows. I've always wondered why my mother named me after the heroine of such a sad tale. And I wonder sometimes—I still do—if a person can be cursed by her own name."

"Why would you think you were cursed, Granny?"

She comes back to the table with her cup of tea and a plate of sugar cookies for me.

"Do you know why your mother sent you here? I mean, surely to get you away from all your troubles, but why here? Why to me?"

"Beats me, Granny."

"Because she knew what you had to learn, and she knew I would tell you. You'll have to learn it over and over in your life, just the way I've had to learn my lesson over and over again. Men and women are different. We're meant to fill in each other's empty places."

326 MARY CECILIA JACKSON

"Granny, I'm sorry. You're talking in riddles. Just tell it to me straight."

"All right, then. You men want to fix everything that's broken in your lives, and in the lives of the people you love. You see a problem, you think you're the one who can solve it, that you can make everything right again. There's nothing in the world wrong with that; it's the way you are. It's in your blood. But women know that some things need time to fix themselves. And some things can never be mended. I've had to learn that lesson many times."

"I still don't get you."

"When your father died, you can't imagine how helpless I felt."

"I can, Granny."

"No, darling," she says softly. "You can't possibly. I was his mother. He was my only child. My one and only beautiful boy, and even though he was a grown man when he died, when he was lying in that hospital bed, all I could see was my baby, the way he was when he was small. I saw his scraped knees and his sweet freckles and the cowlick that always plagued him and the scar he got from falling out of a tree when he was nine. Mothers are supposed to ease the suffering of their children. What kind of mother was I, when I couldn't fix what was wrong with my boy? When I couldn't cure him or ease his pain or stop him from dying? What kind of woman was I, if I couldn't keep my own child alive? I couldn't fix him. There was nothing in the world I could do."

A tear trickles down her cheek, trembling on her chin before it falls into her lap.

"And you, darling. With your Sparrow. You want to fix her, to make her whole. You want to ease her suffering. But it isn't yours to do, is it? It's hers, and hers alone. You cannot do her hard work for her. And if you try, you'll take something important away from her. You won't be helping her, you'll be shielding her, and she needs to face her own truth, in her own time."

She takes a sip of her tea, which is probably stone cold by now. The cookies remain untouched.

"Granny, it was my fault she got hurt. If I'd said something, if I'd ratted Tristan out to her father, then she never would have gone with him that night."

"Were you the one who raised your hand to her, Lucas? Were you the one who hurt her?"

My voice cracks. "No. No, I wasn't."

"Of course you weren't. There's only one person at fault here, and it's that awful boy. As far as Sparrow is concerned, all you can do now is be her friend."

"But that sucks, Granny."

"Lucas, sometimes we just have to let things go. If you want to help her, then do her the honor of believing she has the courage to mend herself."

"But what if she can't? What if she never gets better?"

"She can and she will. Something tells me that she's never had the chance to show anyone how brave she really is."

"She doesn't think she's brave."

"Ah, well, that's a shame. Maybe she thinks that way because she's afraid. The truth of it all is that you can't be brave until you're frightened out of your wits and still do the thing that needs doing. You have to be scared to be brave."

"So I just stand around and watch?"

"You wait for her to invite you in. What you do is up to her, not you. Believe in her. She's not helpless. She's a survivor.

"Now, I know I'm your doddering old grandmother, but have I managed to shoehorn some sense into that thick head of yours?"

I stand up and put my arms around her. Violets and tea and sugar cookies and face powder.

"Granny Deirdre, I love you. You know that, right?"

"I do, darling. I love you too. And I'll tell you something else, something everyone who loves you already knows."

"That I'm a dingus?"

"Hush now. You are, in every good way, just like your father. My heart has ached a little less with you around to remind me of him. We live on in those who loved us. And your father, my darling boy, lives on in you."

She reaches out and strokes my cheek.

In my granny's warm kitchen, I feel my dad with me, inside my beating heart.

Sparrow

And all my mother came into mine eyes.
And gave me up to tears.

WILLIAM SHAKESPEARE, *Henry V*

34

Field Trip

I'm curled up on my window seat, looking out the bay window at the sun shining bright and golden on the high ridges. It's the last week of February, but even though it's super-cold and there's still snow on the ground, tiny brave buds have popped out on some of the trees. The mountains are starting to look fuzzier. Like puppy fur.

Lucas has been home for a week, and it's almost like he never left. With my forehead resting on an icy windowpane, I whisper the best part of his poem. It's in the book he sent me for Christmas. He'd had it for a long time, and the pages are scribbled with notes in the margins, underlines, and snarky comments. I love that; it feels like we're having a conversation. He marked his favorite with a silver clip, one with a little bird at the top.

I say the words every morning. For courage.

Though much is taken, much abides; and though
We are not now that strength which in old days

Moved earth and heaven; that which we are, we are;
One equal temper of heroic hearts,
Made weak by time and fate, but strong in will
To strive, to seek, to find, and not to yield.

When Lucas pulls into the driveway, Delaney is leaning out the passenger window like a beagle on a road trip. She's wearing her puffy blue parka and black cowboy hat. She sees me at the window and waves, and I run down the stairs, calling out to Sophie that I'll be back in time for dinner.

The heat in Lucas's Jeep rattles like a smoker's lungs, wheezing and gasping through the vents. Delaney's in the back now, not wearing her seat belt so she can scoot up and talk to us.

"Laney," Lucas says. "You realize that if I skid or stop suddenly, you're going to Peter Pan through the windshield, right?"

"So don't do that, dork. I'll put it on in a minute. Bird Girl, are you sure you want to do this?" She's leaning between the front seats, so close that I can see her earrings. Silver horseshoes, studded with bits of turquoise.

"Nice earrings," I tell her.

"Thanks. I'm asking for a horse for my birthday. I know I swore I'd stop, but that was almost a year ago. One day very soon, my friends, I will wear my parents down and emerge victorious. Now quit stalling, and tell me the truth. Are you sure about this cheerful little field trip?"

"I don't know, Laney. Are you sure about those earrings?"

She sits back and takes off her blaze-orange mittens, glaring at me.

"Well, maybe you're sure, bird brat, but I'm not sure, not at all."

We're quiet for a while, looking out over the deep snowy valley on our left, dotted with white church steeples and tiny houses, watching little whirlwinds of snow rise in front of us, a gift from the eighteen-wheelers laboring up the steep incline.

Delaney says, "So I've been writing poems again, right?"

Lucas points out the windshield. "Look! A giraffe!"

"That trick worked once, you turd, when we were, like, six, so knock it off. You guys want to hear a poem or not?"

"Not," Lucas and I say.

"You guys suck."

"Not as much as some of your poems," Lucas says.

"Lucas," I say, trying not to smile, "that was mean. Tell her you're sorry."

"But I'm not even close to sorry. I speak the truth."

It feels good, the three of us together again. The sound of conversation doesn't terrify me anymore; I'm not freaked out because someone's sitting too close. I haven't flinched once when Delaney touches me. I know this could change in a hot second, but right now I feel mostly normal. Like peace is out there in the distance, waiting for me. Maybe happiness is standing beside her.

Delaney's cradling her journal in her lap, the one she's had for years, crammed full of notes and crumbling autumn leaves and pictures torn from magazines—the things that inspire her. Sometimes, when she thinks no one is looking, she runs her hand reverently over the worn leather cover, like the pages are filled with prayers.

Right now she's wrestling with the thick rubber band that holds the book closed. Balancing the book on her knee, she snaps the band around her coffee cup, spilling half the contents on the floor. She always takes the lid off. She always spills.

"Oh geez, thanks for that, you spaz," says Lucas. "How am I going to get the smell out?"

"Like you'll even be able to tell. This ride smells like petrified tacos and feet. I just made it better, so quit whining."

Even though I know it will hurt my heart to even imagine it, I have to ask.

"How's *Swan Lake* coming?"

"You tell her, Laney."

Delaney groans. "Oh God. We're a train wreck. It's killing me. Caleb, too. We don't have what you guys had, that magic juice, and it's bumming us out. Sorry to complain, especially to you guys."

It must kill Lucas not to be dancing Siegfried.

As though he's reading my mind, he says softly, "I missed way too much. And Caleb and Laney worked super-hard while I was gone. I'm one of the hunting party guys now. It's all good, Birdy, really. I'm lucky Levkova let me come back. I couldn't have done it anyway."

He turns to look at me.

"Not without you."

"Lucas—"

"Also, when were you planning to tell us about New York?"

My face flushes. I haven't told a soul, but Sophie and my father are singing like canaries in a coal mine. "I was going to tell you later."

"Right."

"No, I was, seriously. I just wanted to keep it to myself for a while. I only heard, like, three days ago. It doesn't seem possible. It doesn't seem real."

"Oh, it's real, Birdy. You got into the summer intensives! Five bucks says you'll be in the company of the Manhattan Ballet within a year."

Talking about what I've dreamed of all my life with anyone right now, especially after—after Tristan—is terrifying. I'm afraid someone will find a way to rip it away from me. I put my hand up to my throat, like there's something stuck there. Lucas sees.

"Okay, Birdy. No worries. Let's change the subject," he says. "So how long's it been since you were at St. Monica's?"

"Not since her funeral."

Delaney takes off her seat belt again and breathes coffee breath into my face.

"Are you serious? You really haven't visited your mother's grave in twelve years?"

"None of us have."

"Not even your dad?"

"I don't think so. If he has, I don't want to know about it."

Lucas nods. "I mean, seriously, why would you? No way I'd go. But are you really sure about today? I can turn around and we can go to Nora's and stuff our faces."

"Actually, I'm not sure. But I'm doing it anyway."

"Okay, then. We're in."

"'We few, we happy few, we band of brothers,'" Delaney crows.

Lucas and I roll our eyes.

"Shut up, Delaney."

St. Monica's looks exactly the way it does in my nightmares. Though I haven't been here in more than twelve years, I haven't forgotten a thing. The church is pretty, but creepy pretty, like those Thomas Kinkade paintings. Too perfect, too sweet. My mother should have been buried somewhere dark and Gothic, with pointy arches and flying buttresses splayed out like spider legs.

Lucas pulls into the empty parking lot. It's Sunday afternoon, and there are no other cars here. He cuts the engine and looks out at all the gray stone and pristine snowdrifts piled up against the walls. Ivy climbs between the scarlet and blue stained-glass

windows, and fresh magnolia-leaf wreaths hang from white ribbons on the red doors. A square bell tower rises into the pale
blue sky.

Behind the church, the graveyard is surrounded by a wrought-
iron fence encased in a thick layer of ice. Lucas tugs his Sherpa
hat down over his ears.

"I don't know about this, Birdy. It's *über* weird out here. You
should let us come with you, at least."

"No, Lucas. I need to go alone. I won't be long, I promise."

Delaney scoots up between the seats again.

"Lucas is right. It looks kind of sketchy to me."

"Guys, it's a church. We're the only living people here."

"Exactly," says Delaney, looking over her shoulder at the rear
window. "You don't know what's out there."

I open my door, and biting wind swirls into the car, instantly
numbing my face.

Looking back at their wide eyes and grim expressions, my
heart softens.

"I'm fine, honestly. If I'm not back in ten minutes, you can
come get me."

"Okay, okay," Delaney grumbles.

Lucas says, "Ten minutes, Birdy. Dassit."

When I get out of the car, I'm enveloped by the hushed, muf-
fled silence that comes with snow. My footsteps crunch across the
parking lot, shattering the stillness.

Closing the gate behind me, I look out at the rows and rows
of tombstones. The quiet here is heavy and deep, and I try not
to think of all the people under the earth, sleeping in their silent
beds.

I had to ask my father to remind me where she was buried.
He didn't want to at first, but when I told him I'd just read every
last stone and search grave by snowy grave, he relented.

I walk as quickly as I can to the corner farthest from me, but it's hard. The snowdrifts are deep, almost up to my knees in places, and my foot aches in the cold. I walk between the rows, trying to distract myself by reading the words engraved on the stones.

Precious Son, Cherished Brother. Devoted Wife, Beloved Mother. Dearest Father, Ever Faithful.

My mother is all by herself, in the corner just beyond the last row. On the other side of the icy fence, the skeletal branches of a huge sweet gum tree reach out to shelter the graves beneath.

My hands tremble as I brush the snow from the top of her stone, then step back to read what my father had carved into the dark pink granite.

CAROLINA JANE ROSE

1968–2005

THE SALVATION OF PARDON IS GRANTED

THE PENITENT.

ALLELUIA. ALLELUIA.

It's part of the "Pilgrim's Chorus." From *Tannhäuser*, my father's favorite opera. I stare at the words, clutching the gift I've brought her, the one that's been in my pocket for two days.

My horror, my torment, my curse of a mother doesn't deserve the beautiful words. She isn't penitent. She hasn't earned those alleluias.

"I hate you," I whisper. "All the terrible things in my life flow like a polluted river straight back to you."

I don't pray. I don't cry. I take the plastic lemon out of my pocket and place it on top of her stone. It looks garish and harsh in the muted winter landscape, lurid and out of place.

I close my eyes and remember the mother I saw in the hospital, the mother with the feathered throat, the black wings, the mother who wept stones. I remember the way I saw her on that last day, her pale arms, her white capri pants, her pointed pink fingernails. Her red lips and white teeth. I imagine her now, deep in the dark below, trying to find me with her empty eyes. I hear her.

Come to me, come to me, come to me.

"Damn you," I say, a whisper that rises to a shriek.

"Damn you to hell, Mama! You made me this way! I've been afraid all my life! You told me to keep my mouth shut and smile and smile and smile and never tell anyone what you did. Now look at me! Look at me, Mama! Look at what you've done! Because of you, I loved a monster. My heart is broken, my body is broken, but you broke them before he ever did. You hurt me, Mama!

"I was your little girl!" I sob. "You were supposed to love me, but you hurt me!"

Tears run down my face as I grab the lemon and unscrew the cap with my teeth, just like she did when I was five. I throw it hard at her stone, aiming for the alleluias. It bounces off and lands in the snow.

But it's not enough. Not nearly enough.

I kneel and start pushing the snow off her grave, my hands numb with cold, until I reach the frozen earth. I squirt the lemon juice into the ground.

"How do you like it, Mama? I hope it burns into your dead eyes! I hope you can feel this where you are. I hope you know how much I hate you! How I'll always hate you! Feel it, Mama! Feel all the terror, all the sorrow I've carried with me every day of my life because of you!"

I sob weakly, clutching the empty lemon in my fist.

"I will never, ever forgive you. I'm telling everyone now, Mama. Everyone will know. You hear me? I'm telling. I'm not prey anymore. I'm not, and you can rot in hell forever. I will never forgive you."

I stand and kick her tombstone over and over again. I pound it with my hands until they hurt and begin to bruise. The sounds coming out of me are choked and terrible, all my nightmares boiling out of my throat.

Suddenly Lucas and Delaney are behind me, wrapping their arms around me. I fight them at first, stopping only when all three of us lose our balance and fall to the ground in a heap. I sink, exhausted, into their arms, crying so hard I doubt I'll ever be able to stop. Lucas rocks me back and forth. I let him hold me.

Delaney strokes my cheek. "Oh my God, Sparrow. It's okay, sweetie. We're here. Stop now. Hush, we've got you. I promise, we've got you."

Eventually I stop, hiccupping and wiping my eyes with the sleeve of my scratchy wool jacket. Lucas and Delaney let go, and we stand up together, jeans wet and crusted with snow, our faces red and chapped.

Lucas rewinds his scarf around his neck, finds his hat where it fell in the snow, and jams it back on his head. He says, all quiet and intense, "Birdy. You want me to dig up your mother's rotting bones and light them on fire? Just say the word. I have matches."

Delaney looks at me, eyes wide. Lucas is serious as a heart attack, but his hat is on crooked. And there in the snowy cemetery, with the cold seeping through my soaked jeans, I laugh. I laugh so hard that my stomach hurts, so long that I start to cry again. We walk back to the car, holding on to each other, all three of us weak in the knees.

I dig at the bottom of my purse for Violet Bell's card and hand it to Lucas.

"What's this?" he asks.

"It's that detective. She's pretty much given up on me, even though she talks to me every week. Could you call her for me? I'm afraid I'll chicken out if we don't do it right now. Can you tell her we're on the way? And then—can you guys drive me to the police station?"

"Holy crap, Birdy. Are you sure?"

"No. I'm scared out of my mind to talk about it. But I'm sick of being a victim. I'm not going to live the rest of my life in her shadow. Or his. And I'm freaking tired of keeping my mouth shut."

Delaney puts her arm around me and pulls me close. "Do you think you can talk about him now? About what happened?"

"I don't know. I thought I could make it all disappear if I pretended it never happened, if I just tried to shove it all away. Because that's worked so well for me in the past, right? It will be horrible, talking about it. But I know it will be worse if I never do."

Lucas digs his phone out of his pocket and punches in the number. While he talks to Violet, I pull Delaney aside.

"Laney, would you call my father and Sophie and tell them to meet us there? I don't want to get into a big hairy discussion. I just want to do it and get it over with."

"Done and done," she says.

She holds my hand all the way back.

Lucas parks across from the police station, behind a row of gleaming cruisers. My father, who's standing on the top step of the station's entrance, sees us and jogs across the road. It's getting dark, and the streetlamps are beginning to blink on. I roll down my window, and he leans in and kisses me. I smell his bay rum cologne, and instantly my heart slows a little. I'm safe. I'm surrounded by people who love me.

I say it in my head three times. Then three more, counting on my fingers until I get to nine.

All will be well, all will be well, and all manner of things shall be well.

My father smiles and says, "I won't tell you how brave I think you are, because I know you hate that. So instead I'll tell you that I'm proud of you. Not just for this, but for everything. I think you're my hero, honeybunch."

"Dad, stop. You're totally embarrassing me."

He leans in and kisses me again. "Guess what? I don't care."

"Besides," I say, looking at the uniformed officers going in and out of the station. "I'm scared out of my mind."

Lucas tugs on my sleeve. "Birdy, you know what my granny Deirdre says?"

"No clue."

"She says you have to be scared to be brave."

My stomach is climbing into my throat, and I feel like I might throw up. How will I ever say it out loud? How can I possibly say all the terrible things? Where will I find the words? The strength?

Tears prick behind my eyes and I tilt my head back, automatically, reflexively.

Lucas squeezes my hand. "Birdy Bird, don't. Let them fall."

And I do. The tears flow down my cheeks, hot and fast, but when I speak, my voice is clear. "If your grandmother is right," I say, "then right now, I am definitely the bravest person on the planet."

Violet Bell meets us inside the front doors, shaking hands with my father and Sophie. She's dressed in a dark blue suit, and her hair is pulled back from her face.

"Sparrow," she says, taking both of my hands in hers. "It took a lot of guts for you to come here today, and we're grateful. Are you ready?"

My mouth is dry, and for a second I think about turning and running out the front doors, across the street, and deep into the woods until I'm lost. Until I'm sure no one will ever find me or make me talk or ask me any questions ever again.

"I think so."

She leads us into a windowless room with a long rectangular table and six chairs. There are bottles of water at each place, and at the far end, a video camera is set up on a tripod. The little red light is on.

"Sparrow," Detective Bell says. "Don't worry about the camera. Don't even look at it, okay? It's there to make sure we get your words exactly right. Just look at me and forget it's even there."

Sophie and my dad take the seats at the far end of the table. Violet sits at the head, and I take the seat on her right. We make small talk for a little while, how am I feeling, is my foot better, have I started dancing again, what Madame Levkova's like.

Then she says, "Sparrow. Who hurt you last August?"

My heart pounds, and my hands are shaking so hard that I tuck them under my legs so no one will see. I look down the table at my father, who's leaning forward, his eyes filled with love and encouragement. Sophie puts her hand over her heart and mouths, *Love you*.

When I speak, my voice is strong and steady. I sound like someone else, someone sure of herself. Someone unafraid.

You are innocent. You are beloved.

I look Violet straight in the eyes. I say his name.

"Tristan. Tristan King."

Lucas

*Hereafter, in a better world than this, I shall desire
more love and knowledge of you.*

WILLIAM SHAKESPEARE, *As You Like It*

The Sparkles

"Hey, want to see what I found?"

I take off my headphones, and Ralph Vaughan Williams fills the air.

"Hang on, Mom." I pause the music, then set the piece to start at the beginning when I pick it up again.

"You don't have to lurk out there in the hall like a stalker. I swear I took all the toxic waste out to the trash."

"Good. Because a person could catch Ebola in here."

"That was yesterday. Today's special is cholera."

"Nice, Lucas."

She walks gingerly into my room, tiptoeing over tights and slippers, bending to pick up the huge plastic cups whose insides are coated with the remains of chocolate protein shakes.

"Lucas, the dirty clothes on the floor are bad enough. But if you keep these cups in here, we're going to get roaches and mice. And then, kid, you and I are going to have a serious issue."

"Come on, Mom. If we didn't have at least one serious issue going on, we wouldn't be, you know, us."

She laughs and sits on the edge of my bed.

"True. But look what I found when I was looking for books to give to the hospital library."

She hands me a huge, heavy book, one of those things you're supposed to put on a coffee table and never read.

"Oh my God, I forgot all about this! You aren't going to give it away, are you?"

"No. I thought maybe you'd like to have it."

It's a book of paintings by American artists. When I was a kid I loved it so much that we kept it in the kitchen, between the coffee maker and the toaster. My mom and I looked at it together every day after breakfast.

"Mom, remember the Sparkles?"

She smiles and opens the book to the page she's marked with a bright orange Post-it.

"How could I forget? You loved that painting. You must have looked at it for hours. I've always liked it, but you were absolutely obsessed. I could never figure out exactly why."

The painting's real name is *Nocturne in Black and Gold: The Falling Rocket*, by the same guy who painted a picture of his creepy mother sitting in a chair doing nothing.

I called it the Sparkles. It's not a picture of a person or a river or a bowl of fruit or anything recognizable. It's just flecks of gold and smudges of white on an inky black background. But when I was little, I thought somebody had painted what it would be like to stand inside a shower of stars.

"I think I liked it so much because it made me go all quiet inside. You know what I'm talking about?"

"I do, honey. Not exactly peaceful. More like calm."

"Yeah. I felt like maybe I understood why the guy painted it, but only a little, and not for long. Like it was trying to tell me something, and if I looked at it long enough, I'd figure out some big secret."

"And did you?"

"Mom. In the past seven months have I given you any reason to believe I've stumbled on some deep secret of the universe? Pretty sure if I did, I probably wouldn't have acted like such a jerk to you and Anna."

I close the book and put it beside me. I know for sure I'll be looking at it again, long and hard. Maybe while I listen to Vaughan Williams.

"Oh, honey. It's been a terrible time for all of us. Have you forgiven me?"

"What, for sending me into exile at Granny Deirdre's?" I smile, to take the sting out of the words.

"Yes. Maybe it wasn't the right thing to do at the time, but I was at my wits' end. If you'd stayed, something bad was going to happen."

"Something bad did happen. A whole lot of bad somethings."

"I mean something bad was going to happen to you, something nobody could fix. I felt like one of those mothers in a fairy tale, sending her child off to the wise woman in the woods."

She goes to the window and looks out over our street, which is always super-quiet on Sunday mornings.

"I'm so glad the snow is gone," she says. "This was the longest, coldest winter I can remember. And now look. There are buds on the forsythia, and I can see crocuses poking up their little heads. Spring always feels hopeful to me. For the first time in a long time, I think maybe we'll all be okay."

"Yeah."

We're both quiet for a while.

"Well, I'll leave you to your music, sweetie. Let's go out for pizza tonight, okay? We need to do something fun."

"Wait, Mom."

She turns at the door, and I see, I don't know, this naked hope in her eyes.

"She was the wise woman in the woods, you know. Granny. I'm glad you made me go, though I was super pissed off at the time."

She smiles and returns to her perch on my bed.

"I think I remember you were a bit irritated. I'm glad it was good for you, Lucas. I think you and your grandmother have something special now. I hope she sticks around for a long time so Anna can know her the way you do. And me too."

I pull the book of paintings into my lap, not to look at, just to hold. Its weight and heft are comforting.

"Mom, you know how Delaney's got that whole Western thing going on?"

"Those boots are kind of hard to miss, honey. Along with the feathers and the silver and the turquoise. And the attitude. I love that about her. It makes her so different from everybody else, so interesting. I wish I'd learned to carve out a place for myself, to not care about what other people thought when I was seventeen. I was in my thirties before I figured it out. She's a smart girl."

"Ha. She's a smart-ass if you ask me."

"That makes her the perfect friend for you."

"Haha. So last week, when we found out that Tristan's been charged with assault and a whole bunch of other stuff, and he's probably going to jail for a long time, Delaney got all these people together in the cafeteria, and they did one of those line dances. She has, like, four hundred country-and-western stations on her phone. They were whooping it up and celebrating. It was pretty funny, you know how Delaney can always get a crowd going, but . . ."

"But what?"

"It made me feel bad."

"Like how?"

"I don't know. It was weird. Like, I still hate his freaking guts, don't get me wrong about that. I hope he rots in jail, because he deserves it. But I keep remembering what Granny said to me the night I got there. I almost argued with her about it, but you know, she's an old lady, and I didn't want to give her a heart attack or anything."

"Wise choice. What did she say?"

"She was talking about boys in Ireland. I mean, not really directly, you know how she never does, but I could tell. She said when you stop seeing your enemy as a human being, you give yourself permission to do great harm. And I think that's what I did when I beat the shit out of Tristan. I gave myself permission to hurt somebody, because I thought I was right and he was a monster. I mean, I still think he's a monster, but I feel like crap for what I did. So when Delaney started, you know, celebrating that he was going to jail, I mean, celebrating that he's eighteen and he's destroyed his whole life, it made me feel, I don't know."

"Sad? Unkind?"

"Well, that's the nice way of putting it, but yeah. And I don't want to be that guy."

I'm expecting a lecture, or at least some wisdom from my mother, but all she does is scoot closer, wrap her arms around me, and hug me real hard.

"You've learned your lesson, honey. I'm so grateful to your granny, because she helped get you where you are right now. Part of me feels sorry for Tristan, even though I can barely stand to think about him. Still, I can't help wondering how he got so lost, what it must be like to have so much darkness in your soul. No one becomes a monster overnight."

I'm quiet. There's nothing I can say that will be right, that will convey how much I still despise Tristan King, and how sorry I am that I beat him up.

My mom pats my leg and smiles.

"Look at your painting, honey. Maybe now that you're older, you really will learn all the secrets of the universe."

"I'll let you know what I find out."

"Do that. You meeting Delaney later? Tell her hey for me."

"Will do."

"Bring her to dinner if you want. I sure do love you, Lucas."

"Of course you do, Mom. Everybody loves this guy."

"You and Caleb crushed it the other night, Laney."

Delaney slides into the booth across from me, her braid swinging over her shoulder. She takes off her dark John Lennon sunglasses. No feathers today, no leather vest, just the ever-present boots, a T-shirt that says *Don't Make Me Whip Out My Fouettés*, and the silver sheriff's star.

"We did not suck. That's about the best I can say about the whole thing."

"Also, that T-shirt is seriously lame."

"Tell me about it. My grandmother came for the performance. She gave it to me this morning, and my mother made me wear it to make her happy. I know it's heinous, trust me."

"Okay. I thought maybe you'd lost your fashion sense."

"Not a chance. This is completely coerced. Go on about how we didn't suck."

"Y'all were really, really good. I was there, remember? Prancing around with a fake crossbow?"

"Yeah, but you looked gorgeous in that black vest, and those boots were crazy-hot. Your prancing was perfect. Speaking of hot, did you even see how much I was sweating? Like, it was dripping off my chin!"

"I did. We were all pretty ripe by the end, just like always. But all I know is that it felt amazing to be back on that stage. It wouldn't have mattered if I had to dress like a swan princess and do stands, like those poor girls in the *corps*. I saw one of them crying backstage. Ouch."

Nora brings our lunch. We were so hungry we called ahead. We are definitely chowing down big-time today, since the gala is behind us and the June Showcase is more than two months away. Bacon cheeseburger with mushrooms, avocado, and a side of fried okra for me, huge pulled pork sandwich with slaw for Laney, and a massive plate of fries to share.

Nora beams at Delaney.

"Darling, you were such a beautiful Swan Queen. That costume was gorgeous, and you danced like a dream. I almost cried when you made your entrance."

Delaney blushes.

"Thanks, Nora. You're sweet to say."

"I speak the truth, love. But, Lucas, I couldn't tell which hunting boy you were! There were so many of you!"

"You mean you couldn't see my manly thighs and chiseled jaw from the orchestra? Geez, Nora. Way to break my heart."

She laughs and gives my shoulders a squeeze. On her way back to the kitchen, she tells Stephanie, her new waitress, to bring us both chocolate peanut-butter shakes, on the house.

Delaney squeezes half a bottle of ketchup onto the fries and pops one into her mouth. She closes her eyes and groans.

"Oh my God, this is so good I'm going to lie down and die."

"I get so freaking tired of protein all the time. Carbs are life. And sugar. Sugar is also life."

"So, can I ask you something?" she says.

"You know you can."

She waits while Stephanie carefully sets down our milk-shakes, which are piled high with whipped cream and topped with three cherries each.

"Thanks, Steph. These look . . . daunting."

Stephanie smiles. "Dare you to finish them," she says.

When she's gone, Delaney says, "Anyway. You guys. You and Sparrow. When is she leaving for New York?"

"The day after the showcase. That's what you wanted to ask me?"

"I'm working up to it."

"Laney. Just spit it out."

She takes a sip of her shake, sucking in her cheeks like a little kid. Nora's shakes are so thick it's like trying to drink ice cream.

"I know you're in love with her. I mean, you were. Crap. This is coming out all wrong. I just want to be sure your heart isn't broken and you're not going to crater or jump off a bridge or anything."

"I'm done cratering. I'm okay. Almost fine. I think."

She waits for me to say something stupid, to make a joke.

"I mean, I still love her. I probably always will, one way or another. But it never would have worked. The timing was all wrong. Maybe someday she would have loved me back, who knows? What I do know is that it wasn't fair for me to push it, to push her. That's the last thing she needs. Another boyfriend. She has a lot of work to do, and I don't want to be out there, waiting, hovering over her like a vulture. Also, I actually do have some self-respect. I don't want to be that pathetic guy, moping and whining about a girl who doesn't love him back."

"Are you being straight with me?"

"I think so. Besides, I can still dance with her, at least until June. We'll always have that. We were good together."

"Yes, you were. You are."

I drag some fries through the ketchup, making swirly patterns on the plate.

"I'll miss her, though. I hope maybe she'll miss me. I also hope she doesn't miss me. I hope she's so busy and everything's so new and different that Hollins Creek and everything that happened here seem light-years away."

She spoons some coleslaw onto my plate.

"Let's not talk about endings anymore," she says. "It makes me too sad."

She looks at me and smiles, not her usual snarky Delaney smile, but a smile that goes all the way up to her eyes.

"So tell me about the big surprise in June."

"Laney, come on. If I tell you, then it won't be a surprise."

"Oh, come on, Lucas. It's just me. I'll know once we start rehearsals. Are you and Sparrow dancing together one last time? You can trust me. I won't tell a soul."

"Oh, right. It'll be all over town in five minutes."

"No, it won't! I'm good at keeping secrets! Not as good as Bird Girl, but nobody should be that good."

"I'm not telling you anything, except that the music will slay you hard-core. But I'll give you a hint. *Master and Commander*."

"What, that boring movie with those old-timey boats? The one with all the cannons and storms and the little kid who gets his arm cut off?"

"That's the one."

"What about it?"

"The music, Laney."

"There's a lot of music, doofus. It's called a soundtrack."

"Sorry, that's all you get."

"Ugh, that movie. Never again, not even for you," she says, shaking her head. "My dad made me watch it with him one night, and it made me seasick. I almost ralphed in my popcorn. You can have your little secret all to yourself."

She points to the sheriff's star pinned to her shirt, then kicks me under the table with the pointy toe of her turquoise boot.

"But Sheriff Delaney's going to be all over you like a cheap suit, morning, noon, and night. I will not rest until you give it up, every stinking detail."

I reach across the ketchup-smeared plate and take her hand. She looks up, surprised.

"Swan Queen. I'm counting on it."

Finale

I'm shirtless in front of a lighted mirror, sponging on foundation, using bronzer to highlight my cheekbones, pencil to darken my brows, and black eyeliner above and below my eyes to make them look bigger.

Out in the house, the audience is arriving. People are greeting one another, studying their programs, strolling down to the orchestra pit to watch the musicians tune.

In here, we're all praying that we don't screw up.

I run some gel through my hair and spray almost a full can of hair spray on it, to make sure it doesn't fly all over the place. Then massive quantities of deodorant, which will be useless after ten minutes in the lights. I inspect my face in the mirror and dab on some lip stain. I'm a super-exaggerated version of myself.

The assistant stage manager knocks, opens the door a crack, and studiously avoids looking at us, a bunch of jittery half-naked dudes.

"Lucas," she says, checking her clipboard. "You've got less than an hour before your cue. Forty-five minutes. Sparrow's already backstage. You might want to hustle."

"Okay, thanks, Harper."

She gives me a thumbs-up and walks away, talking into her headset.

I slather on more deodorant, pull on my shirt, and make my way backstage to the costume rack. The dressers are waiting with needles and thread to reinforce hooks and seams and fix any last-minute disasters. My costume is so simple that I don't need them tonight, but they check me over anyway. When they're finished, I bend and stretch and jump up and down, to get my muscles warm and loose.

The chaos backstage pumps me up. The sight of dancers flying offstage and bending double, panting and sweating, the others waiting nervously in the wings to go out, the smells of rosin and hair spray, the whispers of the stagehands, the music rising and receding like a tide.

When I'm finished jumping, I walk over to the big table where the ballerinas mutilate their pointe shoes. Sparrow's already there, sewing the knots in her ribbons to make sure they stay tight. She smiles when she sees me.

"Hey, you."

"Hey. You ready to kill it tonight?"

"For sure. I'm excited. Also nervous, like always. You?"

"Same. More nervous, I think. You look great. Good call on the costumes."

She's wearing a pale pink camisole and a floaty white skirt. I'm wearing black tights and a dark gray shirt. She's got a thin jeweled headband over her short hair, but that's the only thing that sparkles.

"I wanted it to be just us, you know? No tutu. If this really is the last time we dance together, I want to remember all those times in the studio. Like it was that day we were rehearsing, remember? When *Swan Lake* finally clicked?"

"Damn, that was a fine day. I asked Levkova if she'd let me wear my favorite shirt. You now, the gray one with the holes in it? She did not see the humor."

"It's your trademark. I can't believe that thing's still in one piece."

"I'm giving it to you to take to New York."

"Seriously?"

"Seriously. I can't let you go without something to remember me by."

"Right. Like I could ever forget you."

"This is way too serious just before we go out."

"You started it."

I try to smile, but it's tough to do with my eyes going all blurry.

She stands up and tests her shoes, bending each foot back and forth. I follow her to the rosin box, and we take our places in the wings, watching Charlotte and Ainsley doing *chaînés* turns around the stage.

Sparrow stands beside me, breathing slowly, centering herself. I know she's nervous, so I rub slow circles down her back, like I always do before a performance. It's the last time I'll ever do this for her.

"Birdy, there's a lot I want to tell you before you go tomorrow, and I may not have the chance. Your dad will be all crabby, loading the car, and Sophie will be packing food like there's nothing but a barren, starving wasteland between here and New York."

She smiles.

"What happened to the lighten-up plan?"

"I'm ignoring it. I just—I just want to make sure you know some stuff."

"Okay."

Suddenly all the things I was going to tell her fly right out of my head. All but one.

"So, my grandmother told me something while I was with her last winter."

"You never told me about that whole thing. I guess I never asked. I'm sorry."

"God, Sparrow, you had so much to deal with then. I didn't expect you to ask me about my grandmother."

"You sure you don't want to wait until after?"

"No, I need to say it now or I'll chicken out. My grandmother told me that when you love somebody who's battling demons, it doesn't help if you stand in front of them, trying to shield them from the pain. She said that makes them powerless and you presumptuous."

"Your granny is pretty smart."

"She said it's better if you stand beside them, holding their swords."

"Is that what you're doing, Lucas? Holding my swords?"

"Always. For as long as you'll let me."

"Thank you," she whispers. "For everything."

Charlotte and Ainsley and Caleb fly into the wings. We're up next. She reaches out and squeezes my hand.

"Merde."

"Merde."

We dance, Sparrow and me, the way it's been for three years, the way I wish it could be forever. The music washes over me and fills me up, so achingly beautiful that I feel the soaring violins, the weeping violas like they're coming from inside me. I will see her face, I will breathe her honeysuckle hair, I will feel the softness of her skin, the strength of her muscles every time I hear this, the "Fantasia on a Theme by Thomas Tallis."

I try to remember everything, but like all turning points, it's over way too fast.

The speed of her footwork, the brilliance of her turns, the impossible boneless arms, the warmth of her breath on my face, the feel of her hands in mine.

My turns are sharp and quick and perfect. My jumps are high and strong, with more *ballon* than ever, that illusion of effortlessness, of opening up and hovering in the air for a beat before I land.

Near the end, a fish dive so beautiful, so perfect, that the audience gasps.

Sparrow holds on to my hips with her legs, her face inches from the floor. I open my arms wide.

I embrace it all, the pain of the last ten months, the rage, the helplessness, the hope.

I know that this, right now, is goodbye for us, not tomorrow when I wave and watch her car disappear. I've loved her for so long I'm not sure I'll know how to stop. She is the bravest person I've ever known. If this is the last time we do this together, if it's the last time I touch her face or hold her in my arms or lift her high over the stage, it's enough. Because it's everything.

I'll keep a room inside my heart for Sparrow. It's hers forever. No matter how wrinkled and old I get, no matter where we go or what we do, even if she forgets my name and I forget hers, even if Levkova's eyes and the smell of rosin and the sound of the music all fade away into the dark, we will never, ever forget that we had this. It was ours.

Goodbye, my Birdy Bird.

I love you.

The music soars.

Author's Note

When I began *Sparrow* more than six years ago, I was struggling to finish another novel when a terrible news story went viral. A high-school girl had gotten drunk at a party and passed out. While she was unconscious, a group of boys took naked pictures of her and posted them on Facebook. I was so horrified by the cruelty of those boys that I felt sick for days. I couldn't stop thinking about that girl. I dreamed about her. I wept for her. Just before sunrise one morning, I put aside the book I'd been working on and wrote the first line of the first draft of *Sparrow*: "I am not the kind of girl who tells."

During the course of those years, as I wrote and revised and Sparrow's story evolved, I began to learn about dating abuse in teen relationships. I read about young women who had been physically hurt by a boyfriend or girlfriend who professed to love them. I learned about young men who had been abused by dating partners and were too ashamed to tell anyone. And I learned that teens who experience violence in their dating relationships are at higher risk for substance abuse and eating disorders and attempted suicide. Teen dating abuse exists in big cities and small communities, regardless of gender, sexual orientation, race, or religion. Women and men—both teens and adults—who are in physically and emotionally violent relationships almost always live in a state of constant fear and anxiety, as though they are walking on eggshells every moment of every day. This breaks my heart.

If you are in a violent relationship, you may feel isolated and alone. You may feel scared and invisible. You may feel that no one will believe you or care enough to try to help, that there is nowhere for you to turn. But there *are* people—many, many people—who will listen and care. I encourage you to confide in someone you trust—a close friend, a parent or other family member, a school counselor, a pastor, or a coach. Below you will find a list of resources you can reach out to right now, in safety and confidence, staffed by professionals and volunteers who will hear you and believe you and help you.

I see you. And I care.

Resources

National Domestic Violence Hotline
www.thehotline.org
www.ndvh.org
1.800.799.7233

For information on dating abuse and how to recognize the signs:
www.loveisrespect.org
www.breakthecycle.org

Rape, Abuse, & Incest National Network (RAINN) Hot line:
1.800.656. HOPE (4673)
www.rainn.org

There are also state coalitions against domestic violence in each
state. For a list, contact www.ncaav.org/state-coalitions.

Acknowledgments

Thank you to my former agent, Lindsay Mealing, who loved *Sparrow* from the moment she pulled it from the slush pile. Thank you also to my current agent, Mandy Hubbard, who saw me through to publication.

Thank you to my brilliant editor, Susan Chang, who encouraged me to dig deep, unearth the true bones of the book, and give them flesh.

Thank you to Elizabeth Saathoff of San Antonio's Performing Arts School of Classical Ballet, who helped me ensure that the ballet scenes were accurate. Any errors or exaggerations are my own.

Thank you to attorneys Maurine "Mo" and Barrett Shipp, who provided me with detailed explanations of police and legal procedure in domestic violence cases. Though much of that information does not appear in the book, I remain deeply grateful for their enthusiastic and gracious assistance.

Thank you to Heather Plank for making me laugh out loud every day. Thank you to Helen Sachdev, who sends wisdom from London. So much love to Chris Englehart, dearest sister of my heart.

My father, Francis Joseph Jackson, took me to the ballet in the years when I was awkward and shy and ashamed of my height, my thick glasses, and my hideous braces. When it mattered most, he filled my eyes with stars.

Thank you to my stepmother, Nancy McMahon, who never failed to tell me that my writing was glorious, even when it was a raging dumpster fire.

Thank you to my lovely stepdaughter, Lacey Triplett Thistle, and her delightful husband, Joe, for their unwavering support, kindness, and generosity of spirit.

Endless love to my magnificent sons, Alexander, Nicholas, and Joshua, who never doubted that their mom could write a book. Guys, Lucas is a love song to the three of you. When I finished the first draft, I realized that I'd given him your kindness, your bravery and intelligence, your humor, your compassionate and loving hearts, and your fierce loyalty to friends and family. I will love you forever, and I am so proud of you.

Finally, I owe so much—everything, really—to my wonderful architect husband, William. His steadfast love and support sustained me during the six years I wrote and revised *Sparrow*. I'm grateful to him for so many things: For listening to me read early drafts and not throwing up. For telling me—and everyone he meets—that he's proud of me. For taking me to the nearest bookstore, no matter where in the world we were, and buying me notebooks I did not need and books that I did, when revisions were daunting and I was discouraged and disheartened. William, my hero, my dearest love, you are my North Star.

Thank you, thank you, thank you.

My heart is full.